LIVING
WITH
RISK

The British Medical Association Guide

LIVING WITH RISK

The British Medical Association Guide

A Wiley Medical Publication

Published on behalf of the British Medical Association by

JOHN WILEY & SONS
Chichester · New York · Brisbane · Toronto · Singapore

Living with Risk

A report from the BMA Professional and Scientific Division.

Project Director: Dr John Dawson

Written by: Dr Michael Henderson

Production: David Morgan

Graphics: Team Leader, Clive Yeomans
                 Artists, Lesley Whale and
                 Polygraphics
                 Photography, Clive Yeomans

Editorial
Secretariat: Hilary Curtis
                 Audrey Porter

British Library Cataloguing in Publication Data:

Living with risk : the British Medical Association guide. — (A Wiley medical publication).
   1. Environmental health — Evaluation
   I. British Medical Association
   363.7   RA566

ISBN 0 471 91598 X

Printed in Spain

Contents

Contents ————————————————————————————

Preface

The British Medical Association is interested in risk because it touches upon every single aspect of health and human welfare. As doctors, we try to do the best for those who entrust themselves to our care, whether as individual patients or as whole communities. Their appeal to us is to keep the risk to them as low as possible. "What are my chances, doctor? Is it safe?"

Responding to that appeal, doctors have traditionally sought a balance between risks and benefits. As finding this balance has increasingly become a formal process of scientific analysis over recent years, we believe that patients should be involved in making the choices which define the level of acceptable risk. Further, because we all live in a world where technology makes the choice of action not only much wider but also more complicated, it will help us all if we understand how risks are assessed and managed.

Human values, different for each of us, influence our perceptions in such complex ways that at no time will all of us agree on a single level of acceptable risk. But if people can agree upon the way risks are measured, and on the relevance of the levels of risk thus represented to the choices we must all make, then the scope for disagreement and dissent is thereby limited.

This book, therefore, sets out to make the following points.

First, we live in a complex, technological world, and everything we do, or is done to us, carries some risk to our health and welfare. *There is no such thing as zero risk, absolute safety.* Many of the risks we face now are new, and different from those faced by our ancestors. They are not necessarily higher—overall, they are probably lower—but their very unfamiliarity makes them seem more threatening. Second, the way we perceive risk is much influenced by our own preconceptions and beliefs, as well as by the media; the world we see through the television screen or read about in the tabloids can be a very alarming one. Many risks are in fact far lower than they seem, but some are higher. A wide selection will be described in this book. Finally, risk can be managed and controlled; scientific principles can be used in association with full appreciation of human values to fulfil the aim of all of us—to gain the greatest possible benefit to mankind at the lowest possible cost.

This is not a comprehensive textbook of medical or environmental science. It is intended simply to present a selection of arguments and examples in a manner which is easy to absorb. Its emphasis is on risk to the person rather than the environment, which reflects our bias as practitioners of medicine; our concern as individuals is for all aspects of risk. In any event, many excellent texts are already available on environmental risks. We have concentrated on the big risks which affect almost all of us, as well as on a wide selection of smaller risks which are of particular public concern or of particular personal importance.

References are listed at the end of the book, citing literature to support statements in the text which appear to us to require validation, or which seem to be particularly contentious. For the sake of easy reading, we have kept the number of references to a minimum, but included among them are several review papers (as opposed to the source documents we would expect to find listed in a truly scientific publication) which will open up the subject for the interested reader. We have also described a selection of books which seem to us to be particularly good examples of further reading on matters of risk.

This publication was prepared under the auspices of the Board of Science and Education ,of the British Medical Association. The members of the Board are as follows:

Sir Douglas Black—Chairman
Professor J P Quilliam
Dr M Goodman
Major General J M Matheson
Professor J P Payne
Dr J M Cundy
Mr K C McKeown
Dr G M Mitchell
Dr V Moens
Dr H M White
Dr P G R Godwin
Dr P Hendy-Ibbs

Introduction

There are few things that are certain in this uncertain and complex world. One of the certainties is that we are all doomed to die. For each one of us, the death rate is 100%. Death is not a preventable occurrence.

It follows that most of us seek daily to make our lives as long and enjoyable as possible. But the purpose of life is not simply to avoid death. In the words of the author and adventurer Jack London: ''The proper function of man is to live, not exist. I shall not waste my days in trying to prolong them. I shall use my time''. So, it is the choices we take, and the decisions we make, which help us to make the most of what life has to offer. To minimize the risk of unnecessarily early death or illness, while at the same time maximizing the happiness of life, is one of mankind's most fundamental imperatives.

In the wider world, other people are also deciding things that affect the quality and length of our lives. In such cases we probably know little about how decisions are reached. Yet they affect matters which touch us every day, such as transport, electrical power, health services, even the food we eat. One might ask, how would it affect me if a nuclear power station was built nearby, rather than a coal-fired one? If I collide with that car over there, would I be safer inside it or inside my own? Or should someone have made sure that both are less dangerous to crash in? How often does someone check the brakes of the train I am travelling in tomorrow? Why have this level crossing; wouldn't a bridge over the railway be better?

All the time, then, we are faced by the dilemma of risk, the threat to our health and well-being which is posed by the world's hazards. We accept many risks, such as a chest X-ray or driving to work, because the benefits in so doing are immediately obvious. But if the risks become too high, we may have to forego all sorts of benefits. In such ways our fear of risk can come to determine so many of our decisions and activities in life.

But if we perceive risks as higher than they really are, then we may find ourselves foregoing benefits quite unnecessarily. And there is also the other possibility that we might wrongly perceive risks as being less significant than they really are. Thus, if we think smoking would do us no harm, we would be more likely to choose to smoke. We might decide not to wear seat belts in a car, because we believe we drive better without them and see little risk that we will be involved in a crash.

In a world where technology rules such a large part of our lives, where so many decisions are taken out of our hands, we may feel threatened by our simple inability to do much about anything. Indeed, many people do think that technology is imposing a whole set of new risks on us which our forebears did not face, such as the burgeoning use of synthetic chemicals, artificial additives in food, air and water pollution, and nuclear radiation. Does the convenience of the family car justify the road death rate? Can the benefits of manned space exploration possibly justify the fiery death of astronauts? Do the cures offered by new medicines and complex new operations really justify the ill-health caused by their unwanted effects?

The extraordinary rate of technological change increases the potential for the introduction of risks which we cannot assess until perhaps too late. About 1,000 new chemicals are produced each year, for example. Further, there is a decreasing time between the identification of a new technological development and its widespread use in the community. Most people think they are more at risk today than they were yesterday; they fear disaster, lack of personal control, potentially irreversible effects and risks to their children. Scientific debate is construed as scientific confusion. Accordingly, some categories of risk are especially feared: nuclear power generation, aircraft crashes, pesticide use and acid rain, for example. Such risks are fundamentally *different* to those faced in the past. In the public eye, they overwhelm in importance those more familiar risks we have faced for generations.

Yet it is the familiar risk which may be more important. Though exceedingly popular and widely used, both tobacco and alcohol are addictive and carcinogenic in different degrees, and they would certainly be banned if application was made for approval as foodstuffs or medicines.

''Experts'', these days, are widely distrusted: they always seem to disagree. ''Statistics''? We all know what lies they can be used to tell. ''Science''? May not be worth the candle; perhaps we should return to a gentler, simpler, non-technological way of life. These are all common attitudes. How do we know what to believe?

In order to make sensible decisions about the risks we run in our present way of life, we need information. To provide it is the purpose of this book. To the extent that available data permit, it represents an attempt to put risk in perspective, and to put numbers on a selection of risks as far as is possible. It is not its purpose to make choices for people, but only to present some of the facts on which those choices may be based. It does not seek to make judgements, because the *quantification* of risk—expressing it in numerical terms—is essentially an objective exercise. On the other hand, the *significance* attached by individual people to risks which have been thus quantified is indeed a subjective matter, a matter for personal concern and fundamental to judgement reached at all levels: individual, administrative

and political. But without reference to and agreement on essential information, any personal or community decisions reached are likely only to lead to conflict. Information is the key to consensus.

Chapter 1 traces the emergence of a logical train of thought in the pursuit of health and the conquest of disease. That has been a great deal more successful in some fields of human endeavour than others, and changing patterns of mortality show how different are the risks which our ancestors faced from those we face today.

The nature of risk is examined in more detail in Chapter 2. Its relationship to the concept of ''safety'' is examined, and injuries and disease brought together in a logical framework. The measurement of risk is the subject of Chapter 3: some occurrences and some outcomes are easy to measure, some virtually impossible. The handling of statistics and experimental data are outlined, and the way that analysts identify and quantify hazards described. The degree of risk may be expressed in several ways, and a selection of such expressions is discussed.

Chapter 4 identifies the main causes of death today, including heart disease, cancer and injury. Factors which appear to affect the risk of premature death from these causes are identified. Some important risk factors, such as smoking and the excessive use of alcohol, affect the outcomes of so many activities that they have Chapter 5 to themselves.

In Chapters 6 through 13, a wide variety of activities are described: work, play, transport and medical care. The risks associated with these activities are outlined and compared. Risks in the home, and risks posed by the production of electrical power and through the use of chemicals all receive individual attention.

In the final analysis, as we have already noted, what determines action at an individual or group level is the risk that is *perceived* by those affected, which may or may not be the same as that enumerated by analysts. This is the theme of Chapter 14. There is, in addition, a big difference in human value between a risk which is ''acceptable'' and a risk which is ''accepted'', either voluntarily or involuntarily, and such differences are examined.

Risk can be managed. Indeed, if by its management the overall level of health and welfare can be improved, most would agree that it should be. Some management techniques are outlined in Chapter 15 along with discussion of standards set for safety measures and devices, and the systems existing for regulatory control. To a large extent, we can manage—and thus control—the risks we face in our daily lives, and some guidelines are outlined.

Reductions in risk—improvements in the degree of safety—do not come free. Generally, the higher the standard we seek, the greater the cost. The balancing of the triad of risk, benefit and cost is also the subject of Chapter 15.

In the preparation of a publication such as this, a large number of sources have to be consulted. References to these sources are identified by numbers throughout the text, chapter by chapter, and are listed in a separate section towards the end of the book, together with some suggestions for further reading. Any good library will be able to obtain copies for the interested reader.

It is likely that advances in science, including medical science, are likely to lead to longer lives, led at a generally higher level of well-being. But it is also likely that the public awareness of risk, and concerns about risk, will continue to increase. Risks can be managed, reduced; but not all of them, and none to zero. It seems important, therefore, that our increased capacity to identify, measure and control risks should be accompanied by a high level of public understanding of their significance. To that end the book is aimed. As put so nicely by Lord Rothschild in his 1978 Reith Lecture: ''There is no point getting into a panic about the risks of life until you have compared the risks which worry you with those that don't, but perhaps should.''

Chapter One

History and Background:

THE TIMES ARE CHANGING

The word ''risk'' is probably derived from the Greek word ''rhiza'', the hazards of sailing too near to the cliffs: contrary winds, turbulent downdraughts, swirling tides. The idea of risk and its management was well understood by the ancient Greeks, who, with the Romans, identified many common hazards and potentially effective ways of minimizing their capacity to cause harm.

As long ago as Roman times, it was known that some substances and activities were hazardous, and that the risk from them could and should be reduced. The reduction of risk is one aspect of risk management.

Hippocrates was one of the first. He wrote in the 4th Century BC that sharp objects were more likely to cause injury because of the concentration of forces exerted by them on the human body; to spread the loads, he concluded, would reduce the chance of injury[1]. The Roman writer Vitruvius observed, also well before the birth of Christ, that workers exposed to the fumes of molten lead suffered disorders of the blood, and concluded that water should not be carried in lead pipes if it was to be wholesome[2]. In Deuteronomy, builders of new houses were urged to place parapets round roofs, lest otherwise visitors fall and bring ''the guilt of blood'' upon the home. Traffic safety was of active concern in ancient Rome, where non-essential wheeled vehicles were segregated from pedestrians during the hours of daylight. All these ideas were simply and effectively connected to the reduction of risk.

However, following the decline of the Greek and Roman civilizations, there was little progress during the next few hundred years towards a greater understanding of the links between hazards and harm. Few could comprehend basic biological and physical processes. Techniques for the systematic collection and analysis of data were yet to emerge. The scientific principles of formal experimentation were hardly developed at all. But these barriers could not resist an underlying imperative, a drive for the arrangement of facts into logical structures and for the classification of all things, animate and inanimate. When such pressures were coupled with the laying of the foundations of the theory of probability by Blaise Pascal in the mid-17th Century, a true revolution in intellectual development became possible. The *likelihood* that events would come to pass was at last a subject for scientists, not soothsayers.

During the Middle Ages, property damage and personal harm were regarded as inevitable consequences of certain courses of individual action. Efforts to prevent losses of this kind were thus concentrated on the behaviour of those men and women who were identified as "causing" the harm, and thus "to blame". Today, we accept that there are mechanistic links between hazardous behaviour and harm: weaving in and

out of dense traffic increases the risk of a crash, and setting aside the guard on a metal-working machine increases the risk to the hands of the worker. But three and four hundred years ago, the association between behaviour and harm was often regarded as having a supernatural basis. Hundreds of thousands of people were, after careful analysis by Church dignitaries, put to death as witches; to the satisfaction of such analysts, witchcraft by their victims had been proved responsible for a wide variety of small and large disasters, including crop failures, floods, droughts and diseases.

When it was finally proved that "witchcraft" was an illusion, that burning witches had no good effect on the incidence of loss and harm, and that most of the accusations were false and could not be substantiated by independent evidence, the burnings stopped. Logical thought had prevailed. Similarly, the concept of probability brought logic to the study of the likelihood of events, frequencies and averages. In the practical and competitive world of commerce, an emerging class of merchants needed to be able more precisely to calculate the chance that a planned venture would lose money: its risk, in other words. Mathematical theories of probability were soon being employed to develop tables showing how long people might be expected to live, and the practice of life insurance thus received its foundations.

Burning witches was an irrational response to the risks perceived as arising from dreadful hazards, such as plagues and famine. Nowadays we try to identify hazards more precisely and manage risks through science rather than the supernatural.

These developments created a far better understanding of the incidence and distribution of disease and injury in the community. They were paralleled by many studies aimed at identifying cause-and-effect relationships between the things people do that could be hazardous, and the adverse health effects which could result. By the end of the 19th Century, the following linkages had already been demonstrated[3]:

—London smoke and respiratory disease;
—celibacy and breast cancer;
—tobacco snuff and cancer of the lining of the nose;
—child chimney sweeps and cancer of the scrotum;
—arsenic and cancer;
—slum living and illness generally;
—sunlight and skin cancer;
—aromatic amines and cancer of the bladder;
—contaminated water and cholera.

The establishment of the link between water supplies and cholera is of particular interest because it illustrates so much of what is important in the study of disease in the community: of "epidemiology".

In the late 19th Century William Farr, in England, and Lemuel Shattuck, in Boston USA, recognized quite independently of each other that in order to understand hazards to life and to minimize the risks they posed, the systematic analysis of information on births and deaths was a necessary step. Information on the cause of death, not available in mass form before the 1840s, was crucial to Snow's identification of water as the carrier of cholera.

John Snow studied as a surgeon, but became a famous epidemiologist as the protegee of Edwin Chadwick, Secretary of the Poor Law Board and a pioneer in what he called "the sanitary idea". Chadwick believed that man could, by studying disease, determine causes and seek ways to prevent it. His great service to mankind was to replace fatalism by a new faith in science, in the control of the physical environment. It was Chadwick who secured the new law for the registration of the causes of death, and it was he who selected William Farr to administer it.

Conditions in crowded urban areas in the late 1800s were truly foul. It is hardly surprising that the many epidemic diseases were believed to be caused by "atmospheric impurity", miasmas generated by rotting organic filth. Although the miasma theory was subsequently shown to be false, it was constructive in that it encouraged improvements in sanitation. One of the main pioneers of urban sanitation was William Duncan, reputed to be the first Medical Officer of Health in Britain. He was appointed in 1847 in Liverpool with the principal purpose of controlling epidemic disease. Although unaware of the causes of infection, he recognized that overcrowded and insanitary housing was associated with increased risk of disease. The miasma theory was disproved for cholera by Snow, who had long believed that cholera was actually transmitted from people to people in some way, but it was not until 1854 and a vicious outbreak of cholera in Soho, London, that he was able to prove it by way of a natural experiment. Over 500 people within a radius of 250 yards died within 10 days. Snow plotted the deaths on a street map, and saw that the mass of them centred on a public water pump in Broad Street. He had the handle of the pump removed and the epidemic, already declining, ceased soon thereafter.

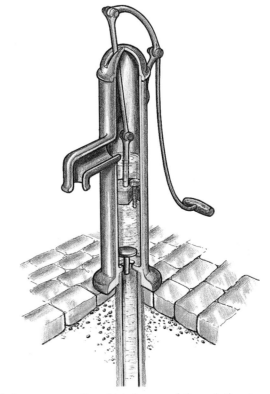

Cholera was once thought to be spread through the air. But it was found by careful study that the disease was carried by water. Control of the disease was possible by managing water supplies, including measures as simple as removing the handles from water pumps. Thus, control was possible long before the actual cholera germ was identified.

Snow also found that no cholera occurred among people living in the affected area, but who used water from sources other than that pump. Further, he discovered a few cases in suburbs miles away, among individuals who liked the water from the Broad Street pump so much they had it specially delivered to them.

Taking his analysis a further step, he then used Farr's data to study the results of a huge natural experiment. Water for most of London south of the Thames was supplied by two companies, the Lambeth Company and the Southwark and Vauxhall Company. The former furnished water from Thames Ditton, far above the massive outflow of sewage from London into the Thames, whereas the latter used water from the Thames in London. Water was piped by the companies in parallel, and consumers could choose either. The water from both sources was filtered to remove visible impurities. A cholera epidemic which had started in 1853 continued into 1854, and whenever a death occurred, the source of the water was identified. Over a four-week period, there were 71 deaths for every 10,000 houses serviced by Southwark and Vauxhall, and only 5 for every 10,000 houses using Lambeth Company water. The average for the whole of London was 9 deaths per 10,000 houses. Conclusion: cholera was being carried by sewage in the water.

Snow's work exemplified so much of what is important in epidemiology today, and is directly relevant to the assessment and management of risk. He included large numbers of people in his studies, so that confusion by chance factors was minimized. He used groups for comparison which were similar in all ways except for the influence of the supposed harmful agent—in this case, the water under study. He showed that not every individual exposed to a harmful agent will necessarily succumb to it. And, importantly, he showed that control of the harmful outcome did not necessarily depend on precise identification of the mechanism of harm: the only thing he could actually prove was that the disease was carried by water in some way that was invisible, but he could still control its spread by removing the handle of the Broad Street pump. The actual agent of harm, the cholera bacillus, was not identified until 30 years later. Knowledge of ''cause'' is not always needed in order to control the ''effect''.

The sanitary revolution which was so stimulated by those such as Chadwick, Farr and Snow (and not forgetting their eminent contemporary Dr William Budd, who did for typhoid what Snow did for cholera) initiated a complete change in the study of the pattern of disease. It was increasingly recognized that scientific investigation of the occurrence of disease, including the manner of spread from person to person, held the key to effective prevention. William Pickles, a general practitioner in Wensleydale, was a systematic student of infectious disease. From 1928 onwards for over 25 years he recorded every occurrence of a number of diseases within the villages that made up his practice. This rigorous attention to method enabled him to detect the long incubation period of infectious hepatitis, as well as contributing to the understanding of epidemic myalgia, chicken pox and other infections. As a result of the work of men like Snow, Budd and Pickles, concepts of quarantine and isolation became widely accepted. Acute infectious diseases, once the leading causes of death, were brought under control, so that their importance became minor. Jenner's observation in 1792 that vaccination with cowpox would prevent smallpox started a chain of events that allowed the World Health Organization to announce in 1979 that the disease was conquered completely. The onslaught on infectious disease has continued in recent years through the use of antibiotic drugs and the development of new vaccines directed against poliomyelitis and the childhood diseases. Sadly, however, in parts of the developing world the living conditions are still so bad that the patterns of disease have not changed, and infectious diseases are still killers.

The way we think about risks to life, limb and well-being today are manifestly very different from the way our ancestors thought about them, at least in the developed world. Major changes in the pattern of disease have occurred, and there have also been substantial changes in the social and political environment. Life expectancies have altered because of this shift in the distribution of risk. It is thus to these changes that we now turn our attention.

Trends in mortality

Thanks to the efforts of Chadwick and Farr, 1841 was the first year for which comprehensive mortality statistics were collected in England and Wales. The ''crude'' death rate (numbers of deaths per number of population) has about halved since then. The big fall was from 21.4

Trends in mortality, 1841–1980

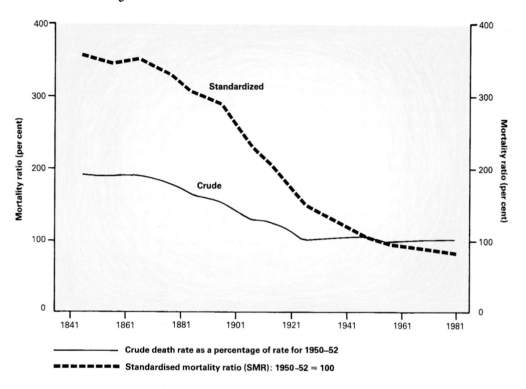

Crude death rate as a percentage of rate for 1950–52

Standardised mortality ratio (SMR): 1950–52 = 100

The crude death rate is the number of deaths per head of population. It is shown here to have fallen until 1921, since when the age and sex structure of the population has changed in such a way as to obscure death rates. The Standardized Mortality Ratio expresses the number of deaths per year as a percentage of those expected, if the age and sex distribution of the population stayed the same. It has continued to decline since records began in 1841.
Source: references 4 and 5

deaths per thousand people in the decade 1871–80, down to 12.1 deaths per thousand in 1921–30[4]. Since then, the crude death rate has stayed about the same, but this is because of changes in the age distribution of the population. To take account of such changes, the Office of Population Censuses and Surveys uses for standardization of rates the ''Standardized Mortality Ratio'', SMR, which expresses the number of deaths registered in a particular period as a percentage of those expected in a given year, had the age and sex mortality rates operated in the year of interest. The SMR calculated with 1950–52 as a base has declined from 344 in 1841–45, through 145 in 1926–30, to 81 in 1976–80.

There has been a very marked reduction in infant mortality during this period, from 148 per thousand live births in 1841–45 (one in seven) to 13 per thousand in 1976–80 (one in 77). This is just one part of a general pattern: the younger the age group, the greater the reduction in death

rate over the years. Among children and young people the death rate is now less than one-tenth of what it was in the 1840s, while it has been about halved for those in their sixties and reduced by around one-third for the oldest groups.

Clearly, then, while the expectation of life has increased generally, it has done so much more among the young than among the old. Life insurance was introduced in a rudimentary form in Roman times, and despite some opposition from the Church—whose authorities once considered that what was in effect gambling against the will of God was immoral—it became a flourishing industry in England from the 17th Century on, and led to the derivation of ''life tables''. The expectation of life can be tabulated in such a way that account is taken of changes in the age and sex distribution of the population over time, and the expected age at death has changed greatly from the time of Farr to modern days. Gains to the benefit of the young are the most obvious.

5

Expectation of age at death, 1841–1981

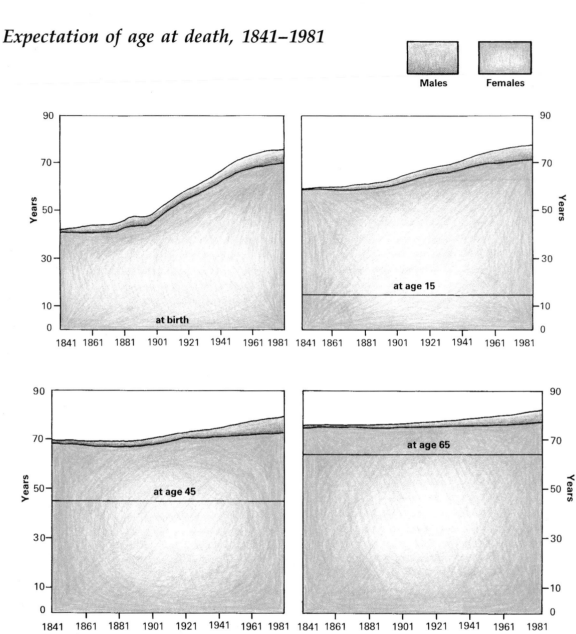

The bulk of the improvement in life expectancy has been due to very greatly reduced death rates in the very young. The figure shows that a male could expect to live to age 35 when born in 1841, but to 70 when born in 1981. However, the life expectancy of a man aged 65 has not changed much during the same period, although it has improved a little for women.
Source: references 4 and 5

What these figures mean is this. Out of a group of babies born in Victorian times, a high proportion would die in the first year, and even those children who had survived that period would continue to die in large numbers, well into their teens. The image of the dying child is in sharp focus in Victorian literature, which is hardly surprising—nearly half all those dying were children. Now, to lose a child is rare: only about 2% of all deaths occur between birth and

14 years. A far higher proportion of those being born these days, therefore, are surviving through the middle years. Not that the ageing process can, at present, be beaten; for thousands of years those who have survived the longest have finally succumbed at about the same age, not greatly extended from the "three score years and ten" of the Bible. The overall effect of all this is that many more of those being born now will still be alive 50–70 years on than was the case in Victorian times.

A corollary of this is that the more people can be saved from dying from a premature death, the more people will die from what we used to call "old age". The care of the aged, and the management of the hazards to which they are particularly susceptible (such as falls and extremes of temperature), will be a major challenge in future years.

The life tables show a consistent difference between the life expectancies of males and females, and this is confirmed by examination of death rates for different age groups. The gap between male and female mortality has been widening in recent years. In the age group 15–19, the mortality among boys for the decade 1961–70 was 150% higher than among girls, an entirely new pattern since the Second World War. In the age group 55–64, male mortality in 1961–70 was 100% higher than female, compared to 28% higher in 1901–10 and 12% in 1841–50.

These changes must be influenced by environmental factors and the way we live, including different patterns of smoking between the sexes, alcohol use, and (often related) accidents. They therefore reflect a shift in the pattern of risks faced by men and women over the last century. If male death rates could be reduced to female levels, fewer than half the men now dying below the age of 65 would do so in the future[5].

So, what *are* people now dying from, compared to past years?

The relative importance of the main disease groups as causes of death in 1930, 1950 and 1982 has changed to an extraordinary extent. The striking feature is the virtual disappearance of mortality due to infectious disease, of which the most important used to be tuberculosis, the "captain of the men of death". Some of the reasons for this (the "sanitary revolution") have already been outlined. "Maternal causes" of death have also almost disappeared; but once upon a time, giving birth was a dangerous business. There have also been reductions in the relative frequencies of deaths from disease of the lungs, guts and genito-urinary system.

Percentage excess of male over female death rates by age, 1841–1980

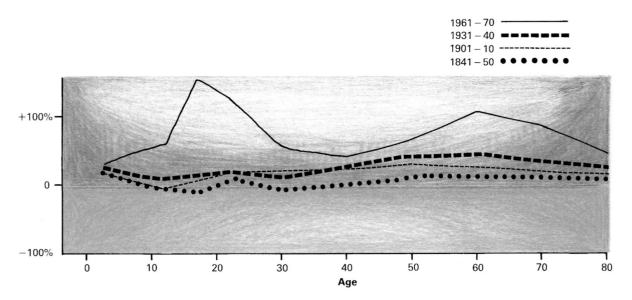

This shows, for each age group, the percentage excess of male mortality over female. In the group 15–19 years, the mortality among boys is 150% higher than among girls, an entirely new pattern since the Second World War. At ages 55–64, male mortality in 1961-70 was 100% higher than female, compared with 28% in 1901-10 and 12% in 1841-50.
Source: reference 7

Relative importance of causes

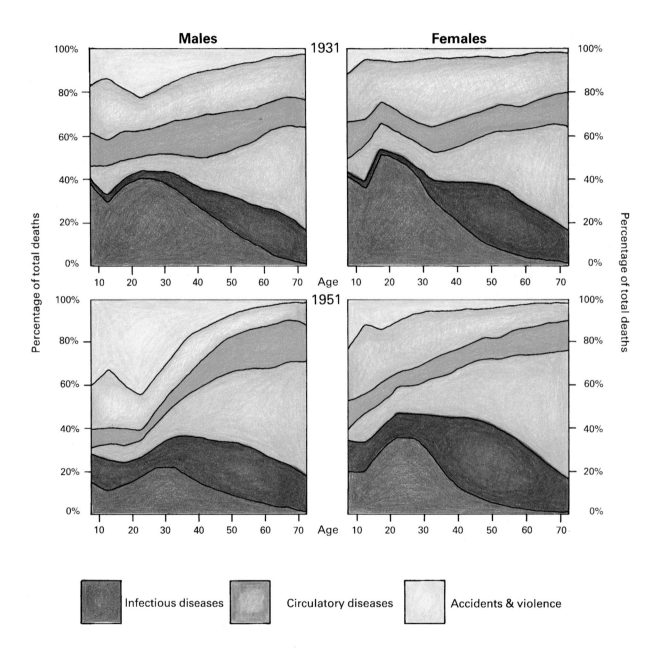

Males   1931   **Females**

Percentage of total deaths

1951

Age

Percentage of total deaths

Infectious diseases   Circulatory diseases   Accidents & violence

The relative importance of various causes of death is shown for different periods. At each age, the percentage of all deaths is shown; so, for example, in 1931 among men aged 20, about 36% of deaths were from infective disease, 4% cancer, 7% circulatory, 14% respiratory, 6% digestive, 3% genitourinary, 10% other, and 20% accidents and violence. The

# of death, by age, selected years

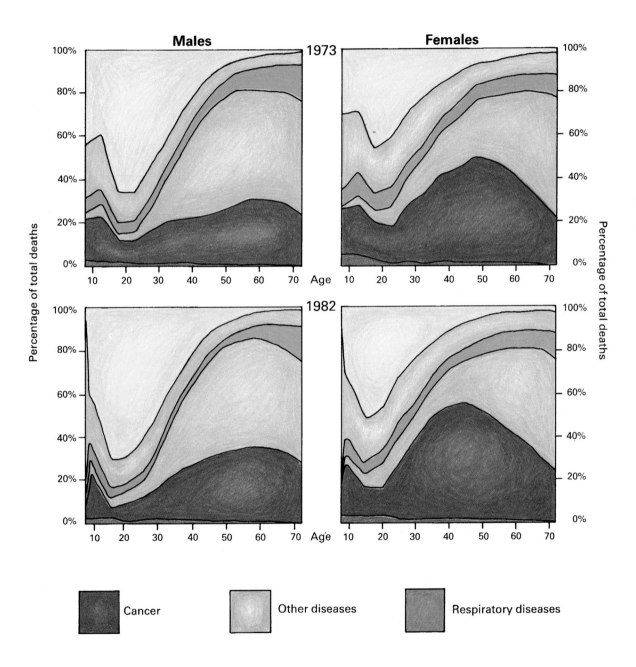

important feature is the virtual disappearance of death due to infectious diseases and the massive increase in the relative importance of accidents and violence among the young, especially males.
Source: OPCS and DHSS statistics

Causes of death, England and Wales 1984

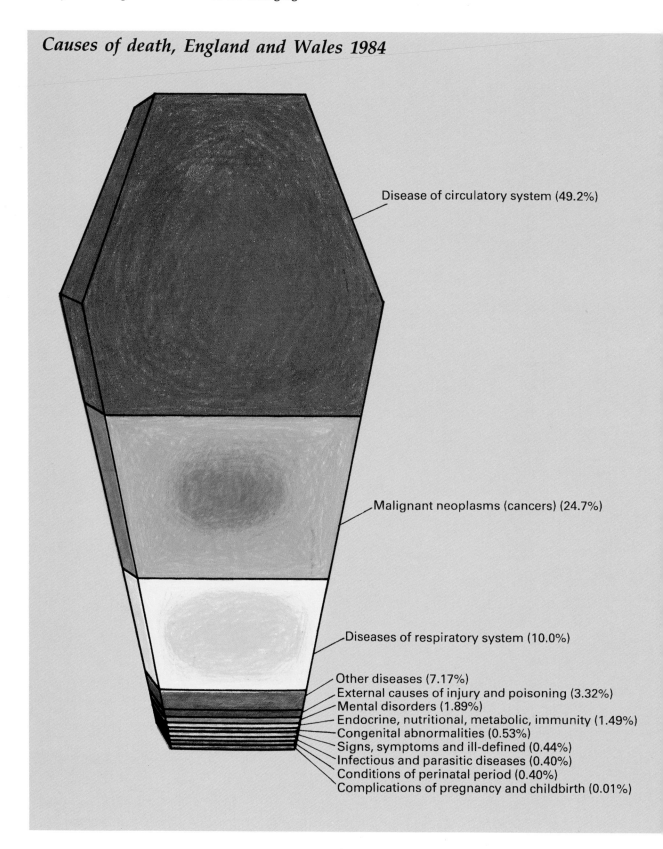

Disease of circulatory system (49.2%)

Malignant neoplasms (cancers) (24.7%)

Diseases of respiratory system (10.0%)

Other diseases (7.17%)
External causes of injury and poisoning (3.32%)
Mental disorders (1.89%)
Endocrine, nutritional, metabolic, immunity (1.49%)
Congenital abnormalities (0.53%)
Signs, symptoms and ill-defined (0.44%)
Infectious and parasitic diseases (0.40%)
Conditions of perinatal period (0.40%)
Complications of pregnancy and childbirth (0.01%)

On the other hand, there have been relative *increases* in mortality in three groups: diseases of the blood circulation system (including heart attacks and strokes), cancer, and accidents (unexpected violent injury and poisoning). Between them, these causes now account for three-quarters of all deaths.

The increase in accidents and violence has dramatically mirrored the decrease in infectious disease as a relative cause of death. This is especially the case for males. Two-thirds of all male deaths around the age of 20 are now from accidents and violence, which are still accounting for half of all male deaths right up to the age of nearly 30 years. They are not overtaken by circulatory disease as the single most important cause of death until well into the fourth decade of life.

The above are, of course, *relative* causes of death. Overall, for all violent deaths the crude death rate (deaths per million in the population) has declined since the turn of the century from 480 (about one death for every 2,000 people every year) to 406 (around one in 2,500 each year) in 1931–35, and 299 (one in 3,300 per year) in 1976–80[4].

So, what we die of now is summarized in the accompanying figure. About half all deaths are caused by diseases of the heart and circulation, of which three-quarters are classified as heart disease (mostly coronary artery disease) and one-quarter as blood vessel disease. People die from these diseases at an increasing rate at increasing ages. Cancer, the second commonest cause of death, now kills nearly one in four of us.

Accidents and violence are responsible for the deaths of a lower percentage overall, at around 3%, but because they are the most important cause of death among the young they are responsible for a large proportion of premature deaths and great loss of productive life.

No other single disease causes more than 2% of all deaths.

Overall, what this chapter shows is that there have been dramatic reductions in the risk of premature death since Victorian times, when measurements first became possible because deaths began to be assigned to causes and counted. The risk has been reduced by the systematic application of scientific knowledge, so that human lives have been saved. While we may worry about hazards imposed by new technologies, we should not forget that the hazards faced by our ancestors were certainly not less terrifying than those we face now, and killed relatively far more of them at earlier ages. The

ICD Number	Cause of Death	Number	Percentage
390-459	Disease of circulatory system	278,849	49.2
140-239	Malignant neoplasms (cancers)	140,101	24.7
460-519	Diseases of respiratory system	56,828	10.0
E800-E999	External causes of injury and poisoning	18835	3.32
520-579	Diseases of the digestive system	16,980	2.99
290-319	Mental disorders	10,744	1.89
320-389	Disease of the nervous system	10,483	1.85
240-279	Endocrine, nutritional, metabolic, immunity	84,999	1.49
580-629	Diseases of the genito-urinary system	7,731	1.36
710-739	Diseases of the musculoskeletal system	4,943	0.87
740-759	Congenital abnormalities	3,017	0.53
780-799	Signs, symptoms and ill-defined	2,534	0.44
001-139	Infectious and parasitic diseases	2,295	0.40
760-779	Conditions of perinatal period	2,289	0.40
680-709	Diseases of the skin	601	0.10
630-676	Complications of pregnancy and childbirth	52	0.01
Totals		566,881	100.0

By the late 1980s, diseases of the heart, circulation and lungs, together with cancer, were responsible for most deaths. Killer diseases cannot be prevented for ever. But their influence on the length and quality of life can be reduced as far as possible. Changing risk factors can help do this. *Source:* OPCS, *Mortality Statistics, Causes of Death*, 1984

way of life might have been simpler then, but it certainly was not safer.

In studying risk, therefore, the above very simple analysis indicates that on a priority basis we should be most concerned about factors which affect the risk of heart disease and cancer, which are the leading causes of death overall, and factors affecting the risk of accidents and violence, which, for the young in the developed world, have taken over from infectious disease as captains of the men of death.

However, as we shall see later, society places a very high priority on causes of death which, in terms of total numbers, appear to be of much less significance than those we have briefly reviewed so far. The deaths of a lot of people at one time from natural and ''man-made'' disasters is an example which comes readily to mind. Risks associated with such causes receive a high level of attention, and so from the point of view of risk reduction are of commensurate importance. Before turning our attention to such matters in more detail, we should now discuss the nature of risk itself.

Chapter Two

The Nature of Risk

Difficulties often arise when scientists and technical people use jargon, especially when quite common words are used differently from everyday chat. "Risk" is such a word.

The way the word is used in this book, and the way that most scientists believe the word should be used[1], is as an expression of the *probability*—the likelihood—that something unpleasant will happen. If the consequence of throwing a six when you roll a dice is that you receive an electric shock, then there is a one-in-six *risk* of being shocked.

A *hazard* is a set of circumstances which may cause harmful consequences, and the likelihood of its doing so is the *risk* associated with it.

A speeding car is a hazard. The faster it howls through a village, and the more children there are playing at the roadside, the higher the risk that it will kill a child. Tower Bridge is a hazard by its very existence: there is a risk that a vessel may be damaged when swept against it by the tide, and there is a risk that a road vehicle may fall into the gap when the bridge opens. Both risks are low, but the events have happened.

Harmful outcomes vary. Worrying about human health and welfare, we may be most concerned about losses such as death, illness, or injury to human beings. The loss of trees is an outcome of exposure to acid rain. The loss of amenity results from the collapse of a bridge. So, there are many kinds of *losses* resulting from many kinds of hazards. Losses can be represented as *costs* to society, and costs are also incurred when we try to reduce risks.

The degree of risk, then, can be changed. Risk can be *managed*. The probability that occurrences may cause harm can be increased or decreased by the influence of "risk factors". Which brings us to another example. The process of birth is a *hazard* to the child. There is a *risk* that the child will suffer *harm*, including death. Various *risk factors* are known to be associated with an above-average probability of the baby dying; and, by way of comment on the preceding chapter, it is clear that these risk factors have changed dramatically in England during the last century in such a way that the risk of death is much lower than it was.

Naturally, the word "risk" is often used pretty casually. We are familiar with the general idea from childhood. We risk burning our hands if we touch the stove. We risk skinning our knees if we ride our bikes too crazily. So we learn to change the ways we behave, taking due account of risks while we work out ways best to enjoy ourselves.

There are those who are generally "risk takers" and those who are generally "risk avoiders" by temperament. As they age, people may ease across from one category to the other. At one extreme, there are those who see real benefit in accepting and facing risk, even when this quite substantially increases the probability of a premature death. Mountain climbing, motor racing and hang gliding are all examples of activities carrying very high risk and very low "utility", or usefulness in terms of benefits to mankind. That does not make them worthless. An Everest climber[2], answering the question "why climb Everest?", has given as a reason the fact that Everest climbing *is* very risky and very useless. "The risk taker", he argues, with tongue only partly in cheek, "anxious to expand the pure aesthetic scope of his preferred style, could not ask for a more perfect objective". The risk avoider, on the other hand, is positively repelled by the very same values that the risk taker finds attractive.

So, although people shade between these extremes, at any given time an individual will have a view of the world, and a view of risk, which is strongly influenced by personal opinion and social context. This does not mean that one individual is "right" and the other is "wrong". There should be plenty of scope for such differences in the wider social context. A great deal of argument about risk (whether to humankind or the world) is not so much about objective measurement of hazards and disease rates as it is about different moral and social values. In a study of beliefs about risks to the environment, the views of industrialists as well as conservationists were sought. It was found that industrialists saw much lower risks generally than the conservationists, with a random sample of the public falling somewhere in between[3]. The groups at each extreme did not differ in the amount of information available to them, but "risk" translated into very different orders of "danger" for each group because of their very different views of the world in general. The way such perceptions may be important in making personal decisions on health are explored further in later chapters.

Risk cannot ever be reduced to zero, and for many voluntary activities such as climbing, risk adds to the spice of life. We are prepared to accept much higher risks if we choose to face them voluntarily than if we are put at risk by others involuntarily. If we understand how risks compare with each other we can make sensible judgements about avoiding and reducing those we find unacceptable.

On the *facts* of a situation, there may be little disagreement. Mountain climbers, Grand Prix drivers and ocean sailors know, at least as well as those who would avoid such hazardous activities like the plague, that they are a great deal more likely to die prematurely than if they had stayed at home and watched the television. That does not mean the risk takers want to die; there is a huge market for ''safety equipment'' for use in dangerous sports, exemplifying risk management at the personal level. And it is not a matter of financial inducement; the vast majority of those who voluntarily engage in hazardous activities pay heavily to do so. And the few top professionals are rich enough to stop if they wanted to.

As individuals, risk takers and risk avoiders may simply observe each other's activities with amused detachment or varying degrees of tolerance. But when risks spread, when people are exposed to risks involuntarily, those are other matters altogether and the measurement, evaluation and management of risk becomes a subject of community concern. But it is as well, at that stage, that protagonists in any debate agree on the ground rules and the basic objectives.

Many people feel uncomfortable with the whole concept of ''risk''. They would be much happier thinking about ''safety''. Genetic engineering may be good for crops and all that, ''but is it safe?'' That is a great new car, ''but is it safe?'' Nuclear power may not use scarce fossil fuels, ''but is it safe?'' That medicine may help my arthritis, ''but is it safe?''

There is no such thing as ''safe''. It is an absolute term. Varying degrees of risk can be compared with varying degrees of safety; the two concepts are mirror images in a way. But what we are trying to do is minimize the incidence of unwanted consequences, and so it is *risk* which is the most appropriate concept. We discuss the ''risk'' of a wet weekend, not (usually) the ''risk'' of the sun shining.

It might seem that we could be absolutely safe—and avoid all risk—by simply not doing things which force us to confront hazards. But in the real world we can never do better than exchange one risk for another. By not going swimming we totally avoid the risk of drowning; but by staying at home instead, we may increase the risk, if only to a small degree, of heart disease resulting from inactivity. Choosing to travel to work by train instead of car may make us a lot ''safer'', in terms of lowered risk to life and limb

each trip; but it does not make us ''safe''. Risk can never be reduced to zero.

What ''safe'' means, to most people, is that for a given activity the associated risks have been reduced to ''negligible'' levels, and to make something ''safe enough'' is to reduce the risk to the level of ''acceptability''. To the idea of ''acceptable'' risks we will return towards the end of the book. But first, let us examine a little more closely the nature of harm, because it is to reduce harm which is at the very heart of all risk management endeavours.

The nature of harm

The harm that results from a given hazard is commonly expressed in terms of death. This may seem to over-emphasize the importance of death as an unwanted outcome, but there is a reason which is partly historical and partly practical.

As we have seen, the first public health statistics to be gathered in England and in the United States were those concerned with the immediate *cause* of death, as a result of an understandable focus of priority on the *prevention* of death. Now, as then, the most complete and the most reliable data we have are on deaths and their causes. However, as a growing proportion of the population extends life into the middle-age groups, it is of increasing importance to collect and analyse information on community *morbidity* (illness and non-fatal injury), as well as on mortality. But apart from much higher numbers involved, this is very hard to do. Much illness goes unreported, let alone unrecorded; diagnostic classifications vary from doctor to doctor; and so on.

Nevertheless, the Department of Health and Social Security does monitor morbidity on a sample survey basis (as opposed to the 100% coverage of death statistics). For example, the Office of Population Censuses and Surveys annually processes a 10% sample of discharges from non-psychiatric hospitals in England. Cancers are registered in terms of sex and site on the body. Surveys of morbidity reported during visits to general practitioners are periodically undertaken. Not surprisingly, the patterns of disease associated with care by the general practitioner are different from those associated with hospital care, and both are different from the pattern of diseases which cause death. For instance, heart disease and lung cancer are common causes of death in males and females over 65 years of age, but are less predominant among those discharged from hospital or visiting the general practitioner. Injuries comprise a higher proportion of discharges from hospital than either deaths or contacts with the general practitioner[4]. Chronic disorders with low mortality, such as arthritis, are more often seen by the general practitioner than the hospital specialist.

The study of risk in its widest sense implies an intent to reduce *all* sorts of harm, and not only the rate of mortality. In any event, some might argue that death was not the worst conceivable outcome, compared for example with a lifetime in complete paralysis, or a terminal period in great pain and distress. In discussing the avoidance or minimization of risk, it is as well to keep in mind that harm to the human being may be measured and perceived in many different ways.

Several attempts have been made over the years to develop an "index of harm", to take into account several effects and outcomes within a single measure. For example, the International Commission on Radiological Protection[5] wished to compare the risk of occupational exposure to ionizing radiation with risks in other occupations. They proposed a comparison based on the loss of years of life or normal activity, as a result of death, non-fatal injuries and occupational disease. But this treats cancer, genetic defects, fractured skulls and lacerated faces all on the same basis, as it does for loss of activity for whatever reason and at whatever age. Death, compared to a year off work, is weighted by a factor of 10. Most would agree that there are too many disparate elements in this type of index to help individuals make decisions on what they choose to do, although it may assist planners with limited money to reduce risk where it is most necessary. The fundamental aim is to embrace measures showing *quality* of life as well as *quantity*.

Such attempts have been taken further, to include estimates of monetary value for the losses entailed. The element of subjectivity is strong, but to assign hard costs can force the use of logical thought before making decisions, so that the process may be helpful in assessing priorities for action.

Injuries, and measures to reduce them, are commonly viewed as falling into a different category from "disease", and the reduction of the risk of injury as a task which is independent of the normal activities of public health and medical

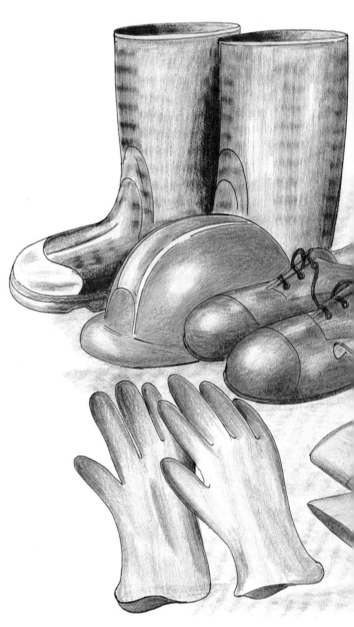

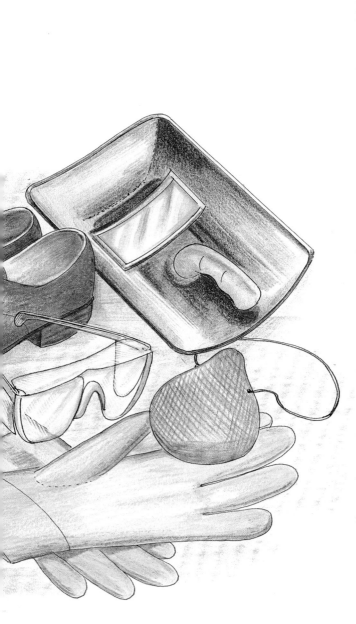

We can reduce the risk of physical injury by using all kinds of protective equipment. Injury is just like disease: we can reduce the risk of its causing us harm by choosing from available protective measures.

specialists. There is no logical reason for this to be so. Communities and individuals have for centuries sought to reduce the risk and degree of injury by an extraordinarily wide variety of control measures: airport control towers, traffic lights, electrical fuses, seat belts, ambulance services, gloves, shoes and fireguards are a tiny selection of them. Injuries have always been endemic (widespread in large numbers over a long period of time throughout the community), and in many ways their epidemiology is directly analogous to that of infectious disease: there are epidemics (shorter outbreaks of large numbers), seasonal variations, well-established long-term trends, and known distributions within geographic, socio-economic, and rural-urban categories. This has been well established for nearly 40 years[6]. There is nothing very "accidental" about such a non-random and uncapricious distribution of events.

In classical epidemiology, within a given *environment, vehicles* and *vectors* carry *agents* of harm to susceptible individuals in such a way as to cause disease. In a suitably damp environment, for example, the mosquito (the vector) carries the malaria parasite (the agent) and injects it into the victim. Comparatively recently[7], injury has been placed in the same context, except that the *agents* of injury are the various forms of energy. Mechanical energy is the commonest, and others include heat, chemical and electrical energy, and radiation. The energy is carried by vectors such as cars and guns, and may be stored in structures such as high buildings and dams for later release.

Notions of individual blame, and the overriding importance of the control of individual behaviour, have since the turn of the century retreated into insignificance in the control of widespread disease. Such a shift in approach has been slower to occur in the case of injury, which is one reason why injury is now such an important cause of death, but it would be more widely accepted if injury control were to be more closely related to classical approaches to public health. Perhaps because of the very close association in time between individual actions and resulting injury, attention does tend to concentrate on the need to change individual behaviour in the search for injury control. But in essence, there is only a difference in time between lung injury caused on the one hand by years of inhalation of coal dust and, on the other hand, lung injury caused by impact against a vehicle dashboard in a crash. Yet it is much easier for most people to conceive of a wide array of measures at community and personal levels to control black-lung disease than to control impact injury.

Injury is such an important contributor to premature death, and the risk of injury so central to discussion of risk in general, that it is essential to consider injury risk in the same context as we consider the risks associated with heart disease, cancer and other diseases, and not single it out as a special category of harm for a different style of intervention.

The mosquito is a link in the chain which puts us at risk of malaria and other disease. To control this risk we can tackle the mosquito and the environment where it breeds, or give drugs to people which kill the parasites in the bloodstream. There are many ways to control a single risk.

Chapter Three

The Measurement of Risk

RISK ASSESSMENT

If we really want to understand how important to us a risk may be, sooner or later we will have to express it in quantitative terms: to put some numbers on it, in other words. The science of risk assessment brings together two disciplines: mathematics, and in particular the theory of probability; and epidemiology, particularly the identification of causes of death, illnesses and injury.

The trouble is, for many risks the numbers are simply not available. Risks fall into different classes[1]:

—risks for which plenty of statistics are available, and for which information on harm can be accurately collected;

—risks for which some evidence may be available, but for which the relationship between hazard and harmful effect for any given individual cannot be estimated with certainty (for example, cancer developing some years after exposure to a chemical);

—risks of harmful events which have not yet happened, and estimation of which is thus based on forecasts and probabilities (for example, collapse of a bridge, or reactor failure in a nuclear power station).

When plenty of data are available, the process of *"risk assessment"* can proceed without real difficulty. It is often divided into two stages, as follows.

1 Risk estimation

This relies on scientific activity and scientific judgement. When information is available on harmful events that have already happened, it can be used to build a bank of statistics, with numbers large enough to be reliable ("statistically significant", with an identifiable range of doubt). These statistics can then be used to predict both the magnitude and the likelihood (the risk) of harmful events in the future.

2 Risk evaluation

This relies on social and political judgement, and is aimed at determining the *importance* of hazards and the risk of harm from the point of view of those individuals and communities who face the risk. It would appear to be self-evident that a risk of high probability and large magnitude is consequently an important one; but it may not be seen to be by those affected. Accordingly, this aspect of risk assessment includes aspects of the perception of risk and the trading-off of perceived risks and benefits, which are both the subjects of later discussion.

Collection of data

Counting deaths has been a way of putting numbers on risk since the emergence of epidemiological method nearly 150 years ago. Deaths are absolute, and easy to count if efforts are made to do so. The problem is, death rates can only give a crude indication of the process of harm and the extent of risk. Harm, as we have already stressed, may be represented in many other ways: by disease, injury and disability to people, effects on experimental animals and wildlife, damage to plantlife and the environment, financial and material loss, or loss of social amenity. Although all these outcomes are much harder to measure than death rates, for the purpose of assessing risk they may have every bit as much validity.

Deaths usually occur shortly after exposure to the hazard, and the chain of factors causing the death can comparatively easily be identified. A child is run over in the street; the car which struck the child was moving at 30 mph, the damage to the car and child is visible and measurable, the car driver had a measurable level of alcohol in the blood. If all such factors are measured often enough, the relationship between, say, speed in urban streets, driver blood-alcohol level and child pedestrian fatalities can become well established and thus predictable. Factors linking illness with long-term exposure to a toxic gas or chemical may be far harder to elucidate, and several years may pass between the time of exposure and the diagnosis of disease.

To count deaths alone is not in itself sufficient to give a "rate", as Farr realized at the outset. By using census data to define the population as a whole, he was able to publish death rates in terms of age and sex for each disease; more recently, other measures such as marital status, occupation and area of residence have also been included in mass statistics. This enables, for example, comparison of death rates for stomach cancer among middle-aged males in Liverpool and London; but it does not permit further analysis including, say, examination of dietary, drinking and smoking habits. This would require more detailed study, usually by setting up special research projects. But large, cross-sectional data do often signal the need for further research on risk, by raising questions that need answering.

Remembering our child pedestrian for a moment, to assess the *true* risks to children in the street or that street in particular, we need to know a bit more about the situation. First, we must know more about exposure. We need an idea of the number of cars that use the street by day or night, and it would be helpful to know the range of speeds at which they are travelling. We also need to know about the children: how many, what ages, how much time do they spend in the area, how much time crossing over the road or playing in it? Given these data, we can quite realistically put a measure on the actual risk to a child of being hit by a car in the street. The simple fact that one child has been hit by a car shows that a risk exists; it does not show how great it is. And bear in mind that once a child *is* hit, then public perception of the risk will jump dramatically and understandably, although the *actual* — that is, as measured — risk has not changed at all.

Causal factors are similarly linked together in complex ways when it comes to death, injury and disease suffered as a result of occupation.

To assess risk, we need to know about the type of work and the machinery used, and how many individuals are engaged in similar labour. What of the individuals themselves? What of their social, personal and psychological characteristics? Is an observed high incidence of lung cancer linked to carcinogens on the job or the incidence of smoking? Or both; maybe the factors multiply, rather than just add together?

Given the data, they can be worked through in at least two ways[2]. The first is to concentrate on each occupation to see whether there are any peculiar features of the mortality pattern observed. Are the death rates from any particular causes especially high?

Second, causes of death can be examined in order to see whether particular occupations appear especially commonly, and whether there are characteristics which are shared by different occupations with high death rates from similar causes.

As this century moved into its second half, several studies were mounted throughout the world which aimed to track groups within the population throughout their life, properly documenting exposure to all kinds of hazard. The smoking habits of a large group of doctors, for example, were followed for many years, enabling the first really accurate assessment of smoking's risk to health; the point was that non-smokers in the same group were also followed and documented, enabling proper comparison to be made. Similar studies have been performed among workers in rubber and chemical plants, and among asbestos workers.

Similarly, but from the point of view of the disease rather than the occupation, a large number of Americans are now volunteering personal information over a very long period for years, in order to try to define what roles are played in the genesis of cancer by various factors in daily life, including smoking, diet, work and several aspects of lifestyle. The problem here is to ensure that research is asking the right questions; if at a late stage in the study a suspicious factor emerges unexpectedly, it is too late to go back and start again.

For the assessment of risk, it is important to stress the need for study of the whole population at risk, or at least a representative sample of it. If that is not done, the results of study can be grossly misleading.

For example, in several countries which have introduced laws requiring the use of seat belts, concerned doctors have identified an apparent *increase* in the severity of crash injury following the legislation. Their concern, reflected in the media, has often caused great confusion. Do seat belts *increase* the risk of injury? The reason for this misapprehension, however, is that doctors will see a relatively high incidence of severe injury

after such legislation because seat belts have their greatest beneficial effect in crashes at moderate speed, so that those who would have been "moderately" hurt have their injuries prevented altogether. Thus, the doctors never see them. But they still see the more severe injuries received in the more violent crashes. Also, in very bad crashes, many of those who might have been killed without seat belts instead survive with severe injuries; previously, the doctors had never seen those who died. Furthermore, seat belts

The interested eye is so often turned to the victims of harm that it is easy to forget those who escape it. We can have no idea of the size of a risk if we look only at those affected by it. We must always compare those who are harmed with those who are not.

cannot protect in some kinds of crash, such as impact from the side, and because these commonly result in rather severe head and chest injuries, their relative importance to the doctors appears to increase. Overall, therefore, the puzzled doctor finds that he is treating worse injuries than before.

The point is that to assess risk, *it is not sufficient merely to study the victims*. The survivors, the non-victims, the population as a whole—all these also need to be counted if the assessment is to be valid.

Studies of the type outlined so far can provide a great deal of risk information to answer questions such as, does activity A or drug B cause injury C or cancer D? But there is a good deal more to be answered. For example, the relationship of smoking to lung cancer has been the subject of the most detailed epidemiological studies imaginable, but we still do not really know very much about the risk of exposure to small amounts of smoke, or whether there is some threshold level below which smoke does not trigger the cancer process. As more detail is required, more complex investigations are needed. How is the "dose" of injurious agent (poison, radiation, mechanical energy) related to the human response? Should death be treated as a separate entity, or as an aggravated form of illness?

The risk posed by many types of hazard is not primarily that of death. Deformation of a baby, or sterility in an adult, are outcomes which represent a substantial degree of harm, yet mortality statistics cannot measure them. For so many such cases, when a given agent is suspected to represent a great risk, the actual probability of its causing harm is unknown because not enough is known about the prevalence of the disability or illness in the population *not* exposed to the agent.

Individual susceptibility further complicates the matter. Individuals with Alzheimer's disease (premature senility) have been found to have a higher level of aluminium in the brain than those of similar age and sex without the disease. Could the use of aluminium saucepans be a risk factor for Alzheimer's disease? To even start answering such a question, one would need to know the relative proportion of aluminium saucepan users in the Alzheimer's and non-Alzheimer's groups and then, if the link was confirmed, to determine how much aluminium saucepan-using represented how much risk, and whether there was a level of use so low that

the risk was negligible or non-existent. This hypothetical case serves to illustrate how hard it is to develop "dose-response" relationships for chronic illness, especially when death is not necessarily the final outcome.

The description of risk

Throughout this book will be found a wide variety of different ways of expressing and describing levels of risk. This is because "risk" can mean such different things, depending on the context and the population "at risk". For example, say (for the purpose of a totally unreal hypothesis) that a nuclear facility was so radioactive that two men a year died from acute radiation sickness working in it. What, then is the risk—the threat to health and welfare—of operating the facility?

The *immediate* risk to the workers in the *plant* might be expressed as two deaths a year per so many workers in the plant. For workers in the *industry* throughout the country, the average death rate would be two deaths from radiation sickness per year among all of them; but, obviously, the risk is grossly unevenly distributed and would not in practice be faced by the vast majority.

The workers are only exposed to the radiation while at work. Maybe, therefore, the risk should be expressed not in terms of numbers of people, but in terms of *time exposed* to risk? This has, in fact, been used as an index of comparison of industrial safety records.

But these hypothetical workers are not exposed only to the risk of immediate death, but also to delayed death from illness such as cancer. Perhaps it would be more realistic to express the risk in terms of illness rates? Or, as is quite often attempted, in terms of life-years lost?

And then there is the public outside the plant, let us suppose also exposed to radiation. They, too, face the risk of delayed illness and a premature death—can we possibly express the risk to them in such terms? Do we know enough to *predict* the level of risk before anyone has died? The risk will be highest for those who live nearest. It would clearly be absurd to express the public risk in terms of death or illness for the entire population. But where to draw the line? At one mile radius? Ten miles? One hundred miles? At the county border?

Such questions are unanswerable. Indices of risk are best chosen on an individual basis, depending on the event or activity, and preferably using simple numbers; say, one in 1,500 rather than 66.7 per 100,000, which means the same thing but is less immediately comprehensible.

An important proposal to make sense of risk levels was recently put forward by Urquhart and Heilmann in their book, *Risk Watch*[3]. In looking at a particular risk, they take all the people exposed to it, and divide this number by the number of victims of the hazard over a defined time span. Examples would be, the risk of a water skier being killed in America is one in 384,000 per year, and the risk of a snow skier being injured is one in 150 or one in 500 per day on the slopes. Very many examples of this style of representation will be found in this book. But Urquhart and Heilmann take their proposition a step further.

Risks using the "one in . . ." expression can be ranked from one in one, one in ten, one in 100, one in 1,000 and so on, through to one in a million, up to any number of noughts needed. They then take the logarithms of these numbers: 0 when the risk is 1:1, 1 when it is 1:10, 2 when 1:100 and so on up to 8, eight noughts, or 1:100,000,000. These log numbers then represent the risk, and are called "Safety Degree Units", or SDUs. It works this way. Say the death rate among motorcyclists is 10 per 10,000. So, the SDU for motorcycling is 3. The SDU for smoking at age 35 is between 2 and 3. The SDU for a fatal lightning strike in Britain is just under 7. The higher the number, the lower the risk.

This is a sterling effort to get people accustomed to something like a Richter Scale, which is a very well-accepted logarithmic expression for earthquake intensity. But it is unlikely to be much easier in practice for people to get used to a logarithmic scale than a "one in . . ." scale, and it lacks flexibility. Comparing traffic risks, for example, it is more valid to express risk in terms of mileage rather than on the basis of population at risk, as will be explained in the relevant section.

To return to our "one in . . ." comparisons for a moment, here are a few examples. In the relevant chapters will be found a great deal more detail, but, roughly, these are the average risks of an individual dying in any one year from an arbitrary selection of causes:

Risk of an individual dying in any one year from various causes

Smoking 10 cigarettes a day:	one in 200
All natural causes, age 40:	one in 850
Any kind of violence or poisoning.	one in 3,300
Influenza:	one in 5,000
Accident on the road:	one in 8,000
Leukaemia:	one in 12,500
Playing soccer:	one in 25,000
Accident at home:	one in 26,000
Accident at work:	one in 43,500
Radiation working in radiation industry:	one in 57,000
Homicide:	one in 100,000
Accident on railway:	one in 500,000
Hit by lightning:	one in 10,000,000
Release of radiation from nearby nuclear power station:	one in 10,000,000

THE PREDICTION OF RISK

The assessment of risk based on past events can be very accurate, given reliable information on past harmful events and on the population exposed to the risk. When it comes to the assessment of risks which exist but which have not yet caused harm, or of risks which are very small but with potentially disastrous consequences, different techniques are required. Examples of activities carrying such risks are the introduction of a new therapeutic drug, the building of a new bridge, and the launching of a space rocket. In the case of such endeavours, past harmful events have not occurred, or have occurred in numbers too small to allow reliable predictions to be made.

Biological risk estimation

In the case of biological risks to man, laboratory experimentation is one of the most important ways to measure them.

Biological risks arise from the use of therapeutic drugs, chemicals in industrial processes, additives in food and drink, pesticides, cosmetics and environmental toxins. They may also arise from the use of chemicals voluntarily self-administered, such as smoking, drinking and drug taking.

In most of the above examples, individuals are exposed to risk without being able to make any choice in the matter. The public demand, therefore, is for such risks to be very low indeed, and governments generally mandate the level of risk by defining testing procedures and permitted levels in the form of regulations. For therapeutic drugs, people are inclined to accept a degree of risk, given the degree of benefit perceived, and for voluntary activities such as smoking and drinking, despite much higher risk, people are content to make choices for themselves.

Analysis of the toxic effects of chemicals is in the first instance undertaken in the laboratory. Unless careful measurements have been taken over the course of many years, which is rarely the case, historical data are likely to be pretty useless. Much of the toxicological experimentation involves animals, and those animals most commonly used in the laboratory are small rodents, usually rats and mice. Larger animals, including primates, are used in some studies, particularly when high doses of the potentially harmful substances are to be administered to man. The reliability of

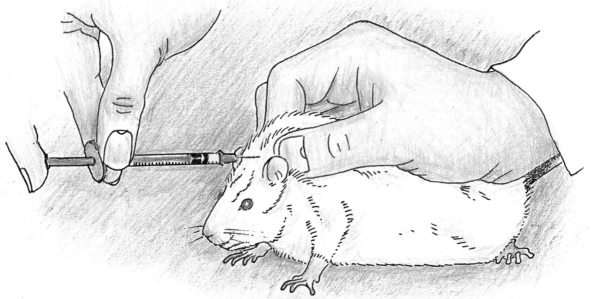

Some risks can be assessed by measuring what has gone before. But some risks must be predicted, either because they are so low that harmful events hardly ever happen, or because they are new and measurement on people could cause illness. This is the case for new chemicals, including possibly lifesaving medicines, and animals are used to represent humans.

conclusions drawn from animal experimentation depends on physiological considerations (which affect the validity of conclusions reached on human response), and on the number of animals used in test and control groups (which affects the strength of the statistical conclusions). The relationship between various levels of "dose" and the resulting nature and extent of response has to be determined with the greatest possible precision for substances to which populations may be exposed daily for many years, such as food additives and environmental contaminants; rather less precision is needed for substances such as pesticide residue, exposure to which would normally be limited and of short timespan.

Initially, chemicals are administered in order to gain a basic idea of their distribution in the body organs and on "acute", that is immediate, toxic effects. Animals are also used to determine the capacity of a chemical to irritate the skin and sensitive membranes, although there is a possibility that these tests will be replaced to a much greater extent in the future by techniques using artificial cultures of living cells.

The next step is to determine whether the chemical has the capacity to change genetic material in the cell, its "mutagenic" potential, because of the association of cell mutation with some types of cancer. Screening tests for mutagenic potential can be performed using cell cultures, but animal tests will be necessary for the reliable prediction of effects from chemicals offering real potential benefit, such as therapeutic drugs.

Further studies will then be needed over part of the whole of the lifetime of experimental animals to identify and measure toxic effects and study the way the animal's body disposes of the chemical. Reproductive studies are undertaken to determine the effects of the chemical on mothers and embryos.

There are limitations to such toxicological studies. While in broad terms toxic effects can be identified—abnormal bleeding, enlargement of the liver, cleft palate in the embryo, for example —it is not possible to put precise figures on the extent to which such effects will be seen in humans, or the relationship of effects to dose. Some harmful consequences in humans, such as deafness or behavioural effects, are hard or impossible to measure in animals. The immune system of animals and humans are sufficiently different to prevent use of animal data to estimate effects on humans: allergic reactions, hyper-sensitivity and immune deficiency syndromes are

examples. Estimation of effects at low dosages (such as people might be exposed to in the case of environmental pollution) may be difficult when high doses have been used on these animals: after *high-dose* testing with a hazardous gas, estimates for its risk of causing cancer in rats at low dosages ranged from one per 1,000 per lifetime right up to 551 per 1,000[4].

As experimental techniques change and become more sophisticated, interpretation of the results of testing must change also. Once upon a time, the objective of the testing was to establish a dose below which no adverse effect could be *detected*: the "safe" dose, or "no-adverse-effect level" (NEL) based on some easily observed criteria. But our ability to detect things is improving: so many effects can now be measured, the significance of which for humans will usually require yet more detailed experimentation and observation, that risk estimation has become not easier, but harder. Again, the very sophistication of the technological processes seems to "create" new risks, the importance of which then needs further analysis to determine. It is quite a treadmill we are on.

At present, for practical purposes, the NEL dose for animals is expressed in terms of milligrams per kilogram (mg/kg) of body weight, and extrapolated to man. An "acceptable daily intake" (ADI) is established, in mg/kg per day, a figure which has proved helpful in estimating the risk of most of the environmental substances to which man is exposed, and defines "acceptable" levels for (among other chemicals) food additives, pesticide residues, and dietary and environmental contaminants. The ADI has the advantage of putting a numerical value on exposure for the purpose of regulatory control, but, for the reasons outlined, the NEL based on animal testing has a large degree of uncertainty.

Other indices are also used in Britain for the extrapolation of animal and other laboratory data to humans. For the exposure of a working population to risk, "threshold limit values", or TLVs, are placed on industrial chemicals. These values represent amounts of the chemical to which nearly all workers may be exposed without harm. Because of the minute concentrations involved, and the often limited quantity of experimental data, TLV values—like those for the ADI—should only be used for guidance, with the general underlying objective of lowering exposure to as far as possible below the values they represent.

For chemicals which it is intended to administer directly to man as medicines, the next stage in the assessment of risk is the process of experimentation called "clinical trials". Most national governments have closely defined licensing procedures for the control of such trials, which will be approved in humans only after the laboratory and animal experimentation has provided adequate information on toxicity and potential therapeutic effect. The extent to which such testing is defined as "adequate" depends to a large extent on the type of drug under trial. If it represents a long-awaited "breakthrough" or a cure for a serious illness, trials in humans will usually be allowed at an earlier stage in development (thus accepting a higher risk in return for great potential benefit) than if the drug is closely analogous to an existing medicine with a known degree of success and a well-established body of information on adverse effects in humans.

In the classic clinical trial, patients with a given disease are administered either the new medicine or a dummy "placebo" in a "double-blind" manner, whereby neither the patient nor the researchers know (until codes are broken at a later stage) what each individual patient is receiving. Groups of patients are chosen to be as homogeneous as possible, but there is inevitably a range of response to the drug. Therefore, the larger the number of patients in the trial the better. A large number of patients is also required if the incidence of rare adverse effect is to be properly enumerated, as we describe in more detail later (see Chapter 11).

In summary, biological risk assessment of new chemicals is becoming much more complex and expensive — in the order of half a million pounds for lab and animal tests for one single chemical[1]. A very cautious eye is cast on the results; if salt and sugar were being tested as potential food additives today, and if judgement of acceptability was to be based purely on the laboratory and animal testing, it is unlikely that either would be permitted for use in food. Further, adverse effects in man may become apparent only after many years of exposure, and the situation is even more complex when cancer or threats to the unborn are involved. The assumption that there are levels of exposure below which there are no adverse effects is nowadays hard to sustain. More information is needed on man's susceptibility to potentially harmful chemicals and on normal variations in such susceptibility.

Engineering risk estimation

There are numerous substantial risks where the hazard is mechanical, and the risk analysis is performed by engineers rather than biologists. Engineers go about risk estimation in ways rather different from biologists, although the mathematical statistics they use in order to assess the strength of their conclusions are just the same.

As in the case of biological risks, the analysis of previous events can allow prediction of the future. Road crash statistics have already been employed by way of examples. Similarly, a particular type of engineering structure, such as a bridge, may have a known rate of failure under given conditions over time. But for new engineering techniques, the problems of prediction of risk are not the same. It is usually unacceptable to allow a failure to occur in order to predict future failures; especially where human loss is concerned, we need to be able to predict the risk of failure.

The first step for the engineer is to identify potential hazards associated with the particular installation or system, survey the way the operating system is to be managed, and assess the consequences of deviation from the system. To identify a hazard is not the same as to identify a risk. So, to assess risks, the engineer takes his analysis further to include considerations of reliability and study of the consequences of failure.

"Reliability" is a measure of the probability that a component will perform as desired. The reliability of a system depends on the reliability of its components. Among the most popular ways to examine the failure of a system are "fault trees" and "event trees".

A *fault tree* works back from a particular event, say the failure of a cooling plant, through a chain of all the failures of the bits and pieces which made the final event inevitable; back, say, to a stuck control valve or a faulty pressure gauge. Fault trees are much used for risk estimation studies in the aeronautical and energy-production industries. In a way, the use of a fault tree is simply an exercise in applied logic, but in addition to the contribution they make to the quantification of reliability, and therefore of risk, fault trees are highly effective in providing insight into the requirements of sound engineering. Critics, however, claim that the fault tree cannot take sufficiently into account human error and stupidity, or external hazards such as deliberate and hostile attack from vandals or terrorists. The relevant example of Chernobyl will be examined in Chapter 10.

Event trees specify a range of all possible outcomes of a given failure. So, if the frequency of a given failure is known, the probability of a given outcome can be predicted by computing the frequency and consequence of all the events in the intervening chain: an "accident sequence".

The use of such analytical chains over a period of time allows increasing precision in the assessment of risk. If the probability of failure of a number of minor components becomes more precisely known, the predictions of the effects of failure of a critical component, or of an entire system, can be quite accurate although such failures have never in fact occurred.

UNCERTAINTIES IN RISK ESTIMATION

In several chapters of the book we give examples of the risks estimated for a very wide range of diseases and injuries. It should already be clear that the precision of any estimation depends

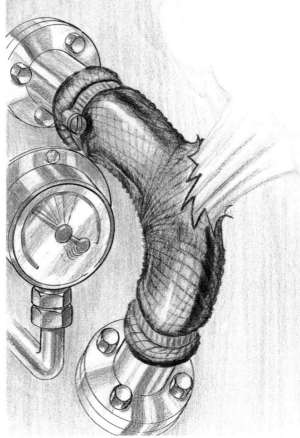

fundamentally on the reliability of the data used to do the estimating; it is because deaths are quite reliably counted that it is deaths which are so often the subject of risk assessment.

The first thing to understand is that the importance of a given degree of uncertainty depends on the level of risk involved. Let us assume that for a given risk, say the failure of a pressure hose which could start a chain of events leading to a fire, our estimation could be wrong by a factor of five times. This sounds pretty inaccurate, but does it matter? It does if the risk is high: a range of failure rate of between, say, once a year and five times a year represents a substantial difference. But if the risk is low, giving for this example a range of between once and five times in 10,000 years, the degree of uncertainty is far less important.

Another aspect of uncertainty is that risk estimations tend to be used to predict events more pessimistically than justified by subsequent measurement. This is for two interacting reasons. First, if a range of uncertainty exists, the pessimistic end of the range is likely to be used in planning; and, second, events which *actually* occur are more likely (by definition) to fall into the high probability/low consequence category. Thus, it may be estimated that release of a given amount of toxic gas *could* kill 1,000 people; but in practice it is usually found that release of the gas occurs in smaller quantities than assumed for the purpose of calculation, and deaths are rare because few people are around.

One example of an extremely wide range of uncertainty was that of the US National Academy of Sciences, whose report on the emotional subject of saccharin concluded that over the next 70 years the expected number of cases of human bladder cancer in America resulting from daily exposure to 120 mg of saccharin might range from 0.22 to 1,144,000! A range of this size is influenced by personal values, and the good scientist will strive to produce tighter conclusions that are both scientifically supportable and usable.

Risk estimation is not always a precise procedure, and comparisons of risk between and within various categories can only be approximate. The realities of risk analysis should be understood. However, it is a useful and influential technique for planning and placing facilities and systems with the potential for causing harm. It aids the drafting of sensible regulations. And it helps those who are not technically inclined, and who may be exposed to harmful consequences, to assess for themselves the extent of risk and thus make decisions on personal action based on the best available information.

Chapter Four

Main Causes of Death

CARDIOVASCULAR DISEASE

Diseases of the heart and circulation (''cardio-vascular'' disease), together with cancer, are the commonest causes of death. They represent, in a most general sort of way, the biggest risks to life of all. Naturally, we all must die. But the risk we want to avoid is of dying before we need to, of *premature* death due to raising the risks to ourselves in ways we need not. In particular, disease of the coronary arteries, which feed the heart muscles with blood, has become an extremely important cause of premature illness, disability and mortality.

Coronary artery disease (or coronary heart disease, CHD) accounts for about 80% of all heart disease in developed countries. The actual changes in the arteries supplying the heart muscle include the thickening and stiffening of the walls of the blood vessels and narrowing of their interior by depositions of fat (a process called atherosclerosis). The reduction in blood flow to the muscle may result in sudden death, or may damage the heart muscle in such a way that although the individual remains alive the heart cannot perform the work required of it (a state known as ''being in heart failure''). Reduction in the coronary artery blood flow can cause severe pain in the chest on exercise (angina).

Cardiovascular diseases are particularly impor-tant as a cause of death in developed, industrial countries, where they are responsible for 40–80% of all deaths. Now, however, they are becoming a health problem in developing countries too.

A bright note is that in a few countries death rates from diseases of the coronary arteries are stationary or beginning to fall, after years of rising[1]. These improvements are contributing to greater life expectancy, and show that the technological world is not inevitably doomed to suffer heart disease as a result of modern lifestyles. In most nations, however, the trend is still upwards. And there are many other types of cardiovascular disease. For example, high blood pressure is common in all industrial societies and in many developing countries; it contributes to the risk of stroke as well as to coronary heart disease. In the developing world, the infectious disease rheumatic fever, with consequential rheumatic heart disease, is still a major cause of illness and death; indeed, it has been estimated that the commonest cause of heart disease among young people in the entire world is rheumatic fever and that in some countries it is responsible for about a third of all deaths from cardiovascular disease[2].

Because of their prevalence and importance, cardiovascular diseases have been the subject of a massive amount of research over recent decades. Countries have been compared, one with another. Migrants have been surveyed to see if their rate of heart disease changes when they have moved from one country to another. People have been carefully studied within given countries, and controlled experiments under-taken with various forms of intervention and changes in life style. Taken together, the results of this research support the view that the major cardiovascular diseases as causes of *premature* death are substantially preventable[3].

Death rates for coronary heart disease, other major cardiovascular diseases

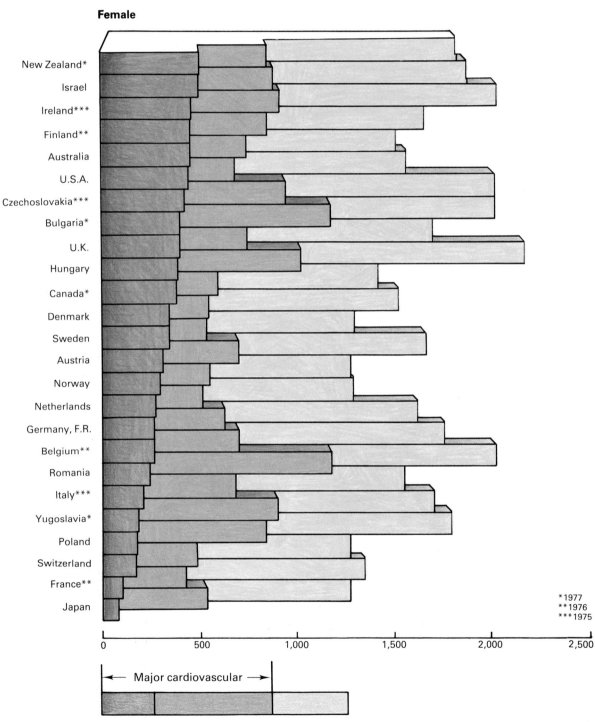

Female

New Zealand*
Israel
Ireland***
Finland**
Australia
U.S.A.
Czechoslovakia***
Bulgaria*
U.K.
Hungary
Canada*
Denmark
Sweden
Austria
Norway
Netherlands
Germany, F.R.
Belgium**
Romania
Italy***
Yugoslavia*
Poland
Switzerland
France**
Japan

*1977
**1976
***1975

0   500   1,000   1,500   2,000   2,500

←— Major cardiovascular —→

Coronary   Other cardiovascular   Other causes

Male

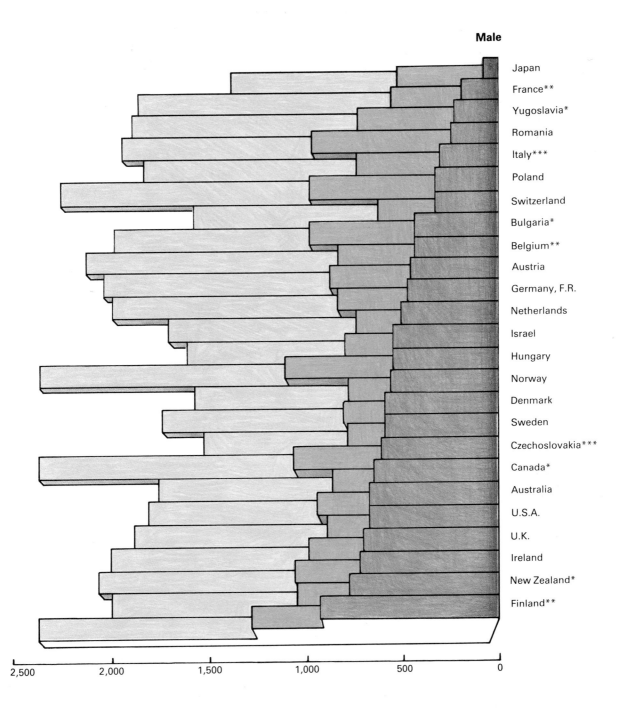

Japan
France**
Yugoslavia*
Romania
Italy***
Poland
Switzerland
Bulgaria*
Belgium**
Austria
Germany, F.R.
Netherlands
Israel
Hungary
Norway
Denmark
Sweden
Czechoslovakia***
Canada*
Australia
U.S.A.
U.K.
Ireland
New Zealand*
Finland**

2,500   2,000   1,500   1,000   500   0

Death rates from heart disease vary greatly, country by country.
Source: adapted from Fraser G E, *Preventive Cardiology*, 1986

There are large national differences in death rates from coronary heart disease. Among the countries with highest rates are the eastern European ones, plus Finland, Britain, Australia and New Zealand; among the lowest, Japan, Switzerland, Italy and France. But national differences should be treated warily. Although the *International Classification of Diseases* classifies disease, when heart disease is combined with other conditions at the end (as it often is), then doctors in different countries may tend to record the actual cause of death in different ways.

The World Health Organization has studied changes in death rate during a recent ten year

Death rates from coronary heart disease, 1950–1975, males and females, United States, Australia and United Kingdom

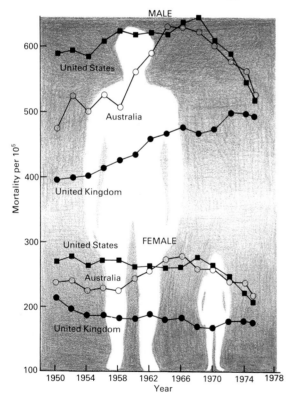

The death rate among men with coronary heart disease was rising in most developed countries until the late 1960s. Since then, the death rate has dropped in the US and Australia, but not in the United Kingdom. It is possible that some risk factors are being tackled more aggressively and successfully in some countries than in others.

Source: adapted from *Preventive Cardiology* (US)

period for the high-risk (for heart disease) age group 40–69 years, in 27 developed countries and areas[1]. To take Japan as an example, during the 1970s cardiovascular mortality rates in men and women of this age group declined by 36% and 42% respectively. In the United States of America the equivalent rates were 28% and 30%. Taken as a whole the figures seem to indicate that it is the developed countries outside Europe that have been most successful in reducing the cardiovascular death rate over recent years, albeit from a higher base level. The countries of western Europe have been successful to some extent, but less so. The countries of eastern Europe are still showing an upward trend in the cardiovascular disease death rate.

Similar trends are shown for coronary artery disease and cerebrovascular disease (stroke) when they are specifically singled out. Because cardiovascular diseases are such an important cause of death overall, they influence the trend for all causes of death put together. The effect is that in Poland, Hungary and Bulgaria, for example, there is a continually increasing *overall* death rate which is fuelled by rapid increases in the rate of death from cardiovascular disease.

The risk of rheumatic heart disease, which we have already noted as an important cause of death in the developing world, is high where there is overcrowding and poverty, and the incidence has thus been declining throughout this century in industrial societies. The reduction in risk from this disease is associated with social and economic changes, in the same way that the incidence of cholera started to fall in England in the time of Chadwick and Snow.

In the developed world, general affluence permits a lifestyle which appears to increase the risk of cardiovascular disease. But affluence and lifestyle are not inevitably linked together. The countries which are now tackling the problem with determination are succeeding in lowering cardiovascular death rates, through reduction in the incidence of the disease and better medical treatment of coronary heart disease, cerebrovascular disease (causing strokes) and childhood heart disease. These reductions have not been accompanied by an increase in mortality from other diseases, and they are most evident among the richer and better educated sections of society. The effect of this has been that in the most highly developed societies it is among groups of lower socio-economic status that the highest rates of cardiovascular disease are now to be found.

Research into coronary heart disease has linked a large number of risk factors with the incidence of the disease. Experts now feel able to make firm recommendations on reducing these risks.

Any nationwide and comprehensive strategy for controlling and reducing the incidence of CHD requires an awful lot of activity, including alteration of personal lifestyles and the nature of the environment of the population at risk. It means the bringing of preventive care to individuals at especially high risk, and the treating of those with the disease in such a way that fresh heart attacks are prevented and the quality of life maintained as far as possible.

Nutrition is the principal subject of attention by governments making attempts at reducing risks. Many individual countries have now set nutritional and dietary goals, which are based on relationships between what people normally eat, levels of cholesterol in the blood, and CHD. Most countries see a need for reduction of the average level of cholesterol in the blood throughout the population. There is also a need to prevent future rises in blood cholesterol in populations where levels are currently quite low. A WHO expert committee's recommendations[2] included the

suggestion that saturated fatty acids should contribute no more than 10% to the total energy intake, which implies that for many countries, including the UK, the total fat in the diet should be reduced to 30% of total energy (calorie intake). Achieving this objective can be assisted by replacing some of the saturated fat in the diet by monounsaturated and polyunsaturated fats, which may have favourable effects other than the lowering of the total amount of cholesterol in the blood.

National dietary goals also aim to lower the incidence of high blood pressure (hypertension)

Dietary factors have been identified as important in affecting the risk of heart disease. A diet which is low in fat and high in fibre is better than one high in fat and low in fibre.

and obesity, which will indirectly reduce the risk of coronary heart disease. Salt intake should be minimized because high salt intakes are linked to high blood pressure, and the consumption of large amounts of alcohol is best avoided. Taking the population as a whole, the best way of reducing obesity is to encourage people to increase their physical activity and reduce the calorie content of the diet by consumption of food with a relatively small quantity of fats and sugars.

Distribution of coronary heart disease in England, 1968–78

There is a sharp contrast within the pattern of coronary heart disease in England, with low mortality in the south and east and high mortality in the north and west. Dietary and other lifestyle factors (including smoking) affect the risk, and this is reflected geographically.

Source: adapted from Gardner M J, *et al. Atlas of Mortality from Selected Diseases,* John Wiley and Sons 1984

This advice would lead to the emphasis on foods of plant origin and on a wide range of nutrients including carbohydrates and dietary fibre. Fish, poultry, lean meats, non-fat and low-fat dairy products, and the limited use of fats in food preparation all help to reduce both the total amount of fat and saturated fatty acids in a given nation's diet.

It follows that at the national level, agricultural policy and food production are intimately related to the risk of coronary heart disease. Many such policies are based on concepts of health and nutrition which were developed well before the risk factors for cardiovascular disease were properly identified. Nevertheless, evidence for the fact that governments, industries and food technologists can respond quite rapidly to consumer demand for new and nutritionally better foods comes from the development and intense marketing of low-salt and low-fat foods in the USA and Europe over recent years. Further, there have been great improvements in the labelling of foods for their nutritional content in many countries, although much of this labelling is not readily understood by the people for whom it is intended.

All the above issues are for governments, whose policies thus determine the risk for individuals. At the individual level, people have the choice of many actions which directly determine their risk of developing cardiovascular disease.

The first and perhaps the most important of the risks voluntarily accepted, and thus responsive to individual initiative, is smoking. Because smoking also carries the risk of increasing the likelihood of several other diseases it receives a special section in this book (see the next chapter), so what follows are only the most important aspects of its association with cardio-vascular disease.

Both among adults and young people, the relationship of cigarette smoking to CHD has been documented in several population studies[5], although exactly how the one causes the other remains uncertain. Within measured groups of people the risk of CHD has been found to be strongly related to the number of cigarettes smoked each day. The relationship is consistent, appears to be independent of other risks and can be used to predict CHD rates. Therefore, although there are few experimental data (that is, from laboratory tests) to confirm the relationship, and the actual mechanisms are unclear, the relationship between smoking and CHD is generally regarded as being one of cause and effect. Further, smoking acts together with other factors which also raise the risk of CHD so that even light smoking may increase the risk.

Relative risk of coronary heart disease

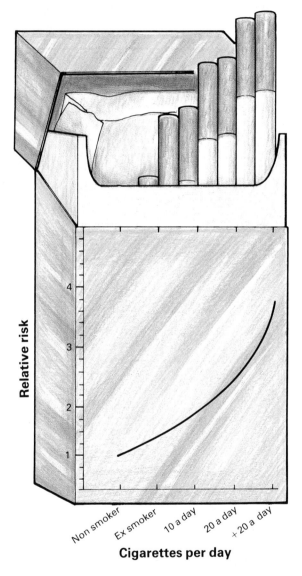

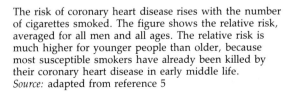

Cigarettes per day

The risk of coronary heart disease rises with the number of cigarettes smoked. The figure shows the relative risk, averaged for all men and all ages. The relative risk is much higher for younger people than older, because most susceptible smokers have already been killed by their coronary heart disease in early middle life.
Source: adapted from reference 5

When smokers give up, they reduce their risk to less than that for those who continue to smoke[6]. However, the benefit in relation to ischaemic heart disease of giving up cigarette smoking is rather gradual, and ex-smokers are always at higher risk than those who have never smoked[7].

Several studies have suggested that moderate exercise may reduce the risk of CHD and improve the likelihood of survival from a coronary attack. It may be that regular exercise increases the capacity of the cardiovascular system for work and reduces the demand of the heart muscle for oxygen at any given level of physical activity. But it would be nice to have good studies comparing the risk in reduction of heart problems with the risk of increase in bone and joint disability, which is also well documented. Exercise carries its own risk, too.

Turning to other risk factors for CHD, it may be of some comfort that alcohol does not appear to increase the risk of CHD when used in moderation. Indeed there have been some reports that moderate use of alcohol can reduce the risk of cardiovascular disease[9]. The evidence for this is inconclusive, while it is known that alcohol in excess may damage the heart muscle and increase the risk of irregular heart beat.

Oral contraceptives have been linked with an increase in incidence of CHD and other vascular diseases[10]. They appear to be related to raised blood pressure, abnormal amounts of fat in the blood, and clotting of the blood within the blood vessels. There appears to be a multiplying effect with other risk factors, in particular the smoking of cigarettes, especially in women after the age of 35.

There are other potential risk factors which have been studied for their relationship to CHD, but for which the links are unclear and if anything rather weak. Certain psychological factors, including the possession of a so-called type A personality with an over-developed sense of urgency, drive and competitiveness, appear to be related to an excess of coronary heart disease, but the mechanism seems to be that type A people are particularly affected by established major risk factors. In the environment, the hardness of water, trace metals in the air and water, climate and air pollution have all been studied for the risk of CHD, but any evidence which does exist is incomplete and fragmentary.

CANCER

Cancer is a terrifying word to many, bringing to mind gloomy notions of a long illness terminated by a lingering and painful death. Many people believe that a diagnosis of cancer is a death warrant. It is hardly surprising that a set of diseases associated with such strongly fearful emotions have generated a powerful mythology. Among such popular myths is the idea that we are now experiencing an epidemic of cancer caused by pollution, additives and chemicals whose presence we cannot detect and against whose influence we are utterly powerless. In fact, as we will see, cancer death rates (with the exception of the lung) are really rather steady, and there is no more reason to fear cancer than any other potentially fatal disease. As we said at the beginning, we all have to go somehow.

What is cancer? Cancer is a blanket term embracing a very wide variety of diseases, all characterized by uncontrolled and disordered growth of abnormal cells. Cancer cells displace or destroy the normal cells of the body and, if not stopped, can spread to other parts and to different organs. For cells to grow and reproduce is perfectly normal, of course, but cells in cancer tissue grow faster and divide more rapidly than in the normal tissues from which they are derived.

Cancer cells spread through the body in many ways. The first is by direct extension into surrounding tissues, sometimes forming spidery outgrowths which give meaning to the use of the word "cancer", or "the crab". Cancer cells may also be carried to other parts of the body through the system of channels which carry lymphatic fluid, which is why the lymph glands (in places like the armpit and neck) are so often affected when cancer spreads. Cancerous cells can also be carried in the blood, which may take them to distant parts of the body where they form new growths called metastases.

Cancer is predominantly a disease of middle age and later, and is rather rare in children and young adults. Over 80 it is a commoner cause of death than diseases of the heart and lung but, overall, about three times as many people die from cardiovascular disease as from all the cancers put together.

As countries develop, incorporating the better public health sanitation and medical care systems which, as we have seen, have their greatest effect on diseases *other* than cancer, the death rate from cancer can, apparently, rise. This is simply because more people are living longer and have thus more chance of developing the disease. It does not mean that the risk of getting cancer is being increased by new or more potent external hazards.

In the last 50 years the only cancer which has increased dramatically in incidence is cancer of the lung, and that has happened in both sexes[11]. (A point to be stressed in tracking death rates for cancer over the years is that allowance has to be made for the gradual ageing of the population which, as noted above, appears to increase the incidence of the disease.) While lung cancers have increased in incidence, two types of cancer which have shown a steady decline in the same period are those of the uterus and the stomach.

Cancer death rates, males and females, England and Wales, 1921–74

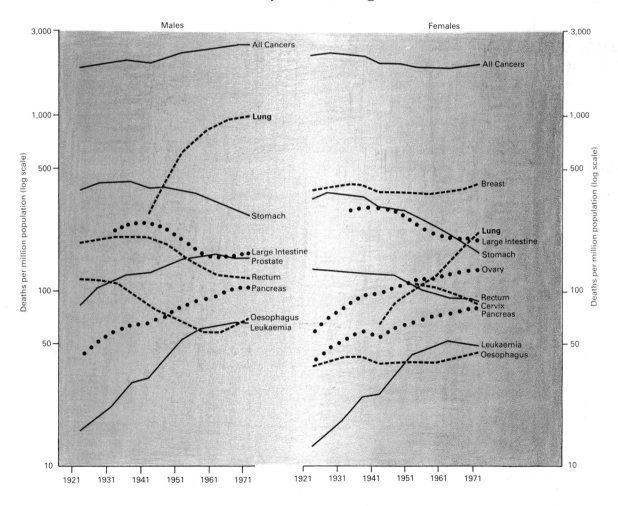

The death rates for individual types of cancer have changed over the years. The most striking change is for cancer of the lung (bronchus); in the last 25 years there has been a threefold increase. The lung cancer death rates reflect changes in smoking patterns some 40 years earlier.
Source: reference 11

In the case of stomach cancer, no-one really knows why there has been this decrease, as the success of medical treatment has not improved very much over the period. However, this is not so for cancer of the uterus the decline in the rate of deaths for which is related to greatly improved methods for early diagnosis and treatment. The best known technique for early detection is the sampling and analysing of cells from the cervix. It is now possible to recognize changes in cell structure which may lead to frankly malignant (cancerous) growth of the cells, and this in turn has opened up the possibility of early, comparatively simple surgery which removes small amounts of potentially cancerous cells from the cervix of the uterus and prevents more extensive surgery later.

Apart from lung, stomach and uterine cancer, the incidence of most cancers has stayed about the same for the last 30 years. The commonest are cancer of the breast, the bowel (colon and rectum) and prostate gland. The incidence of breast cancer has changed very little over recent years, although the latest techniques of treatment which combine surgery (generally less dramatic and disfiguring these days), X-rays and chemo-therapy (treatment with anticancer drugs) have brought about a small improvement in the proportion of sufferers surviving for four years after diagnosis[12]. The death rates for cancer of the pancreas, liver, and bladder have been rather constant for many years now. Leukaemia (cancerous changes in the blood cells) is now gradually declining in death rate after a slow rise up to 1960.

Cancer in children is far less common than it is in adults, and there have been recent striking advances in treatment. Between 50 and 90% of those diagnosed as having the commonest childhood cancers now survive for two years after diagnosis[13].

The steady rise in the overall death rate from lung cancer is easily the most worrying aspect of this group of diseases. The main increases recently have been among females, with only the youngest women showing a decline in death rate over recent years. What we are witnessing now is the heavy price we must pay for the large number of women who started to smoke in the nineteen twenties, thirties and forties, because of the long time which exists between exposure to a given carcinogen and the development of the disease. Smoking as a cause of lung cancer and other diseases will be discussed in much greater detail in a following section (see Chapter 5).

The causes of cancer

When a man slips into a pothole and breaks his ankle, the cause of the injury is easy enough to ascertain. Similarly, he might have a pretty good idea of what caused his cold if he came down with the symptoms three days after being sneezed on by a spluttering child. The relation-ship between cause and effect is clear. But years pass between exposure to potential carcinogens and the development of cancer. Some carcinogens may cause cancer in different parts of the body. Identical carcinogens may cause cancer in some people and not in others. Some carcinogens are widespread and powerful and cause lots of cancer, some are rarely encountered and are responsible for a very low incidence of the disease.

For all these reasons and others, to *prove* that a given carcinogen has caused a given cancer (a "causal" connection) is exceedingly difficult. It took decades before it was proved that smoking caused lung cancer, and this was through the accumulation of a large quantity of evidence rather than by direct (and impossible) human experimentation. An important effect of these difficulties is that "minor" causes of cancer are extremely hard to untangle from the "major" causes. For example, it might be suspected that a pollutant from a factory chimney is responsible for increasing the incidence of lung cancer. If it is indeed doing so, but only does to the extent of causing one extra death in a population among whom 100 are expected to die from lung cancer due to smoking, the influence of the pollutant would be exceedingly hard to define with any precision at all, let alone "prove".

By the same token, it is difficult to *disprove* claims that a suspected carcinogen is causing an extra incidence of cancer in a population where the disease is reasonably common anyway. There are normal fluctuations in incidence. Say, for example, that a chemical analogous to (but different from) fluoride could be introduced into public drinking water supplies in order to completely prevent tooth decay. Meanwhile, cancer of the throat will be found to rise and fall from one area to another throughout the country as a result of perfectly normal fluctuations. By careful selection of areas to be surveyed, it would be possible to show an association between the introduction of the new chemical and rises in cancer of the throat in every one of the selected areas. It would seem to be obvious that this association is *not* proof that the chemical caused the cancer, but uncritical linking of cause and effect has been responsible, over the years, for creating much unwarranted fear of the disease and of all the factors that could conceivably raise the risk of it.

Another statistical trap is "clustering", groups of occurrences which can occur as part of a perfectly random distribution of events. If a dice is thrown again and again, at irregular intervals the same number will come up consecutively — three sixes in a row, perhaps, or (more rarely) six sixes. In the same way, if a disease is randomly distributed in a community, there will be occasional clusters of that disease. "Small" clusters will be commonly observed, and "large" clusters rarely. In the same way that random pressing of the keys of a typewriter would sooner or later (a lot later) write Macbeth, there is a very low chance of occurrence of spectacular "clusters", and it will take careful analysis to disentangle the "chance" factor from all the other possible causes of this apparent outbreak of a disease.

An estimate of the risk of cancer attributable to different classes of environmental agents was undertaken by British scientists Doll and Peto for the US Congress Office of Technology Assessment[12], and is summarized as follows.

air, food and water, or occupational exposure.

The only cause of cancer whose effect is both large and reliably known is tobacco (see page 54). The role of diet will be described in more detail in a following section (see page 64); Doll and Peto's estimate of risk is (as they admit) highly speculative, and dietary factors are not yet reliably identified. There are many indications, nevertheless, that dietary factors do influence the risk of stomach and intestinal cancers.

None of the other factors listed in this study even approach the definite importance of smoking or the probable importance of diet. Of the larger remaining groups, sexual behaviour affects the incidence of cancer of the breast and reproductive and genital organs (such as the cervix of the womb).

While the percentage of cancers influenced by each of the other causes is small, so that they have little effect on the incidence of cancer in the population as a whole, they are of course of particular importance to sections of the population on whom the risks are concentrated.

To take two important examples the relationship of *chemicals* to cancer is discussed at some length in Chapter 13. In the case of *radiation* and cancer, because it affects the assessment of risk in so many aspects of life (smoking, indoor

No.	Factor	Best estimate (%)	Range of acceptable estimates (%)
1	Tobacco	30	25 to 40
2	Alcohol	3	2 to 4
3	Diet	35	10 to 70
4	Food additives	<1	−5 to −2*
5	Reproductive and sexual behaviour[†]	7	1 to 13
6	Occupation	4	2 to 8
7	Pollution	2	<1 to 5
8	Industrial products	<1	<1 to 2
9	Medicines and medical procedures	1	0.5 to 3
10	Geophysical factors[§]	3	2 to 4
11	Infection	?10	1 to ?
12	Unknown	?	?

*Allowing for protective effects of antioxidants and other preservatives.
[†]Multiplicity of sexual partners predisposes to cancer of the uterine cervix.
[§]In addition to the small percentage of sunlight-induced skin cancers that are fatal, there is a much larger number of non-fatal cancers of similar origin.

Easily the largest estimates relate to the effect of tobacco and the diet, and these authors comment that they know of no figures to support the common belief that most cancers could be prevented by controlling chemical pollution of the

pollution, power production and medical treatment are some examples), it is more appropriate to describe the association at this point in the book.

Radiation and cancer

A lot more people know that radiation can cause cancer than know that smoked meat can do so. Radiation is about as terrifying as cancer itself, and because of the high risk that many people believe is associated with radiation from nuclear facilities, we will examine the links between radiation and cancer in some detail.

The whole world and everything that lives on it is built up of atoms. The nucleus of the atom is made up of protons and neutrons, with the number of protons defining the substance. The atoms of carbon, for example, always contain six protons. The number of neutrons can vary, so that there are varieties of the same substance. Carbon-12 has six neutrons (six protons plus six neutrons) and carbon-14 has eight neutrons and six protons. These varieties are called "isotopes" of carbon.

Most atoms have a nucleus which does not change and they are referred to as being "stable". Other atoms, however, have a nucleus which changes by itself, a process which is known as "radioactivity". Thus, "radioactive isotopes".

During the radioactive process, the atoms may throw off alpha or beta particles or gamma rays. Alpha particles, for practical purposes, only damage the body if they are breathed into the lungs or swallowed, in which case they can be very dangerous. Beta particles are smaller and faster, can pass through the skin and may cause more generalized damage (such as burns) than the localized injury caused by alpha particles. Gamma rays consist of radiation rather similar to light or X-rays, and can pass completely through the body. A proportion of the rays are stopped within the body, and when they do so they emit an electron with the same properties as a beta particle, which is what then causes the damage.

As atoms go through these radioactive changes they are said to "decay". The speed of decay is represented by the "half life" which is the average time taken for half of any group of atoms to decay. Elements with a very long half life may not necessarily be particularly dangerous to humans because of their low level of radio-activity, whereas elements with a short half life can be virulently radioactive and much more hazardous for the time that humans are exposed to them.

During the process of decay the properties of the elements change and a radioactive atom may eventually become stable. For example, uranium-238 decays through a chain including radium-226, radon-222 and polonium-218, all radioactive, and ends in lead-206, which is stable. Uranium-235 and thorium-232 also decay through chains of radioactive substances until they finally become stable forms of lead. The rate of decay is a measure of the quantity of radioactivity, and two units are used to represent them. One is the *becquerel*, which is one decay per second, and the other (now being superseded) is the curie. Radioactivity can be represented in terms of volume (air or milk, for example), weight (kilogram of food) or area (square metre of ground).

The *dose* of radiation received by people or things is measured in terms of *grays* (previously *rads*). A given dose of so many grays of beta, gamma or X-rays has rather similar effects, but alpha particles are much more dangerous, gray for gray. Because what we are interested in is the biological effect of a given dose of radiation, we take into account the differing capacities of radiation to cause damage and state the result in *sieverts* (previously *rems*); the biological effect of one sievert* of alpha particles is the same as one sievert of X-rays and so on. For a given number of sieverts, the wider the body area exposed to radiation the worse the likely effect, so that, say, four sieverts (400 rems) to the whole body is likely to lead to death whereas the same dose to a leg would only lead to some localized and hopefully temporary inflammation of the skin. Such large doses could only happen in wartime as a result of nuclear explosions, or in peacetime as a result of the sort of catastrophic accident in the nuclear industry which has not yet occurred. With particular regard to radiation as a possible cause of cancer, we are interested in much lower doses than this, applied over longer periods of time.

As in the case of chemicals, because of the long delay period between exposure to radiation and the onset of cancerous changes, it was only comparatively recently that it was realized that low doses of radiation could be dangerous. Before about 1950 it was considered acceptable for a radiologist (a doctor working with X-rays) to be exposed to one-tenth of a rem (1 mSv) each *day*. However, studies began to show that cancer and leukaemia rates among radiologists who had

*In practice, one *sievert* is a very big dose indeed, rather inconveniently so for the purpose of discussion. The superseded *rem* (often still encountered) is the same dose equivalent as one-hundredth of a sievert (0.01 Sv) or 10 *millisieverts* (10 mSv). Previously, doses in the real world were most conveniently expressed in terms of one-thousandth of a rem, or *millirem* (mrem); 100 millirems are equivalent to 1 mSv.

been working in the profession before 1921 were much higher than among medical practitioners who were their contemporaries, but not working with X-rays. In the 1920s a number of protective measures were initiated, and radiologists who joined the profession after this period have been found to have a death rate from cancer which is not significantly different from other doctors.

For some serious diseases, therapy includes the giving of known doses of radiation. It has been found that an increased risk of leukaemia develops, and this is roughly proportional to the dose of radiation received, indicating that there is no dose so small that it offers no risk. Leukaemia rates have also been studied among the survivors of the atomic bomb attacks on Hiroshima and Nagasaki, also indicating an increased incidence of the disease which is proportional to the dose of radiation received.

The human body is, nevertheless, an incredibly resilient machine. It is far from being the case that all the survivors of the atom bomb attacks got leukaemia, even those who had received doses of radiation hundreds of times higher than that to be expected from natural causes. In fact, only 1% died of leukaemia as a result of radiation in the 30 years following the explosion. Only another 3% died from cancers of all types caused by the radiation[14].

The International Commission on Radiological Protection (ICRP) was established in the late 1920s to advise on radiation in industry and make recommendations on appropriate limitations. This organization has estimated the extra risk of dying eventually of cancer as a result of radiation[15]. For every 10 mSv (one rem) of radiation received on the whole body, it suggests that the extra risk of dying of cancer as a result is about 1:10,000. This figure is averaged over all ages (an individual aged 20 has most of a life time to develop cancer, whereas his grandparent of 80 has very little time left in which to do so if they are both exposed to radiation on the same day). It seems likely that if the dose is delivered at a very fast rate over a short period of time, its damaging effects are worse than if the same dose is given over a longer period.

Given what we know now, it is reasonable to assume that this increased risk is proportional to dose. Accordingly, if the risk is 1:10,000 per 10 mSv, then 10 times that dose represents an increased risk of 1:1,000 of dying from cancer. If one million people receive 10 mSv each, then about 100 extra deaths will be the result. The ICRP has also estimated the cancer rates to be

expected for individual organs of the body, given that they were irradiated at the worst possible age. Totalled, these estimations give a figure of 125 extra cancers per million people per 10 mSv, slightly higher than for the whole-body dose, but the difference is not significant.

In practical terms, the ICRP estimate of risk represents the following. The current chance of dying of cancer in Britain is about 22%, or just over one in five. If you receive a dose of 10 mSv over your whole body this will add one extra chance in 10,000 to your existing chance of dying of cancer, raising your chance to 22.01% from 22% assuming that you are around the mid range of life (and thus have time to develop cancer at all). Extending this figure to population groups, it follows that if a given number of people are exposed to a given dose of radiation, then an estimate can be made of the extra cancer deaths that may result from such exposure. Radioactivity is not different from other environmental pollutants in being dependent for the damage they do on their amount!

However, any figure derived in this sort of way can only be an approximation. It is simply not possible to conduct controlled experimentation on humans for obvious reasons, and animal experiments and measurements of Hiroshima survivors have their obvious limitations; for example, it now appears that earlier studies may have over-estimated the dose received by the survivors, which would lead to under-estimation of the cancer risk. Expert groups other than the IRCP, together with several individual academics, have expressed disagreement with the IRCP estimates, with a range of uncertainty of about three times in either direction, and according to some critics the ICRP is under-estimating the risk by 5–10 times.

That said, it is still more useful for most people to have some idea of an additional risk than it is to have no idea at all, and new estimates were expected from the ICRP in 1987. In 1986, the ICRP was stating that it was prudent to limit the *lifetime* exposure of members of the public to 1 mSv each year, with 5 mSv permissible for some individual years provided that average annual lifetime exposure was less than 1 mSv. For workers in the radiation industry, 50 mSv per year was the limit, with special investigations mandatory if exposure exceeded 15 mSv in one year. From the aforementioned ICRP figures it will be seen to follow that a dose of 1 mSv implies an extra fatal risk of cancer of about one in 100,000. The *actual* average for workers in the radiation industry is about 1.4 mSv in a year, giving an average risk of cancer which is lower than the average risk of fatal accidents in all industries.

Mutation

Many of the pregnant women who were irradiated during the atom bomb attacks on Japan lost their babies, and many of the children whose mothers were irradiated at an early stage of pregnancy were born with major physical defects. (These abnormalities were *"congenital"*, meaning that the developing foetus was injured in the womb after conception. This is different from damage resulting from mutation (changes) in the nucleus of germ cells, which can result later in *"genetic"* abnormalities which are inherited through the generations.) Surveys were then conducted of children born more than nine months after their parents were irradiated and, apparently confirming the fear of mutation, a much higher rate of physical abnormality was recorded than had ever been seen before. However, it was also found after further study that even the most minor abnormalities were being detected during this research, and counted for the first time. In fact, the actual rate of abnormality, when severity of defect was taken into account, was the same among babies later born to parents who had been irradiated as it was among babies in cities similar to Hiroshima but well outside the zone of radiation[16].

Follow-up studies among scores of thousands of children born to irradiated survivors during following decades have shown no increase in hereditary defects, although there has been a tiny, and probably insignificant, decrease in the proportion of males to females. Radiation may indeed be causing mutations, but if so, it is to such a small extent that it cannot be detected.

Low level and natural radiation

We live in a radioactive world, and this has little to do with nuclear power or nuclear weapons. In Britain, the annual average dose received from normal background radiation is about 2 mSv[17], or 200 millirems. About 0.3 mSv is due to cosmic rays, 0.35 mSv from gamma radiation from the soil and building materials, and 0.38 mSv from the natural radioactivity of the body. More biologically damaging is the 0.97 mSv we receive each year from radon and thoron inhaled into the lungs. Differences in average doses from one locality to another may exceed 5 mSv.

Cosmic radiation varies with altitude, and terrestrial gamma radiation varies enormously depending on where we live, with normal values between 0.1 and 1 mSv per year. The higher levels of radiation are associated with granite rocks, such as in the far south-west of England and in Scotland.

In some places, as will be described more fully in the section on indoor pollution (see page 93), radiation from radon and its decay products can range up or down by a factor of some three times, and in a few places radiation levels have been measured as much as 100 times the 0.97 mSv average. Residents of some poorly ventilated buildings constructed over granite can thus annually be radiated at a level comfortably above the top *limit* for workers in the radiation industry, or 70 times more than the average dose received by these workers.

Of all the radiation we receive, an average of about 87% results from the above natural sources, and an average of 11.5% is received from the medical use of X-rays. (If an individual is never X-rayed, of course, he does not share in this population average.) The remainder, about 1.5%, results from non-medical, artificial sources. The Chernobyl accident in April 1986 added to this total a proportion of about 3% for the year May 1986 to April 1987, and a declining proportion in subsequent years.

Assume that there are about 50 million people in Britain and the average dose is 2 mSv each year, distributed among the total population. Taking the ICRP estimate for whole-body radiation, which is for 100 extra cancer deaths for every 10 mSv distributed among one million people, that works out to an estimate of 1,000 deaths from cancer each year from unavoidable natural background radiation (out of the over 140,000 annual cancer deaths).

While that is an estimate, in practice it is very hard to support or disprove such figures from direct observation. One American study (described in reference 18) did compare rates of cancer incidence State by State throughout the United States where, in each case, the natural background radiation was known. For the seven States with the highest average amount of natural background radiation, all well over 1.6 mSv per year, the cancer death rates were well *below* the average. The two States with the highest background radiation, Colorado and Wyoming, with between 2.4 and 2.5 mSv per year, were found

Average exposure to radiation of people, United Kingdom

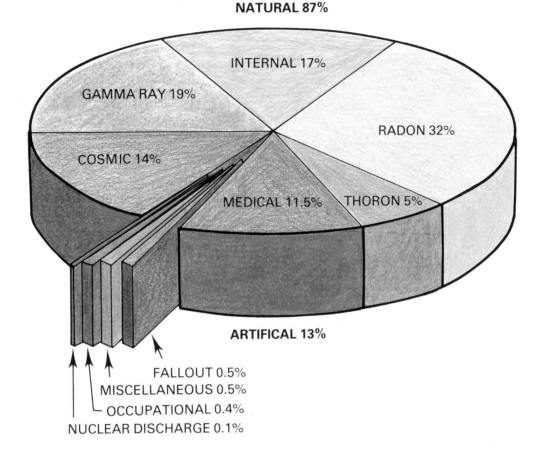

NATURAL 87%

INTERNAL 17%

GAMMA RAY 19%

RADON 32%

COSMIC 14%

MEDICAL 11.5%   THORON 5%

ARTIFICAL 13%

FALLOUT 0.5%
MISCELLANEOUS 0.5%
OCCUPATIONAL 0.4%
NUCLEAR DISCHARGE 0.1%

The overall effective dose from radiation of natural and artificial origin is about 2 mSv (200 millirems) on average. The percentage contribution of each source to the overall value is shown here. Natural radiation contributes almost 90%, with about half of that coming fron radon (see page 95). The radiation contributed by the Chernobyl accident was equivalent to just over 3% of the total for the year May 1986 to April 1987, and will contribute a markedly declining proportion in subsequent years.
Source: National Radiological Protection Board, *Living with Radiation,* HMSO 1986

to have a cancer death rate at the bottom of the range.

Even casual study of these figures shows that if low level background radiation *is* causing cancer then it is doing so at a rate which is swamped by other causes. The most obvious difference between the high radiation/low mortality States and the others is that the former group are all at fairly high altitude, being more than 1,000 metres above sea level. Although there is about the same proportion of city dwellers in the high altitude States as the low altitude States, in the latter case the cities are more closely crowded and subject to much worse air pollution.

This factor is likely to be far more influential on cancer rates than the level of radiation found in the high States, where the cities are a lot windier and less polluted.

Nevertheless, background radiation *could* be causing one in 100 of all cancer deaths. Man-made radiation *could* be causing about one-tenth of that one in 100 and artificial radiation from man's nuclear activities about one-tenth of that one-tenth. It is about *that* last fraction that people are most concerned, and more discussion of the effect of nuclear power stations on cancer rates will be found in Chapter 10.

RESPIRATORY DISEASE

Diseases of the respiratory system, the lungs and airways are the third most important causes of death (after cardiovascular disease and cancer) in most developed countries. If lung cancer is classed as a respiratory disease rather than as cancer, then diseases of the lungs go into second place after diseases of the heart in order of importance.

Respiratory disease has always been a heavy burden on society in Britain. At the turn of the century, easily the commonest lung disease was bronchitis followed by tuberculosis and pneumonia, with a rather low incidence of asthma and a very small number of cases of lung cancer[19]. Since that time the incidence of bronchitis has fallen by about 75%, and tuberculosis and pneumonia have fallen dramatically in incidence as a result of better treatment, including the use of antibiotics. They are now relatively unimportant causes of death from lung disease. Asthma has shown a steady decline this century, but death rates do not correctly indicate the importance of this condition in the community because sufferers rarely die from asthma as such but, rather, from complications including infection.

All the decline in infectious diseases of the chest has been cancelled out by a tremendous rise in the incidence of lung cancer, starting in the 1920s and levelling off only recently, so lung cancer is now easily the commonest cause of death from respiratory disease and more than twice as important as bronchitis.

To reduce the risk of premature death from respiratory disease we may look to infections, socio-economic factors and toxic agents in the air as possible causes which might be open to counter-measures.

In the case of bronchitis, the decline in incidence which has been observed does not appear to have a great deal to do with the availability of antibiotic treatment. Chronic bronchitis is more frequently found in cigarette smokers and in dwellers in densely packed population centres, which indicates that cigarette smoke and environmental pollution are more important than infection. Recent falls in the incidence of bronchitis in Britain are likely to be due to the influence of legislation related to clean air, or to a reduction in smoking by older men, or to both.

Along with bronchitis, the other disease of the chest which lays a heavy burden on society is lung cancer, and as will be shown in more detail in the next chapter cigarette smoking is the most influential single cause. If lung cancer is to be reduced in importance, then smoking will have to be reduced also.

At work, many people over the years have been exposed to toxic agents which have affected their lungs. In Britain the coalmining, iron and steel industries have caused exposure to dust which has resulted in chronic lung disease. However, under present conditions, the evidence is that the exposure to industrial dust of this kind contributes little to death or illness, being completely overwhelmed by the importance of the workers' smoking habits[20]. Only in the slate industry in Wales has dust disease been at least as important as smoking in recent years.

Asbestos

Workers with asbestos have been known for many years to have a relatively high incidence of lung disease including asbestosis, lung cancer, mesothelioma (cancer of the lining of the lung), and several lesser conditions. (The association of asbestos with other cancers has not been confirmed.) Doll and Peto have recently reviewed the health effects of asbestos, and what follows is based on their conclusions[21].

Precautions now being taken in industry have virtually eliminated severe asbestosis leading to early death, but less severe disease may increase the death rate from other respiratory and circulatory disease, particularly as asbestos acts together with smoking to produce non-cancerous lung disease.

The risk of mesothelioma increases with exposure to asbestos up to a period of 20 years, thereafter staying about the same. Several studies have shown that brief exposure produces relatively little risk.

In relation to lung cancer, even under conditions of heavy exposure little if any risk is produced for at least five years, with the relative risk then rising progressively with continuing exposure for at least 30 years. Observations on short-term exposure to asbestos have produced conflicting results.

Cigarette smoke and asbestos dust multiply each other's effects. Whether exact multiplication occurs is unimportant in practice, as the absolute risk of asbestos to non-smokers is certainly small, even after heavy exposure.

Limits to exposure have been set for industrial use of chrysotile asbestos in industry, suggesting that a man who begins work at 20 years of age and is exposed to an average exposure of half the limit will increase his existing risk of lung disease by about 0.4% for 15 years employment and 0.87% for 35 years employment. The extra risk for non-smokers is relatively lower.

In buildings, the effect of general environmental exposure to asbestos is hard to estimate because the levels are extremely low. Exposure to the levels which have been measured in buildings can very roughly be calculated to cause one premature death a year in the whole of Britain.

ACCIDENTS AND VIOLENCE

Death rates for accidents and violence, both sexes, 1901–80

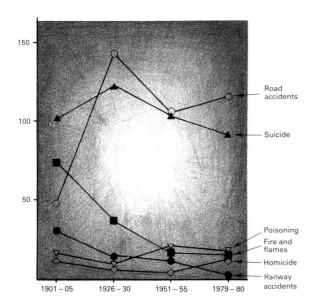

In England and Wales, the actual number of people dying from accidents and violence has changed little this century. The death rate has therefore dropped in terms of population numbers. But there has been a big increase in the death rate from road accidents, moderated by improvements over the last 40 years or so.
Source: adapted from reference 19

Along with the decline in infectious disease, the relative importance of accidental death has greatly increased during the course of this century. It has now become the single most important cause of death among young people and the biggest single cause of lost years of potential working life.

A major part of this book is devoted to specific activities and events, all of which carry some risk of illness or injury (see Chapters 6 to 13). In addition, a separate section on poisoning follows immediately after this one. What we wish to do here is to review the accidental injury scene on a large scale, comparing the incidence of various causes of injury and briefly reviewing national and international trends.

In England and Wales the absolute number of people dying each year from accidents and violence (including poisoning) since the turn of the century has changed very little[19]. In the five-year period 1901–05 just under 100,000 people were killed from these causes, and in the five-year period 1976–80 just over 100,000. With the increase in population over this period the death rate from injury per million has actually fallen during this century by one-third, from 480 to 299.

Averaged on a population basis, therefore, the risk of dying from accidental injury, violence or poisoning is now about one in 3,300 each year.

Of all individual causes of accidental death, the only one which has shown a dramatic increase during this century is road transport accidents, which were responsible for the death of 8,190 people in the five years 1901-05 and 30,600 in 1976-80. In terms of the death *rate* per million population, however, the situation is by no means as bad now as it was 40 or 50 years ago. In the period 1936-40, there were 164 people killed on the roads for every million in the population, and the equivalent figure now is 124. So, the present risk of dying is a traffic crash in any one year averages out at one in 8,000.

The death rate in railway accidents has fallen this century from 26 to 2 deaths per million population, down to an annual risk of one in 500,000. The other big fall this century is in deaths from accidents in fire and flames, from 74 per million to 14 per million.

The rate of suicide and self-inflicted injury has fallen from 101 per million at the turn of the century to 83 per million (one in 12,000 each year), with a peak in the years 1931-35 of 135 per million. The suicide rate is very much higher than the murder rate, which was 9 per million at the turn of the century and is now 10 per million (one in 100,000) having varied between 4 and 10 per million during the course of the century.

Taking a closer look at the last 20 years or so, the total number of accidental deaths in Britain has fallen from around 20,000 to 15,000, with reductions in deaths in all categories for this period. More detail of the classification of death in accidents occurring other than in association with transport are shown in the table opposite.

It will be seen that a very high proportion (over 40%) of non-transport accidental death occurs among the very elderly, those over 75 years of age. About three-quarters of these accidental deaths among the aged occur at home or in residential institutions.

Turning now to the rest of the world, as usual we find huge gaps in the data available. For example the *WHO Annual of Mortality Statistics* has no information on causes of death of any kind for India, Pakistan, the USSR or China, or for almost all of South America or Africa. Assuming a worldwide population of about 4.5 billion people, injury expert Professor Julian Waller estimates that approximately 375,000 deaths a year occur from unintentional injury[22]. Among

countries that do report to the World Health Organization, the available figures indicate that no matter what the state of development of the nation, deaths from injury represent some 3 to 10% of all deaths in all countries. There are great difficulties in assessing the significance of death rates for various types of injuries within countries, let alone in comparing country to country. As Waller points out, if a person with a disease has a dizzy spell, falls, breaks a hip and dies from cardiovascular complications of lying immobile in bed, there will be considerable differences between various administrations as to whether the death will be attributed to the fall or to the heart disease.

Deaths from Violence and Poisoning Selected Causes, England and Wales, 1984

ICD number	External causes of injury		Age					
			Total	0–14	15–44	45–64	65–74	75&over
E800-E999	EXVII EXTERNAL CAUSES OF INJURY AND POISONING	M	11,197	654	5139	2568	1188	1648
		F	7,638	336	1465	1457	1111	3269
E800-E807	Railway accidents	M	76	2	48	18	6	2
		F	10	0	5	3	2	0
E810-E819	Motor vehicle traffic accidents	M	3,547	286	2112	547	277	325
		F	1,465	151	504	217	240	353
E820-E825	Motor vehicle non-traffic accidents	M	67	7	47	11	0	2
		F	11	1	3	2	2	3
E826-E829	Other road vehicle accidents	M	50	5	15	11	10	9
		F	32	6	10	9	3	4
E830-E838	Water transport accidents	M	49	5	32	10	2	0
		F	5	0	4	1	0	0
E840-E845	Air and space transport	M	29	0	23	6	0	0
		F	0	0	0	0	0	0
E850-E869	Accidental poisoning	M	384	18	235	85	24	24
		F	258	11	83	93	34	37
E880-E888	Accidental falls	M	1,416	49	201	235	238	693
		F	2,512	9	43	122	264	2074
E890-E899	Accidents caused by fire and flames	M	318	55	56	68	46	93
		F	323	34	43	47	43	156
E910	Accidental drowning and submersion	M	215	50	102	43	10	10
		F	88	14	15	22	20	17
E919-E919.2	Accidents caused by machinery	M	139	2	82	54	0	1
		F	4	0	3	0	0	1
E922	Accident caused by firearm missile	M	13	1	9	3	0	0
		F	1	0	1	0	0	0
E950-E959	Suicide and self-inflicted injury	M	2,859	1	1341	960	321	236
		F	1,456	1	403	584	257	211
E960-E969	Homicide and injury purposely inflicted by other persons	M	188	27	104	41	10	6
		F	153	23	71	28	17	14
E980-E989	Injury undetermined whether accidentally or purposely inflicted	M	917	27	454	270	103	63
		F	646	19	224	214	85	104

Source: Office of Population Censuses and Surveys *Mortality Statistics, Causes, 1984*, OPCS 1985

POISONING

Poisoning is an important cause of death in all countries and throughout all age groups. The average death rate worldwide is in the order of 7 to 15 deaths per million each year, or an annual risk of 1 in 140,000 to 1 in 70,000. Just what it is that people get poisoned by varies from age to age and country to country, with much depending on the level of technological development. In England and Wales, accidental poisoning is the fourth commonest cause of ''violent'' death, after traffic accidents, falls and suicide. The death rate is currently around 15 per million (one in 70,000). In addition, many suicidal deaths are as a result of poisoning. For all deaths from poisons which have been swallowed, medicines and non-medicines are quite evenly split as the two causes[23], and carbon monoxide gas accounts for nearly as many deaths as each of those two categories. Accidental death by poisoning (other than gases) is most commonly from the ingestion of alcohol, followed by painkillers and illegal narcotics. In nearly one-quarter of accidental poisonings not due to alcohol, alcohol was used in association with the other poison. Among suicidal poisonings, pain-killers are the most commonly employed agents, along with drugs used for the treatment of depression and sleeping pills. The list of ''non-medicinal'' poisons (apart from alcohol) shows no particularly significant single substance, almost everything conceivable having at some time poisoned somebody.

Separate statistics for England and Wales are also published with respect to the death by poisoning of children. Surprisingly, the total number recorded as dying accidentally this way is very small, with 12 children under 15 years being poisoned in 1983. The increasing use of child-resistant containers and medicine cabinets is important in keeping this particular risk low.

In the United States, two-thirds of those who die from poisoning by solids and liquids do so as a result of the ingestion of pharmaceutical preparations, including aspirin and sedatives. The most common liquid to cause poisoning, as in England, is alcohol. Of gases and vapours that cause death by poisoning, motor vehicle exhaust is easily the commonest, followed by carbon monoxide from other sources.

While deaths from poisoning are reasonably well documented, the incidence of poisonings

Throughout the world, about one person in 100,000 is poisoned each year, or about one in 70,000 in England. The vast majority are adults, most commonly dying from poisoning by alcohol and drugs (medical and otherwise).

that do not result in death is hard to assess. The main reason is that there is a big difference between the simple ingestion of a substance which causes alarm and the seeking of medical help, and the actual damage to body tissues by such ingestion. The difference is, of course, clearly related to the type and quantity of the material ingested. In the United States the substance most commonly reported to have been accidentally ingested (non-fatally) is aspirin, followed by bleach, paraffin (kerosene), chocolate-like laxatives and drain cleaners[24]. Of course, many of these reportings are as a result of genuine but unwarranted concern rather than actual damage, but even when the number who are hospitalized (as a proportion of all those who have reported) is taken into account, aspirin is still the most important cause of non-fatal poisoning. Nearly 40% of all those who have ingested paraffin remain in hospital after reporting, whereas only 6% of those who have ingested laxatives do so. Children are at risk from poisoning because their natural curiosity is aided and abetted by an apparent unconcern for unpleasant taste. It has also been found that children who have been poisoned are more likely to have shown behavioural difficulties over the years than other children. Among adults, the commonest liquid poison is a very large dose of alcohol, commonly ingested by those who already have problems with drinking.

Among factors in the environment which add to the risk of poisoning are ease of access to poisons and their attractiveness to children. The use of child-resistant caps for containers for hazardous chemicals and pharmaceutical preparations has greatly reduced the risk of childhood poisoning, with the use of such packaging being associated with substantial drops in poisonings by aspirin, cleaning compounds and other products.

Poisoning from gas, apart from the carbon monoxide emitted by motor vehicle exhaust, is usually as a result of poorly maintained or badly vented cooking and heating appliances. Changing the type of gas piped to homes in the United Kingdom from coal gas to natural gas, which is almost free of carbon monoxide, resulted in a 70% drop in male deaths from unintentional gas poisoning and a 75% drop in female deaths[25].

Poisoning from animal and insect bites is rare in developed nations and urban areas, but still very common in the tropical and developing parts of the world. Each year, there are about 300,000 snake bites each year, resulting in 30,000 to 40,000 deaths. Most of these occur in South-East Asia and South America.

INFECTIOUS DISEASE

We have seen how, in the developed world, deaths from injury and violence have taken over from infectious diseases as the most important causes of death for the first half of life. As we approach the end of the 20th Century, however, it is clear that this picture certainly does not apply in the developing world and, moreover, it may no longer be true for the developed world within a few years.

In the developing world, infectious disease still runs rife. We have already pointed to the high incidence of rheumatic fever and subsequent rheumatic heart disease. In far too many areas of the Third World we will find very much the same conditions as were common in the dark days in industrial Europe, one hundred and more years ago. There are enormous shortcomings in medical attention, sanitation and nutrition, especially in Africa, Asia and Latin America. In Britain and the United States, we have virtually conquered epidemic diseases such as polio, measles, tetanus and diphtheria, but only in the case of smallpox can world-wide success be claimed. All the other infectious epidemic diseases run rife. Simple diarrhoea is the largest single killer in the third world. The effects of the classic tropical diseases, of which malaria is still the most important, continue to be devastating. The overall world malaria situation has not improved for 15 years, and is deteriorating in poorer rural areas. River blindness, schistosomiasis and sleeping sickness still afflict millions of people in tropical areas. In the poorer nations infectious diseases will continue easily to outweigh the importance of diseases of lifestyle and environment for the foreseeable future.

Comparatively recently, a new infectious disease has been added to the list of those which are already scourges of central Africa, and has become a problem of extraordinary enormity. This is Acquired Immune Deficiency Syndrome, or "AIDS", which is now also spreading rapidly throughout the developed world and threatens by the end of the century to exceed accidents and violence as the commonest single cause of death among the young, and be by that time the single biggest cause of loss of productive years of life.

AIDS

At astonishing speed AIDS has become an international problem. In addition to illness and death, the risk of AIDS is now a source of widespread fear. Unfortunately, many of those who fear the disease the most may not be at very great risk, and many of those who are at risk do not fear the disease sufficiently. While it is a life-threatening disease and a major public health issue, it is in principle preventable[26].

The Acquired Immune Deficiency Syndrome is just that, a syndrome; in other words, a collection of conditions rather than a single disease. A person who has AIDS is in the final stages of a series of health problems caused by a virus which has attacked the body's immune system. Without the defence against disease offered by a functioning immune system a person becomes vulnerable to infection by a wide variety of bacteria, fungi, other viruses and cancers.

The AIDS virus has had a few changes in name during its short history, but is now referred to as the human immunodeficiency virus, or HIV. At present no cure is known, and there is no vaccine to prevent the virus taking hold.

After infection, people may remain apparently perfectly well. They may have attacks of symptoms a bit like flu, and may suffer from swollen glands. If the symptoms get bad, they may be termed "AIDS related complex" or ARC. After infection the body tries to defend itself against the invading virus by formation of antibodies in the blood, and these can be identified by laboratory testing. However, there may be two or three months between infection and the appearance of antibodies.

Estimates of the proportion of individuals who are carrying antibodies who go on to develop the full-blooded syndrome vary up to 75%, and an exact prediction is at present difficult because the symptoms sometimes take up to nine years to appear, and the length of time people have had antibodies is the major factor known to determine the risk of developing AIDS[27]. The best estimate at the end of 1986 was that some 30% of those infected with the AIDS virus will develop the illness within five years.

AIDS first appeared in America in the summer of 1981, and the first case in the United Kingdom was reported in December of that year. Retrospectively, it is now clear that the disease had already appeared in Africa in the late 1970s. The World Health Organization estimated that by late 1986 in Africa there were 2–5 million infected people and some 50,000 cases, with 200,000 to 1.5 million cases to be expected in the following five years, these cases being in people already infected. However, workers in the field have estimated a figure of several hundred thousand, and that as many as five million Africans could be carrying the virus[28]. Accurate estimation is impossible in Africa, because officials are reluctant to concede the high

AIDS: estimated new cases in Britain

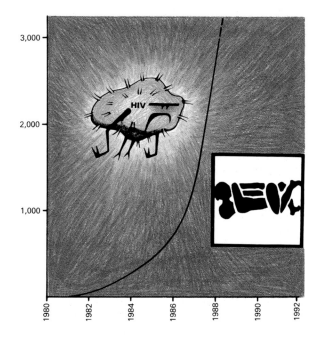

The explosive growth of the new infectious disease of AIDS is shown here. Unless controlled, by the end of the century it will well exceed road accidents as a cause of death and have replaced violence as the main killer of young people.
Source: reference 30

incidence of the disease in many countries or, indeed, may be prepared to deny its existence completely.

In late 1986 the number of people known to have the full syndrome in the United States was over 25,000, of whom about half had died by that time. At least 145,000 deaths (including 3,000 children) were expected in the following five years.

In Britain, by the end of 1986, 610 cases and 293 deaths had been reported. Based on the rate of increase during earlier years in Britain and other countries, the estimated number of new cases in Britain in 1987 would be 1,300 and, in 1988, 3,000[29]. Soon after, there would be as many new cases annually as there were deaths in road accidents.

AIDS is a sexually transmitted disease. During the early stages of its spread in various countries where it has been monitored with some accuracy, it has primarily been a disease of the homosexual population, but as it becomes well established the proportion of women to men who are infected increases. In the United States, for every woman infected there were about 30 males by late 1986, although in some areas the ratio was 1:2. Among potential recruits for military service in 1986 the ratio was one in 2.5. In Africa, however, the disease is spread evenly between men and women and is now spread predominantly through heterosexual relations or passed from mother to unborn baby. It is now, therefore, acting like other sexually transmitted diseases such as syphilis and gonorrhoea, with the difference being that at present AIDS is inevitably fatal.

The AIDS virus is carried in the blood and is also found in the semen and female genital secretions. It is not, as viruses go, a particularly infectious one, but sexual intercourse by way of the anus or vagina will transmit it, as will use of drug addicts' needles contaminated by someone else's blood.

The risk of AIDS is distributed very unevenly throughout the community, and is affected to a very great extent by personal behaviour. Individuals, therefore, have considerable choice in the extent to which they are at risk of infection. The initial discovery of AIDS was in the homosexual community, and men who have sexual relations with other men are especially at risk. The risk of infection increases according to the number of sexual partners: the more numerous the partners the greater the risk. The limited epidemiological evidence available in 1986–87 indicated that the rapid spread of AIDS among homosexual men may have been due to the influence of a small minority who were very promiscuous.

For those at risk who choose not to change their lifestyles, "low risk sex" is now being urged by authorities and health care groups. The use of a condom during intercourse acts as a barrier to the transmission of infected fluids. When one of the partners is at high risk, mouth contact with the penis, vagina, or rectum should be avoided, as should all sexual activities which could cause damage to the membranes of the rectum, vagina or penis.

Infection spreads from the homosexual to the heterosexual community through the activities of bisexual people and drug addicts, although by the end of 1986 the disease in Britain and the United States had spread to only a very small extent outside the groups at recognized risk. Addicts who inject drugs into the veins are at high risk and already have high rates of infection by the AIDS virus. In America, indeed, users of intravenous drugs made up 25% of cases of AIDS in late 1986. The virus is carried in contaminated blood in the needles of syringes, and if these implements are used again the live virus is injected straight into the vein of the next user. The only preventive measure for these people is to use a clean previously unused needle, syringe and other implements necessary for the injection of the drug solution.

If a woman is infected with the AIDS virus and becomes pregnant she can pass the virus to her child. Approximately one-third of babies born to AIDS infected mothers will also be infected, and most of the babies will die.

A very small number of people have been infected by the AIDS virus through transfusion with infected blood, but in Europe and the United States, blood donors are now screened and blood that has been collected for use is tested for the presence of antibodies to the AIDS virus. The risk of being infected this way, therefore, is now exceedingly low (in the order of one in a million), although not zero. As it happens, the risk in 1986 was about the same as dying from a prescribed drug or from a vaccination. In less developed countries, however, the blood may well not be screened for antibodies, and where the rates of infection are high, blood from local donors should be avoided unless the transfusion will definitely save life. Some 10% of blood stocks in Zambia are contaminated, but a blood screening test costs around £3.50 and in Africa the entire annual health expenditure per head of population is in the order of £1.20.

There is no recorded case of AIDS resulting from casual social contact such as shaking hands, hugging, social kissing, crying, coughing or sneezing. AIDS has not been contracted from swimming pools or hot tubs or from sharing bed linen, towels, cups, straws, dishes or any other eating utensils. It is impossible to catch the infection from toilets, door knobs, telephones, office machinery or household furniture, or from massages or any non-sexual body contact. *Donating* blood carries no risk whatsoever: all equipment used for blood collection is sterile and is used only once.

There is no risk in visiting a patient with AIDS or caring for him or her. Normal hygienic practices will provide full protection.

No cases of transmission of the AIDS virus have been recorded from child to child in school or between child and adult, by flying insects to people or from pets. Although the virus has been found in tears and in saliva, no instance of transmission from these body fluids has been reported.

In the United States about 2,500 health workers who were caring for AIDS patients while they were sickest have been carefully studied and tested for infection with the AIDS virus. These people have been exposed to the patients' blood and other body fluids, but only three of them, all having accidentally stuck themselves with a needle, had a positive antibody test for exposure to the virus. It is therefore clear that the virus is not transmitted by casual contact, even when this involves considerable exposure to patients and their body fluids.

People who engage in high risk sexual behaviour or who use drugs intravenously are risking infection with AIDS virus, and are risking their lives and the lives of others. The full impact of AIDS on society is as yet unknown, and it is clear that an enormous challenge to public health lies ahead of us. However, witch-hunting and panic will not help, any more than it did in the case of cholera, plague or leprosy in the past, all diseases which were regarded with superstitious terror but which were all successfully brought under control by rational and scientifically valid public health measures.

Chapter Five

Major Risk Factors

SMOKING

Smoking is the greatest single self-imposed risk to health of all. This is true throughout the developed world, and it is true for most of the developing world as well. Smokers have greatly increased rates of death and illness compared to non-smokers, especially for diseases of the heart, blood vessels and the lungs. Although the greatest relative risk is that relating to cancer of the lung, the impact on the total community of smoking is of the same order of magnitude in regard to cardiovascular disease because, although the increase in risk is less than for cancer, there are so many more people with cardiovascular disease. Indispensible reviews of the subject are the recent reports by Royal College of Physicians of London[1] and the Surgeon General of the United States[2].

In Britain, tobacco has been smoked in one form or another since Elizabethan times. British men rapidly increased their consumption to a maximum by the end of the Second World War. Women have followed the same pattern of increase, although forty years later on. The rate of smoking among men stayed rather constant between 1945 and 1975, and since then has been dropping[3]. Between 1976 and 1984 the average daily consumption by adult male smokers fell from 18 to 16 cigarettes, and from just over 14 to

just under 14 among females. In 1972, 52% of men and 41% of women were cigarette smokers, but by 1984, these figures were down to 36% among men and 32% among women, a faster fall for men than women. Unlike male smokers, female smokers in every socio-economic group smoked more cigarettes in 1984 than they did in 1972.

In 1982, for the first time, smokers were a minority in every social group and this was still the case in 1984. However, men and women in the "manual" socio-economic groups were much more likely to smoke than people in the "non-manual" groups.

In the United States the first decline in cigarette consumption was seen in 1954 after 40 years of increase, and this was the year that the first American Cancer Society report showed that cigarette smokers suffered a relatively high death rate. There has been a decline in smoking in that country since 1973 among men, but smoking among women has steadily increased and in 1984 for the first time in American history, more women were smoking than men. That same year, the death rate among women from lung cancer in the United States first surpassed their death rate from breast cancer.

The association of smoking with cancer of the lung has been known for over 30 years. More recently, evidence has hardened on the link between smoking and chronic bronchitis, emphysema, coronary heart disease, narrowing of the blood vessels in the limbs, and damage to the unborn babies of smoking mothers. Tobacco accounts for some 15–20% of all deaths in Britain throughout all age groups. In 1981 there were about 70,000 deaths from lung cancer, bronchitis and obstructive lung disease, of which at least 90% were attributable to smoking (say 63,000 deaths, or over 5,000 *a month*). There were about 180,000 coronary heart disease deaths, of which perhaps 20% will have been related to smoking (say 36,000). These figures, together with a few deaths due to miscellaneous other causes related to smoking, give a total of over 100,000 deaths, well over 8,000 premature deaths every month.

This figure dwarfs the number of deaths resulting from any other voluntarily or involuntarily imposed hazard.

The Royal College of Physicians has pointed out that among 1,000 young male adults in England and Wales who smoke cigarettes, on average about:

1 will be murdered,

6 will be killed on the road,

250 will be killed before their time by tobacco.

Smoking is the biggest self-imposed risk of all. Among 1,000 young male smokers, about 250 will die from the effects of tobacco, compared with 6 who will be killed on the road and one who will be murdered. In Britain, at least 2,000 people die before their time from smoking each and every *week*.

Death is not the only outcome of smoking. It also causes prolonged ill health, loss of working time, and a substantial cost to the nation. About 50 million working days are lost each year as a result of smoking-related illness, or about quadruple the time lost from strikes. The National Health Service is required to carry the cost of hospital bed occupancy, sickness benefits and medical treatment at a total cost which was estimated by the Office of Population Censuses and Surveys to be £370 million in 1984.

It was observations on the rapid rise of lung cancer after the second world war that stimulated concern about the effects of smoking[4]. Lung cancer accounted for fewer than 10 deaths every 100,000 men each year at the beginning of the century, but by the early 1960s, among men aged 45 to 64 years, the rate had peaked at nearly 200 deaths per 100,000. Today, lung cancer is the commonest killing cancer in Britain.

The confirmation that it was cigarette smoking which was responsible for the enormous rise came through a special study by Professors Doll and Peto of a part of the population who gave up smoking in hordes, doctors. Between 1954 and 1971 the proportion of all male doctors who were smoking cigarettes halved from 43% to 21%, while that for all other men in England and Wales remained the same. Over this period, the death rate in men from lung cancer fell by 25% among doctors, while in the general population it increased by 26%[5].

Lung cancer death rates in men and women in England and Wales

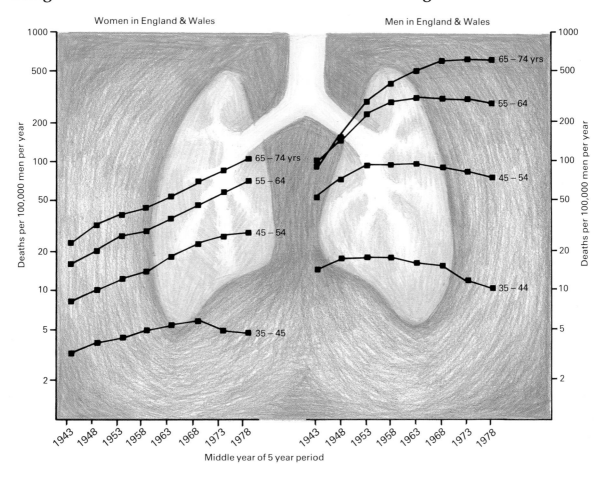

Death rates per 100,000 per year between 1943 and 1978 are shown for four age groups, each covering a span of 10 years. The recent decline in mortality seen in all except the oldest men is only just becoming evident in the youngest women. We are paying a fearful price for the women who started to smoke some 40–50 years ago.
Source: reference 1

Cancers of the mouth, larynx and oesophagus have all now been associated with smoking, and among pipe and cigar smokers as well as cigarette smokers. Associations have also been found between smoking and cancer of the pancreas gland and of the urinary tract.

Chronic bronchitis and emphysema, already discussed earlier in the context of respiratory disease and themselves significant contributors to death overall, are responsible for an enormous number of days lost from work through disabling breathlessness. The death rate from chronic bronchitis is six times as great in smokers as in non-smokers, and those smoking 25 cigarettes a day have 25 times the risk for non-smokers.

As also previously described, coronary heart disease is now one of the leading causes of death in all developed countries. Cigarette smoking adds to and interacts with existing factors which predispose to the disease and, overall, smoking accounts for around one in three to one in five deaths from coronary heart disease. In other parts of the body, blood vessels are also affected by smoking, with regular smokers accounting for something like 95% of all patients with serious disease of the arteries of the legs (which causes pain when walking and may lead to amputation).

Smoking causes ulcers of the stomach and duodenum, with male smokers having twice as many ulcers as non-smokers, and with ulcers which are harder to cure and more likely to kill.

The ill effects of smoking follow about 20 years behind the use of cigarettes, so that although smoking among women is now decreasing, lung cancer deaths are still rising.

In the early 1970s concern was expressed about the adverse effects on the unborn child if a mother-to-be smoked. Even when trying to become pregnant, women who smoke are more likely to be infertile or take longer to conceive than those who do not. Smoking increases the risk of a miscarriage to an extent that the risk is doubled among women smoking 20 or more cigarettes a day, quite independent of other factors which are known to pose a risk of miscarriage. Children born to women who smoke are on average half a pound lighter than those born to non-smokers. There is also a slightly increased risk of the baby dying at around the time of birth, a risk which is doubled among heavy smokers. However, suggestions that the risk of congenital abnormality is increased have not, in general, been confirmed.

Smoking interacts with the contraceptive pill in such a way that the ill effects of both are increased. The risk of heart disease and stroke in young women is increased by about three to four times by either the pill or by smoking, but when the two are combined the joint risk is about ten times higher, and worse again for those over 45 years of age.

Children know about cigarettes from a very early age. Three out of four of them are aware of cigarettes before they reach the age of five, whether their parents smoke or not. At ten years of age, as many as 40% of boys and 28% of girls have tried a cigarette, but it is not until adolescence that smoking may become a regular habit. By the time they reach 16, one in four boys are regular smokers with the figures for girls only slightly lower.

Passive smoking

Non-smokers are commonly exposed to other people's irritant and carcinogenic smoke, whether they like it or not. To what extent, then, are these "passive smokers" exposed to the risk of lung disease, as well as to annoyance and discomfort?

Several epidemiological studies have been mounted in order to try to answer the question, are non-smokers living with smokers at higher risk of lung cancer than non-smokers living with non-smokers? The findings of these individual studies were inconclusive because most were too small to detect excess risk, but a recent review by Professor Nicholas Wald combined the results of all of them. His team concluded that there is clear evidence that non-smokers who live with smokers face a 35% higher risk of getting lung cancer than those who do not[6], and that breathing other people's tobacco smoke *is* a cause of lung cancer. Wald estimates that in the United Kingdom around 300 non-smokers die each year of lung cancer induced by tobacco smoke.

In the United States, a recent National Research Council report concluded that: (i) young children are at 20–80% greater risk of respiratory problems that require medical attention if they are raised by smoking rather than non-smoking parents; (ii) adults who have never smoked are significantly more likely to get lung cancer if married to smokers than if they are not; and (iii) many people suffer severe eye and nose irritation when exposed to tobacco smoke[7].

Many risk issues remain unresolved, but the implication of what is known today is that smoking is not only a voluntarily accepted risk, but also an involuntary risk for some, including children who are in no position to counter it.

The risk as seen by smokers

In a later chapter we will discuss the sometimes very wide differences that exist between, on the one hand, the degree of risk for a given activity as measured using objective criteria, and on the other hand the risk which is generally perceived. For smoking, because of the extremely high risk it poses and because of the degree of choice involved in whether or not an individual smokes and thus exposes himself to risk, this risk perception gap is extremely important. A rather gloomy finding is that the knowledge of smokers about the risks they run is imperfect and incomplete[8]. Many smokers flatly reject any link between smoking and disease. Forty-five per cent deny that smoking causes heart disease and 33% that it causes lung cancer, and among many others there is only a qualified acceptance of these links. Further, even among those who do believe that smoking is harmful, there are not many who think that smokers will help themselves by giving up, which is contrary to the truth.

For smokers, then, smoking is an acceptable risk, but in practice the risk they are prepared to accept is assessed by them as being a lot lower than it really is. Even when people accept that the consequences of smoking *can* be severe, the probability of those consequences ever arising is perceived to be low and the risk therefore acceptable for that reason. People who are doubtful about the link between smoking and disease will easily be swayed by advertising which plants the idea in their heads that the debate is still an open one, with scientists evenly split on the matter and definite conclusions not yet reached.

The preventable epidemic

It is research in the developed world which has drawn attention to smoking as a potent risk to health, but smoking is an international problem and the developing countries are now faced by an epidemic of disease which ought to be almost completely avoidable[9]. It is a deliberate and overt policy of the international tobacco industry (which is based in the developed world) to encourage smoking in the Third World[1]. In this way, the developed world is deliberately imposing a substantial risk of premature death and disease on their less developed neighbours. There is an almost ludicrous lack of public and international concern regarding the deliberate imposition of this risk upon others, in comparison with, for example, the imposition of risks posed by acid rain and radioactive fallout. At a time when the growth rate in the cigarette market in the developed world is very small or indeed negative, it is still very substantial in developing countries. Because of the time-lag before disease is established, it is tomorrow's epidemic. Surveys in developing countries are hard to undertake, but one study of 18 year olds in southern Brazil showed that 38% of them smoked. There appear to be few contrary influences. Among male medical students in Lagos, 72% were found to smoke, and 40% of all *doctors* in Bangladesh do so.

While tobacco in many developing countries is a major source of employment and cash income, the growing of tobacco takes up land that might otherwise be available for crops that are more socially beneficial. Unfortunately, immediate risks to economic well-being are likely to be perceived as more important than remote risks to community health and welfare. People of the Third World are even more poorly informed about the dangers of smoking than people in countries like Britain and the United States. A leading cigarette brand in Africa is called "Life".

In the words of the Royal College of Physicians, "the international tobacco industry can be expected to oppose and hinder efforts to reduce smoking. In doing so, it will be directly responsible for fostering the deaths of thousands in the 20th Century's most avoidable epidemic".

ALCOHOL AND OTHER DRUGS

Alcohol

Humankind has a striking capacity for identifying natural and man-made substances which are "psychoactive" and alter the mind so as to stimulate and intoxicate. These are eaten, drunk, chewed and smoked in order to bring about the desired effects. But at any given time, between and within various communities, there will be found very wide differences of opinion on the desirability of each of these mind-altering substances. In Europe and North America it is alcohol which is the most popular intoxicant, although it is by far the most potent psychoactive substance now legally available without prescription. Its competitors, including opium and its derivatives (morphine and heroin for example), cannabis, cocaine and so on are illegal, yet in many ways they are similar: their use is very pleasurable for many people, but they all have substantial disadvantages both to individual users and to the rest of society. It is not surprising, therefore, that ambivalent attitudes are common, as indeed they have been for centuries[10].

Tobacco, which contains the highly addictive drug nicotine, has also been greeted at various times with widely differing degrees of enthusiasm, ranging from optimistic descriptions as a remedy for all diseases to its characterization by James I as a "loathsome custom". Less than 300 years ago the penalty for smoking in some parts of Germany was death. In the Americas, on the other hand, it was alcohol that was seen as the root of all evil, and even now, several counties in the United States are "dry". Its use was also punishable by death in pre-Hispanic Mexico. Many western governments currently regard drugs such as cocaine and heroin in much the same sort of light, and marihuana (cannabis) was described by a high government official in the United States in 1953 as "one of the most dangerous drugs known". Yet in Britain both opium and cannabis could be bought perfectly legally until 1868, and at around the turn of the century a Royal Commission on opium concluded without hesitation that no extended physical or moral degradation is caused by its use.

In its excellent book on alcohol[10], a special committee of the Royal College of Psychiatrists points out that almost every psychoactive drug known to humanity, from alcohol to opium, has been regarded by some government and society as a dire threat to public order and moral standards, and by another government and another society as a source of harmless pleasure. Further, nations and governments sometimes change their views completely. Almost every society has at least one drug whose use is tolerated, while drugs used in other cultures are generally viewed quite differently and with deep suspicion. Mexican Indians may have disapproved of alcohol, but they used mescaline. Most Muslim cultures forbid alcohol, but they tolerate cannabis and opium.

Therefore, for the purpose of this brief discussion of the effects on risk of psychoactive drugs, they are treated together as one group.

Alcohol is so popular that it is easy for most westerners to cast a more favourable eye on it than on other mind-altering substances, despite the fact that it is probably the most important single factor in affecting the risk of injury, impulsive crime, violence in the home, and socio-sexual difficulty. Its very popularity has led to the availability of far more information on its use, misuse and effects than is easily available for other psychoactive and addictive substances (other than tobacco, discussed above).

The annual per-capita consumption of alcohol has risen steadily in the United Kingdom since the early 1950s. Between 1960 and 1981 per-capita consumption of beer rose by over 50%, of spirits by a factor of two times and of wine by about five times. The total per-capita (15 years and over) intake of absolute alcohol rose from over five litres a year in 1960 to over nine litres in 1984. This is a faster rate of increase than throughout the rest of Europe, but slower than in Australasia and North America. To the extent that alcohol represents a risk factor, therefore, it is increasing annually.

It is not possible to put precise figures on the prevalence or incidence of drinking which causes direct personal harm, and only the crudest estimate can be made of the true cost of alcohol-related problems. However, some idea of the magnitude of the risk the drug represents to society may be obtained from an estimate that the total cost of alcohol misuse in England and Wales in 1983 added up to over £1,500 million, with costs for Northern Ireland and Scotland being proportionately greater since the extent of alcohol misuse appears to be rather higher in these parts of the United Kingdom[11]. The way these costs were calculated indicates that overwhelmingly the highest proportion of costs, about 87%, are represented by the social cost to industry. The social cost to the National Health Service is about 6% of the total, the cost of traffic accidents 5.5% and criminal activities 2%. A tiny fraction of the cost is represented by expenditure on national alcohol agencies and research.

Costs of alcohol misuse, England and Wales, 1983

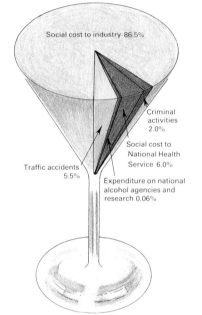

The total cost of alcohol misuse in England and Wales exceeds £1,500 million, with the greatest part being borne by industry through absenteeism, alcoholism and accidents. The costs are felt not only in money terms but also in misery, illness and death.
Source: reference 11

Total costs of alcohol misuse in England and Wales, 1983

Category	Cost in £ millions
Social cost to industry	1396.8
Social cost to National Health Service	95.9
Expenditure on national alcohol agencies and research	1.0
Traffic accidents	89.2
Criminal activities	32.2

Source: McDonnel and Maynard 1985 — 33

Even the heavier types of "acceptable social drinking" carry some risk of shortening life expectancy, and there is certainly a high mortality rate among heavy drinkers identified by doctors as being dependent on alcohol. The actual age-related death rate of a group of 935 patients diagnosed as being alcohol dependent and who were followed up after 10 to 15 years was about three times higher both for men and women than would have been expected in the general population[12]. The particular causes of death which spring into predominance as a result of dependence on alcohol are cirrhosis of the liver, suicide, accidents, poisoning and violence.

However, individuals do not have to be dependent on alcohol to be faced by increased risks to health and welfare resulting from drinking. Drinking problems are related to an interacting complex of factors and do not result from alcohol as a single cause. The actual type of problem that may result from drinking depends on the characteristics of alcohol as a depressant drug, the characteristics of the drinker, and the context of its use. In the United Kingdom many alcohol-related problems are a result, not of heavy drinking over a long period, but of acute intoxication.

After drinking, alcohol is absorbed quickly. Absorption is faster if the concentration of the alcohol in the stomach is high, and slower if it is diluted before drinking or by the stomach contents, including food. The quicker the absorption, the higher the peak of the blood alcohol concentration and the greater the consequent effect on behaviour and performance.

Although the concentration of alcohol in different drinks varies, the actual amount in each one is about the same, which makes the "standard drink" or "unit of alcohol" (same thing) concept useful. British measures of spirits contain 8–10 grams of alcohol, about the same as in a sherry-glass of sherry or port, a standard glass of wine, or half a pint of beer. (After many years of popular sale in countries such as Australia—despite its "macho" beer-drinking image—low-alcohol beers are at last becoming available in Britain, and these of course fall outside the standard drink category).

One or two drinks will raise the blood alcohol concentration (BAC) to 50 milligrams per 100 millilitres of blood, commonly abbreviated to 50 mg%. At this level, measurable alteration of judgement occurs, and careful vehicle accident studies show that the risk of crashing starts to rise for many people. Mood and the ability to maintain concentration both start to change. At the legal limit for driving in Britain of 80 mg% it is possible to say that every road user—driver, cyclist, pedestrian—is at a higher risk of injury than when sober. Studies of the epidemiology of other injuries is sadly less detailed than for car crashes, but an analogous picture is emerging.

Alcohol-related injury (other than on the roads) has not been studied in any great depth in Britain, but research in many other similar countries has associated alcohol use with drowning, injuries at home, and accidental falls.

About half of the admissions for head injuries at a hospital in Glasgow were found to be under the influence of alcohol, with an average blood/alcohol level of more than two and a half times the legal limit for driving.

Alcohol is related to injury resulting from personal violence as well as accidental injury, and has been linked to a wide spectrum of aggressive behaviour and crime ranging from fights outside pubs to mass hooliganism. However, alcohol is rarely or never a single cause[13], and it would be helpful to have far more information on alcohol drunk by offenders and by matched groups who do not offend. No such statistics are now gathered in Britain (except for alcohol-related road accidents), although studies of young people in Scotland and the United States have shown high alcohol intakes among juvenile offenders[14].

A special case of alcohol-related crime is drinking before driving to an extent which raises the blood alcohol level above the prescribed limit of 80 mg%. A more detailed discussion of this relationship will be found in Chapter 7, in which risks in transport are described. Briefly, at the UK prescribed limit the risk of crashing is about twice the risk for the same driver when sober, by 150 mg% the risk is ten times normal, and by 200 mg% the risk of crashing is about 20 times the sober level. Not only does the risk of crashing increase with increasing levels of blood alcohol, the severity of the crash increases also.

The importance of alcohol to industrial production has been shown by the estimate of costs outlined above, and some occupations have been shown to have exceptionally high rates of alcohol problem. These high risk jobs include the drink and catering trades, the Armed Forces, the Merchant Navy, the fishing industry, the medical profession and journalism. Drinking contributes to a high rate of absenteeism and is (as would be expected) a frequent contributing cause to accidents at work.

The psychological effects of alcohol, including the slow development of mental distress in association with consistent heavy drinking, have been identified by the Royal College of Psychiatrists as contributing to the appalling high rates of suicide which are associated with dependence on alcohol, leading to a risk of suicide which is least 50 times higher than in the general population.

Alcohol also increases the risk of physical illness in several ways and excessive drinking can damage nearly every organ and system of the body and thus contribute to premature death. Accurate figures are hard to obtain, because alcohol-related deaths are substantially under-reported. It has been traditionally assumed that alcohol-related physical damage only occurs after the long-time daily consumption of alcohol in excess of 80 grams a day (about eight to ten standard drinks a day). But it has become increasingly evident that the risk of physical damage rises among people drinking regularly at a more moderate level than that. The risk is higher for women, because they achieve significantly higher blood alcohol values than men at given levels of intake because the total amount of water they have in their body is significantly less.

The risk of cirrhosis of the liver is widely known to be high for heavy drinkers, and indeed the majority of individuals who are dependent on alcohol will show microscopic changes to the liver at some stage of their lives. Daily intakes of 40 grams of alcohol a day by men, and 20 grams by women, have been linked with a significant increase in the risk of developing cirrhosis. Up to 10% of patients with alcoholic cirrhosis will develop cancer of the liver as a late complication, but stopping drinking does reduce this risk. Severe inflammation of the liver can kill, but people reducing their alcohol intake after an episode of this disease have an 80% chance of surviving the next seven years, whereas of those people who continue to drink only 50% can expect to survive the next seven years.

The risk of developing cancer of the throat (oesophagus) is increased in those drinking 80 grams or more of alcohol a day, and this risk is multiplied by the use of tobacco. Excessive drinking is also associated with an increased risk of cancer of the upper throat and mouth, and with inflammation of the lining of the stomach. Alcohol may destroy the pancreas gland, which severely disrupts the digestive process.

Heavy drinking can upset the rhythm of the heart beat and may cause disease of the heart muscle. There appears to be a lower incidence of death from cardiovascular disease among people who drink a little alcohol, compared with those who either drink none or larger quantities. However, taking all the studies together, the conclusion that alcohol in moderate amounts might possibly protect against coronary heart problems is hard to sustain, as the moderate drinker may be the sort who leads a life which in many other ways minimizes his or her risk of unnecessary disease.

Women who drink heavily during pregnancy risk harming their offspring. However, while maternal drinking during pregnancy is associated with a risk of abnormalities to the child, so too are other factors, some of which appear to be more important than alcohol. These include the age of the mother, her social class, the use of tobacco and illegal drugs, the use of medicines, and her diet. Moderate drinking in itself does not appear to harm the baby.

While most people are aware of the increased risk of harm posed by alcohol for various particular circumstances, there is a comparative lack of awareness of the *total* picture. This is comprised of a mass of problems of risk of varied origin, to each of which alcohol contributes to a greater or lesser extent. There are still many gaps in the evidence and little comprehensive monitoring of the health costs, which are deficiencies unlikely to be remedied until the broad picture is brought into sharper public focus.

Other drugs

As outlined at the beginning of this chapter, at the present time public and political concern is much more outspoken when it is directed at the problem of *illegal* rather than *legal* drug use. Naturally, part of the reason for this is the presentation of drug problems on the media, with the television screen and much of the press presenting a very distorted picture of the drug-taking world. Heroin is the illegal drug in Britain which is perhaps the one subjected to the most publicity, and indeed the government has spent millions of pounds on public education campaigns directed at its use, and on attempts to stop it entering the country.

The illegal drug available in the largest amounts, and the one which is often the first introduction to illegal drug use, is cannabis (marihuana). The sniffing of glues and other solvents provides another route into experimentation by young people with drugs used illegally, the use of which currently includes substances such as the amphetamines, cocaine, barbiturates and tranquillizers, LSD and other hallucinogenic chemicals, as well as over-the-counter preparations which can be bought legally from chemists.

Taken together, deaths from drug use in the UK each year total just over 200, which should be compared with the tens of thousands that die annually from alcohol use and smoking. As is the case for alcohol and tobacco use, the contribution of illegal drugs to premature death is unlikely to be adequately recorded, because the recorded ''cause'' of death is likely to be an illness which is not *necessarily* related to drug use but which in the particular case will probably have been suffered because of dependency. Examples are infections and diseases of the blood. Even if it is not already the case, it is likely soon to be so that the commonest reason for the death of an intravenous drug user is AIDS.

Unfortunately, the application of epidemiological research to drug abuse is relatively recent, despite the long history of drug abuse in society. Such studies have really only begun within the last 20 years.

Risk factors for drug use change. The factors that placed people at high risk of heroin abuse in the sixties and early seventies have changed during the eighties[15]. In the earlier period a profile of a heroin addict was a male in the middle to late teens who was initiated into the use of the drug during the previous few years. By the mid-eighties, the heroin addict population was still composed primarily of males but in their early- to mid-thirties, the majority of whom had a history of heroin abuse extending back for a decade or two. They are, in fact, the early group but grown older.

As implied above it is the *consequences* of drug abuse which are likely to draw attention to it and the pattern of consequences changes over time. For example, the growing risk of contracting AIDS, as well as a host of other diseases and consequences, can change with routes of administration and the ways that drugs are used in combination.

In the United States, surveys have been used to monitor the prevalence of drug use and trends.

For example, it has been found that while the extent of marihuana abuse does not change much after children leave school, the abuse of cocaine increases dramatically. However, data from a recent survey[15] suggested that the use of marihuana was decreasing for both males and females between 1979 and 1982, with decreases which were greater for males. However, the same study showed that females were more likely to start using marihuana at an earlier age.

serious chronic effects over time, just in the way that the long term use of cigarettes can do so.

The study of heroin is exceptionally difficult, partly because its use continues to be a relatively rare event and involves a population that prefers to remain hidden. Epidemics of heroin abuse occurred in the United States in the 1960s, the mid-1970s and the early 1980s. Various estimates of the heroin addict population in the country have been surprisingly similar in spite of the

It is marihuana which is the most widely used illegal drug in the United States, with 1985 studies showing that at some time 24% of 12 to 17 year olds have used marihuana, 60% of 18 to 25 year olds, and 27% of those aged 26 years and more. An increase in the percentage of older people who have ever used marihuana is as a result of the younger ones growing up, and it now appears the the use of marihuana in school children reached a peak in 1978 and 1979 and has declined through 1984. There is an interesting association of the peak incidence coinciding with the highest *perception* of the risk posed by marihuana use. The lowering in use has coincided with a lowering in the perceived risk for occasional use. Marihuana does, in fact, have a serious impact on social functioning and on health. Long-term abuse of marihuana can have

inherent difficulties of definition and measurement, and for the most part have ranged around half a million people over the last 20 years (one person in 500 in the population). It does seem that the preponderance of current heroin abusers were initiated into the habit in the sixties and seventies. A variety of risk factors have been related to heroin abuse, including new types of heroin and its potentially lethal combination with the consumption of alcohol. The most dramatic issue of the day, however, is the association between the intravenous use of heroin and AIDS, and as we have already noted it is drug abusers with AIDS that are likely to form a bridge across which the disease can cross from the homosexual into the heterosexual population.

In the case of cocaine, the age of risk appears to differ in the United States from other drugs.

Since 1974 the proportion of US citizens who have ever used cocaine has quadrupled, although the proportion of full-time college students who have used cocaine in the last 12 months has hardly changed over the five-year period 1980 to 1985. Unlike marihuana, increases in cocaine abuse have been found in older populations, but the current increase in cocaine use in older people does not match the very rapid increases which were noted in the late 1970s.

Recent reports of heart attacks in relatively healthy individuals have been attributed to the abuse of cocaine, and have heightened awareness of the risk of using a drug which was once thought to be rather benign. (Popular literature of some decades ago treated the use of cocaine quite casually. Sherlock Holmes, after all, was a regular user, and one of the characters in the golfing stories of P G Wodehouse was offered cocaine casually at a social gathering.) In 1984, it was reported that admissions to emergency treatment centres in the United States were as a result of cocaine use in almost 14% of all patients, and if problems secondary to the use of cocaine were included, more than a quarter of all emergency patients had a problem with cocaine.

The risk of cocaine changes with the route of administration. In the past, inhaling the drug has been the predominant mode of administration, but it now appears that more potent physiological and psychological consequences can occur from smoking it or using it intravenously. The increasing problems may well be associated with the introduction of a form of cocaine intended for inhaling known as "crack", which, on the streets of America, is a great deal cheaper than older types.

DIET

The preceding sections of this chapter, covering the use of tobacco and psychoactive drugs, are about substances that have the capacity to kill. It may seem a little strange, therefore, to follow them by a section on diet. And it is certainly not our intention to imply that food is in the same "killer" category, rather than being a necessary and usually highly enjoyable part of our daily existence.

However, a brief discussion of risk is appropriate in the context of diet, because epidemiologists have data which indicate that dietary factors can contribute to the incidence of cancer, cardiovascular disorders and other diseases. Official interest in the matter is indicated by the publication, in the United Kingdom, of nine major reports on diet and health within the last ten years[16].

The hunter-gatherers who were our evolutionary forebears ate what was by present standards a pretty healthy diet: one which was high in fibre, low in fat, and with no added milk, sugar or salt. It would have been rich in polyunsaturated fatty acids. With continuing evolution, diets have changed and so, as we have seen, have patterns of illness and death. It is easy to jump to the conclusion that this association is one of cause and effect, but this logical trap should be avoided. Diseases which are common today, such as those of the heart and circulation and cancer, are—as we have already demonstrated—the result of several interacting factors, rather than just one (in the way, for example, that the influenza virus is the cause of flu). Diet is one of these factors, and in the last chapter we discussed some aspects of eating habits which appear to be directly related to the incidence of these common twentieth-century diseases.

Originally, interest in the influence of food on illness arose from observation of the fact that deficiencies could cause specific diseases, so that, for example, a diet deficient in vitamin C caused scurvy. These days, most of the deficiency diseases still to be found in the UK or North America occur within poor families and are rather rare, and the food problems which face most of the population result from eating too much and relying on diets which are out of balance.

The proportion of the population that is overweight is increasing. Massive collections of data, such as those that are gathered by the insurance industry, can be used to associate the risk of illness with an individual's height and weight. Tables have been generated which indicate a range of "desirable" weights, and a working definition of "obesity" is that it is a weight more than 20% above the upper end of the desirable range. Recent surveys have suggested that the prevalence of overweight (outside the desirable range) in Britain increases from 15% in 16 to 19 year olds up to 54% in men and 50% in women aged 60 to 65 years. If all adults are considered, then 39% of men and 32% of women are overweight, with 6% of men and 8% of women being classified as obese.

The risks associated with excess weight are not confined to those who are substantially obese. Reductions in expected life span and increases in illness are measurable with even small increases in weight above the acceptable range. Being too heavy is associated with an increased risk of disease of the gall bladder, of coronary heart disease, high blood pressure, increased fat in the blood, diabetes and a number of cancers (in particular, those of the intestines and gall bladder)[16].

At any given time, some 65% of women and 30% of men are trying to reduce these risks (or to seek aesthetic benefit) by reducing their weight. To do this a permanent adjustment in diet is required, with a shift towards food which is high in fibre and low in calories, such as cereals, vegetables and fruit. Foods rich in fat and sugar need to be restricted.

The relationship of diet to coronary heart disease has been covered in more detail in the section on that disease, and there is no need to press the point further at this point. The difficulty facing public health administrators is that it is difficult to prove, without doing impossibly large-scale controlled trials, that actually *changing* the diet reduces the existing risk of developing coronary heart disease.

The role of diet as a factor in the causation of cancer has for many years attracted a great deal of scientific and public interest. The British epidemiologists Doll and Peto have estimated that around 35% of all cancer deaths in the United States could be attributed to dietary factors[17], but they do emphasize that this figure is highly speculative and chiefly refers to factors in the diet which have not yet been reliably identified. From experimentation and epidemiological studies, there are many indications that diet can be of great importance in determining the risk of cancers of the stomach and intestinal tract and some cancers of the female sex organs, but as yet, there is little firm evidence on which conclusions can be based. It is probable that the most important factors will turn out to be those related to nutrition as a whole, including the total balance of diet, the presence of vitamins and minerals, and other microscopic elements of the normal diet which may either enhance or inhibit the formation of cancer. Less likely to be important is the ingestion of tiny traces of powerful carcinogens which to most people are the main source of worry.

The difficulty is that there is no precise and reliable evidence on what changes in the diet could change the incidence of cancer. One indicator is that mortality from both cancer of the large intestine and cancer of the breast in different countries shows a strong relationship with the overall consumption of fat, but even this tentative finding is confused by differing levels of fibre in the national diets. Diet which is low in fibre is associated with inflammation of the intestine and the formation of little balloons in the intestinal wall (a condition called diverticulitis) which may be due to the higher pressure in the intestine caused by foods which are low in fibre. A deficiency in fibre may also be related to cancer of the large intestine.

A diet which is high in sugar and low in fibre substantially increases the risk of dental caries. Sugar in the diet helps to generate acids on the teeth which can attack the enamel. Chemical sweeteners which replace sugar are not only less likely to cause excessive weight gain and the diseases which result from that, but can also reduce the incidence of tooth decay.

The way our food is produced, preserved and brought to us these days is as heavily influenced by technology as all other aspects of our lifestyle. Most food, one way or another, is "processed", and the risks attributable to processing are the subject of much public concern. But there is a great deal of benefit also associated with this processing. Here again, we find ourselves in the position of having to balance the benefits against the risks[18]. Most concern centres on whether modern foods are contaminated by undesirable residues of the chemicals used in agriculture, and whether the foods are treated with unnecessary and possibly harmful additives.

As far as environmental contamination is concerned, there is no benefit and some risk in the presence of these chemicals in our foods, and as a matter of principle every effort is made to minimize their presence. Regulations are written to reflect this aim. More discussion on the risk associated with these chemicals will be found in Chapter 13.

Additives, of course, are placed in food quite deliberately, and the benefits they offer cover a range from obvious to non-existent. The level of risk, therefore, which we are prepared to accept depends once again on the benefit. Where there is no benefit from an additive, then no significant risk is acceptable either. Most additives are synthetic chemicals, and in their case also there is more discussion on the risks they may present in Chapter 13.

Lest anyone should assume otherwise, it is not true to say that ''natural'' foods which are grown without the aid of agricultural chemicals and to which no synthetic additives are added are for that reason alone free of risk. Very many foods contain substances which, if presented for evaluation as a possible food additive, would certainly be banned. Again, there is more discussion of this point in the context of food additives generally in Chapter 13. Everything in food that is not a pure nutrient constitutes some risk, whether it is natural or is synthetic, and whether it is present under normal circumstances or has been added during processing. In most cases this risk is very small, and there is no reason why the eating of food should not be one of life's great joys. In the developed world we should count ourselves very lucky that the main risk to health we face from food is eating too much of it.

Chapter Six

Occupational Risks

A man or woman at work runs some risk of death or injury which is directly attributable to that occupation. Maybe the risk is lower than if the same individual had stayed at home, and it probably *is* lower than the risk of driving to work. Nevertheless, risks that people face at work do fall into a special category. This is because to a large extent they are involuntarily imposed risks which the worker simply has to face in order to make a living, and over the level of which he has limited control.

Occupational risks show up in two main ways. First, there may be an association of a particular occupation with a disease which appears among its workers to an extent greater than would normally be expected, given allowance for age and other non-work factors. Second, a worker is exposed to some risk of injury from the unexpected release of energy (mechanical, chemical, electrical, radioactive and so on) which accounts for "accidents". As in the case of road traffic crashes, the word "accident" (implying something that happens by pure chance, and is beyond human control) is a poor one to describe events which are not only highly predictable in the statistical sense but also well within the bounds of human control.

The influence of occupation on death rate was first studied in Britain by William Farr, starting in 1841 (see Chapter 1), and his tradition has been upheld over the years. Farr's earliest reviews included comments such as: "Miners die in undue proportions, particularly at the advanced ages when their strength begins to decline . . . Tailors die in considerable numbers at the younger ages . . . Labourers' mortality is at nearly the same rate as that of the whole population . . . " The continued importance of standardizing death rates for age is shown by the current use of the Standardized Mortality Ratio (SMR) in official statistics[1]. The SMR is the ratio of the observed deaths in an occupation to those expected.

There are also lifestyle factors which need disentangling in order truly to identify the links between occupation and disease, and it is hard to do this in routine statistics. For example, smoking rates differ from occupation to occupation, and have their own influence on mortality; the highest smoking levels are in transport and related occupations for men, and in metal and electrical manufacturing and repairing occupations for women. Excess alcohol consumption also raises death rates for some diseases, but the diversity of drinking patterns makes it difficult to relate drinking precisely to occupations and death rates.

Using the SMR, recorded in statistics published by the Office of Population Censuses and Surveys as a basis, the highest death rates are in the transport and related occupations, metal workers, storemen, security services, and in the group encompassing catering, cleaning, hairdressing and other personal services[1]. The lower rates are in the professional, educational and scientific groups.

A relatively high death rate from injury and poisoning is found in the farming and fishing industries, the catering and other services group, mining and transport. Comparatively low rates from accidental death are to be found, again, in the professional and scientific occupations.

More detailed information on accidental deaths and injuries is collected and published by the United Kingdom Health and Safety Executive[2]. The highest rate of death and injury (taken together) is to be found in the construction industry, with about 230 workers being killed or injured each year for every 100,000 employees in this sector (one in 430 each year). Another industry with a relatively high risk is mining and quarrying, with a similar rate of death and injury to construction.

Average Annual Accidental Death Rates at Work in UK per Million at Risk (1974–78 except as stated)

	Deaths per million at work	Ratio of workers per death
Manufacture of clothing and footwear	5	1 : 200,000
Manufacture of vehicles	15	1 : 70,000
Manufacture of timber, furniture, etc.	40	1 : 250,000
Manufacture of bricks, pottery, glass, cement, etc.	65	1 : 150,000
Chemical and allied industries	85	1 : 12,000
Shipbuilding and marine engineering	105	1 : 9,500
Agriculture (employees)	110	1 : 9,000
Construction industries	150	1 : 7,000
Railway staff	180	1 : 6,000
Coal miners	210	1 : 5,000
Quarries	295	1 : 3,000
Non-coal miners	750	1 : 1,500
Offshore oil and gas	1650	1 : 600
Deep sea fishing (accidents at sea only, before 1970)	2800	1 : 360

Showing figures for the late 1970s, this demonstrates the high death rate from injury among fishermen, miners and construction workers.

Sources: Royal Society, *Risk Assessment*, 1983; Health and Safety Executive; Office of Population Censuses and Surveys

Manufacturing industries in general have a death and injury rate not far from the average for all industries, but metal manufacturing kills or injures over 200 employees per 100,000 each year, or one in 500. The timber and furniture industries, with an annual rate of over 180 per 100,000 (one in 555), and the bricks and cement sector at about 150 per 100,000 (one in 670) are also notable for the degree of risk faced by their workers.

Royal Society summarized the average annual accidental death rates at work in the UK, per million at risk, as shown in the accompanying table. The very high (relative) risk of death faced by fishermen, offshore workers and miners is again apparent.

The risk faced by deep-sea fishermen is worth discussing in more detail, not only because this seems to be the highest-risk occupation of all, but also because their case throws up several points of general importance in risk analysis and management.

First, fishing at sea has *always* carried a high risk of death[4]. Figures for a hundred years ago on the death rate of Grand Banks fishermen indicate that more than one man in 50 was lost each year, and among fishermen out of Hull during the same period more than one in 100 were lost annually (a death rate in the order of that of Grand Prix racing drivers today). Today, however, death rates (although still high) are much lower than they used to be, having dropped by four or five times to a rate which is now "accepted", even if not "acceptable" (see Chapter 14).

The second point is that the mortality rate among seamen is grossly under-estimated if only "routine" death statistics are used, because they do not include deaths *at sea*. The inclusion of deaths at sea raises the ratio of fishermen's death rate from two or three times the average for men in England and Wales to 17 times.

Third, it was not until the truly high rate became appreciated in the late sixties, when at the same time there was the disastrous loss of three trawlers and 58 fishermen from Hull, that public concern was sufficiently aroused to do something about the safety of deep-sea fishing boats.

So, the fisherman's story shows the following: a severe safety problem can exist unrecognized for a long time; reliable statistics are essential for recognition and control of the problem; some individuals will be prepared to accept very high risks of death and injury; public perception of risk depends more on disasters than routine statistics; a high *perceived* risk may be necessary for any action to be taken.

Turning from this specific case to the general international scene, and in comparing countries which do keep occupational-injury statistics, many similarities in the general trends can be seen. Deep-sea fishing, mining, quarrying, heavy engineering and working on docks are jobs which are always associated with high rates of death and injury.

One feature of occupational injury rates (shown by the example of the fishermen) is that many of the occupations which carry an exceptionally high risk involve comparatively few individuals, so that the actual number of deaths and injuries which occur are quite low by national standards, and thus rather easy to ignore unless special studies are made. And a related feature of accident statistics in industry is that there is a tendency to concentrate on large manufacturing operations at the expense of smaller concerns. It is also easy to ignore injury involving transport vehicles, which are in fact involved in about 40 of all deaths resulting from work injury. Even in manufacturing industry, more employees are killed by vehicles of one sort or another than by fixed machinery.

There are some who believe that statistics on mortality and injury rates do not truly represent the relative risks of occupations, because the immediate drowning of a fisherman (say) is very different from the delayed death of a worker who contracts a disease (black-lung disease, say, or cancer from radiation) as a result of working in a particular industry. Researchers at the National Radiological Protection Board, for example, have tabulated the days of life expectancy lost as a result of hazards in various industries[5]. They argue that calculating the extent to which hazards shorten life is more meaningful than expressing risks in terms of fatal accidents per person per year.

Their calculations indicate that to be a deep-sea fisherman for one year at the age of 20 reduces life expectancy by 51.4 days, while the corresponding risk in the paper, publishing and printing industry is only 0.5 days. A fisherman aged 20 who plans to fish until retirement at 65 reduces his life expectancy by over 3.5 years, with the equivalent reduction in the paper trade only 12 days. Only the individual reader can decide which is the most understandable way to give this sort of information, remembering (as discussed further in Chapters 11 and 14) that what people perceive to be the case depends very much on how the facts are presented.

For practical purposes the only useful statistics on occupational death and injury are gathered in the developed nations. In the developing countries groups of workers are usually quite small, and they commonly work under circumstances which pose an exceedingly high risk of death and injury. However, in the absence of good and consistent information on work practices in such areas, it is difficult to discuss injuries in any useful detail. But to give some idea of the size of the problem, it was found that in a rural population in Punjab, India, 24% of all injuries and 22% of all deaths were of occupational origin. There were no deaths recorded in the Punjab area from transport injury because the only vehicles available were boats and animals. Another Indian study indicated that 80% of all injuries were suffered at work, mostly through agricultural activities[6].

Metal manufacturing is an example of an industry of high hazard, with risks reducible through matching workers with suitable tasks, equipping machines with guards and safety interlocks, and providing operators with protective clothing.

Risk factors in occupational injury

For an occupational injury to occur, a hazard has to exist in association with a particular pattern of worker behaviour. In occupations with a high level of hazard and a complex task, all else being equal, the risk of injury is higher than it would be in an occupation where the hazards are low and the task a simple one. Similarly, for a given degree of task difficulty, the worker whose performance is impaired by fatigue, alcohol or inexperience is more likely to be injured.

Several human factors have been studied for their influence on the risk of death and injury at work. The first and most obvious one is age, which, of course, interacts with experience. Overall, injury rates are highest among males in their late teens and are lowest in the middle years. However, this tendency is affected by the number of years the individual has been working at the particular job in question. Young men with some years of experience at a given task have been found to have a similar risk of injury to older men doing the same task, whereas young men coming fresh to the job have much higher injury rates. It seems likely, therefore, that it is the sort of *task* to which a young man is assigned which determines the likely risk of injury, rather than his age. Younger workers are at a disadvantage in tasks requiring considerable judgement and anticipation of unexpected conditions.

Death and injury rates tend to rise again among older workers. As in the case of the youngsters, this may well be a matter of assignation to the right kind of tasks. Older workers generally do less well with complex tasks which require a fast response.

Overall, female employees generally have lower rates of death and injury than their male counterparts, although differences are small in some industries. Some studies have indicated that injuries among women tend to occur during the premenstrual and early menstrual period.

There are, of course, several differences between men and women which are insufficiently taken into account by the designers of tasks and of machinery. Such discrepancies range from the layout of pedals and levers and the strength required to move them to the relationship of hand tools to hand size.

The relationship of alcohol use to work injury is a matter of serious and increasing concern. Many large enterprises now have facilities for the identification and treatment of employees with problems with alcohol. Unlike injuries on the roads, no system exists for the systematic collection of data associating alcohol use with industrial injury. One would expect that the use of alcohol is grossly under-reported and its importance, therefore, considerably under-rated. There have been several research studies which have attempted to make more precise measurements but the range of findings is very wide.

In industry, as with other fields of activity, there has been much interest shown over the years in the concept of "accident proneness" as a risk factor. Overall, it does seem to be the case that in a given period of time, a rather small proportion of employees is involved in a rather large proportion of accidents. The problem is that this finding is of little *practical* use in assessing and managing risk. The group containing the "accident prone" individuals changes from time to time. Identification of the individuals before the fact of the accident is not only difficult but also inaccurate, so that, for example, to exclude all potentially accident prone individuals from a given job would mean excluding from work a very large number of people most of whom would not, in fact, have had an accident. It is a much more practical proposition to match the worker with the job in such a way that the task he is expected to undertake is within his capabilities.

Generally speaking it is environmental factors which determine the risk of a given job or activity, rather than the "human" factors associated with the people who perform those jobs. As already noted, the commonest single hazard is transport vehicles, which are responsible for about 40% of all work-related deaths in the developed world[7].

Apart from the use of motorized vehicles, a low risk work environment will be "controlled". The type of machinery involved in industry clearly influences the risk to the workers. Hazardous machinery is the type of equipment which exposes human flesh to the risk of cutting, tearing, pinching and puncturing. Farm machinery is notable for its effectiveness in such respects[8]. Protective guards are often employed in farm and other machinery in order to separate operators from the dangerous bits, but are not in action when the machinery is being repaired. During repair, many of the worst injuries occur. Another way in which machinery can increase the risk to operators (and in many cases the public) is if it is not designed in such a way as to minimize the task load which the operators face. It has been realized for years, for example, that a row of dials whose needles all move in the same direction are easier to read than a row of dissimilar dials, and that the markings on dials should be clearly visible and not open to confusion with other information presented. Control levers, dials, knobs and switches should be designed with the needs of both male and female workers clearly understood, and such mismatching has been identified as an important cause of injuries among female workers.

Fatal accidents, farms in Britain, 1981–84

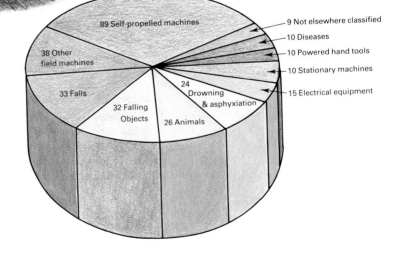

89 Self-propelled machines
38 Other field machines
33 Falls
32 Falling Objects
24 Drowning & asphyxiation
26 Animals
9 Not elsewhere classified
10 Diseases
10 Powered hand tools
10 Stationary machines
15 Electrical equipment

A total of 296 fatal accidents happened on British farms in the four years 1981–84. The biggest proportion occurred in association with self-propelled machines such as tractors, with the commonest single accident being a tractor overturning. *Source:* Health and Safety Executive, *Agricultural Black Spot: A Study of Fatal Accidents*, HMSO 1986

The chemical industry

Workers in the chemical industry are exposed to a rather special set of risks. Not only are the injurious events often manifest by illness a long time after exposure to the chemical, but the industry itself is being increasingly questioned as to whether the benefits offered to society by its products are justified by the risk imposed through their use. Public risks from the chemical industry are the subject of a separate section (see Chapter 13).

The *rate* of fatal and major injuries in the chemicals sector of British industry is slightly above the average for all manufacturing industries, although the actual *number* of people who die from injuries is very small. Many of the accidents which occur in chemical works are not related to the process itself, but are similar to those which occur in other factories and result in injuries such as those suffered in falling, moving and handling materials. Nevertheless, a special study of incidents in the chemical industry in 1983[3] showed that 65% were indeed related to the process of manufacture. In just over a third of the incidents investigated, people were adversely affected by the release of chemicals which were toxic, corrosive, or harmful in other ways.

Workers in the chemical industry face the special hazards of toxic chemicals as well as the normal hazards of industry. However, although the rate of fatal injury in the chemical industry is about the same as in manufacturing, the actual number of workers killed annually is very small.

Chapter Seven

Risks in Transport

ROAD TRAFFIC RISKS

As already shown, transport accidents have represented an important cause of death for the population of Britain for at least the past hundred years. Although attention is now placed with some justification on the risks of road transport, it should not be forgotten that moving around has always been a potentially dangerous business. To compare one mode of transport with another in terms of risk requires information on exposure, such as miles travelled, hours spent travelling, or some other similar index. Using such measures, it may well be that the hazards we now associate with travelling by car are not as bad in historical terms as we might think. Before road transport systems were highly developed, one of the most important ways of moving was by sea. The swiftly tidal waters and changeable weather in the area of the British Isles have always meant that sea travel was a dangerous business, and an immense number of ships, carrying many hundreds of people, have been wrecked on these shores. Unfortunately, the lack of exposure data prevents a true comparison of the risk of travelling by sea in the old days and travelling by modern motor vehicle now.

Throughout the world there are at least a quarter of a million deaths on the roads each year[1]. There are big differences between the various countries of the world, with the more developed countries having an average of one-tenth of the rate (in terms of vehicle numbers) of deaths in the developing countries.

Generally, characteristics of road traffic crashes are rather similar throughout the developed world. Crashes resulting in death are predominant in rural areas as opposed to urban areas in the ratio of about 2:1, with the opposite being the case for crashes resulting in non-fatal injuries. The death rate in terms of miles travelled is about three times as high at night as it is during the day, with about one-half of fatal crashes but only one-third of all crashes occurring in the night-time hours. About half all fatal crashes occur between the period Friday through Sunday. In countries with lower rates of vehicle ownership the proportion of fatal accidents occurring among the pedestrian population is relatively high and, of course, where two-wheeled vehicles form a substantial part of the vehicle population, they are over-represented in the statistics.

Road crashes in Britain

Taking one example of the pattern of road crashes in a developed western country, let us take a closer look at crash statistics in Britain[2].

Ask a man in the street to look up from his newspaper and think of a road accident, and he is likely to conjure up in his mind a picture of a heavy goods vehicle plunging into a mass of cars on a motorway, causing fire and the death of many vehicle occupants by burning. But this picture would be an extraordinary misperception. Heavy goods vehicles actually have the lowest overall rate of involvement in traffic crashes of any type of vehicle. Motorways have the lowest rates of crashes of any type of road. Fires very rarely occur as a result of crashes and death by burning is exceedingly rare. In actual fact, therefore, the picture that builds up from statistical analysis of the rates of various kinds of traffic crash in Britain is very different from the stereotype.

Before examining some of the characteristics of this picture in more detail, it is worth reviewing how different rates can be used for expressing different risks. The measurable *outcomes* of road crashes include the number of deaths, the number of injuries and the number of crashes. Deaths are counted reliably and quite accurately. Serious injuries are counted fairly accurately, but a large number of minor injuries are not counted at all, and definitions of the various categories of injury tend to be inconsistent. A very high proportion of all crashes that do not result in injury go unreported.

Then, in *terms of what* shall these outcomes be expressed? Take death for an example. The number of road deaths *per head* of population expresses the problem in public health terms. A country with few cars and few deaths will have a small traffic crash "problem". But this expression does nothing to explain the level of *risk* to individuals. To do this, a better way is to use the *number of vehicles* in a population, which does give some account of how well a country is managing its traffic in order to minimize risk. A better expression of individual risk is to determine the *mileage covered* by each category of vehicle and express outcomes in terms of that measure. In a country with a very low crash rate in terms of vehicle mileage, a driver will be at a lower risk of crashing (his journey will be "safer") than if he is driving in a country with a high crash rate per mile travelled. (That said, pedestrians still need to be treated differently in

Fatal and serious casualties by type o

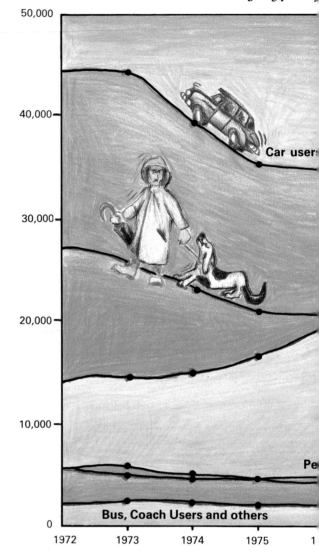

Over recent years the number of road users killed and injured has
Source: reference 3

the statistical sense, because their "mileage" is qualitatively as well as quantitatively different from that of other road users.) Further, it would be desirable to count the number of people in each vehicle, the time each vehicle is on the road and so on, but such information is systematically gathered in very few places indeed.

Road crash statistics for Britain were first collected in 1909. In that year, there were 1,070 fatal accidents and 101,000 motor vehicles, or one crash for every 90 or so vehicles each year. This translates to a rate of 106 fatal accidents for every 10,000 vehicles. It is quite some contrast that

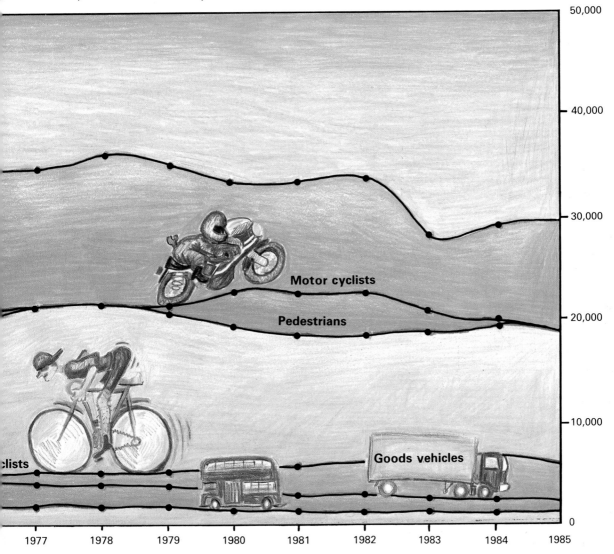

declined, despite the greater numbers on the roads, so that the risk for each individual road user is lower.

in 1985 there were 4,768 fatal accidents and 21,166,000 motor vehicles, representing a rate of 2.25 fatal accidents for every 10,000 registered motor vehicles (one for every 44,000). So, there has been a huge reduction in the risk for an individual of being involved in a fatal accident while operating a particular motor vehicle, but a massive increase in the average risk of involvement in a fatal crash for the community as a whole. Because more than one person is killed in some crashes, the actual number of people killed in 1985 was 5,165.

Since the late 1950s, not only has the popula-tion of Britain risen, but also has the number of vehicles as well as the number of crashes and casualties. However, the number of vehicles and the total mileage driven have risen much faster than the number of crashes and casualties. Indeed, the actual number of people killed on the roads in Britain reached a peak of 7,985 in 1966, since which time the absolute numbers of deaths, injuries and crashes have gradually but steadily declined. Of those road users that are killed in Britain, the largest proportion (44%) are the occupants of cars, followed by pedestrians (35%), motorcyclists (15%) and pedal cyclists (5.5%).

These proportions have changed quite markedly over the years, as might be expected. The number of pedestrians killed on the roads was not exceeded by vehicle occupants until 1965. In the twenties and thirties far more motorcyclists were killed than car users, and motorcycle deaths exceeded deaths among other vehicle users until 1959. In 1941, 4,781 pedestrians were killed, nearly as many as the entire count (5,165) of road deaths in 1985; the blackout may well have caused more deaths than it saved lives.

In terms of risk to road users, the safest roads per kilometre travelled are motorways. In 1985, the motorway crash rate was 12 reported crashes (of all severity) for every 100 million vehicle kilometres travelled. For other roads, the lower the quality the higher the crash rate, with the rate for A-class main roads being 78 reported crashes per 100 million vehicle kilometres, for B-class roads 109, and for other roads 140. The rates on all roads put together have fallen over the last ten years by about 25%.

Not only is the risk of crashing much lower on a motorway than it is on a lesser standard road, the actual number of crashes is probably lower than most people believe, certainly if the basis of the belief is reports in newspaper. Only about 4% of all fatal crashes occur on motorways, with 96% on other roads.

Looking at risk from the point of view of the road user rather than the type of road that is used, those at highest risk are motorcycle riders, with 12 of them being killed in 1985 for every 100 million kilometres travelled by motorcycles. Motorcyclists reached a peak rate of 22 killed per 100 million motorcycle kilometres in 1977. Pedal cyclists, another vulnerable group, were killed at a rate of 6.2 per 100 million pedal cycle kilometres travelled in 1985, with this rate having dropped very slightly during the previous ten years. The death rate among car drivers was 0.5 per 100 million vehicle kilometers in 1985, having dropped from 0.9 in 1975. The death rate among drivers of other vehicles, mostly the drivers of heavy goods vehicles and buses, is lower than for car drivers. Rates of reported non-fatal injury follow the same trends.

Pedal cycles have their lowest rate of involvement on minor roads, particularly in non-built-up areas where they meet slower-moving traffic than on main roads. The rate of crash involvement among pedal cycles is highest on A-class main roads, and has shown a recent tendency to increase.

The risk of motorcycles crashing is highest on built-up B-class main roads, but the rates for these vehicles remain higher on every road class than those for any other vehicle type. Even on motorways the involvement rate of motorcycles in 1985 was around nine times higher than the average vehicle involvement rate. The crash rate for passenger cars is at its highest in built-up areas, especially on B-class roads and minor roads.

Casualties by hour of day and day of

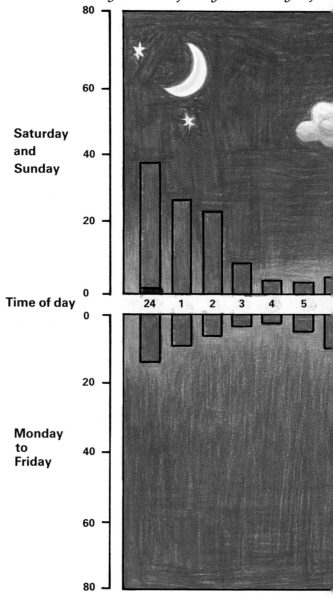

On average, more than 14 people are killed every single day in Britai happened day after day. But, because the deaths are widely distribut number of deaths and injuries as all the rest of the week put togethe

Youth, which interacts with experience, is closely related to crash rate, with a peak in the late teens and early twenties and a steady decline thereafter.

The number of casualties by hour of day depends on the day of week, with the peak number of casualties per hour occurring between 11 and 12 p.m. on Saturday and Sunday nights. From Monday to Friday, the peaks are at the rush hours, but even so there are more adult casualties per hour around midnight at the weekends, although far less traffic is on the road.

Again as a function of enthusiastic reporting in the media, it would be easy to assume that the holiday periods are the most ferociously dangerous for road users. In fact, this is not the case. Both actual holiday days and holiday periods, whether considered separately or as a whole, generally have lower accident and casualty figures than comparable days and

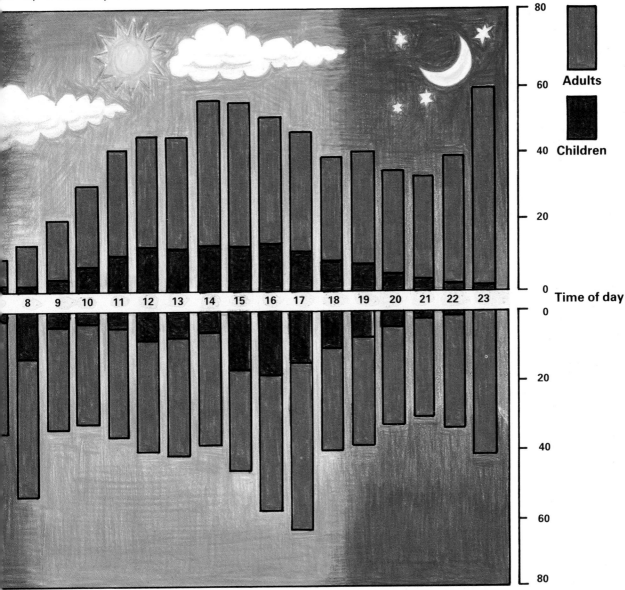

equivalent of a half-full bus. If a bus crash killed 14 people on a motorway, there would be horror, let alone the outrage if it
d mostly occur one at a time, we hardly even notice. This figure shows that Saturdays and Sundays account for about the same
st casualties occur in the afternoon and evening, with the worst single hour being between 11 and 12 p.m. at the weekend.

periods which are not holidays. In particular, there is a particularly low relative risk of crashing during the Christmas holiday period in comparison with comparable periods in December, which would appear to suggest that it is the build-up to Christmas which is the period of high risk, and not, as is sometimes supposed, the holiday period itself.

For a given driver and type of vehicle, the risk of crashing that he faces is determined far more by the total amount of time that he spends on the road than by what day it is or whether it is a holiday. It is the relentless addition of deaths to the road toll, every single day of the year, that adds up to the final figure, not deaths resulting from groups of crashes which are reported in gory detail by the media.

International comparisons

Overall, by world standards the risk of dying in a traffic crash in Britain is rather low, whether measured in terms of the population, the motor vehicle population, or by vehicle mileage. Motor vehicle mileage is not very reliably measured

in many countries of the world, and the ways that the measurements are performed differ widely. Among countries that do undertake such measurement, the United States, Japan and Sweden have notably low death rates, as do the other Scandinavian countries (at about the same level as Britain). On the continent of Europe the death rates are rather higher, and in Greece and Spain several times as high. Most countries do count the number of motor vehicles quite reliably, and differences of a similar extent can be seen when this figure is used as a measure of risk.

There are quite substantial differences in the number of pedestrians killed as a proportion of all road users, with 18% of deaths in the United States being among pedestrians and only 10% in Sweden.

Risk factors in traffic accidents

The scope of this book does not extend to the detailed description of all the factors which can be modified to reduce the risk of death and injury on the road. In Chapter 15 there is outlined a set of strategies for dealing with injuries generally,

Increasing risk of crashing with increasing levels of blood alcohol

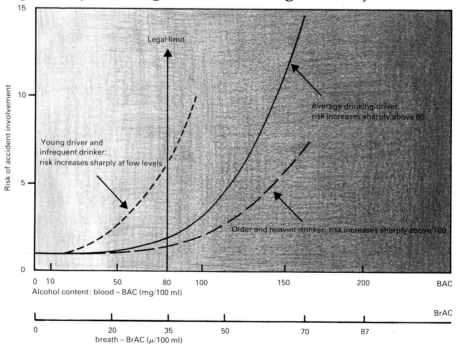

The risk of being involved in a crash in traffic starts rising after one or two drinks, then goes up at an increasing rate at increasing levels of blood alcohol. Young and inexperienced drivers are more likely to be involved in crashes at lower blood alcohol levels. On average, the higher the blood alcohol level, the worse the crash.
Source: adapted from references 3 and 4

and examples related to traffic crashes will be found there. Some particular factors, however, are outstandingly important and the first of these is the use of alcohol by road users. Its role has been well established in the United States, Canada, Britain, Australia and Scandinavia.

From the results of breath testing it is known that in Britain most driving by those who have been drinking occurs at the weekend, and peaks at around midnight on Fridays and Saturdays. In recent years, just over one-quarter of all drivers or motorcycle riders killed have been found to be over the legal limit in Britain of 80 mg per 100 ml blood. The peak ages of drinking drivers are in the range 20 to 40 years, and the worst hours of the day between 10 p.m. and 4 a.m. In total, it is estimated that in Britain some 1,400 to 1,500 road accident deaths each year are associated with alcohol use (including drinking by pedestrians) which represents around one quarter of all road deaths[2].

This would mean very little in terms of risk if one-quarter of *all* road users have been drinking before involvement in a crash. However, studies in many countries in the world have shown that this is *not* the case, and that the actual proportion of those who have been drinking is very low (under about 5% even during the bad hours). It is therefore possible to assess the increased risk

which alcohol use poses, with some estimation also possible of the extra risk on top of that which results when other factors such as age and inexperience interact with alcohol use. An early study conducted in America was of seminal importance in establishing this risk[3], which has been thus well documented for over two decades.

Another potent factor in determining the risk of injury among those who have crashed in motor vehicles is whether or not they were restrained by seat belts. Overall, the evidence is that the wearing of such devices reduces the risk of all kinds of injury by about 25%, of serious injury about 50% and of fatal injury about 65%[4]. Most countries now compel the wearing of seat belts, a measure pioneered in Australia in 1971.

The major cause of death and permanent disability from motorcycle crashes is head injury, the risk of which can be markedly reduced through the use of crash helmets. In 1972 in Britain, some 52% of motorcyclists who ended up in hospital suffered from head injury, but by 1980 this had fallen to 31%[5]. Patients in hospital as a result of crashing in *other* types of vehicle, or having been pedestrians or pedal cyclists, are now relatively more likely than this to be suffering from head injury. In the United States, between 1966 and 1969 laws requiring the compulsory use of helmets became effective in

Effects of compulsory seat belt legislation in Britain

Seat Belt Law	
Reduction in deaths:	
Drivers	– 17%
Front passengers	– 25%
Reduction in deaths and injuries:	
Drivers	– 22%
Front passengers	– 29%

In an individual crash, the wearing of seat belts can more than double the chance of survival. However, when the wearing of seat belts became compulsory in Britain the number killed in cars was not halved, because a high proportion were wearing belts already and some high-risk drivers did not comply with the law. There was, nevertheless, a big drop in deaths following the legislation, which saved around one occupant in five. Further reductions can be expected from the use of seat belts in rear seats and from child safety seats.
Source: references 3 and 5

40 states and the US fatality rate per 10,000 motorcycles dropped from 13 down to 7 (the same as for Britain in 1985). However, between 1976 and 1979 27 of these states repealed or weakened their laws and the national fatality rate rose again to 10, with the increase being accounted for by those states that had changed their laws back again.

The cost of road crashes to Britain in 1985 was estimated by the Transport and Road Research Laboratory to be £2,820 million, or about £60 a head for every man, woman and child. More than one in every 10,000 people in the country is killed on the roads every year, and this relatively high risk is faced by almost every citizen. One hundred people are killed every week, more than a jumbo jet-load a month. There could hardly be a better example of a risk which is so familiar that it is almost totally disregarded.

RISKS ON RAILWAYS

In contrast to road travellers, the risk to passengers of travelling in a railway train is exceedingly low[6]. Indeed, in Britain in 1985 not a single passenger and no member of the railway staff died in a train crash, and in five of the previous ten years no passengers had been killed in train crashes. The six people who were killed by trains in 1985 were all users of road vehicles including, in one case, a motorcycle.

The total number of people killed in UK railway operations during 1985 was 74, compared with an average of about 69 during the five years before. Thirty-one of the people killed were passengers, and 16 of these fell from the train while it was in motion. Indeed, so few members of the public are killed in association with train operation that the sort of event which is quite often referred to in this book as being "not impossible but highly unlikely" is thrown into sharp focus. For example, in one such event, a foot bridge over a railway was damaged by vandals who left a hole in the walkway. Walking over the bridge in pitch darkness someone fell through the hole and was killed when he fell into the empty hopper waggon of a train passing underneath.

In terms of miles run, the number of "significant" train accidents is about half the number of injury-producing road accidents per mile. However, far more passengers are carried per mile, and the rate of death from such accidents is very near zero. In very great contrast to road accidents, virtually all train accidents are reported, so that the real difference in risk between road and rail is even greater than indicated by these figures.

Train accidents for every million miles run, Britain, 1966–85

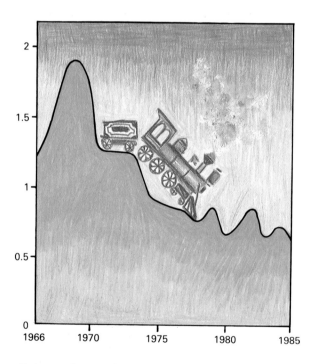

Train travel is very low risk, and getting lower. Not a single passenger or railway staff member died in a train crash in 1985. The figure shows a jump in accident rates in the late 1960s due to a spate of derailments among old and overworked goods wagons, now replaced. The accident rate is declining despite an increase in the average weight and speed of each train.
Sources: reference 1 and 8

Running trains is a complicated business, and the consequence of human failure can be very severe. The system is being adapted to take human capacity into account. For example, much of the scope for error by signalmen that existed in old-fashioned signal boxes has all but been eliminated from the modern power signal box. However, the driver of a train is still dependent on his ability to observe, interpret and react correctly to the coloured light signals along the line. The provision of radio communications will ease the task for the driver to some extent, and the provision of expensive automatic train protection systems, such as are now being used to some extent on the continent of Europe, is being considered for Britain. If they are installed, it will be a demonstration of how community pressures act, in some cases (but not others), to reduce very low risks even further. It will also show that the closer the risks come to an irreducible minimum, the higher the costs of reducing them will get.

Level crossings will remain a vulnerable part of the railway system for some time. As old-fashioned gated crossings were being replaced by automatic crossings, it was found that the risk of crashes at the old kind was consistently higher than at the new, so that, overall, risk throughout the system was being reduced. However, now that the new automatic crossings are widely employed, more road vehicle/train crashes inevitably are occurring on them, and these crashes tend to be dramatic and well reported. So, in early 1986, following two fatal crashes (in one of which nine people died), a ban was placed on this new type of crossing; this ban, however, can be expected to result in a *higher* risk than necessary throughout the system overall, because of resulting delays in the replacement of the higher-risk old crossings.

In other developed countries, the risk to passengers in trains is also extremely low, with passenger deaths at an average of less than 10 per year in the whole United States[1]. There is a very different picture in the less developed parts of the world, where unprotected railways run close to densely populated urban areas, and where familiarity with risk can lead, again, to its being disregarded.

AIRCRAFT

To many people air travel is the very epitome of low-risk transport. To others, having queued to take out extra life insurance at the airport and now sweating nervously before takeoff, exactly the opposite is true. It is one of those cases where man is venturing into an alien environment, and perception of risk depends very much on how alien the environment is actually felt to be by the individual concerned.

Aviation can be divided into two categories, the first being passenger-carrying "commercial" aviation, and the other being so-called "general" aviation, mostly using smaller aircraft in operations including pleasure flying, executive travel, crop spraying, land surveying and so on.

The International Civil Aviation Organization tries to collect and collate international information on fatal aircraft crashes, but receives no such data from the Soviet Union and very limited information from many other parts of the world. According to the figures which this organization does receive, the average annual number of crashes in commercial aviation (almost certainly an underestimate) was 1,383 between 1975 and 1980, and 6,750 in general aviation[1]. These resulted, on average, in 1,425 and 1,893 deaths annually for commercial and general aviation respectively. There was an average of some 30 crashes each year in which passengers were killed, a rate of 0.36 fatal crashes per 100 million kilometres (0.66 per 100 million miles) and 0.14 passenger fatalities per million passenger kilometres (0.23 per 100 million passenger miles).

In the United States, for every 100 million passenger miles travelled, the death rate for scheduled air transport services is about 0.04, with the equivalent figures for buses being 0.15 and for cars 1.30. The US aviation fleet carries about 40% of all paying passengers in the entire world.

With respect to crashes involving aircraft on the British register, the number of fatal accidents is so small that it is difficult to compare rates directly, although they are of the same average order of magnitude to those in the United States[7]. In the years 1976 to 1985 there were only four fatal accidents involving British passenger-carrying planes of over 2,300 kg. These occurred in 1976, 1979, 1980 and 1985, and were responsible for the deaths of 63, 17, 146 and 55 people (passengers and crew) respectively. During these years a total of 657,478 million passenger kilometres were travelled, giving an average rate of 0.04 deaths per 100 million passenger kilometres (0.07 deaths per 100 million passenger miles), or about one death for every one and a half thousand million passenger miles, a very long way indeed (about eight times to the sun and back, or 60,000 times round the world).

Figures relating to miles flown or hours in the

air are not really very meaningful, because the most dangerous phases of any one flight are takeoff and landing. So, for most passengers, a figure relating to the risk of crashing on a given flight is more helpful. In Britain ''reportable'' accidents are those in which people are killed or injured or the aircraft incurs structural damage. Again, the rate of such crashes is very low, averaging, over the ten-year period 1976 to 1985, a fraction under one reportable accident for every 100,000 flight stages. The figure for fatal accidents

the United States and Britain, is generally very similar to the picture of recreational car or boat use, with operators getting into trouble because they exceed their capabilities, a problem often compounded by the use of alcohol. Studies of light plane crashes in the United States have shown a degree of alcohol use which is comparable to that found in drivers in fatal car crashes. It does seem that the greater the extent to which the aircraft is being used like a car, the greater the extent to which incapacitation by

Death and accident rates, large and small aircraft

Deaths per 100 million passenger miles		Reportable accidents per 100,000 hours flown	
Scheduled air transport	0.04	Aircraft over 2,300 kg	0.55
Buses	0.15	Aircraft under 2,300 kg	29.84
Cars	1.30		

Rates of death and injury in commercial air travel are very low, and the risk of a flight ending in disaster is much lower than one in a million. Flying in a light plane is much higher risk in terms of hours flown, and as a hazard is more like a private car. Alcohol is frequently incriminated in light-plane crashes.

is subject to a wide range of error because the number of these is so small, but works out at fewer than one fatal accident for every 1.5 million flight stages, well under the one-in-a-million risk which, for most activities, people equate with being no risk at all (see Chapter 14).

The figure is rather different when we turn to the smaller aircraft used in general aviation. In Britain, figures comparable for all aircraft are available for estimated flying hours, with the number of reportable accidents per 100,000 hours flown averaging 0.55 for aircraft over 2,300 kg (averaged over the ten-year period 1976 to 1985) equivalent to one accident for every 182,000 hours flown, or nearly 21 years in the air. The equivalent figure for aircraft under 2,300 kg was 29.84 reportable accidents over the same period, one accident per 3,351 hours, or about 4.5 months in flight. There has been, however, a general tendency for this figure to decrease, having been 24.4 in 1985. This 50 to 60-fold difference between large and small aircraft is also reflected in the number of fatalities for every 100,000 hours flown.

In fact, the picture of pleasure flying, both in

alcohol is likely to be raising the risk of crashing.

In a crash at equivalent speed, the passengers of a small aeroplane are at far higher risk of injury than in a modern small car, and there is much that could be done to make the risk of dying in a light plane crash lower than it is today. It is commonly the case that occupants in light plane crashes have received unnecessarily fatal injuries, although the cabin structure has remained essentially intact. The fatality rate per 100 million general aviation passenger miles is at least seven times higher than that for passenger cars.

Even when big planes crash, the outcome for their occupants is not inevitably fatal. Passengers have died in survivable crashes because the cabin materials have burnt and released highly toxic fumes. There have also been reports of injuries during emergency evacuation. A hopeful sign is that over the last decade, crashes involving modern widebodied jets have resulted in approximately three times *fewer* fatalities per number of passengers than was the case for piston-engined aircraft[8], although at least part of the reason for this is the present use of much better emergency services and hospital facilities near airports.

Chapter Eight

Risks
in the
Home

HOUSING

The next time someone reflects on some newly discovered risk to health and well-being in the great outdoors, and reflects that the only truly safe place to be is at home, perhaps in bed, he should be reminded that that is almost certainly not true. Falls kill more people from unintentional injury than anything except traffic accidents and most falls occur at home[1]. Most deaths from burning happen at home. The average house is full of high energy appliances that can wound by cutting, ripping, puncturing, and hitting the human body, and more energy in high concentrations is available in electrical outlets and from hot water taps. The air may be far more polluted than can ever be found outside. A general proposition is that housing is a public health responsibility because poor housing increases the risk of premature death.

In the broadest sense, people's living environment obviously affects and reflects the quality of their life. As populations drift towards the cities, the more affluent tend to move to the newer suburban areas, and this reduces the amount of money available for the support and renewal of inner urban areas. Crowded and insanitary conditions increase the risk of communicable disease, including tuberculosis, especially in the relatively poor parts of the world. Inadequate structures and poor maintenance increase the chance of injury. Naturally, the interaction between people and their environment includes their dwelling places. Strictly speaking, to put

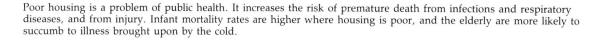

Poor housing is a problem of public health. It increases the risk of premature death from infections and respiratory diseases, and from injury. Infant mortality rates are higher where housing is poor, and the elderly are more likely to succumb to illness brought upon by the cold.

hard numbers on the extent to which poor housing increases the risk of injury and disease, people would need to be randomly allocated to various types of housing and their health outcomes measured over a period of many years. This is manifestly not possible. Nevertheless, it is possible to identify many factors which do increase risk, but before doing so let us spare a thought for those who have no homes at all. Out of the approximately 1.6 billion people aged under 15 in the world today, as many as one-quarter have never lived in anything better than temporary shelter, and many may continue in this way for the rest of their lives. The World Health Organization has estimated that there are 100 million people worldwide living on pavements, rubbish tips and railway platforms and in open fields. Most are in the developing nations, but many thousands are in the big cities of the developed world. Practically no information is available on the ways these people are injured or are otherwise at risk, although a fair guess would be that their risk of injury is high and in most parts of the world their chance of receiving medical treatment is very low.

Injuries at home

In Britain in 1984 during a three-month survey period[2], 1% of all males and 2% of females had an accident at home sufficient in severity to cause attendance at hospital or a doctor's surgery. The proportions were highest among children under 5 and elderly women, particularly those aged 75 and over. This roughly translates into an annual risk of one in 12 (females) and one in 25 (males) of suffering an injury at home which needs treatment.

Figures for fatal injury at home are shown in the following table. They include deaths from accidents in residential accommodation. About one-half of the males and 80% of the females who die in accidents in the home or residential accommodation are aged 65 or over. More people die from injuries received at home than on the roads.

Deaths from accidents in the home and residential institutions, England and Wales, 1983	Males	Females	Total
Accidental falls	936	1,973	2,909
Fire and flames	292	304	596
Accidental poisoning	304	216	520
Accidental suffocation	219	177	396
Other causes (including undetermined whether accidental or deliberate)	209	215	424
	1,960	2,885	4,845

Source: reference 1

After falls, the commonest cause of death from accidents in the home is fire, with the elderly again over-represented. Poisoning comes next, followed by suffocation, usually from inhaling food.

The annual death rate from injuries and poisoning in the home and residential institutions is now around 12 per 100,000 population, a risk of death of one in 8,500 each year distributed evenly (which, as is apparent, it is not; the risks for the very old and the very young are much higher than for other age groups).

In the United States also, about one-quarter of all deaths from injury occur at home and well over one-third of all non-fatal injuries do so[3]. The death rate (standardized for age) from injuries at home in the US has been declining consistently for many years, having come down from nearly 30 per 100,000 population in the 1930s to 10 per 100,000 (1 in 10,000) in 1980. For minor injuries, the rate is now rather steady, having been 10.7 per 100 in 1959–61 and 12.2 per 100, equivalent to more than 1 in 10 each year in 1980 and, again, very much of the same order of that recorded in Britain.

Otherwise, internationally comparable figures on domestic injury are virtually impossible to obtain, although a special World Health Organization study some 20 years ago[4] did attempt to make such comparisons for countries in the industrial world. The range of recorded injury rates is large, extending from Japan, where about one-third of women who die from injury do so at home, to Scotland and Norway, where about two-thirds do so. For men, in Japan and Finland about 12% who die from injury are killed at home, ranging up to 21% in England, 23% in Norway, and 27% in Scotland. (However, the usual caveats on international comparisons must apply: differences in classification and so on.)

As for so many other causes of unintentional injury, the factors which increase the risk of injury at home are linked to a combination of hazardous products, environmental factors, and human inability to cope with tasks demanded of them. Among the individuals at high risk in this situation are the very young, the very old, those affected by alcohol and those impaired by ill health, but in the best of all possible worlds even the most incompetent of these individuals should not be exposed to a high risk of injury when "safely" at home. Infants should not be able to stick metal pins into power plugs or suck exposed electrical wiring. The drunken reveller should not be able to walk through a glass door or fall from a third-floor window.

The shaky and poor-sighted grandmother should not have to fall the length of a flight of stairs because the hand rail is too thick for her arthritic hands to grasp. Death and injury are too high a price to pay for not being "careful"[5].

In the United States the Consumer Product Safety Commission has established a nationwide electronic injury survey system which gives consistent and reliable data for that country on domestic injury, information being gathered from people visiting the emergency departments of hospitals.

A 1980 survey[6] of such hospital visits following injury from parts of buildings showed that stairs were easily the commonest source of injury at 333 per 100,000 population each year (about 1 in 300). Glass doors, windows and panels accounted for 91 visits to the emergency department for every 100,000 people (1 in 1,100) with fences and baths following along as also rather common sources of injury.

The average garden shed is packed full of high-energy appliances with the capacity to maim or even kill. The risk can be minimized by careful attention to operating practices and the use of protective clothing.

About 600 deaths occur each year in England and Wales from mishaps on stairs, about 12 per million people of all ages and 108 per million in the group of highest risk, females over 75 years of age (one in 10,000 in this group each year). The commonest picture is that of an elderly or handicapped individual who wrongly judges the height of a step while descending the stairs and falls forward.

Doors are another hazard in all sorts of ways. Glass in doors can be broken by children, or young adults in a hurry or affected by alcohol. It is usually children whose fingers or arms get trapped between the door and the jamb, or injured when the door swings unexpectedly. In the case of windows, it is the glass which causes most of the injuries, typically among children who fall on to or through it. Another common cause of injury is breakage of the glass while trying to open a stuck window. In the United States there is one injury for every 3,800 windows in use each year, or one serious injury each year for every 250 houses.

Electrical systems in the developed world are not responsible for a very high proportion of domestic injury, probably because from its very introduction electricity has been recognized as a hazardous form of energy and thus properly managed from the outset. Installation has long been subject to strict codes, which cover aspects such as insulation and fuse design. The latest types of fast-acting fuses should further reduce the risk of electrocution. Some figures indicate that the risk of electrical injury is lower in countries such as the United States and Canada, where 110–120 volts are used in domestic systems as opposed to 220–240 volts in Britain and the rest of the world.

Nearly half all the injuries which occur in baths or showers are suffered by children under 10, and three-quarters of those who die from their injuries are in this age group. The slips and falls which are the commonest reason for injury are distributed otherwise quite evenly thoughout age groups, with the elderly surprisingly not being over-represented. One possible explanation is that having a bath is just too difficult for many of them and they simply forgo the luxury.

Most features of building design and construction which affect the risk of injury are covered by various regulations and codes, although these vary very widely throughout the world and even from place to place within large developed countries. Unless information is gathered systematically and consistently over a long period it is very difficult specifically to employ the codes as ways of reducing the risk of injury let alone to measure any beneficial effect that the codes and regulations might be having.

By contrast, many of the furnishings, appliances and toys which are used within domestic dwellings and which pose a risk of injury are not covered by any regulations at all.

In the case of furnishings, problems which contribute to the risk of injury include instability, the presence of joints and pivots which can trap and pinch limbs, gaps (such as those between the rails of baby cots) which can trap body parts, heavy lids, slippery surfaces, sharp edges and flammable coverings. A related issue is that of placement. A shelf which can be easily reached poses no substantial risk, but if it is a high one which a perhaps impaired or elderly person can only reach by standing on an unstable stool, then the additional risk of injury can be quite substantial.

Many appliances used in the home pose a rather obvious risk of causing injury. These include cooking stoves, radiators, electric fires, irons and the like. There are less obvious sources of potential injury such as washing machine wringers, and electrical appliances which can too easily be tipped over.

In the garden shed and workshop there are a mass of appliances which can cause severe and disabling injury. In most cases the parts which cause the injury are the bits that do the work, such as saw blades, knife edges, drill bits and so on. Domestic tools of these kinds are less likely to have adequate guards than their equivalents used in industry, and the protective devices that do exist are less likely to be used and more likely to be put out of action deliberately.

Injuries from heat and cold

Burning is a common cause of injury and death, as already noted in Chapter 4, and many burning injuries are caused by the type of appliances we have just reviewed. In England and Wales in 1983 a total of 747 fire-related deaths occurred in the home. In the United States it was found that fires occurred between midnight and 6 a.m. with smokers being found to be the main culprits. In Britain, many deaths also occur from the use of matches, cigarettes and so on, but there are too many "unspecified" causes of fire to make much sense of relative risks from published statistics.

Information on domestic burning injuries is very poor for countries in the developing world, but it is reasonable to surmise that the rates are very high. Factors increasing the risk for people living in such nations (and in poor areas in richer countries) include crowding, the widespread use of highly flammable building materials, open fires, the use of appliances which are inherently unsafe, and the presence of very large numbers of children. When fires do occur they are unlikely to be quickly extinguished, and the injuries are relatively unlikely to be quickly and successfully treated. Burn injuries which do not result in death have most commonly resulted from contact with hot surfaces in the home and from scalding water and hot fat or oil.

Elderly people are under-represented in non-fatal burn injury statistics in terms of their numbers. However, at the individual level, people with the disorders of coordination and consciousness which are more common among the elderly are at particular risk, and treatment of the old for burns is less likely to be successful for a given degree of severity. The death rate from burns among the elderly is therefore relatively high.

Children, as would be expected, also have high death rates from burns around the home in proportion to their numbers in the population. Their natural curiosity is in hazardous combination with their inexperience with hazard, and with their small size and poor coordination. Among adults, those who drink heavily and smoke heavily are also relatively likely to be injured by burning and, of course, heavy drinkers tend also to be heavy smokers. One-half to two-thirds of adults killed in fires have alcohol in the blood, most well over the legal limit for driving[7]. In a study of home fires in Montreal[8] it was found that the single most important factor associated with serious fires was the number of alcohol drinkers per household, and for minor fires the most important variable was the number of smokers per household.

The people most likely to be burnt at home are those who smoke and drink heavily. Well over half the adults killed in home fires have alcohol in the blood sufficient to make driving illegal. About 750 people each year are burnt to death at home in England and Wales.

The risk of burn injuries changes as the general pattern of home heating changes. For example, as the number of coal fires decreases, the number of children injured by falling into such fires will obviously decrease as well. On the other hand, in the United States there has been a swing back to "low technology" wood-burning stoves with which the present generation has very little experience, and the number of burn injuries as a result of using these has increased markedly.

Similarly, as clothing styles alter, patterns of burn injury change, as do regulations and their influence. The decrease in burn injuries among female children in the fifties in England was probably associated with a rapid move away from flowing nightdresses and highly flammable materials which occurred at that time, following mass publicity about the risk associated with such clothing.

At the other extreme, deaths from cold, 131 women and 93 men were recorded as dying from "excessive cold" in England and Wales in 1984. Of these, 84% of the women and 60% of the men were aged 70 years or over, indicating the "hypothermia" hazard that can arise in the English winter among elderly people living in inadequately heated homes or none at all. This number does not, of course, include the cold-related illnesses which may have been the immediate cause of death for many others. In all countries, the overall death rate is somewhat higher in the winter than the summer, and this difference is more pronounced in Britain than in other developed countries, including colder ones. Among elderly women, cold is well exceeded by falls, but only just by fire, as a "non-disease" cause of death at home.

INDOOR POLLUTION

The energy consciousness of the seventies has had an unexpected consequence for the eighties. With the laudable objective of minimizing costs to ourselves as well as keeping down the long-term demands on the world's reserves of fossil fuel, householders in the developed world have made strenuous efforts to improve the insulation of their homes and to eliminate draughts. A living room in which an open fire is burning completely replaces the air in it every few minutes. Even without a fire burning, the stagnant air inside an average home in the sixties and seventies would have been exchanged with the outside air every hour or so. Now, with improved insulation and sealing of windows and doors, the air exchange rate in many houses may be as slow as once in every 10 hours.

The effect of this is that an enormous range of pollutants can gather in the household air, and many of these have been linked to respiratory disorders and even to cancer. Even if the actual concentration of pollutants is rather low, the fact remains that most people spend a very large proportion of their total lifespan inside their homes, so that the dose of a potentially dangerous pollutant, when taken over many years, can be quite high.

Of course, this is not only a problem for people in the developed world. In simple dwellings in many countries, fires are burnt in open spaces in the interior, as can be seen by the liberal coating of soot on the roofs and walls. These fires may be fuelled by charcoal, wood, animal dung or petroleum products, and concentrations of dangerous pollutants easily exceed anything to be found in the outside air.

Many indoor pollutants are below levels at which they can be detected without instruments, although long-term exposures may cause increased rates of illness and even death. There is, overall, a rather patchy collection of information on the distribution of this problem, the characteristics of buildings which make it worse, the actual concentrations indoors, the patterns of exposure of people to the pollutants, and on the actual degree of health risk which is suffered. Nevertheless, on first principles there is much that is now known that bears careful consideration. Evaluation of indoor as well as outdoor exposure to air pollution is essential if we wish realistically to assess the health effects of either. In fact, studies have already found that the total exposure of people to pollutants is often better related to indoor concentrations than those found in the outdoors[9]. Just one effect of this is that even if outdoor pollution were to be eliminated completely, the ill effects of air pollution on people would not cease.

There are several pollutants from indoor sources which can affect human health[10].

The indoor burning of various heating and cooking fuels can generate carbon monoxide, carbon dioxide, sulphur dioxide, formaldehyde, hydrocarbons, nitrogen oxides and a variety of types of particulates (smoky matter). Very high levels of, for example, nitrogen dioxide have been measured during ordinary cooking operations, and exposure to this gas can cause the formation of fluid in the lungs and wheezing. Carbon monoxide has already been referred to in the section on poisoning because it is so often involved in fatal accidents. Levels in the air well short of those that will kill but that are,

nevertheless, dangerous have been found in houses where gas cookers have been used for heating purposes, which is not uncommon among the urban poor. High concentrations have also been found in public buildings and offices which have attached or underground garages.

Tobacco smoke can contribute some 2,000 compounds to the air in homes and buildings used by smokers and non-smokers alike. Many of these compounds are known to be carcinogenic. The health effects of breathing other people's smoke have already been discussed in the smoking section, but to recapitulate, there is little doubt that the adverse effects do include lung cancer and other respiratory disorders.

Bacteria which cause disease, as well as a wide variety of biological material giving rise to allergic effects, are also found in the air within buildings, and within ventilation and air-cooling systems. Legionnaires' disease is a well-known example, but minor illnesses are far more common and when totalled over the entire population probably represent an enormous cost in lost time, particularly from respiratory illness. Again, reductions in ventilation and the increased use of recirculated air which is not treated and filtered may increase the concentrations of bacteria and allergens.

Many building materials contain formaldehyde resins, which are a sort of glue, and formaldehyde can be released as gas. High levels of formaldehyde concentration have been found in the United States and in Europe, and especially in mobile homes in America. Formaldehyde is known to be mutagenic and carcinogenic in rats. It is also an extremely irritating and unpleasant gas generally.

Another potentially dangerous pollutant of the indoor air is asbestos, which can cause skin irritation as well as a variety of cancers with a long period between exposure and development of the disease (see Chapter 6). There is also the possibility of asbestos combining with other contaminants, in particular cigarette smoke, in a way which multiplies the risk of cancer.

An increased consciousness of the risk posed by asbestos over recent years has, however, reduced the actual chance of hazardous exposure to it in public buildings and dwelling places to a very tiny level.

Pollution of the indoor air is for most people a much higher risk than pollution outdoors. Indoor air can carry cancer-causing compounds from cigarette smoke, oxides from cooking fumes, bacteria and allergy-causing dusts. Poorly ventilated buildings contain high levels of radon gas, which is a radioactive product of uranium.

Radon

Comparatively recently recognized as a carcinogenic pollutant of indoor air is the gas *radon*. Radon is part of the decay chain between uranium-238 and lead-206. Uranium and its decay product radium-226 are found quite naturally in rock and soil, and turn up in building materials such as bricks. Outside, radon gas seeps out of the ground quite naturally, but is instantly so diluted in the air that its concentration is very low. Inside buildings, however, radon gas seeps into the indoor air from the ground, from the building materials or even from water used in wells. The concentration of radon indoors, therefore, as well as the concentration of its decay products such as thoron (which are also radioactive), will increase to a level which is balanced by its removal by ventilation.

Concentration levels of radon and its decay products have been measured in buildings in many developed countries, including private homes. Concentrations in houses in Sweden have been found to average about three times the concentrations reported for houses on the east coast of the United States, and 20 to 30 times the concentrations reported for houses in the warm states of California and Texas. In Britain a wide variety of concentrations has also been found and, of course, they depend in part on the rate of ventilation and how and where the buildings are built.

On the basis of existing measurements and an average of one change of air per hour, the National Radiological Protection Board has estimated[11] that the average annual dose of radon received in Britain is equivalent to a whole-body dose of nearly 1 mSv, which is of the same order as all of the other sources of natural radiation put together, in other words half the total. At this level of risk, it could be responsible for about 500 deaths from cancer each year in Britain. In the United States, estimates have ranged up to 10,000 for the number of excess lung cancers occurring as a result of exposure to radon gas in the home. Radon exposure must be, for most people, a greater source of biological hazard than any other natural source of radiation. It is a rather nice paradox (and an example of swopping one risk for another) that an individual who reduces the ventilation of his home in order to contribute to energy conservation, as a step towards minimizing reliance on nuclear power and its attendant risk of radiation, may actually be increasing the average level of radioactivity to which he is exposed.

However, in terms of the total number of cancer deaths each year, the extra risk posed by radon gas in the home is really very small. It has arisen as a side effect of our perfectly justifiable aim to make our use of energy more efficient, and to counter it in a precipitate manner would incur immense costs in construction, reconstruction, relocation or reduced ventilation. Techniques for reducing radon ingress from the ground are being studied in several countries, including the United Kingdom. The point here is not that we should immediately dispense with all home insulation activities in order to reduce radon levels but, rather, that there are some risks we simply cannot avoid. Once again we are faced with the need to balance substantial benefits against a measurable risk, and to compare this risk with all the others we are faced with.

Chapter Nine

Recreational Risks

As lifestyles have steadily changed over the years, an increasing proportion of the population come to be at risk from injury and death during recreational activities. This is, naturally, especially the case among Europeans, Australasians, North Americans and Japanese, and while the same may or may not be true among the less developed nations the information currently available allows no real analysis of such risks to their people.

Nobody sincerely believes that all recreational activities can be made free of risk. Indeed, some degree of risk is manifestly one of the attractions of many kinds of recreation, and it is clear that people in general are prepared to accept far higher levels of risk in recreation than they would be prepared to at work, say, or as a result of the operation of a nearby industrial facility.

Millions of people worldwide are involved in various kinds of recreational activity and competitive sport, but to analyse death and injury *rates*, on either an individual or a comparative basis, is difficult. While for some organized activities quite good statistics are gathered for deaths and injuries, the less organized and the more personalized the activity, the less likely it is that reliable figures will be available. Further, to determine the risk of injury, the population at risk needs to be known; again, with few

exceptions, the number of participants in the various activities is hard to estimate with any accuracy.

Moreover, it is difficult to rate risks in sport in terms which make a lot of sense to everybody. Take, for example, one activity which results in a large number of injuries, some of them very severe, namely diving. Practically every person who swims at some stage dives. The population at risk could therefore be regarded as the entire population of swimmers, but it is probably more realistic to concentrate our concern on those who treat diving as a sport in itself, as opposed to swimming generally. The population of divers in a controlled environment, such as a given pool, or in a given competitive team, might well be known. But this would not include most non-competitive individual divers. And the number who dive off river banks and trees in the countryside is never likely to be known. It could be argued further that the diver is only at risk during the instant of the activity, and that therefore risk should be assessed in terms of the number of dives undertaken during a given period of time. However, when studying risk with this level of precision, account will need to be taken of the interaction between individual skill and the task that is attempted. A skilled diver might undertake complicated manoeuvres off a high board, whereas his less skilled friend will content himself with simpler dives from lesser heights. The result from the point of view of the individual divers is that they are choosing to face very similar levels of perceived risk. All this can mean that there are nearly as many ways of expressing ''risk'' as there are people exposing themselves to it.

In practice, most assessments of risk in sport take some account of the people exposed to risk during a given period of time, expressed in terms such as the number of injuries for every few thousand man-hours of play. In Britain, as well as in the United States (where much more comprehensive statistics have been gathered), it is team sports involving violent body contact which result in the highest risk of non-fatal injury. The martial arts have a lower rate of injury, but when an injury does occur it tends to be more serious and necessitate a longer time away from the sport. What many people see as ''feats of daring'', such as mountaineering, motor racing, sport parachuting, and hang gliding, have lower injury rates overall but much higher death rates.

As well as risks of specific injuries, some sports carry a risk of gradual or cumulative damage to health. Boxing is particularly dangerous, as repeated blows to the head cause progressive and irreversible brain damage.

There are several general features of recreational activity which determine the risk of injury. For the individual participant the state of physical conditioning will be an influential risk factor for most sports, as will be the degree of natural talent and extent of experience and learned skill.

The nature of the equipment used, such as protective clothing, crash helmets, boots and the like, will have a great infuence on the injuries of the user and of other participants. The equipment will, necessarily, be in interaction with the nature of the environment which, in many cases, is inherently hazardous. This is especially the case for underwater divers, mountaineers and hang gliders. That the environment is hazardous is evident in these cases, but the relationship is less clear for other sports which involve vastly more people. A hard and unforgiving playing surface for football is one example.

Finally, the risk of injury is affected by the extent to which the actual infliction of harm is part of the sport and sanctioned by its regulations. Boxing is an obvious example, and some forms of football are arguably in the same category.

WATER SPORTS

Drowning is the third most common cause of death from unintentional injury among all ages and ranks second for the ages 5 to 44. In the United Kingdom around 1,000 people die from drowning each year. About three times as many men drown as women.

Under the international classification of diseases, drowning falls into two groups, one involving the use of boats and the other not. Apart from drowning and near drowning, the other injuries which occur in water sports include disruption to bones and flesh caused in diving and waterskiing, injuries (mostly bites and stings) received from dangerous marine animals and decompression sickness from diving with self-contained underwater breathing apparatus (scuba).

Drowning is a risk to people who are swimming in artificial pools or natural bodies of water, to children who fall in, to people who are caught up in flood waters and to people who suffer sudden illness while in the water. About one-quarter (in England) and one-third (in the US) of drownings involve boating activity and about another third swimming or diving. Most of the remainder have slipped or fallen into the water unexpectedly. Drownings from scuba diving, skin diving and surfing together account for no more than about 2% of all drowning deaths, so that when exposure is not taken into account, the activities which appear on the face of it to be the most dangerous do not in fact account for many deaths.

Figures relating to deaths and injuries in association with recreational boating are not gathered in a very reliable manner anywhere in the world. From 1970 to 1976, the average annual number of deaths in the United States associated with recreational boating was 1,480[1]. The number of such boats was estimated as 0.3 million, giving a death rate of 17.9 per 100,000 boats (one death for every 5,600 boats each year) or 0.5 per million occupant hours. If the average period for a day out on the water is ten hours, this represents an average risk of death in the order of 1:200,000 for each outing.

An analysis of the year 1980 showed that about 1,200 drownings involved the use of pleasure boats. Almost 60% of these were less than 16 feet (five metres) long and the majority were open power craft. Capsizing or falling overboard caused almost two-thirds of the deaths[2].

About 40% of these deaths occur while simply "pottering about", about 20% while fishing and 10% while drifting. The typical picture is of an open outboard motor boat or boat under 16 feet long with no motor (excluding sailing boats) on a pleasant summer weekend afternoon with a light wind, in non-tidal calm water. The boat is most likely to have only two people aboard, with ages in the twenties.

By definition, drownings are fatal events. The number of "near drownings" is not known, but one American estimate is that for every drowning there have been nearly 2,000 "near-drowning" episodes, defined as an event perceived by those concerned as a serious risk of drowning, but not necessarily involving the aspiration of water or severe shortage of oxygen[4]. In the same survey it was found that out of every 100 people admitted to hospital for near drowning which did in fact involve severe shortage of oxygen and complete submersion, 13 people subsequently died. A British estimate, using different criteria, is that about ten times as many people come close to drowning as actually die[5].

The overall death rate from drowning is highest in children, with the very highest rate among children aged under two years. The vast majority of deaths in this group of little children result from falling into water and drowning in the bath. Several small children have even drowned in buckets of water.

Drowning is the third commonest cause of death from unintentional injury, and kills about 1,000 people each year in Britain. About one in five drownings are from boats, and the typical picture before tragedy occurs is of a happy afternoon in an open boat. Alcohol is a risk factor in drowning.

In the United Kingdom, it is many years since a comprehensive study of drownings was conducted, but in 1961 it was shown that of a total of 1,029 fatal drownings, 161 (16%) were related to the use of a boat, categorized in the following manner: motor boats 58 (36%), rowing boats 38 (24%), canoes 28 (17%), and sailing boats 5 (3%)[3]. Of these deaths, 49 occurred during work rather than recreation.

In countries where home swimming pools are popular, they pose a real risk to small children and there is an increasing tendency to mandate the use of fences and gates which limit their unsupervised access to the pool. An Australian estimate is that there is a one in 20 risk that a child will die, or almost die, in any particular unfenced pool during a period of 20 years, and that fencing will cut that risk by at least half[6], and a British study has concluded that about 80% of all pool drownings could be prevented by fencing regulations[7].

As for so many other kinds of violent death, alcohol use has been linked with drowning in several studies. As an example, in one study in America, it was found that alcohol was in the blood of 11 of 14 people who had drowned while swimming, with blood alcohol levels in most of them being more than double the legal limit for driving in England[8]. The same study reported alcohol in four of seven people who drowned while boating, and in Finland it has been estimated that over half all water traffic deaths involve alcohol[9]. Pre-existing medical conditions may also play a part, including strokes, mental retardation and heart attacks.

The ability to swim is obviously linked with the risk of drowning, but the association is far from being a simple one. If everyone could swim, that would not mean that no-one would drown, because swimmers take risks in the water which non-swimmers would not even dream of doing. In America it has been shown that black males, who often cannot swim, have higher drowning rates than white females, who usually can swim; but they also have higher drowning rates than black females, who are even worse swimmers than black males[4]. Clearly, a number of factors must interact in order to increase the risk of drowning.

Quite apart from drowning, there is another group of injuries associated with recreational use of the water, namely impact injuries suffered from striking hard surfaces. In the United States, only about 7% of spinal cord disruptions occur during recreation, but three-quarters of these involve swimmers and they are usually young men who become paralysed as a result. About 45% of these have resulted from diving into a river or stream, 27% into swimming pools and 28% into lakes, reservoirs or the ocean[10]. Once again alcohol has been implicated as a risk factor, in this case for diving into water which is too shallow[11].

High diving, in itself, does not appear to pose more than a small risk to those who are skilled and experienced. Severe injuries are extremely uncommon among competitive divers, although several do suffer strains of the joints and soft tissues. In Acapulco, Mexico, a group of local people dive for the enjoyment of tourists from heights of 100 and 130 feet, around 1,000 times a year. X-ray examination of their necks has shown no more than very minor damage and with no arthritis or other long-term effects.

Another water sport which is responsible for impact injuries is surfing, but for fairly obvious reasons there is very little information available on injuries except from Australia and Hawaii. Overwhelmingly the commonest type of injury is laceration, about half of which are caused by hitting the surfboard itself, with fractures being the next commonest type of injury. The type of injury depends on the type of surf, with serious spinal injuries sometimes occurring when, on steeply shelving beaches, waves break very suddenly and "dump" surfers on the sea bottom. Overall, considering the very large number of individuals who enjoy this individualistic sport, the number of deaths and severe injuries appears to be very low. In a consecutive study in Australia[11] of 200 spinal injuries sustained in all water sports (150 of this 200 had consumed alcohol before the injury event), it was found that 159 were due to diving and 19 to body surfing without a board, but that board surfing accounted for only two of the 200 spinal injuries. Similar proportions have been found in Hawaii.

Water skiing is a sport in which large amounts of energy are generated and released, and therefore on first principles may result in a high risk of injury when things go wrong. Generally injuries occur through hitting the water or being dragged through it, running into the shore or shoreside structures, or being run over by the power boat. Because the injuries can be exceptionally severe, they often receive wide publicity and thus the sport may appear to present a higher risk than is actually the case. An American estimate based on coastguard figures from 1977–81 is that about one in 32,000 skiers sustains relatively major injury per year and one in 384,000 is killed[12]. In competitive skiing major injury is rare, but there are plenty of minor cuts, sprains, bruises and pulled muscles. Most of the injuries occur in special events such as jumping and slalom skiing. Serious injuries in this sport can occur as a result of poor handling of the towing power boat, especially in cases when the skier is run down and slashed by the revolving propellor.

Diving underwater with self-contained underwater breathing apparatus ("scuba" diving) has become rapidly more popular since the early seventies. In the United States alone, some 4,000,000 divers were certified between 1970 and 1979[13]. No-one has any idea of for how many years each diver continues to dive, but there is no doubt that the number diving is increasing in that country by about 200,000 each year. Despite this, the number of fatalities has stayed remarkably constant and it is clear that the manifest risks in scuba diving are being increasingly well managed by participants and administrators.

The injuries suffered by scuba divers include drowning, damage to the ears by changing in pressure, decompression sickness as a result of rising from the depth too quickly to the surface, injuries from the sea bed, rocks and coral, and injuries from marine animals. As is the case for so many incidents in hazardous activities, a specific cause in each case cannot be singled out in that many factors may act together to cause a diver's death. A diver who experiences a minor medical or equipment problem at depth may be unable to save himself if he is also cold and then must struggle with rough water when he returns to the surface. The profile of a diver most likely to be killed is of a man of 16 to 35 years, inexperienced and perhaps uncertified by the appropriate authorities, and engaged in general recreational diving or diving in caves or wrecks. Alcohol has also been implicated in some deaths.

A similar pattern appears to exist for non-fatal diving injuries with decompression sickness figuring rather prominently (it is a very rare cause of death).

The most feared marine animal is the shark. But in over 350 years only about 1,000 shark attacks have been recorded, about 800 un-provoked. 730 attacks were recorded between 1941 and 1968 (30 each year), with 29% of them resulting in death (eight a year)[14]. The mortality rate has fallen over the last decade to about 20%. Only about 20 of the 350 different species of shark have ever been known to attack man. Rarely has any creature been more maligned and brutally mistreated as a result of gross misperception of the risk it poses to humans. Sharks are exceedingly common throughout the warm waters of the world, especially in coastal areas, and although it is impossible even to begin to estimate the number of people at risk from attack while swimming or engaged in water sports, just casual calculation will show that in fact there are few risks that are lower than an unprovoked attack by a shark.

TEAM SPORTS

A great deal of energy is generated during team sports, most of which involve body contact as well as impact against the implements of the game and the solid structures which enclose it. The total amount of activity is impressive. In the case of soccer, for example, it has been estimated that mid-field players in top professional teams run about 7,000 meters (nearly 4.5 miles) during a game and that the ball reaches speeds of 140 km/hour (80 miles per hour).

For injuries in soccer, estimates range from around 3.6 to 14 injuries for every thousand hours of adult play, with a slightly higher rate among adolescents[15]. These injuries include bruises, sprains, strains and fractures, but exclude minor abrasions and blisters. About two-thirds of the injuries occur to the legs. Making the rough assumption that for about 40 hours each year a player is engaged in competitive play, and that

the rate of injury is at the high end of the estimated range, the risk of injury works out at something less than one injury for every two years play.

The injury rate for rugby football is of the same order of magnitude, with some estimates giving much higher rates and some lower[16]. (Given the rubbery nature of the figures that are available, it is rather striking that reports of studies whose authors themselves enjoy a particular sport tend to indicate lower injury rates than reports of studies conducted by supporters of other codes!) Injuries in rugby are, as would be expected, rather less concentrated on the legs and include a higher proportion of arm injury and injuries to the head and neck. Injuries to the teeth used to be more common than they are now, and can be almost completely prevented by the use of mouth guards.

Injuries per 100,000 man-hours of play, selected sports

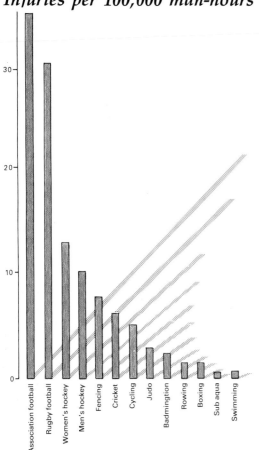

Team sports carry the highest risk of non-fatal injury, with large amounts of energy being generated and released through violent body contact. Most people will accept a far higher risk of death and injury in recreational activities than in other parts of life.
Source: reference 15

In great contrast to the codes popular in Britain, American football has always placed great emphasis on the use of protective equipment and the minimization of injury. However, as another contrast, the rules of the game permit and indeed encourage concentration on the player rather than the ball, so that violent body contact is a deliberate part of the sport. Deaths do occur in American football among the vast population of that country, but have shown a steady decline over the years. There are enormous differences in the number of deaths which are estimated. For example, the US Consumer Product Safety Commission estimated 260 deaths from American football in all ages for the years 1973–80 (37 a year). The estimate for soccer was 11 deaths, or less than two a year, in the US[17]. The American Football Coaches Association, however, estimated that just over 80 deaths had occurred during American football in the same period[18], or just over 10 a year. Considering that deaths are among the more reliably reported outcomes of injury, this three-fold difference indicates that

any comparative data should be treated with the greatest caution. For head and neck injuries, a reporting scheme was set up in 1985[19] so estimates of the incidence of these injuries may be more reliable. The occurrence of quadriplegia as a result of neck injury fell dramatically following a change in the rules in 1976. This illustrates how risks can sometimes be reduced by appropriate action. The overall rate of all injuries in American football was found to be just under 0.5 per player per season in a study in a North Carolina School[20], which is of the same order of magnitude as for British codes of football.

In the United States it is baseball which is responsible for the next highest number of deaths after football, at around 20 deaths per year as opposed to 30. There are millions of baseball players in the United States, and the injury rate appears to be about two per 100 players per year.

Basketball and field hockey have comparable injury rates, at around one injury for every thousand hours of play, or an injury every 2.5 seasons.

INDIVIDUAL CONTACT SPORTS

Boxing is perhaps the prime example of a sport in which the *intention* is to cause harm to one's opponent. In wrestling and the martial arts (when performed as sport) the intention is to cause the opponent to surrender rather than concuss him by causing brain injury. Because the intention of boxing is to injure, measurements of the rate of injury are inherently unreliable and certainly so in comparison with other sporting activities. A rather low incidence of injury is often recorded by supporters of boxing, but the injuries that do occur tend to be serious and cause longer periods of disablement than other sports. While the immediate aim of a boxing match is not to inflict permanent damage, the fact is that repeated concussive and near concussive blows to the head over many years have the effect of causing long term damage to the brain and other parts of the nervous system, often of a profound kind. In one study thirteen out of eighteen modern boxers and former boxers showed unequivocal evidence of brain damage, and all showed at least one sign of possible abnormality[21]. The risk in boxing is essentially different from other sports, as the danger of gradual serious damage is at least as great as that of specific injury. The Board of Science and Education produced a report on the risks of boxing in 1984[22] following which the BMA adopted policy in favour of public education towards an eventual ban on the sport.

Wrestling and the martial arts, such as judo and karate, are associated with high rates of injury, although they seem to cause lower rates of permanent and disabling injury than boxing. Most of the injuries result from impact with the floor or from twisting of the joints. An American study of wrestlers at college[23] indicated an injury rate of 12.7 and 6.2 per thousand bouts for "significant" and "major" injury respectively which, at a bout a week, indicates a risk of significant injury of 1 in 1.5 years and of serious injury of 1 in 3 years. The injury rate in karate appears to be much higher with 25% of all contests resulting in injury in an American study and a similar rate of one injury for every five contests in Scotland in 1974 and 1975. However, protective padding was introduced at about that time, and in 1976 the injury rate in Scotland dropped to one for every 22 contests[24].

In boxing the intention is to cause harm. The risk of injury is accepted voluntarily, with benefits seen to lie in athletic prowess or monetary reward. Some people believe that no benefits can ever justify such risks when the harm is deliberately imposed.

INDIVIDUAL SPORTS

Watching a planeload of enthusiasts returning from a holiday in the Alps will indicate to even the casual observer that the risk of moderate injury in skiing and other winter sports is rather high. Reported rates of skiing injuries range from 2 to 7 per 1,000 days (one for every 140–500 days on the slopes)[25], but would probably be higher if injuries that are not reported are included. The rate does appear to be declining somewhat over recent years. Deaths are very rare events. Most injuries are to the legs, especially in non-competitive skiing; head injury is relatively common in competitive downhill skiing. The use of newer types of equipment appears to be lowering the rate of leg and ankle injury. Ski jumping is by far the most hazardous of the snow sports, with nearly half all participants being injured in any given three-year period and with an incidence of head injury of about 33%.

Several other competitive sports may pose quite high risks of death or injury, although personal combat and body contact with other competitors are not among their aims. Other recreations such as running or riding may or may not involve any competition, but they do involve some risk. The actual rates of injury are not at all well known, although the patterns of injury and the ways in which it can be prevented or managed are now popular subjects for the medical literature. Heat stroke is becoming a problem among competitors in long distance running events, especially among novices who attempt to run long races without proper training. In Canada, about one in 100 runners are admitted to hospital during and after mass participation runs[26]. Another real risk in recreational running is being hit by a car, with an American study showing 30 deaths resulting from 60 collisions in a one-year period[27].

Horse riding is known by its participants to pose some risk, with reports on injury rates ranging around one to two injuries for every 1,000 rides[28]. Head injuries are both relatively frequent and serious, although their incidence can be reduced by the use of protective headgear.

There are a few sports which appear to present an especially substantial risk, in that they challenge natural forces, with the meeting of such challenges being an integral part of the activity. Of these, mountain climbing is probably the most popular. There are about 60,000 mountain climbers in the United States, with about 40 each year being killed, a death rate of 1:1,500 participants[29]. The overall rate of injury is about four times as high. Slips and falls are the commonest causes of mountaineering injury, but at high altitude, fluid in the lungs and freezing pose additional risks.

Hang gliding appears to attract about the same number of participants in America as mountaineering. Estimates range from two to three deaths for every 1,000 participants each year (one in 300–500), a rate which is perhaps slightly higher than for sport parachutists. Risk in terms of frequency of exposure is almost impossible to assess because of lack of information, and in any event there is a very doubtful level of comparability between two sports such as hang gliding and parachuting which, to the average non-participant, appear to be rather similar. The sport parachutist is in the air for only a few seconds or minutes during each jump, the number of which during any given day will be limited. The jumper is also exposed to the risk of the aircraft crashing, arguably greater than during normal flight operations because, for example, the plane may be flown as slowly as possible. The parachute jumper's risk might perhaps be assessed best in terms of injuries suffered for every so many jumps. Hang gliders, on the other hand, may be in the air for up to hours at a time in suitable conditions, and the risk to them is better expressed in terms of time in the air.

Motor racing is perhaps the sport which is most closely associated in the public mind with a high risk of death and injury and, of course, the risk extends to the spectators as well. In the single worst crash in the history of racing, at Le Mans in 1955, a total of 83 spectators were killed. Deaths in motor racing are certainly highly publicized, and the death rate in Formula One Grand Prix racing is extremely high. Out of an average number of active Grand Prix drivers of 35, about six are likely to be killed in a ten year period, a risk of about one in 60 each year[30]. However, taking all other forms of motor sport together, and this will include thousands of participants in Britain alone, the total number of deaths averages something less than four each year in Britain. Recommendations for additional life insurance payments for racing drivers (and thus representing an extra risk of death) range from 0% to 5% for the average weekend club racer, and up to 30% for Grand Prix racing, events for Indianapolis-style racing cars, and for professional sports car racing[30].

In summary, taking the whole spectrum of risks to participants in sporting and recreational activities, it is remarkable how little systematic information is currently being gathered on injury-producing events and on the risk that injury will be suffered. The epidemiology of this group of injuries is one of the major unstudied fields in risk assessment and injury control.

Grand Prix racing drivers face perhaps the highest annual risk of all, whether they are compared to other people earning a living or other people enjoying a sport. They, like many others, seek personal satisfaction in coming to terms with such a high-risk activity. Other forms of motor sport may pose much lower real risks, while still offering the thrill of participation.

Chapter Ten

Risk and Energy Production

S oon after the first man was at last successful in coaxing some flame from unwilling twigs, he almost certainly got burnt. The production of energy has always entailed some risk. Fire burns, and water drowns. The wind has been used for centuries for pumping water and grinding corn, and the building of windmills must have been a dangerous business in a non-technological society. Watermills have been used in their thousands throughout the centuries. Even at the time the Domesday book was compiled, the wheels of watermills were known to be dangerous to those who worked around them. However, deaths and disabilities were not well documented in those early days and the amount of power produced was not very great by the standards of the present. In terms of death and injury per unit of power produced, today's power production facilities are almost certainly very many times less hazardous than those of the Middle Ages. But the amount of power produced is incalculably higher, the number of people involved in producing the power is many times as great, and the numbers of deaths and disabilities are well recorded. In addition, when failure occurs in such a way that many people die at one time, the efficiency of the communications media ensures that huge numbers of people very soon know all about it.

The generation of energy has always been an activity of some risk. Windmills needed the felling of trees for their subsequent construction, the transport of materials, and the maintenance of moving parts.

So we are very much more conscious of the dangers of power production than we used to be. In recent years, the topic has become an even hotter one because of the use of nuclear technology, not only to produce horrendous weapons of war, but also to produce energy for domestic use. It follows that the risks involved in power production have become a major issue, and may indeed be a prime factor in determining how much power will be produced in the future and how we are going to produce it. The whole subject, therefore, is the subject of more detailed attention than the actual number of people killed would seem to justify, but it is worth stressing again that the risk that people perceive is at least as important in determining policy as the risk which is measured ''objectively''. Risk *estimation*, it bears repeating, is a process of analysis and calculation which takes into account factors both measurable and predictable, and levels of uncertainty are as far as possible defined. But then comes risk *evaluation*, which takes into account value systems which cannot be measured

in such ways. It may well be, for example, that the death of just one child from leukaemia is perceived to be a far bigger loss than the death of a hundred coalminers in the depths of the earth. The parents of the child almost certainly feel that way. Perceptions of loss may differ widely from person to person and community to community, but being different does not mean that some of the perceptions are thereby ''irrational'' or ''wrong''.

Nevertheless, in discussions about power production it is clear that many groups are not even arguing from the same numerical foundation, let alone from the point of view of equivalent personal and social values. It is worth seeing, therefore, how risks have actually been assessed for various types of power generation*. The risks we are discussing here, as is usual for this book, are of deaths and illness from injury and disease and, as usual, the best information that is available is for deaths.

It is important to remember that all equipment that generates energy has to be built, maintained and, in most cases, fuelled. Risks arise throughout the entire cycle of energy production. All systems require raw materials and all conventional power producing facilities (using coal, oil and nuclear fuels) require the extraction of the fuels which run them. The fabrication of components and the construction of buildings generates risks common to construction workers throughout industry. Materials have to be transported, with transportation risks (as always) being a substantial proportion of the whole. Operators and maintenance personnel are at risk, and further risk arises in the disposal of waste. Risk to the public health arises from the normal operation of the systems as well as from accidents and mismanagement. The public may also be at risk from pollution of the air and water.

To provide a fair comparison, risks are best expressed in terms of losses per unit of power produced. In practice, risk estimates are usually presented as the number of deaths per gigawatt year (GWy).

A gigawatt is a lot of energy. An electric fire may have a bar which uses electricity at a rate of 1,000 watts (1 kilowatt or kW). If the fire is on for an hour, a kilowatt hour (kWh) of electricity has been used, and the same amount of power could be employed to drive a little car for about

*Two important sources of material for this chapter have been books by Fremlin and Ferguson, references 1 and 2 respectively. These authors have had access to source material not easily available elsewhere.

10 miles. Power stations must supply many houses with many electric fires as well as other appliances, not to mention the substantial demands on industry. To heat 50 to 100 houses will need about 1 million watts, a megawatt (1,000 kW). A thousand megawatts is a gigawatt (GW). Most modern power stations produce power in the range of one-half to two gigawatts (500 to 2000 megawatts), and to put out a gigawatt for a year (one GWy) will be worth some hundreds of millions of pounds.

In the United Kingdom in 1981, about 37% of primary energy was produced from the burning of coal, about 35% from oil, 23% from natural gas, 4.3% from nuclear power, and 0.7% from hydroelectric power[1]. These may be referred to as the "conventional" sources of energy. Of increasing interest is the production of energy from non-conventional sources, which include solar power for the direct generation of both heat and electricity, the use of biological (usually plant) matter to produce alcohol and gas, wind power, and power from the action of ocean waves and currents.

The assessment of risk in power generation starts at the construction phase. Measurement over many years enables analysts to put numbers on the deaths and injuries which can be expected for the production of a given number of tons of steel or concrete, and any large power generating facility, whether it uses conventional or unconventional sources, will be a massive construction enterprise. A small but nevertheless real risk exists simply in the production of the materials needed to build the facilities which are to produce the power.

Sources of primary energy in Britain (1985)

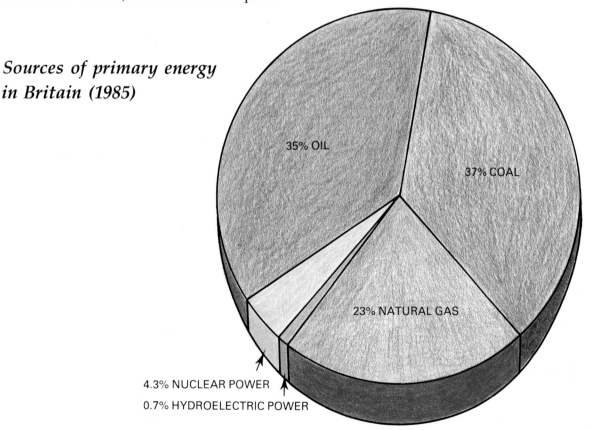

35% OIL

37% COAL

23% NATURAL GAS

4.3% NUCLEAR POWER

0.7% HYDROELECTRIC POWER

"Primary" energy provides warmth, light, food, goods and transport. Total energy use has been declining since 1973. Most energy goes to providing heat and electricity, and about one-quarter to liquid fuels for transport. UK oil and gas reserves are limited. Coal provides about three-quarters of UK electricity, and reserves may last for hundreds of years, but mining it is a hazard for men and burning it is a hazard for the environment. Nuclear power arouses public fears, and nuclear waste has to be disposed of. Hydroelectric dams have the potential for catastrophic failure, but their risk is a very familiar one which causes little or no public concern.

Risks in the extraction, preparation and transport of fuel for power stations

In the early part of this century, coal was easily the commonest source of energy in Britain, being employed in industry, for transport and for cooking and eating in the home. Indeed, until recent years (when homes have increasingly been heated by oil or gas), about half all coal consumed was burnt in private houses, and it was the smoke from fires in such houses which caused the terrible killer smogs in the cities of only a few decades ago.

Practically all the coal used in Britain is mined locally. The output of coal has steadily dropped over the last 30 years, with an increasing proportion of the coal that is mined going to power stations. The number of fatal accidents in British coal mines has dropped also, and at a rather faster rate than the reduction in output would indicate. There were 473 (nearly ten a week) fatal accidents in National Coal Board mines in 1951 and 30 (less than one a week) in 1979-80. The average death rate has dropped from about one death for every half a million tons of coal mined to about one death for every two million tons[2]. The actual number of miners killed is slightly higher than the number of fatal accidents because a handful of (fortunately) very rare incidents result in the death of more than one miner.

Apart from injury, the other main threat to the health of coal miners is the inhalation of dust particles which cause the "black lung" diseases, the best known of these being pneumoconiosis. The risk of developing pneumoconiosis is directly related to the amount of dust inspired, and therefore standards have been set which define the maximum levels to which miners may be exposed. The incidence of pneumoconiosis has dropped, with about 7.6% of miners showing evidence of the disease on X-ray in 1974-77, whereas back in 1959-63, 12.1% of miners showed such evidence. The disease takes about 30 years to develop, so that miners who die with pneumoconiosis as the prime cause of death are likely to do so in their sixties and seventies. There has been a steady increase in the average age of

Coal has long been a popular source of energy. There is risk to miners in its extraction from the ground, with nearly one a week dying in Britain. Like all power stations, coal-fired stations contributed to the killer city smogs of a few decades ago, and although much cleaner they still carry a risk of human and environmental damage through the emission of oxides of sulphur and nitrogen (which contribute to acid rain) and carbon dioxide (which may upset the world's temperature balance).

death from pneumoconiosis and this is now quite close to the average age of death of the male population generally. In 1984, 203 deaths were attributed to coalworkers' pneumoconiosis as the prime cause, the average age of those dying being 75–79 years. This is a drop from 1,160 deaths in 1955 at an average age of 64. Because of the present use of dust control standards it is now rare to see pneumoconiosis in a miner who has been at work for less than 20 years.

Miners are also exposed to a variety of other occupational diseases including skin disease and diseases resulting from radiation by radon and its decay isotopes. In addition, and as another example of exchanging one risk for another, miners run a small risk from the radiation of the X-rays which are used to regularly monitor them for pneumoconiosis.

Oil is also produced at the cost of substantial risks to those involved. In Britain, oil is much less important than coal in producing electrical energy, but it is exceedingly important for the production of the fuels used for transport. The vast majority of the crude oil consumed in Britain comes from oilwells in the North Sea. Most deaths occur during the construction and establishment of oil-drilling rigs. In the years 1974–1978 there were 62 fatal accidents at rigs concerned with oil and gas production, with about 30% being attributed to production activities. Twenty-four of the 62 fatal accidents occurred during diving activities and 11 while drilling.

The fuel consumed by nuclear power stations is uranium, which comes from overseas, mostly from Canada and Africa. Available reports suggest that the rate of fatal accidents among uranium miners is very low, at about one-tenth of the deaths of coal miners per gigawatt years of power produced. Pneumoconiosis is also known to affect the health of uranium miners, though to a lesser extent than coal miners in Britain.

Men mining for uranium are subjected to radiation, with the major risk arising from radon and its decay products. Just as in domestic dwellings the risk of lung cancer arising from the deposition of radon products in the lung is reduced as ventilation is improved, but ventilation alone cannot reduce the concentration of radon to nothing. It was, in fact, the mortality rate from lung cancer among uranium miners in America which was used to define the risk of radon inhaled within buildings. These days, however, various control measures have reduced the mortality rate from radon to extremely low levels in terms of power produced.

The mining and milling of uranium produce radioactive wastes. Liquid wastes are treated to reduce the radium content, but may increase the radioactivity of rivers into which they are discharged. Radioactive particles and radon gas are released into the air. The majority of the wastes are solid and known as "tailings". Piles of tailings continually produce radon from the decay of radium-226, and the radon will escape unless something is done to stop it. The emission of radon gas is greatly decreased if the tailings are covered by soil and rock, but the covering has to stay intact for a long time because radium-226 is derived from thorium-230 which has a half life of about 80,000 years. Many estimates have been made of the risk to the public arising from the sites of tailing deposition, but there is an enormous range of uncertainty. If the tailings are covered, the radon emission is about the same as normally occurs from the ground (uranium mining does not *create* radioactivity: it was there in the ground already) and therefore the extra risk to the public is effectively zero. If the tailings are left uncovered the maximum risk may be in the order of one fatal cancer for each ten years of operation of a big power station, but this is essentially an educated guess based on estimates of how well the tailings are to be managed in years to come. Who can guarantee they will not be disturbed during the next 80,000 years?

Once the fuels have been extracted, an interim phase is entered during which they are prepared for the generation of electricity and transported to the generating site. Coal requires a great deal of transportation, but needs little preparation. Crude oil needs some preparation, but its transport needs are small in comparison with coal. Nuclear fuel does need a lot of preparation and some transport is involved, but the only significant risks are in reprocessing activities. The risks of railway crashes, as we have already seen, are really quite low, but nevertheless, the rail transport of several millions of tons of coal each year does pose some risk to rail workers and to the public.

The routine movement of oil and gas poses little or no risk to operators or the public. The presence and movement of oil and petrol tankers on the road represents some risk to the public, representing perhaps the deaths of 12 people a year in Britain, mostly the occupants of cars in collisions with the tankers.

111

Once uranium has been imported into Britain it is purified and converted to a form appropriate for the type of nuclear reactor. After use, the spent fuel is sent to British Nuclear Fuels Limited (BNFL) at Sellafield for reprocessing. As in the case of uranium miners, workers involved in the manufacture and reprocessing of nuclear fuel are exposed to a limited amount of radiation, and may therefore develop diseases induced by it.

The operation of power stations

Turning now to the actual generation of electricity through the three main sources of fuel, we find that during the 1970s far more fatal accidents occurred at coal-powered stations than oil or nuclear stations. Coal, however, also produced a great deal more power. The actual number of deaths which occurred in coal stations from 1969-70 to 1978-79 was 32, and analysis of the normal fluctuations in number which can occur through chance gives a possible range of about 22 to 45 deaths for such a period. In nuclear stations, two people were killed during this same period (neither from radiation) and one in an oil-powered station.

During the normal operation of all three types of power station, there is some risk, not only from operational accidents but also from radioactive and non-radioactive emissions. Because these may cause delayed illness among workers and public, and because they affect a very wide section of the population that has nothing to do with the operation of the power station and may live hundreds of miles away, these emissions represent the aspect of risk in *normal* power generation (as opposed to accidents) which is perhaps of the most widespread public concern.

Turning first to the burning of coal for the generation of power, the main risk to the public arises from the pollution of air by its combustion products. At its worst, in the first half of the 20th Century, pollution was one of the biggest single killers of all. In the major industrial centres of Britain, mass deaths of epidemic size occurred when the smoke was mixed with fog to cause the notorious ''smogs''. In the London smog of December 1952, 3,500 to 4,000 deaths were estimated to have occurred as a direct result of it, and yet the entire episode lasted no more than some five days. The main culprit in the case of the smogs of the fifties, sixties and seventies was, of course, the open coal fire rather than the electricity generating station and there has been a vast improvement in recent years following the introduction of the Clean Air Act as a result of the 1952 London catastrophe. The more polluting coal-fired power stations have gradually been closed down, and newer stations burn the coal more efficiently and release the emissions at much higher altitude.

The emissions from coal-powered stations of principal concern, apart from the particles which make smoke, are the oxides of sulphur, nitrogen and carbon. Sulphur dioxide is the most injurious of these. It is a gas and does not appear to be harmful in low concentrations, being made harmless by conversion to sulphate in the lungs. When combined with smoke particles, however, tiny globules of sulphuric acid may cause local damage within the lungs before the body's own defensive mechanisms can have any useful effect.

This damage may cause an isolated episode of acute respiratory disease, or, as is more likely for people living in heavily polluted areas, a series of minor episodes which, in the long term, end up as the collection of symptoms we call chronic bronchitis.

In the case of chronic diseases it is exceedingly difficult to link them, with any certainty, to air pollution. Not only is the development of disease a very long term process, but people may move from area to area during the same period that the emissions themselves are changing. Further, personal factors such as cigarette smoking and occupational exposure to other potential toxins also interact with the risk of disease from pollution, and thus seriously upset the precision of any estimates. Simply put, places which are heavily polluted are, in virtually all parts of the world, relatively unpleasant places to live, and have higher death rates than cleaner and more pleasant places for all sorts of social and personal reasons, and these have nothing to do with the pollution itself. Nevertheless, research groups and review organizations such as the World Health Organization have concluded that there are increases in deaths from lung disease when smoke and sulphur dioxide levels rise above defined minimum levels. The rather cautious conclusion of the British Health and Safety Commission in 1978[3] was that ''the small contribution due to the ground level concentration of pollutants from a large fossil fuelled power station may cause a few of the thousands of deaths occurring every year from all causes in the surrounding districts''. When it comes to actual numbers, the range of estimates is almost absurdly wide.

The pollutants emitted by coal-fired power stations include carcinogens although their influence is open to debate. They include chemicals such as benzo-a-pyrene, which causes cancer no matter how dilute it is. The only real certainty is that although chemical carcinogens emitted by coal-fired power stations do cause some cancers, the number is small and the risk very low. The ash remaining from the burning of coal also contains radioactive isotopes, and coal power stations emit radon gas. The risk of cancer arising from these sources of radioactivity is also small but again it does exist.

It is on the operation of nuclear power stations that public concern is currently focussed, rather than on their competitors. Part of the reason may be that nuclear power is associated in the public mind with nuclear bombs and the appalling devastation which results from their use. There is also the horror of the long term consequences of diseases such as cancer although, as we have seen, they can result from the operation of non-nuclear power stations as well. There is an extraordinary block in many people's thinking on this matter. A miners' union leader is reported to have said that he would support nuclear power when it could be guaranteed that not a single person would die as a consequence of it; this, from a man whose industry kills nearly a miner a week in Britain and has killed thousands of citizens in the last few decades.

Nuclear reactors, which are the "furnaces" of nuclear power stations, fall into two groups. The first group, called "thermal" reactors, includes practically all the reactors operating in Britain. They use uranium fuel embedded in a moderating material which slows the speed of the reaction. The second group of reactors uses highly enriched uranium mixed with some plutonium. During the process of reaction, more plutonium is produced and so these types are called "breeder" reactors, because in the long term enough new fuel is produced to generate more power.

In Britain, the series of nuclear power stations commissioned in the sixties were known as "Magnox" reactors because the uranium rods are sheathed in a magnesium alloy which is known by this name. The uranium rods in their magnox sheaths are mounted in blocks of graphite, and this whole assembly is placed in a reinforced steel or concrete container. Carbon dioxide gas is pumped through the reactor container, heated by the reaction, and the hot gas is used to boil water, which then drives the turbines that generate the electricity.

A second generation of gas cooled reactors uses uranium pellets inside tubes of stainless steel, so that the system can be run more efficiently at a higher temperature. These reactors are known as Advanced Gas Cooled Reactors (AGRs).

However, most of the world's nuclear power stations do not use reactors cooled by gas, but rather by water, and these are known as Pressurized Water Reactors (PWRs). Small and efficient versions of these were originally designed to propel submarines, and bigger versions now comprise the bulk of all reactors in the United States and France.

The radiation risk to workers in nuclear power stations arises from the beta and gamma radiation to which they are exposed. But epidemiological studies have so far failed to show an increase in cancer rates among workers in nuclear plants, and what concern does exist is based on conclusions from laboratory and animal experiments.

As far as the public is concerned, nuclear power stations allow very little radioactive material to escape, with any risk to the population also being based on theoretical extrapolations from other data. However, in Britain there is a special case and that is the processing plant at Sellafield, from which a much larger amount of radioactive material is emitted.

The most important hazard arising from the Sellafield plant is radioactivity from the liquid discharges which are piped out into the Irish Sea. Because of the attention these have received there are limits on the radioactivity permitted to be discharged, and these limits have been steadily reduced as a result of improvements in the systems by which the effluents are treated. The problem is that the discharges are concentrated by fish and shellfish which could subsequently be consumed by humans. Also, silt particles absorb radioactive elements and sink to the bottom, and may then move into inland waters and estuaries under the influence of the tides and currents. Another potential pathway of radioactivity back into the human body is a variety of edible seaweed which, until about 1974, was harvested in the area and used in a type of bread. There is little risk of this at present, however, as the seaweed is no longer used commercially for this purpose.

As the amount of radioactive material builds up in fish, the radiation dose to the public very much depends on how much fish individual people eat. Among fish and shellfish eaters the dose of radioactivity they have received as a result of effluents from Sellafield has not exceeded

about half the ICRP recommended limits (see Chapter 4) and is being reduced as a result of new control measures.

Because radioactivity is known to cause leukaemia, much natural concern has been aroused by the number of cases of this disease seen in children and young people in Seascale, a small town on the seaside just south of Sellafield. When identified, the number of cases appeared to be more than would "normally" be expected among that size of population, and to assess whether it was the close proximity of Sellafield which was causing extra cases of leukaemia was the task of an advisory group chaired by Sir Douglas Black[4]. The group asked the National Radiological Protection Board (NRPB) to calculate the dose of radioactivity likely to have been received by young people in Seascale since the 1950s, using data obtained from British Nuclear Fuels Limited (BNFL). BNFL were also asked to include all incidents leading to consequences off the site since Sellafield began operating in 1952. Given the amount of radioactivity it was thus calculated the children would have received from Sellafield, and taking into account that from natural sources, the Black group's conclusion in 1984 was that the radiation would not have been sufficient to cause the extra number of leukaemias seen. The actual number of cases of childhood leukaemia observed in the area was four, and the number of extra cases that it was calculated would occur from the radiation was 0.016, a

difference of some 250 times. The Black group conceded that the children could have received radioactivity from some other and undetected source, but this was regarded as extremely improbable.

However, after the Black group had reported, information came to light on releases of radioactivity from Sellafield in the fifties which had not previously been taken into account, although the NRPB subsequently calculated that the additional information resulted in only minor modifications of their estimates of dosages. Using this newly available information on emissions, the Committee on Medical Aspects of Radiation in the Environment (COMARE) recalculated the risk of leukaemia from the Sellafield discharges using the same methods as the Black Advisory Group[5]. Their calculations did show a risk of leukaemia which was fractionally above that estimated by the Black group, but still well short of explaining the extra cases of leukaemia observed at Seascale. The revelations about previously unknown incidents caused COMARE to stress, as Black had already done, that the possibility could not be excluded that other significant releases from the plant could have occurred but not have been detected during a period when controls and monitoring were more rudimentary than they were by the late eighties. Further, the way in which the new data had come to light undermined confidence in the adequacy of the information available. If information is to play a useful role in the way man manages his environment in order to minimize risk and maximize health, then it is essential to ensure that adequate monitoring data are available; this is as important for factors such as radioactive emissions as it is for measuring the incidence of disease.

Discussion fostered by the Black and COMARE reports stimulated more studies of the epidemiology of childhood and adult cancer in the vicinity of nuclear installations, and sure enough there are "clusters" of cases of childhood cancer (more than predicted by radon distribution) to be found in the vicinity of other nuclear power stations. However, over the whole country there have been identified some 517 such clusters, far more than there are nuclear facilities, so there must be several (so far unidentified) causal factors. Because of the inadequacy of the data during the early days, it is likely that we shall never know whether there is any relationship between leukaemia in Seascale and radioactivity discharges from Sellafield. New research should

enable us, in the future, to determine whether there are other influences on childhood cancer rates. Among these, conceivably, are an especial sensitivity of the tissues of young people to radioactivity, some infective process, the use of insecticides and pesticides, and electromagnetic influences.

Disasters

So far we have been discussing what are nominally the "routine" operations of power stations, nuclear and otherwise. The case of Sellafield shows that even routine operations are associated with "incidents" causing discharges of radioactivity which cause great public alarm when they come to light, even if nuclear scientists conclude that their influence on health is negligible. When people discover that "incidents" are occurring without, it seems to them, causing a sufficient degree of technical and official concern, it is easy for them to pass to the second conclusion that major and potentially disastrous malfunctions ("accidents") are also to be expected as an inevitable consequence of the fact that the power stations are operating in the first place.

This conclusion, of course, is strengthened by the justifiable media and public attention paid to serious accidents such as those at Three Mile Island in the United States and Chernobyl in the Soviet Union. It follows that, in assessment of risk, it is not only the hazards of normal operation which require consideration, but also the risk of major malfunction.

We have made the point on several occasions in this book that when energy is generated and stored, its sudden release may cause great harm if that happens in an unexpected manner, and that management of human behaviour and the environment will probably both be necessary to prevent this harm. The point has also been made that in the real world, it cannot ever be said that something is impossible. A system run by humans cannot be truly foolproof if the fool can manage to conceive of the inconceivable. At Chernobyl, operators quite deliberately inactivated a series of safety features and unwittingly drove the reactor into a situation where a disaster was inevitable.

Among the disasters which are most feared are those that have never happened, and this is a cross with which the nuclear industry, in particular, is heavily burdened. It is the one industry which cannot learn from its mistakes, the serious ones anyway. Other power producing industries have had their share of awful disasters, quite apart from the insidious effects of the air pollution which is known to have killed many thousands of people. Partly because of the publicity that such catastrophic events, quite understandably, generate, very rare incidents which cause the death of a large number of people are responsible for much more fear than much commoner incidents which kill fewer people at one time. A risk of one in a hundred will be perceived very differently if, on the one hand, it results in the death of a hundred people in a mass, but at an interval of a hundred years, and on the other hand results in the killing of one person a year for a hundred years. (This is a point to which we shall return in a later chapter.) And, again, the deaths may be grouped in a way which causes special distress, such as those that occurred as a result of the terrible movement of coal mining wastes during a rain storm at Aberfan in South Wales, which engulfed a school and killed 144 people, most of whom were children of the village. In this case, from the point of view of a very wide section of the population, the outcome was worse than if the 144 deaths had been spread evenly through the whole country. For this reason it is entirely justifiable that extra attention is turned to the reduction of the usually already low risk of the high consequence event, but even then the line has to be drawn somewhere. The aim is to determine just how unlikely an event is, and how disastrous its consequences. The conclusions will determine the resources needed to reduce the likelihood—the risk—to an acceptable level. It is not *impossible* that the wing will fall off a Concorde nine miles high over the North Atlantic, but it is *very* unlikely.

Dams store huge amounts of water for the production of hydroelectric power. Many dams have failed over the years with heavy loss of life, and once again we return to the paradox that public familiarity with these failures reduces fear of them in comparison with the fear of failures in other systems which have never happened. The biggest death toll ever to have occurred as a result of power generation followed the failure of the Gujarat Dam in India in 1979, which killed about 15,000 people. Since 1930 over 100 dams have failed in the USA, although only ll of these were producing electricity. These failures killed about 355 people during the early seventies[1].

A group at the University of California has estimated that up to 250,000 deaths could result from catastrophic failure of the largest of the dams in that State[6]. Historically, large dams have failed at a rate of about one in 5,000 per year, with the risk for some dams being as high as one in 100 per year.

All the major sources of energy used for the production of power in Britain have some risk of causing a major disaster. In the case of coal, the best known actual example is that already cited at Aberfan, but overall, the risk was then, and is now, very small. It is possible to conceive of a massive crash involving a coal-carrying railway train, but in practice most of the accidental deaths associated with the production of power from coal occur among those involved in its extraction from the earth.

The best known disasters associated with the use of oil as an energy source have been those resulting from the wrecking of ships such as the Torrey Canyon, which are carrying enormous quantities of crude oil. Huge quantities of oil and its refinement products are stored at oil refineries, and there is the potential for large loss of life in the event of fire because of the number of people that live nearby. For an average size refinery, one estimate is that there is a one in 91,000 chance of an incident causing up to 1,500 deaths, and a one in 2.5 million chance of an incident causing up to 18,000 deaths[7]. In 1982 an explosion at an oil fired power station in Venezuela killed at least 98 people.

In the case of gas, most accidents are minor ones. In domestic installations liquefied gas is stored in large terminals and when storage tanks split or explode, large numbers of people can be killed, as has happened several times in the United States and Europe. Perhaps the worst such incident was the explosion in an LPG storage depot in Mexico City in 1984, which killed at least 500 people. In Britain, the largest storage centre is on Canvey Island, and because the risks are well recognized they have been the subject of a very comprehensive study and report[8]. The quantitative estimate of the study was that there is about 1 in 100 per year chance of an accident killing ten people and a chance of about 1 in 5,000 of an accident killing 10,000 people. The same report identified several measures which could and should be taken to further reduce the risk of major accidents occurring. In actual practice, although it is to be devoutly hoped that the figures are never actually available, the number of people killed in a given incident is likely to end up less than estimated by such forecasts. All the oil- and gas-related acidents which have so far occurred in the world *could* have killed more people in the worst conceivable case, but did not, and the risks to society of Canvey Island are likely in practice to be over-estimated[2].

As is the case for other sources of power, the risk exists that an accident in a nuclear power station could cause death and disease among the population. As for other industrial activities, reactors are designed to take account of the risk of failure and the risk to the population of radiation (as defined by bodies such as the ICRP). Fortunately, disastrous failures of nuclear power stations are so rare that estimates generally remain just that, as estimates, and risks to the population are based on perhaps inappropriate data such as those obtained from study of the survivors of Hiroshima and Nagasaki. Major accidents are so improbable that at any rate until the accident at Chernobyl in April 1986 technical people have regarded the risk of their occurring as insignificant. After Chernobyl, there is virtually no-one in the industry or among the public who believes that the risk of a nuclear accident, however low, is "insignificant", and Chernobyl has thus caused a complete reassessment of the principles and practice of risk assessment and management in the nuclear industry.

What happened at Chernobyl was the subject of a conference in Vienna and detailed review under the auspices of the International Atomic Energy Agency[9]. The power at one of the nuclear reactors was deliberately run down in order to do a test on one of the turbine electricity generators. Soviet reactors (unlike those used elsewhere in the world) have the characteristic of instability at very low power levels, and safety systems are built in to prevent the reactor reaching a dangerous state. But the operators deliberately switched off the safety devices in order to perform the test; the cooling water in the reactors boiled, the power shot up at an uncontrollable rate, and by the time the operators pressed the panic button it was too late. The resulting explosion disrupted the reactor and blew the containment building wide open.

A heroic team of firefighters, many of whom died from acute radiation sickness, extinguished the flames from the burning building, but the graphite core of the reactor continued to burn, with radioactivity escaping at an undiminished rate. By the end of 1986 over 30 people had died as a result of the accident, with a further 200 receiving medical care. Estimates of the radiation released indicate that the accident was about 100 times worse than the fire at the Windscale plutonium plant in the UK in 1957, and 1,000 times worse than Three Mile Island in the United States in 1977.

About 135,000 people were evacuated from the area of the plant in the following few days, and land within a radius of 30 kilometres (19 miles) was closed to habitation indefinitely. Among those in and around the plant, 203 received doses of over 4 sieverts (400 rems) an exposure which as a general rule will kill 50% within 60 days.

The hot flames lofted smoke over the Soviet Union and Europe, and where it then rained, radioactive dust was washed from the skies to the ground from when it entered the food chain and could remain for 70 years.

Estimates on deaths occurring as the long-term effect of the radiation from Chernobyl vary widely, because of doubts on the validity of the ICRP figure of 100–125 deaths per 10 mSv per million people especially where low dosages are concerned. Calculations based on ICRP estimates lead to a forecast of the number of extra cancer deaths in western Europe arising from the accident of just under 1,000, with 35 or so of these occurring in the UK. For eastern Europe, the estimates were about 1,250 extra cancer deaths, and within the western Soviet Union about 7,500 extra fatal cancers could occur during the next 50 years.

The worst accident ever to have occurred at a nuclear power station was at Chernobyl, in the Soviet Union, in 1986. The reactor overheated and exploded because operators disobeyed safety rules, over-rode automatic safety interlocks, and deliberately but unwittingly drove the reactor into an unstable condition. The lessons have been learnt world-wide and the risk of humans intervening in a hazardous manner reduced to as near zero as possible. The radioactive fallout from Chernobyl in Britain added to natural background radiation by about 3%, reducing later.

However, the extra deaths are a minute addition to the total number of cancer deaths which will occur in the next 50 years. In the UK, for example, where about 140,000 people die from cancer each year (7 million in 50 years), the extra 35 deaths should be compared with the normal annual *fluctuation* of cancer deaths of about 6,000.

Throughout Europe the dose of radiation from Chernobyl was less than 20% of the normal background dose. In southern England the dose was equivalent to what a passenger would receive in a jet plane flying to the Costa del Sol and back. The total extra dose to an individual over the whole 50-year period would be equivalent to a resident of East Anglia (low background radiation) taking a three-week holiday in Cornwall (high background radiation). The limit on radioactivity placed on sheep and lamb meat after Chernobyl was lower than the normal radioactivity of many foods routinely on supermarket shelves, such as instant coffee.

To present such comparisons is not to imply that the Chernobyl accident was of no concern. It was a shocking and very severe disruption of the plant, the most severe nuclear accident ever. But the risks it imposed to health should be kept in perspective, nevertheless.

Could such an accident happen elsewhere? For gas cooled reactors such as the Magnox and AGR types which are used in Britain, the most serious kind of accident is a failure of the cooling circuit. As in all types of reactor, a number of automatic shut-down devices come into action as the temperature rises. An important feature of these reactors is that they can survive sudden and complete loss of pressure in the cooling system, and the most probable outcome of accidental depressurization of a Magnox reactor is that no release of radioactive compounds would occur. In the case of AGRs, even in the case of sudden loss of pressure in the cooling system, the temperature of the fuel would be unlikely to exceed the melting point of the stainless steel in which it is contained. Again, it should be stressed that the fortunate fact is that experience with such accidents is so small that estimates of risk are necessarily rather vague.

In the United States, several studies (and one of enormous scope) have been mounted to define the risk of major accidents, concentrating on the pressurized water reactors (PWRs) which are commonly used in that country. The best known accident actually to have occurred was that at Three Mile Island. What actually happened there was that the main cooling water system failed;

an auxiliary system should have taken over automatically, but did not do so because a number of valves had been left closed after a test of the system shortly beforehand.

From sampling of the water and the air in the area after the accident, it was estimated that the dose to the thyroid gland from radioactive iodine in drinking water was less than 0.002 mSv, and in the air the dose to anyone at the site boundary was estimated to be less than 0.5 mSv over a five-day period. Three workers in the building received dosages between 30 and 40 mSv and 12 other workers received lower doses.

The most pessimistic prediction from a member of the US Nuclear Regulatory Commission is that there is in the order of a 10–50% risk of a core meltdown accident at one of the 100 American plants now in operation over the next 20 years, a risk which could be reduced to "acceptable" levels by spending an average of $50 million on each plant. However, the actual experience (fortunately) of severe accidents at nuclear power plants is so limited that forecasts can only be educated guesses.

In all reactors, risk is managed by building a large number of automatic and humanly controlled operations into the system, a combination of all of which have to go wrong before an incident can occur. The more of these safety features there are, the more "minor" incidents will be measured but the more the risk of major incidents is reduced. Unfortunately, the public perception is generally just the opposite, leading to the belief that the more minor incidents that occur, the more the likelihood of a major accident; further, that the need for all these safety devices simply goes to show how dangerous the whole business is. The only way to overcome this problem is through an open discussion of risks, with full disclosure of information on them as well as on benefits.

What Chernobyl did show was that for reasons which may never be fully clear, a group of well-trained people deliberately embarked on the precise blend of indiscretions that would make an apparently safe reactor blow up. It is this fact, perhaps above all else, which focusses on the need for automatic shut-down devices which are beyond, at least for a period, human control.

Non-conventional sources of energy

Because of widespread public fears of the risk of nuclear energy and the fact that non-renewable sources of fossil fuel will inevitably dwindle, an increasing amount of attention and scientific research is now being brought to bear on what are, at present, regarded as "non-conventional" sources of energy. These sources include energy produced by the force of the waves and the wind, energy from the sun, and energy from the processing of renewable organic sources such as trees and plants (biomass).

In even quite serious discussion of such sources of energy, it is often taken for granted that they are virtually free of risk. Is this so?

Rather few detailed studies have in fact been performed in order to examine this question in any great detail. It is important to realize that, as for the case when comparing conventional sources of energy with each other, the entire fuel cycle has to be taken into account. Wave generators have to be constructed from steel and concrete, which is exactly the same stuff that is used in other power stations. The copper which is used for piping has to be mined by the same men, whether the piping is to be used for conducting solar-heated water or nuclear-heated water. When such considerations are taken into account, the differences in risk between non-conventional and conventional sources of energy are probably less than most people realize.

Solar energy is rather fierce in comparison with man's puny efforts. The power density of solar radiation intercepted by the earth works out at about 170,000,000,000 megawatts.

This energy can be used to produce electricity directly or to heat water. "Photovoltaic" cells are already widely used for generating small amounts of electricity, the example which is perhaps the most commonly seen being the small cells which are used to power pocket electronic calculators. Larger units are used to maintain the charge of low-voltage batteries in houses and boats, and many maritime navigation aids are powered in this way. Assemblies of solar photovoltaic cells provide power for the scores of satellites now circling the globe.

These trouble-free systems are very useful for the production of low voltage electricity, but when it comes to the generation of electricity in power station quantities, difficulties arise. One problem is that of area. In Britain, where sunlight is not what might be regarded as a totally reliable source of power, about 50 to 80 square kilometres (20 to 30 square miles) of solar panel would be needed to produce as much electricity as one modern power station. Because most of the power is produced at a time when there are the lowest demands on it, storage and backup systems will be needed to even out the load. In

Solar energy can contribute usefully to heating and lighting, and can be used to produce electrical power directly. Its main risks lie in the need to provide storage for backup power through for example batteries or conventional generators.

sunnier parts of the world open areas are more likely to be available for establishment of the arrays of solar panels, and cleaning and general maintenance are less likely to be a problem. The cost of solar cells, however, is still very high.

In Britain, sunlight is more effectively used for the direct heating of hot water systems in individual houses, and in countries such as Israel virtually every house and block of flats has a solar water heater on the roof. In making valid risk comparisons the total energy generated by all these individual little systems should be equated with the equivalent amount of energy produced by one centralized water heating system, so that, for example, it would take many thousands of rooftop heaters to produce as much hot water as one power station. For the installation of each rooftop heater several man-hours will have to be spent by installation technicians on the roof, which is not an industrial activity totally free of risk. Further, to the extent that the use of solar systems generates the need for non-solar backup systems, then the risk of construction, operation, maintenance and distribution of power from these backup systems is part of the risk of the solar energy; indeed, to risk analysts, backup systems comprise a high proportion of the total risk from large-scale solar power systems. It follows that the risk posed by a single solar power station will depend a great deal on the amount of backup power that is required and the way that power is generated. To take a very simple example to illustrate the point, a photovoltaic panel which is used to run some electronic equipment on a boat (or a few lights in a house in the Australian outback) needs storage batteries for backup and storage of power, and lead-acid batteries are quite hazardous objects. They are heavy and injurious if dropped, the acid causes burns, the vapour produced during charging can be toxic and is explosive under the right conditions. All these factors contribute to the risk of producing a little electrical power from a solar panel.

Ocean water can be used to produce huge amounts of power through the movement of the tides and the motion of the waves. Tidal barriers are much like dams through which the water passes and turns turbine generators and construction of tidal barriers has much the same degree of risk as the construction of dams to be used to generate hydroelectric power. However, there is a great deal less risk to the public if the construction fails in a disastrous manner. Once operating, the risks posed by tidal systems are quite low in terms of occupational and public health, but the ecological effects are less easy to predict.

Energy from waves requires the construction of wave-powered generators, which will work better in those parts of the world where the weather is generally rather ferocious and will be most efficient of all out at sea. These systems, therefore, pose a high risk during construction and maintenance. A large number of generators are required to produce power by power-station standards, with studies showing an expected long term average power of 48 kW per metre of wave front at distances of 100 km or more offshore.

Energy from the wind is already being used widely throughout the world, and could become a major contribution to energy supplies in Britain. Windmills and windpumps, of course, have been common sights in Europe for centuries, although in England the old ones are now more commonly

seen in the form of bijou residences. Wind machines need to be built in reliably windy places, and if they are to survive a reasonable lifetime, they have to be able to withstand violent storms. Even in windy places the wind does not blow all the time, and backup systems are inevitably required. In the United States, arrays of windmills are now producing substantial amounts of power. Denmark is already producing much power in this way, and Holland is also moving to construct windmill parks. In Britain windmills are being used in projects in Fair Isle and Orkney. As in the case of solar panels, one of the problems is the sheer area that is needed to produce power by power station standards. To replace just one high-output power station with an array of windmills would require about a thousand of them, spread over an area

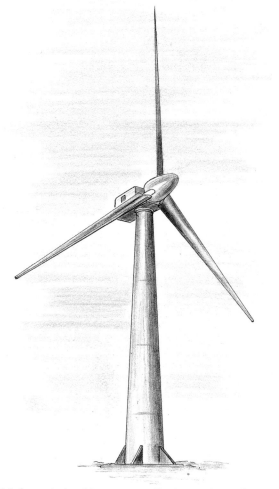

Modern wind turbines are contributing to electrical power to a growing extent. They are needed in large numbers to compete with conventional sources of power, and pose risks in construction and maintenance.

about the size of a small county. Building the wind-generating systems offshore would reduce the need for land space, but would much increase the risk of construction and maintenance.

The conversion of biomass to energy includes the direct production of heat from burning, the production of gas from fermentation, and the production of alcohol (methanol) and charcoal to be used as fuel. The growing, harvesting and processing of special crops poses the risks of agriculture, and a substantial practical problem in the real world is that, although the plants are *supposed* to be renewed, in places where they are actually being used in this way, that is not being done.

Finally, among the more popular non-conventional sources of energy is geothermal power, produced by drilling into the ground where large volumes of water can be naturally heated not too far below the surface. Such systems are operating in several countries throughout the world, but all of them added together now hardly total the output of one large power station. In the future, geothermal power could well comprise a large proportion of the energy produced throughout the world, with risks similar to those involved in drilling for oil and the production of power from that source.

Comparative risks in electricity generation

The UK Atomic Energy Authority requested the Energy Centre in the University of Newcastle upon Tyne to compare the risks from the principal electricity generating systems in the UK, and the resulting report is not only a mine of information but also a major contribution to the field of risk assessment[2]. The author, R A D Ferguson, goes to great pains to stress the width of the range of estimates presented, and the limitations and uncertainties of the data (a constant source of frustration in risk analysis, as will now be clear to the reader of this book).

Nevertheless, the overall conclusion of this report is that all three fuel cycles considered (coal, oil and nuclear) are generally associated with low risk estimates, taking into account the amount of electricity now required by British consumers and industry. The overlap of uncertainties in risk was such that it was not possible to state whether any one of the three was safer than any other.

Several studies have been conducted in the United States, and Ferguson compares his findings with them. Taking into account differences between the studies, the ranges of risk estimated by all the groups generally span the same consensus of opinion.

Only one of these studies attempted to compare the risk to human health from the production of power from conventional and non-conventional sources[10]. The author's main conclusion was that the risk from non-conventional sources can be as high as, or even higher than, that from conventional sources. However, this particular piece of analysis has not only received a great deal of publicity, it has also been subject to great criticism. His main critic pointed out that much information that was needed for proper risk analysis did not yet exist (a common problem) and recalculated the results taking into account what he saw as being the largest errors[11]. The effect of such recalculation was to smooth the differences between risks of the various sorts of power generation, so that, for example, the upper limit of nuclear risks to workers and the public moved into the range for coal and oil, and the health risks of non-conventional sources dropped into the middle of the range of uncertainty for nuclear risks. In other words, after the analyses were done as carefully as present data permit (and given that the door is still wide open to more information), for the fuel cycle as a whole there is not a huge difference in risk between any one type of power generation and another.

From the information now available, therefore, it does not appear that the risk to personal health and welfare inherent in the generation of power, already low by the standards of other risks, can be reduced to any real extent by switching from one kind of generation to another. If society truly demands a lower level of risk, it will have to put up with (or accommodate to) a lesser total amount of electrical power. In the future, policy choices may well be affected by *perceived* risk, which often has little or no relationship to the types of analysis outlined above, or by consensus on potentially catastrophic effects on the environment which could become more powerful as time goes by — promotion of the "greenhouse effect" by the carbon dioxide produced by burning coal, for example.

Chapter Eleven

Risks of Medicine and Surgery

Virtually everybody who seeks medical attention knows that treatment cannot come free of risk. Indeed, no progress in medicine or surgery would be possible at all if no patients were prepared to accept any risk. Everyone who waits for his prescription to be filled at a chemist realizes that the medicines he is about to receive may have effects undesired by both himself and the prescribing doctor. Naturally, all those involved do hope and believe that the benefits of the drug will be enough to overwhelm the risks involved in taking it. Similarly, to undergo a surgical operation is a matter for universal concern if not outright fear, simply because it is perceived as a procedure which *does* carry some risk. And again, it is presumed by surgeon and patient alike that, overall, the benefits of the procedure will outweigh this risk. As we shall see, although new techniques offer new risks, the general tendency is for medical and surgical procedures to be of lower risk as time goes by.

The question is, do we—that is the doctors as well as the patients—truly understand what *are* the risks of medicine and surgery?

The first problem is that it is very hard for an individual doctor to assess risk with any accuracy. This, surprisingly, is because he sees far too few patients. Let us assume, as a working figure, that a doctor sees about 20 patients during a working day, or in the order of 5,000 in a year. Let us also make the unlikely assumption that the patients are all of the same age and sex, that they all have the same disease and that the doctor treats them all in the same way. Now, let us assume that his treatment carries the risk that one in 1,000 patients will suffer adversely from it. This means that during the whole year he is likely to see only five patients, less than one every other month, who have suffered the adverse effect. If he has an excellent memory and record system, the doctor might just be able to identify this effect through personal observation. But if it occurs less often than this, he is very unlikely to do so. Yet this level of risk of an adverse effect is well within the range that would cause a drug to be banned. In practice, the doctor's capacity for recognizing the risk of an adverse effect is far more limited even than this, because his patients are so different one from the other and in their individual reaction to treatment.

Because the individual observations of a doctor are probably unreliable, special investigations are needed for particular drugs and particular procedures in order more precisely to identify the risks associated with them. As it happens, with the exception of the introduction of new drugs, this is a concept which is really rather new. Surprisingly few surgical procedures, for example, have been validated for their effectiveness, either in absolute terms or by comparing alternatives for the treatment of a given disease. To an increasing extent, however, research is being applied in such a way that the outcome of treatment can be properly assessed. This sort of research includes the study of individual patients and comparing what happens to them with the outcome among other patients, who have received different treatment or none at all. Other techniques include the retrospective study of patients who were treated in different ways in the past, and concurrent monitoring of the use of medicines in order to assess their success and their risks of adverse effect. The trouble is that such research cannot give easy or quick answers, because it is so often the case that a considerable time elapses between the event causing harm and the onset of the disease or disability. As in the case of occupational exposures to radiation and harmful chemicals, so often the risk is not of immediate death but rather of delayed disease, so that death rates may well be an inappropriate measure of risk.

Risks of surgery

As to what the actual risks are, and turning first to surgery, a general downward trend in risk has been demonstrated over the years for many procedures. Most surgical operations involve the use of anaesthetic, and indeed for many procedures the risk of the anaesthetic is more significant than that of the procedure itself. However, the risk of receiving an anaesthetic has fallen dramatically over recent years from over 600 deaths per million operations (just under 1 in 1,500) in 1950 down to around 40 per million in 1970 (about one death in 25,000 operations)[1].

There have been similarly rapid reductions in the risk of child birth and induced legal abortions[2]. In the last three decades, the number of deaths among mothers per million maternities has dropped from 500 (1 in 2,000) to below 100 (1 in 10,000). The risk of death associated with a legal abortion has fallen from about 1,200 per 10,000 abortions (about 1 in 8) in the mid-sixties down to around 40 to 50 per million (1 in 22,000) since the early 1970s. These two examples do demonstrate the value judgements involved in assessing ''benefit'' in medicine. The benefit of a life achieved through birth is to most people self-evident. To many, on the other hand, there is no conceivable benefit in abortion, and to them the risk/benefit equation is therefore always negative however low the risk is.

There are several instances in the history of medicine where procedures have been shown to carry more risk than their benefits have been found to warrant. A related matter is that there are great variations in surgical rates throughout the world. For example, a study in 1968 showed that the rate of gall bladder removal was five to seven times higher in Canada than in England and Wales and yet the death rate due to gall bladder disease in the elderly in Canada was double the British rate. The same study showed that although the rate of removal of breast and the surrounding tissue for cancer was 3.2 times greater than in Britain, there was essentially no difference in the death rate from the disease in the two countries[3].

Tonsillectomy was, during the early part of this century, an extremely popular surgical operation, and in Britain during the 1930s some 25 to 30% of all children had their tonsils removed by the age of 14. However, rather belated studies found that the death rate from tonsillectomy was unacceptably high and the popularity of the operation declined. It was then found that this decline was not associated with a rise in ear and throat infections. There are still large differences in tonsillectomy rates between various countries, but unfortunately the medical literature is still lacking in a definitive experiment involving random allocation of children to surgery and non-surgery in order, properly, to assess the benefit of the procedure. Over the years similar doubts have also been expressed for other widely-used operations such as appendicectomy and hysterectomy (removal of the womb).

Number of deaths attributed to anaesthetic and childbirth per million operations

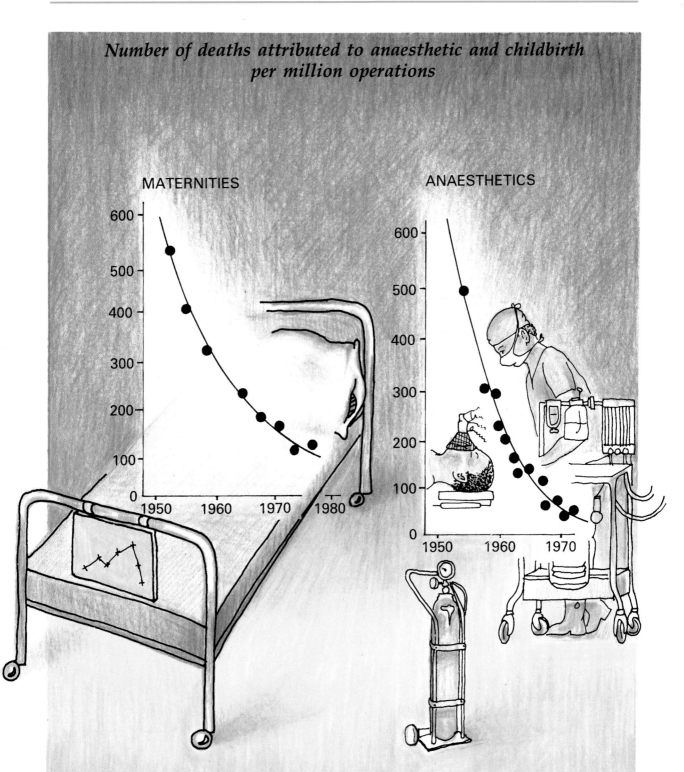

The risk of receiving an anaesthetic has fallen dramatically within the decades through the use of better techniques and high-technology equipment by anaesthetists and their assistants. The risk of giving birth has fallen equally dramatically, again demonstrating the lowering of risk which modern methods and technology can achieve—albeit at extra cost.
Sources: reference 1 and 2

Of course, the success and associated benefit of an operation depends very much on whether the diagnosis of disease was correct in the first place. Obviously there can be no benefit, and there will be some risk, for a patient who is operated on for a disease he does not have. Appendicitis is an example of a disease which has been studied for accuracy of diagnosis, and in one interesting survey it was found that the accuracy of diagnosis by doctors improved when they were being challenged to ''compete'' with computer-aided diagnosis[4]. Under normal circumstances, although the accuracy of the doctors' diagnosis was considerably better than would be achieved by pure chance (tossing a coin), several patients were nevertheless being operated on who were not subsequently found to have appendicitis. The surgeons in these cases were erring on the side of ''safety'' as they saw it, in that their belief was that the risk to the patient was less if he had the operation than if he did not, given that there was indeed a suspicion of appendicitis. But, as we have already pointed out, it is very difficult in practice for an individual doctor to assess the risk of a given procedure.

To generate mass data, the results of large numbers of operations are gathered by the ''Hospital In-Patient Enquiry'' (HIPE) and collated by the Office of Population Censuses and Surveys[5]. The assessment of risk of operation is the percentage of procedures which result in death. Overall, the risk of an operation increases substantially with age and indeed, for this reason, surgeons are reluctant to operate on individuals of over about 75 years.

For all operations taken together, HIPE figures show that there is a risk of death of about 1.6 per cent (1 in 60), a rate which is steadily declining overall. However there are, of course, enormous differences in risk between different operations as well as in the way risks are changing over the years. For example, brain operations carry a risk of death of about 1 in 10 and (given that the numbers are comparatively small and that, therefore, trends are difficult to detect) this rate does not appear to be altering much. In the case of heart and other chest operations, however, there has been a steady decrease in risk over recent years, from about one death in 20 operations to fewer than one in 30. Most ''routine'' operations such as those on tonsils and piles carry a very low risk, from near zero to about one death in 10,000 operations. For such procedures the risk can probably not be reduced

any further, with the remaining risk being essentially that of the anaesthetic, so that the accuracy of diagnosis and assessment of benefit are of paramount importance.

Percentage case fatality for selected operations, England and Wales

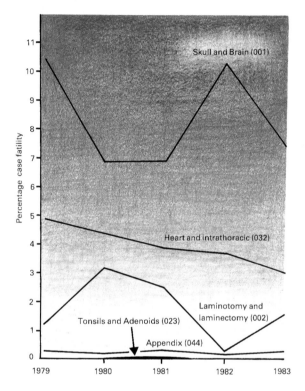

The risk of dying as a result of surgery is reducing steadily, and for some operations is close to no risk at all. Brain surgery is of higher risk, of course, but the benefits can be immense, often lifesaving.

When entirely new procedures are introduced for the treatment of common diseases, it is becoming relatively likely in these technological days that they will be tested for their risks and their benefits. An important example of this is the treatment of coronary heart disease, and specifically the use of coronary artery bypass surgery. In this procedure blocked arteries in the heart are bypassed by connecting short pieces of vein to either side of the obstructed section. During most of the operation the heart's functions are replaced by an external pump, which also provides the blood with new oxygen. This is a complex and costly procedure, but it is becoming very popular and as we have already commented the risk is reducing. The benefit, however, is rather less easy to assess. The aim of the coronary artery surgery is to reduce pain in the heart on exercise (angina) and to decrease the risk of another heart attack and thus to prolong life. As it happens, early hopes (and indeed claims without much scientific justification) turned out to be well justified by measured outcomes. Follow-up research showed that there was no doubt that the pain of angina was reduced partially or completely in the vast majority of patients and to a significantly greater extent than through the use of drugs. However, there was a less significant improvement in the general performance of the heart, in the prevention of further heart attacks or life expectancy[6]. So, what this operation does best, but at great expense and at substantial risk, is to reduce the pain of angina, so that this cost and risk have to be compared with the use of drugs which also usually help the pain but not so effectively.

In addition to the direct risks of a particular surgical procedure there are incidental risks of hospital treatment. The hospital environment fosters the growth of a wide range of infectious organisms, many of which are uncommon elsewhere[7]. The overall risk of hospital admissions for surgery thus depends on the level of infection in a particular hospital as well as the procedure undertaken.

Health system managers would like to be able to reduce risk assessments to numbers for the purpose of maximizing "efficiency" and minimizing unnecessary drain on limited resources, but in practice when such complicated issues are concerned the decisions will probably boil down to an individual choice of action based in each case on what the doctor and the patient feel about it all.

Thoroughly scientific and reliable research can take a long time. Studies which have confirmed that coronary bypass surgery can improve the life of patients with coronary heart disease needed some ten years of bypass surgery in order to generate numbers which were consistent enough in terms of the type of patient and the specific procedure undertaken. Now and in the future, decisions on the use of new and increasingly technological techniques in surgery will have to be based on assessments of risk and benefit, but these do have an inevitable time lag. Even now, to continue with this specific example, ever more sophisticated ways of treating diseased coronary arteries are evolving, so that a whole set of new questions are being posed and controversy continues to be inevitable.

Risks of medicines

The other important group of risks in the treatment of disease are those arising from the use of therapeutic drugs. While most patients will probably accept that the use of medicine must carry some risk, very few (and indeed, not all doctors) realize that until the last 40 or so years, they did not offer much in the way of benefits either.

Public interest in the potential risks in drug use was sharply awakened not long after a new medicine was introduced in Germany in 1956, one which quickly became the most popular sleeping pill in Europe. It then resulted in the only true "disaster" ever to follow the use of a prescribed drug. By 1961 more than 8,000 deformed children had been born to mothers who had taken the drug, the name of which, thalidomide, is now more evocative of the potential dangers of medicine than probably any other single word. It so happened that at about this time the procedure for government approval of new drugs in the United States was very slow, indeed to an extent which was much criticized. For this reason, approval for the use of thalidomide in the States was not obtained during the period it was widely used in Europe, so by the time its awful side effect was identified the US authorities were able to prevent its ever being on sale in that country.

Regulatory authorities all over the world learnt from this that they would receive no credit for speedy approval of a drug which promised substantial benefits but about which people knew nothing, and on the other hand that they risked nothing by delaying the introduction of a new medicine and thus withholding it from those who could benefit. The non-use of a medicine which could save lives is in practical terms equivalent to the use of an ineffective medicine which has death as an adverse side effect. It follows that unnecessary delay in approval of effective new drugs, or to prevent them ever becoming available in the absence of alternatives, costs lives. Yet several drugs have been kept off the market, or banned, on very questionable evidence.

No one disagrees with the proposition that the risks of a new medicine as well as its benefits should be assessed as thoroughly as possible before it is introduced for general prescription. Accordingly, the chemicals used in the drug are assessed in the laboratory and in animals for toxic effects, and first used cautiously in volunteers to study the ways that they are distributed throughout the body and metabolized. Careful trials are first employed among small groups of patients, and comparisons made with similar patients treated differently. As confidence builds, the number of patients in experimental ("clinical") trials (see Chapter 3) is gradually increased.

But, as we have had to stress time and again, a problem arises with the size of the numbers. At present only a relatively small number of patients (up to about 2,000) are exposed to a new drug before permission is given for its release to the market. (In Britain, approval is given by the DHSS on the advice of the expert Committee on Safety of Medicines.) But among this number of patients an "adverse" effect has to be really rather common in order to show up in the statistics, especially as many adverse effects are quite frequently encountered on their own (headache and diarrhoea are two of the many possible examples). If the *spontaneous* incidence of such an effect is one in a hundred, and the risk of the new drug *inducing* it is also one in a hundred, then 2,000 is the minimum number of patients that will have to be exposed to the new drug to detect the adverse effect. If the incidence of the adverse effect is one in 500 but still occurs normally in one in 100 patients then nearly 36,000 patients will have to be exposed to the drug before that adverse effect can be detected[8]. If the incidence of the adverse effect is really rare, then however severe it is, hundreds of thousands or even millions of people will have to be exposed to the drug before its risk can be assessed. The use of a medicine in such numbers could never be termed "experimental" even if its administration was undertaken in a deliberately experimental manner. Thus the existing clinical trial and approval system simply cannot, for mathematical and practical reasons, detect very rare adverse effects of new drugs. That drugs which have been approved do occasionally turn out, after some years of use, to have hitherto unidentified but serious adverse effects, is inevitable if new drugs are ever to be introduced to the market. It is absurd to cast blame and scorn on the manufacturers and authorities responsible

for drug approval under these circumstances.

A curious paradox is that the more effective, and thus popular, a drug is, the more likely it is that pressures will grow for its banning on the basis of a rare side effect. Say, for example, that the adverse effect represents a risk of one in 100,000 of dying (about 10 times the average risk for all drugs put together). If only a few hundred patients are (successfully) treated, this low risk effect is never likely to be measurable. But if two million patients are treated each year, there will be 20 deaths a year as a result, making a good case for shock–horror treatment in the media. Risk information is totally useless unless account is taken of the size of the population exposed to it and the time span involved.

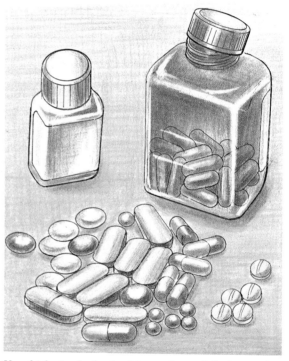

Very high standards of safety are demanded of prescribed drugs. The risks of medicine are discussed much more than the risks of other forms of medical treatment. Medicines which are popular because they are effective may have rare but serious adverse effects which are highlighted in the media, so that the focus is on their small risk rather than on their large benefit. Some risks are so low they cannot be identified by experimentation and can only show up after many thousands of patients have received the medicines. Herbal and other "alternative" medicines are not free of risk, but are not assessed either by laboratory experimentation or after introduction to the market.

The problem of the detection of rare events is, of course, widely recognized by governments and medical scientists, and most countries in the developed world have set up systems for the reporting by doctors of adverse effects occurring in association with the use of new drugs. This system is not free from serious deficiencies. First, notification of adverse effects is voluntary. This means that it tends to be only the most enthusiastic doctors that report them. Also, once an adverse effect is identified, the attention of other doctors will be drawn to it, and subsequent reporting may be at a level which attaches to the adverse effect a significance which is not justified. In other words, voluntary reporting may be a poor indicator of the true risk posed by a new drug.

While biased reporting may disproportionately emphasize problems with particular drugs, in general a voluntary system is likely to suffer from under-reporting overall. Most doctors never report any adverse reactions and, in any event, the relationship of the medicine to the unwanted reaction may well not be one of cause and effect. To compound the difficulty, the fact that a medicine is prescribed does not mean, unfortunately, that it will be taken by the patient exactly as intended.

Nevertheless, despite these deficiencies (and in full knowledge of them) statistical information is published on adverse reactions to drugs, based on the voluntary reporting system.

In 1982 there were 14,701 reports of adverse drug reactions, of which 9.4% were defined as "serious" and 2.3% as fatal[9]. Over the last 20 years or so, the total number of deaths reported has about doubled, but halved as a proportion of all reports submitted. The total number of "serious" reactions has increased slightly over the period, but also declined as a proportion of all reports. In 1965 there were 0.61 deaths reported for every million prescriptions (1 in over 1.5 million) a figure which has fluctuated over the years up to 0.89 per million (one in 1.12 million) in 1982, but during these years the overall reported risk has only once exceeded one in a million. (It so happens that the risk of dying as a result of vaccination is also about one in a million.)

Obviously some medicines carry an inherently higher risk than others, and may be used for the treatment of more serious disease and thus associated with a higher risk of fatal adverse reactions. When medicines are newly introduced, there tends to be a relatively high number of adverse reports per million prescriptions, a figure which quite rapidly reduces as doctors become more accustomed to using the drug. The rate of adverse reports per million prescriptions tends to stay at about the same level over the years for well-established medicines. The proportion of all adverse effects varies between various categories of medicine, but this is as much a representation of the popularity of the drug as it is its relative risk. For example, the group among which most reactions are reported is comprised of aspirin and other anti-inflammatory drugs used for the treatment of arthritis, but they are extremely widely employed.

The balance of risk and benefit of a particular drug cannot be divorced from the circumstances in which it is used. In some cases drugs used to suppress symptoms may mask the features of a disease, making correct diagnosis and treatment harder. For this reason, indiscriminate use of drugs would be inadvisable even if there were no risk of adverse effect.

An important method for the surveillance of new drugs was recently developed in Britain by Professor William Inman at the University of Southampton. Copies of prescriptions for whatever drug is currently being studied are obtained from the office in the Health Department which is responsible for paying for it, and sent to the Prescription Event Monitoring (PEM) study group. This group then sends a questionnaire to the prescribing doctor and asks him in confidence to list the medical events that the doctor's records show have occurred to the patient since the prescription was filled. When there is an event of special interest, more detailed information is sought. This method appears to be capable of identifying adverse effects which occur as rarely as once in 3,000 times, and has the great advantage that it does not depend on the doctors' assumption of a causal relationship between the medicine and the effect. An "event profile" is generated for each new drug of interest. This method of identifying unusual and unwanted effects is quite costly, but a great deal cheaper than formal clinical trials—even if they could be mounted in the numbers (in the order of 10 to 20 thousand patients) involved in PEM studies. This type of analysis is a major step forward in bridging the gap between experimentation and general use and, once expanded, could be used to replace costly and time-consuming clinical trials in such a way that useful drugs are made available earlier than was hitherto possible. The risk to patients overall should be at worst no greater, and at best much lower. Importantly, it enables the *benefits* of a drug to be taken into account as well as the *risks*.

The use of PEM has already demonstrated how misleading media reports on drug effects can be. One example is the short history of the anti-arthritic drug "Opren" (benoxaprofen). In January 1982 it became headline news after eight cases of jaundice had been associated with its use by 6,000 patients. Early follow-up showed that at least five of these cases had nothing to do with the drug, but it was nevertheless removed from the market in July 1982. Inman's team then reviewed, in detail, a total of 24,000 patients who had received Opren, finding only one case in which the drug could probably be blamed for causing jaundice, and that was non-fatal. Another 11 cases were possibly connected. Thus the side effect was truly very rare, and the risk of fatal jaundice immeasurably low, if it existed at all. But following such bad publicity, it would then be impossible to re-introduce the medicine, however great its benefits.

Another anti-arthritic drug, "Zomak" (zomepirac), was withdrawn in the US and Britain after a small number of reports of fatal allergic reaction (anaphylactic shock), one patient being related to the owner of a television network and his illness thus generating vast publicity. There is an existing risk (for all people, all causes) of anaphylactic shock of about one in two million. No death of this nature occurred among patients taking Zomak in Britain. The PEM study showed that patients on the drug had a *lower* risk of death overall, being in some way protected from coronary thrombosis and stroke. And this effect was quite independent of the markedly beneficial pain-relieving effect of the drug, particularly in patients with terminal cancer. But because of gross misuse of risk-related information, the drug is, essentially, gone for ever. And its apparently beneficial effect on the circulation can never be properly evaluated.

Irresponsible journalism can be responsible for much suffering, and unwarranted fear of rare side effects can wash the baby out with the bathwater. Inman has calculated[10] that if *all* drug risks were eliminated, our average life expectancy would only be increased by some 37 minutes! But if this was achieved by banning all effective medicines and vaccines, the cost would be an average loss of life expectancy of 10 to 20 years. The risk of a drug should be balanced against its need (including the availability of alternatives) and the severity of the disease for which it is needed.

Risks of X-rays

A matter of particular interest in balancing the risks and benefits of medical procedures is that of the use of X-rays for diagnosis and treatment.

X-rays were first discovered in 1895 by Wilhelm Roentgen, a German physicist, and the following year Thomas Edison invented the fluoroscope. Bones could be visualized for the first time with magical ease, and the rays were enthusiastically employed for the treatment of almost everything (in the absence of many genuinely successful therapeutic regimes). The "ill" effects of the rays became known almost immediately, and indeed were used for treatment. For example, the heads of children were irradiated so that the hair would fall out and speed the treatment of ringworm of the scalp. Early workers with X-rays became martyrs to the cause of radiology, with several of them losing limbs and suffering severe damage to their irradiated skin. By the turn of the century, the medical literature carried numerous reports of cancers induced by radiation, and some prominent experimenters died in the United States and Europe during the early years of this century. By the early 1920s the amount of damage being incurred was clearly understood, and recommendations were, for the first time, laid down in order to reduce exposure to radiation.

But the use of X-rays for diagnosis and treatment continued to expand dramatically. In the thirties and forties, X-rays were used very extensively for examination of the lungs of patients with tuberculosis, the long term result being that a significant proportion of women subjected to these X-rays later developed breast cancer. By the 1950s it was clear that high dose X-radiation could cause substantial damage to the body, and by the seventies it was clear that there appeared to be no threshold above which cancer could be induced and below which it would not be.

These findings prompted careful re-examination of practices involving the widespread use of X-rays in the screening for disease. Put simply, the question to be answered was whether the X-rays were causing more deaths than they were intended to prevent. For example, a special sort of X-ray of the breast called mammography was widely employed after the 1960s, when the technique was perfected. The intention is to identify cancer of the breast as early as possible, and the subsequent hope is that early treatment will improve the chances of survival. By the 1970s, when it was clear that mammography could be the cause of cancer, it was being argued that the technique, if used widely in young women, would cause more cancer than it would detect. By the late seventies, given the data on the effects of low dose radiation then available, it was possible to conclude that above the age of 50 more cancers would be detected than induced. With modern methods of mammography, using very low doses of radiation, the risk of causing cancer appears to be minimal. However, there is still no evidence that screening is beneficial for women under 50 years old[11]. Studies have been done in Japan, relating to X-ray screening for stomach cancer, which is very common in that country and is very hard to diagnose at an early stage without X-rays. Because of the large numbers involved, by the late 1970s it was possible to estimate with some confidence the number of cancers that might be detected and the number caused, and it was deduced that to screen below the age of 30 would result in a net loss of life expectancy, whereas over that age the balance of risks and benefits would favour screening[12].

Screening, of course, is by definition employed in populations of healthy people and affects a very large number of them. The use of X-rays for diagnosis in individual patients is a rather different matter, and risks require assessment on an individual patient basis. Medical X-rays form by far the largest component of artificial radiation imposed on people generally and every X-ray carries some risk, however small, of causing cancer. Sadly, the process of litigation in the United States is encouraging ''defensive medicine'' and thus the use of routine X-rays in order to be able to answer the question in court later, ''did you take all possible steps to diagnose this patient's disease?''

The average dose of X-ray used in diagnosis is about 0.7 mSv, taken as the effective whole body dose, or roughly equivalent to the smoking of six cigarettes. The average risk of causing a fatal cancer in a man of 40 is estimated to be in the region of four in a million (one in 250,000) which is roughly the same risk as that of a man dying at the age of 35 on any one day. On the other hand, the benefits to patients in the use of X-rays for diagnosis are substantial, and it would be easy to justify the proposition, for example, that many more people's lives would be saved by the use of a million X-rays than premature deaths would be caused (about four). But such considerations, once in the open, do stress the fact that an unnecessary X-ray is an X-ray which poses an unnecessary risk, and one which most informed patients would prefer to avoid. However, without information on risk, it is all to easy for the concerned patient to ask, ''but can't you just do an X-ray to check that it's not broken, doctor?''

The medical use of X-rays contributes substantially to the average amount of radiation received, although modern technology allows less radiation for a given effect. Although radiation can itself cause illness, its benefits include the early identification of treatable conditions, the diagnosis of illness and injury, and the treatment of cancer. The costs and risks of this and other technologies has to be balanced against the benefits.

"Then what's the risk, doctor?"

The way that people perceive risks and the influence these perceptions have on risk management and public policy are the subject of Chapter 14. It is appropriate at this point, however, to point out that the individual's perception of risk is important to the relationship between the doctor and the patient, and the response of that person to treatment.

First, there is the question of the extent to which patients should be properly informed on the risks of treatment and the amount of detail they can understand or, indeed, wish for. In Britain, decisions on such matters are left to the medical profession as part of the judgement its members must exercise in their clinical decision-making. A patient has every right to refuse a procedure such as an operation, but the main source of information will be the surgeon whose opinion will inevitably be asked (by the patient or the relatives) on what the doctor thinks are the chances. That the disclosure of information relating to the risk to the patient is a matter for the judgement of the doctor is a view which has comparatively recently been upheld by the House of Lords[13].

In the United States, however, the situation is very different. Not only have suits for "medical malpractice" become extremely common, but the legal profession operates on the basis of "contingency fees", which means that cases may be taken up on a purely speculative basis. The bigger the award the bigger the cut for the lawyer, and doctors and hospitals have to charge high fees to cover enormous insurance premiums. Accordingly, the "informed consent" doctrine holds that patients should be told of all conceivable risks associated with the procedure, whether the doctor thinks that to do so is a good idea or not.

This principle is being expanded to prescription medicines, so that instruction leaflets for patients are being written in non-technical language to inform the consumer about the potential risks and the benefits of the medicine. Surveys have indicated that the use of drugs which have some risk of causing death, however small, and drugs which are very widely used, such as oral contraceptives, creates a public demand for very detailed information; and, in principle, it is only the most serious and the most frequently occurring adverse effects which are listed on the patient information leaflets. There is little information so far available on how patients' perception of risk is changed by the provision of this information, but what there is indicates that, as might be expected, patients evaluate the significance of rare but serious side effects much more highly than do doctors.

Similarly, patients might assess the risks of surgical procedures rather differently from the doctors if they were provided with more detailed information than is now common in Britain. If all patients were aware that the risk of death was inevitably associated with any operation, however trivial, would they consent to fewer operations overall? Further, patients' attitudes to risk varies in a way that doctors rarely explore. Some patients may be prepared to accept a small risk of an early death in return for a high probability of a longer life. Others may prefer not to face the small risk of an early death but, rather, accept death when it comes even if it might be a little earlier than if the procedure was undertaken. These are, at present, issues which are rarely discussed between doctors and patients, a state of affairs which will inevitably change as the whole concept of risk becomes more widely discussed and understood.

One example to stress this point is as follows. It has been shown that if two alternative treatments are offered, of equal effectiveness and risk, the alternative presented in terms of *survival rate* will be consistently preferred by patients and doctors alike over the alternative presented in terms of *mortality*[14]. This is despite the fact that these outcomes are simply two sides of the same coin. Further, it shows that doctors can be subject to the same distortions of perception as their patients!

Alternative therapies

The balance of risk and benefit is just as important an issue in considering the use of unconventional or "alternative" therapies as it is for conventional medicine. Unfortunately, while data on risks and benefits in conventional treatment are lacking in many ways, they are at least expanding rather rapidly in association with a strong belief that good information, based on valid scientific data, means good treatment. Unfortunately, not only are such data for alternative therapies extremely sparse, but also there is very little emphasis on the need for it. It is, therefore, very easy for therapists and patients alike to under-estimate the risks and to over-estimate the benefits, a combination which inevitably leads to unnecessary harm. The obverse, being an over-estimation of risk and under-estimation of benefit, merely leads to the patient being less well served because of the loss of potentially effective treatment. Either way the patient does poorly because the information is bad. Further, if a patient chooses an ineffective ''alternative'' therapy, in preference to an effective conventional therapy (which carries reliable estimates of both effectiveness and risk), then he is in effect increasing the overall risk of harm to himself. The whole thrust of this book is that for anyone—professional or layman alike—to make rational choices in order to minimize risk and maximize benefit, an absolute prerequisite is reliable information.

The same principles apply in the use of herbal medicines, which are commonly used for minor conditions, many of which recover without treatment. Assessment of their therapeutic value is difficult, and although those that make claims on effectiveness require (in Britain) a product licence before being sold, the granting of a licence does not require proof of effectiveness through clinical trials and the tight quality control which is demanded of conventional medicines. Other herbal remedies make no claim for effectiveness and are classed as food supplements, so need no produce licence although many are promoted for medicinal use.

Because herbal remedies are perceived as ''natural'' it is easy to assume they are ''safe''. But many do contain the same chemicals as are used in conventional medicines, although in varying and often undisclosed quantities[15]. Information is lacking on pesticide levels, the presence of carcinogens such as aflatoxin, and on contamination by metals and microbes. Some of the active principles in herbal medicines have long-term cancer-causing effects in animal tests, and would be banned if intended as food additives. Some may cause abortions, and are dangerous during pregnancy. A wide variety of less serious adverse effects have been reported by doctors under the process described above for conventional medicines.

The effectiveness and degree of safety of herbal remedies is very poorly documented. Information on the risk of conventional drugs may seem to be alarming, but it is at least available. No information does not mean no risk.

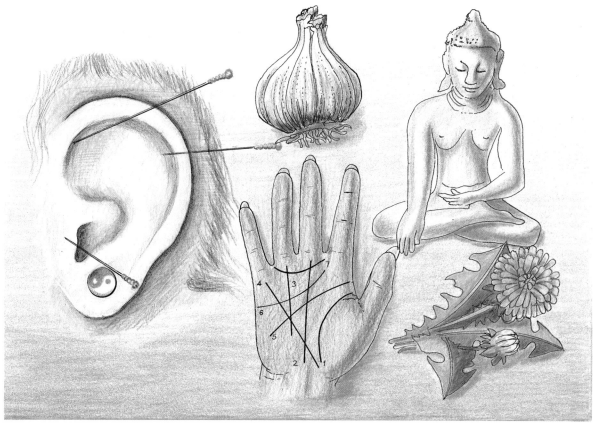

Chapter Twelve

Natural Disasters

Every now and then calamitous events occur which cause a wave of public concern and mobilization of resources. These disasters may be as a result of "natural" events, or they may involve the breakdown of systems designed and built by man. "Man-made" disasters such as the disruption of power stations are described in other parts of this book, and it is those resulting from natural forces which we are concerned with here.

Among the natural disasters which occur most frequently and have a significant impact on mankind are floods, earthquakes, cyclones (tropical revolving storms) and droughts. There are of course others, including volcanoes, avalanches, tornadoes and landslides, but these are less frequent and expose fewer people to risk. One estimate is that each year throughout the world, around 250,000 people are killed in natural disasters which together are responsible for about £18 billion in damage to property.

There is an enormous difference in the distribution of personal risk, with about 95% of deaths in natural disasters occurring in the developing countries. Deaths from natural disasters are rather rare in the developed world, but this, as we shall see, is as a consequence of environmental circumstances rather than the characteristics of the natural event. Accordingly, natural disasters are economically much more important to the developing nations (in relation to the size of their gross national product) than they are to the developed world, and for this reason it is to the former group of countries that we now turn our attention. Before doing so, it is worth noting again how poor the numerical information is for these causes of unexpected death or injury, just as it is for so many other causes.

Over the last few decades there has been a tendency for the number of individuals killed in each disastrous event to increase, and the biggest increase has been noted in the case of earthquakes[1]. The average mortality in the sixties was 750 deaths per earthquake, whereas in the seventies the death toll per event went up to 4,871. The actual number of earthquakes for which international assistance was requested did not change. This big increase was partly due to a massive earthquake in China, which killed about a quarter of a million people, but even if this is allowed for, the average number of people killed in each earthquake for which assistance was requested was 1,780. The average number of people killed in each cyclone and drought-related famine has also increased.

It is a reasonable assumption that the physical nature of these natural events has not altered dramatically in the same period, and that local conditions including a substantial redistribution of population have been responsible for the changes.

Mortality has also increased in terms of the number of people exposed to disasters when the number of events is controlled for. What we are seeing is a steady decline in the resistance of populations to disasters, and the inability of current disaster management policies to reduce the vulnerability of these communities.

The mortality in natural disasters is consistently related to the level of the economy in that, when the number of events are controlled for, there are substantially higher mortality rates in poor countries than in richer ones. It is particularly interesting to compare two particular earthquakes, one of which occurred in San Fernando, California, in 1971, and the other in Managua, Nicaragua, in 1972. Although the California earthquake was rather more violent, caused major damage over a bigger area and directly affected a population 13 times bigger than in Managua, the mortality in the Nicaraguan capital was somewhere around 5,000 deaths compared to 60 deaths in California[2].

What determines the risk of dying in an earthquake is not the strength of the tremor but the quality of the buildings and the urban planning. There is a huge difference in the loss of lives per earthquake between rich and poor countries.
Source: reference 2

When it comes to disease and non-fatal injury, reliable figures are even harder to obtain than figures for deaths. In the few studies that have been done, it seems that easily the commonest injuries are fractures of the legs and arms. Those that are going to die do so within the first few hours after the event, and those that survive the first 24 hours generally live without major bodily harm.

The metropolitan areas of the rapidly expanding cities in the Third World are packed with fragile dwellings in the shanty towns and slums. What would be minor events in the developed world become major disasters in the sort of cities where buildings collapse, transport stops, sewage canals overflow and fires start with little chance that a good flow of water will be available to extinguish them. Clearly, in both earthquakes and cyclones, the structural quality of the dwellings is a factor which largely determines the risk of injury to those within them.

Contrary to popular belief, major epidemic diseases are rather rare events after natural disasters, especially in developed countries[3]. The breakdown in sanitation systems which is relatively likely in the developing countries can provoke epidemics, but these are generally fairly unimportant in scope. More serious epidemics are those generated by famine conditions, such as cholera in Somalia and meningitis in Ethiopia. Outbreaks of disease following natural disasters appear to be related to the level of education and personal income. After a flood in Bangladesh, it was found that among the poorer sections of the community who used canal water for drinking and washing, the incidence rate of cholera was 16.3 per thousand people whereas among families with at least one high school graduate, the incidence was 8.2 per thousand[4].

Characteristics determining risk

There are several characteristics of a natural disaster which directly affect the risk to the population exposed to it. The first is its predictability. Famine related to drought is highly predictable, with almost all important famines since the Second World War having been foreseen for many years. One thing this shows is that the knowledge of an impending disaster has very little to do with whether communities will act to prevent it. Earthquakes, on the other

hand, are rather unpredictable events, although much research is now being done to improve the quality of prediction.

The ''lethality'' of a natural disaster relates to the proportion of the people suffering the event who die as a result, and earthquakes are the most serious in this regard. Generally, lethality is directly related to the magnitude of the event which in turn depends on the amount of energy released through the action of wind, water (or lack of it) and tectonic forces (parts of the earth's crust rubbing together).

Other characteristics of natural disasters, which in part determine the risk to the population exposed to their effects, include the frequency of occurrence, the duration of the episode and the area affected by it, the speed of onset of the event, and its timing (namely, whether it is a regular seasonal occurrence, such as a tropical cyclone, or an apparently random event such as an earthquake).

What people do to minimize the risk of injury to themselves and their families and damage to their properties depends on a wide variety of factors and perceptions of risk. The first thing is, of course, that people have to be aware that the risk of a disastrous event exists at all, and this in turn depends on their appraisal of the information available to them. Where the events are of slow onset, such as a drought, or predictable by time and place, such as a tropical cyclone, then people are more likely to be aware that the consequences can be severe.

However, whether people actually do take action because they are aware of the risk of an impending disaster is another matter altogether. The determination of many groups in the population to act, especially in the developing world, is heavily influenced by factors such as religion and the readiness to accept supernatural explanations for disastrous events. Populations which are highly mobile may well be completely unaware of existing risks in areas to which they are newcomers.

Importantly, people's actions may be influenced by their perception of risk and understanding of risk-related concepts. People who live in crowded urban areas may be so conscious of existing daily risks such as traffic accidents and personal violence that the risk of a comparatively rare disaster can be readily ignored. Further, many people have the fallacious view that disasters come in groups followed by intervals free from such troubles, whereas in fact a catastrophic event with a known probability, even though that probability is low, has exactly the same chance of occurring this year as it had last year.

The classic case of "blocking out" risk is represented by southern California. The 1971 San Fernando quake, 6.4 on the Richter scale, killed 60 people (47 in one hospital, which collapsed), and could have been disastrous. The nearby Van Norman dam nearly failed catastrophically due to liquefaction of the soil, a phenomenon recognized only after its construction. Had the reservoir been full, the dam would have failed, possibly causing 50,000 to 100,000 deaths[5]. Small quakes occur in California every day. At least eight "great" earthquakes have hit southern California along the San Andreas Fault, 30 miles east of Los Angeles, in the past 1,200 years, with an average spacing of 140 years (plus or minus 30 years). The last "great" quake occurred in 1857, and according to the US Federal Emergency Management Agency there is well in excess of a 50:50 chance that a "catastrophic" quake (8.3 on the Richter scale, equivalent to the one which flattened half of San Francisco in 1906) will occur in southern California within the next 30 years. There is a risk of between 1 in 50 and 1 in 20 that it might happen during *any* given year, and the likely consequences would exceed those of any disaster ever suffered in the United States— effects comparable to those of a radiation-free atomic bomb. Yet the citizens of southern California appear to worry much more about comparatively miniscule risks, and the population continues to grow.

Particularly in the developing world, and however high the risk perceived, many people simply do not have the choice as to whether they are able to move out of a hazardous area or not. They are there because they have to be, maybe simply to survive. Indeed, survival in the face of many other day-to-day risks is likely to be seen as far more important than attempts to avoid the low risk of a major disaster, and that does appear to be the perceptual position of the citizens of California.

Measures designed to limit personal and property losses following natural disasters, therefore, fall much more into the fields of activity of governments and public administration than into the field of personal initiative. The planning of land use, although likely to be resisted by the communities affected, is fundamental to such preventive activities. Rickety old buildings and rigid new ones are much more likely to fall down and injure and kill people than dwellings and other buildings constructed in the light of known principles of earthquake design, although such design measures (almost inevitably, one might say) do involve considerably higher construction costs. There are many other guidelines for the planning of disaster management, but the main problem is to get the population concerned to take much interest in the subject.

Man-made disasters

Vast amounts of energy may be released in natural disasters. Energy can also be released in enormous amounts in so-called "man-made" disasters, but in this case the energy has generally been stored, sometimes in stupendous amounts, as part of the process by which man deliberately sets out to manipulate his environment. The people who live at risk of man-made disasters may not, as is the case for natural disasters, have very much freedom to act or to make choices of action in the face of these risks. In practice, too, there are few of man's activities in storing energy with an eye to large future benefits—such as the building of dams for water storage and hydro-electric power—which are fully assessed for their risk to populations who live in the vicinity.

However, risks of low probability but very great consequence, such as those which tend to be associated with new technologies, do tend to rate relatively highly in personal and public concern, because of the unique problems they present. Nuclear power generation is an example of a technology whose risk of disaster does generate a very high level of public concern, and this is in direct contrast to the lack of general concern about risks posed to people in the affected area by the building of dams to produce hydroelectric power.

Risks from man-made disasters are covered in more details in relevant chapters, looking at, for example, power generation, various modes of transport, and so on.

Chapter Thirteen

Chemical Risks

There are about 70,000 chemicals in daily use in agriculture, consumer products and industry and this number is being added to at the rate of about 1,000 a year[1]. Although modern society could not function as it does without many of these chemicals, some are suspected of being harmful or known to be so, and these harmful effects include the causation of cancer and the deformation of unborn babies. Not that these new, synthetic chemicals are necessarily any more toxic than the "natural" chemicals that mankind has already lived with for so long. In fact, the most potent toxins of all are the naturally occurring ones: botulinus toxin, diphtheria toxin, tetanus toxin, aflatoxin and many others.

Fear of chemicals is quite naturally increased after disasters such as that which occurred at Flixborough, in Britain, or at the chemical plant at Bhopal, India in 1984, which claimed the lives of around 2,000 people after the escape of poisonous vapour.

But all chemicals are toxic, so that the very existence of each one represents a hazard. However, as we stressed earlier, there is a fundamental difference between hazard and risk. The actual degree of risk represented by a chemical depends absolutely on the way it is used. In the case of harm to humans, the risk can be reduced to an exceedingly low level, but it cannot ever be reduced to zero. To complicate the matter, as we shall see, our ability to identify the existence of chemicals is constantly improving so that we are now taking into our bodies things we once never even knew existed. It seems to many people, therefore, that the overall risk we face from chemicals is increasing daily, and there is a natural tendency to be scared of chemicals for this reason. This is in contrast with the way that we have come to terms with the existence in our environment of things like bacteria, with which we also come into daily contact, but which do not cause us any harm unless we are invaded by them in unusual amounts or via particular routes.

Types of chemicals

There has been an astonishing rise not only in the quantity but also the variety of chemicals used in the developed world over the last 40 to 50 years. Chemical use, therefore, represents one of the ''new'' risks which are very different from those encountered in the past, and for that very reason (unfamiliarity) may be especially feared. The risks from chemicals are most commonly seen to arise from the disposal of waste, exposure to synthetic pesticides and herbicides, food contaminants and additives, accidents at laboratories and manufacturing plants, spills of crude oil from tankers and threats to the environment from fluorocarbons and acid rain. Many of these new risks are seen as threats for the future as much as for the present, and the risks are involuntary and the harm irreversible. As we will see in the next chapter, these characteristics contribute to a feeling of ''dread'', which can lead to a perception of a level of risk which is far higher than indicated by objective measurement.

Every supermarket in the high street shopping centre carries thousands of products which would not be there if it were not for the use of synthetic chemicals. Chemicals can be put into four categories: structural chemicals, process chemicals, pesticides and medicinal drugs.

Chemicals used for structures are mostly plastics which have taken over from metal, wood and other materials of natural origin. Plastic drains and pipes have taken over from metals such as lead, copper or brass, being safer, cheaper and easier to work. At a more advanced level, plastics are used to build parts of cars, aircraft, ships and yachts. Synthetic fibres are used in textiles, carpets, ropes and so on.

Process chemicals are used in industry to ease various steps in manufacture but are not themselves used as part of the end product. Examples include wetting agents, which are used in the textile and paper industries, detergents used in sewage treatment, and emulsifiers used when making pesticides. More familiarly, process chemicals are widely used in the domestic environment for a variety of purposes, where they have commonly taken over from natural products; they include detergents, polishes and disinfectants without which not only our homes, but also facilities such as hospitals, would not be so clean and free from the risk of secondary infection as they are now.

Without synthetic chemicals, a huge variety of items on our supermarket shelves simply would not be there. About 70,000 chemicals are in daily use, and about 1,000 are being added each year. Although all can cause harm, their risk depends absolutely on the way they are used. Most are much less toxic than the ''natural'' toxins that we have learnt to live with.

Pesticides are used to increase the availability of food, through protection of crops in the field. Herbicides aid by removal of competing plants and the protection of the crop once it is stored. In large parts of the world we no longer see locusts, bugs in apples, or weevils in grain. Pesticides are also used to combat epidemic disease by killing the creatures which carry the disease-causing organisms, such as mosquitoes and snails.

Medicinal chemicals are used either to cure disease or control it, or strengthen the body's defence mechanisms. It is very difficult to put numbers on the benefits offered by chemicals in society today. In some cases, the benefits of synthetic chemicals can be achieved through alternative "natural" methods, but rarely at similar cost. Whether the benefits are apportioned fairly is a matter for individual and political judgement. For example, while chemicals can undoubtedly increase food output, if the only result is that too much food is produced, then the fault lies in the use of the chemical and not in its existence or nature.

Toxic effects

Earlier in this book we have reviewed some of the commoner causes of poisoning, both from natural and synthetic substances. Every chemical carries the risk of poisoning; in other words, it is toxic. But that does not necessarily mean that it *will* cause harm, let alone cause death. Alcohol taken in the amounts used by moderate social drinkers causes no identifiable harm to the body tissues and, indeed, may have some beneficial effect. Yet if the bottle of whisky from which the normal tot is poured is drunk straight off in one shot, it can result in almost instant death. Similarly, chemicals which most people would regard as being highly toxic, such as strychnine and arsenic, were once used in very small amounts for their supposed benefit as medicines, and not so very long ago either. "Toxicity", being the extent of the hazard represented by the existence of each chemical, can be assessed in a number of different ways, and the amount of chemical taken into the body can be related to its effect: the "dose–response" relationship.

The two main approaches to the measurement of harmful effects on the body are through the use of laboratory experimentation and by epidemiology, which is the observation and measurement of groups within human populations. The experimental approach involves the use of animals to estimate the effects on humans, and some approaches to this work have been outlined earlier in the book. The main difficulties arise from the assumptions that have to be made in relating animal response to human response, and making connections between, on the one hand, response to high doses of chemical administered over a short time, and on the other hand the use of low doses over a long time.

Before reviewing in more detail some special aspects of the toxicity of chemicals and the risk to populations which they pose, it is worth stressing again the complications resulting from the accuracy and the precision of analysis which is now possible. If we are setting out to predict what harmful outcome might follow the use of a chemical, we need to know how much of it is present in the compound of interest. There is no such thing as "pure". If the cap is taken off a bottle of solvent in a laboratory, then *some* vapour from the solvent—although not very much—will be present throughout the laboratory building. For this sort of reason, it would not be correct, strictly speaking (although it has been done), to set a zero legal level of blood alcohol level for drivers, because *some* amount of alcohol—although again it may be an exceedingly tiny amount—will always be detectable in human blood. Whether very tiny concentrations such as this are actually detected depends entirely on the sensitivity of the method of analysis which is used. If a contaminant is not found when analysing a substance, then all that can be said is that the contaminant is not present at a concentration greater then the limit of detection of the method of analysis used.

The sensitivity of analysis has improved over recent decades to an amazing extent. To our forebears, a level of purity of 99.5% must have sounded pretty impressive. However, in today's terms that translates to the presence of impurities at the level of 5,000 parts per million. For nearly 30 years we have been able to measure substances at a level of one part per million (1 ppm) and some substances can now be measured at the level of a few parts per billion (ppb, or one thousand million).

One part per billion is not a lot. It is 0.0000001%, about the concentration of two or three grains of salt in a swimming pool, or the thickness of a credit card compared to 1,000 kilometres (over 600 miles). But to the casual ear, 1 ppb is heard as an amount that is definitely more than zero, and it is easy to jump to the probably unwarranted conclusion that a toxic chemical present in, say, food at that concentration poses a risk to health which is also definitely—and perhaps ''significantly''—more than zero.

Therefore, there are no absolutes. There are no chemicals which are free from risk, and there is nothing that is totally ''pure''. Toxicity must be related to *dose*. In most cases an increase in dose brings about an increase in biological response (which may be desired or undesired)

but the relationship may be much more complicated than that. For example, there may be no response at all from the body until the chemical is administered in a quantity sufficient to generate one: the ''threshold'' dose. Similarly, in the case of a medicinal chemical, the desired effect may increase with the dose, but the undesired toxic effects may increase as well, so that a point is reached where the toxic effects overwhelm the therapeutic effects. All these factors are relevant to chemical hazards and to their risks both real and imagined.

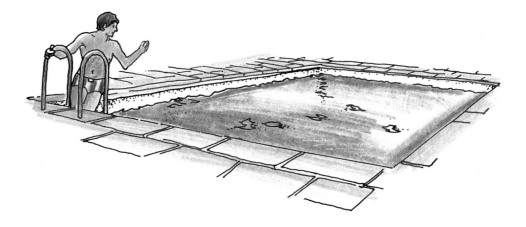

Our capacity to detect tiny amounts of chemicals seems to be adding ''new'' risks daily to the environment, but the real risk of such tiny amounts of even very toxic chemicals is usually immeasurably low. We may be concerned about the presence of a toxic chemical in our food or water at a concentration of one part per billion, and if it caused cancer in animals it might be banned; but that's about the concentration of two grains of salt in a swimming pool.

Chemical hazards

By this stage in the book, readers will fully appreciate that in our complex world we face and cope with an enormous variety of risks, posing some threat of premature death but most of them avoidable or a very small. The contribution of chemicals to the spectrum of risk is also through their potential for causing disease or premature death, including (and most worrying for the majority) their potential for causing cancer.

It is not easy to assess the risks of chemicals when they are superimposed on risks which we live with all the time and which may have nothing to do with technology in general or chemicals in particular. Epidemiological studies are often confounded by the multiplicity of factors which may be interacting to cause a given disease, and by the difficulty of measuring small changes in the incidence of rather rare conditions. For example, we have discussed the problem of "clustering" in relation to cancer caused by radiation, and the same problem is inclined to arise when harmful effects are attributed to the use of the chemicals.

Of course, not all the risks of chemicals are those related to toxicity. Many chemicals are flammable or explosive and may cause damage to people and property in and around laboratories and manufacturing plants. Chemicals require transporting, and whenever transport is involved there is the risk of accidental damage and consequential harm from the release of toxic substances.

Cancer is the harmful outcome which is most generally feared as a result of exposure to chemicals. As we have already seen, the incidence of most cancers is either steady or declining, with the exception of cancers which are directly linked to smoking. If the new chemicals which are being introduced into use *are* causing cancer, they are doing so to an extent which is not measurable in the overall statistics; there is certainly not an "epidemic" of cancer caused by these new synthetic chemicals[2].

Nevertheless, while cancers probably originate from a whole variety of circumstances, exposure to chemicals does contribute to the generation of at least some cancers. These chemical carcinogens may be synthetic or they may be naturally occurring. Naturally occurring carcinogens are found in foods, and in substances such as soot and cigarette smoke. Some natural carcinogens are used industrially, such as asbestos and naphthylamine, a dye which causes cancer of the bladder. But what is probably of most interest to the average individual is the relationship of cancer to the chemicals in food.

Chemicals in food

With very few exceptions (arsenic is one) all chemicals known to cause cancer in man have also been found to be carcinogenic in animals. But the reverse is very far from true. Examples of chemicals found in food which when fed to laboratory animals in large amounts do cause cancer include polycyclic aromatic hydrocarbons (PAH), nitroso compounds, a variety of compounds from plants, and moulds which grow on foods which are going bad.

PAHs are present in many foods and the concentrations are increased by cooking which includes burning (such as barbecuing). Smoked meats contain a relatively high concentration. These chemicals are also found in fresh vegetables and vegetable oils, so that it is not possible to avoid them and they are always part of a "natural" diet.

Nitroso compounds (nitrosamines) have been known to be carcinogenic for nearly 40 years, and are sometimes found in untreated natural food. They are more commonly found as a result of a reaction between compounds which are normally in the food with nitrites or nitrates which are added to slow the spoiling of the food, and hence they are present in fish, sausages, bacon, ham, cheese and so on.

Many compounds known to be carcinogenic in animals are found in plants, including those which are sometimes used in herbal remedies such as comfrey, coltsfoot and sassafras. Bracken has been known for years to be carcinogenic, and indeed cattle that graze on bracken are more likely to suffer from cancer of the gut.

Foods which are normally free of carcinogens may grow moulds which produce these and other toxic compounds (mycotoxins). Toxicity from moulds has been long recognized and indeed has been used for "medicinal" purposes in the past. The fungus ergot contaminates rye, and it causes contraction of the womb. It also causes hallucinations, and the drug LSD was developed from it. Among the most potent carcinogens of all are chemicals called aflatoxins, products of the mould *Aspergillus flavus*, which grows on peanuts. Most countries now have an allowable upper limit for aflatoxin in peanuts intended for sale, indicating that most administrations realize that it is not possible completely to eliminate even carcinogens from the normal diet.

Various chemicals are added to food as preservatives, colouring agents and so on, and regulations are becoming more stringent on the use of those which are suspected of being carcinogens. Food additives are subjected to rigorous and comprehensive laboratory testing throughout the world and are required to meet a variety of national and international regulations. The interpretation of studies which appear to show the potential for tumour formation in animals is becoming increasingly difficult. Some testing procedures are very tightly standardized, but have little relationship to the real world or to use by humans. Other tests are more flexible but difficult to relate one to the other. Indeed, a great deal more needs to be known about the induction of cancer in animals by chemicals before the findings can be confidently related to man. Animals suffer from a wide variety of tumours which are taken to indicate a chemical's carcinogenicity, but few of the chemicals which have been thus identified by scientists appear to be of great concern to those involved with the prevention of cancer, even though regulatory agencies are usually very hard on them.

Chemicals that cause cancer are a diverse group which act in different ways. To classify all of them for the purpose of regulation as ''carcinogens'' is not very logical today, because we really do not know what some of the laboratory findings in animals actually mean, and the mechanism of action of chemical carcinogens in biochemical terms is very unclear. Some of the testing defies common sense. If a chemical is administered to a rat in relatively enormous amounts there will be absolutely inevitable changes in that part of the diet which remains and is acceptable to that unfortunate animal, its metabolism is bound to be altered, and these changes may or may not have as much influence on the animal's illness as the chemical itself.

Because uncertainty is a major source of discomfort in the decisions that must be made by regulators about the safety of food, there has been a tendency to move towards unattainable zero-risk objectives, and this has caused substantial problems in the United States. In that country a group of food safety laws known collectively as the Delaney Clause prohibits the Food and Drug Administration from approving food additives that induce cancer in man or animals. The law does not permit consideration of the extent of human exposure, or the validity of animal data in relation to humans. It makes no allowance for the possibility that a threshold dose exists. Further, it does not provide for balancing benefits against risks so that, for example, when the safety of nitrites came into question, the US government could not take into consideration the role that nitrites play in preventing botulism, a killer disease resulting from one of the most potent toxins known to man.

There is an increasing awareness that food safety regulations must take account of the realities of science, and in particular our now amazing capacity for identifying chemicals in almost unimaginably low quantities and our inability to assess the risk to man of these chemicals. Further, it is important to consider the benefits of food additives as well as their risks. While the benefits of *flavouring* and *colouring* additives may in many cases be questionable, it has been argued that the use of chemical *preservatives* has substantially reduced the risk of cancer overall, knowing as we do the carcinogenic potential of older methods of food preservation such as pickling, smoking and curing.

In summary, then, carcinogens in food are more likely to be there ''naturally' or as a result of traditional preservation methods than by the addition of synthetic chemicals. The significance to human beings of very tiny amounts of carcinogens (as assessed through animal experimentation) is unknown. It would be hard to live on a diet which contained no substances which at some time had been shown by laboratory or animal tests to have carcinogenic properties.

Herbicides and pesticides

Another group of chemicals of especial interest is made up of herbicides and pesticides, the public perception of which is also commonly influenced by popular mythology and sensational presentation of issues in the media.

A particular example is the case of chemicals in the group which includes the herbicides 2,4,5,T and 2,4,D. Commercial preparations of 2,4,5,T are contaminated to some extent with dioxin, which is highly toxic but which does not occur in 2,4,D. These chemicals became notorious following their use in Vietnam, where they were combined in the substance known as Agent

Orange, and it is perhaps the connection with war which has been partly the cause of the fearful connotations which are attached to these chemicals—rather in the way that the nuclear power industry is linked in the public mind with the use of atomic bombs. 2,4,D has been used for over 35 years and 2,4,5,T for nearly as long. Both chemicals are now very widely employed throughout the world, although their use in the United States has recently been restricted following controversy and public pressure on government agencies.

Concern was initially focussed on reports that these herbicides produced birth defects in experimental animals, although epidemiological studies showed no evidence of a link between use of the chemicals and human birth defects in the areas they were used[3,4]. Birth defects are rare, but do occur regularly at a rate of around 1 to 2% in the normal population, and like other rare conditions they can "cluster" in a random manner. Accordingly, in any given country where the herbicide is widely used, there is likely to be a particular cluster of birth defects which has occurred quite normally but which may be linked, understandably, with the nearby use of the herbicide.

More recently, attention has been focussed on contamination of 2,4,5,T by the very much more toxic chemical, dioxin. Dioxin is at least one thousand times more toxic than 2,4,5,T and it is therefore the level of its presence as a contaminant which is more important in determining the toxicity of 2,4,5,T than the latter substance in itself. Chronic exposure to dioxin does produce marked effects on animals, including cancer, interference with the immune system and a skin disease called chloracne. While undoubtedly extremely toxic in animals, the toxicity of dioxin for man is not so clear. Its link to chloracne is well established and when several pounds of the substance were released into the densely populated area around Seveso in Italy in 1976, 134 cases occurred among the total of about 37,000 people who were exposed to the chemical.

While unpleasant and disfiguring, chloracne is not fatal. Although dioxin is about three times more potent in causing cancer in rats than even aflatoxin, there is no evidence, as yet, that the cancer incidence in human beings who have been exposed to enough dioxin to have developed chloracne is any different from normal[5]. Several official and unofficial inquiries, particularly in the United States and Australia, have examined claims by the veterans of the Vietnam conflict that exposure to Agent Orange has caused health problems, including congenital defects in children subsequently born to them. So far, however, service in Vietnam has not been linked to any health problems that might be due to herbicide exposure[6].

In summary, the toxicity of 2,4,5,T is comparable to thousands of other agricultural and industrial chemicals. Dioxin, on the other hand, is extremely toxic, and the essential problem therefore is to minimize its presence in 2,4,5,T. There have been some reports from Sweden on an increase in tumours of the soft tissues (sarcomas) in people who have used herbicides contaminated with dioxin, although none of them suffered from chloracne[7]. No other studies have shown any general health problems among spray operators or the public. If any such problems have arisen, they are trivial compared with most other risks discussed in this book.

Public pressure to limit the use of 2,4,5,T and 2,4,D could, in the end, result in the use of chemicals whose toxicity is far less well understood and which could therefore result in a higher incidence of harm, rather in the way that the abandoning of new, but safer, level-crossing gates in response to public outcry over a single sad incident could result in the continuing use of old but less safe gates. The main problems which we face in lowering risks from the use of chemicals are in ensuring their correct use by individuals so that exposure to toxic effects is minimized, and in disposing of the chemical waste which is now accumulating in large amounts in some parts of the world.

Chapter Fourteen

Perception and Acceptability of Risk

PERCEPTION AND MISPERCEPTION

Decisions have to be made about risks if only to decide whether or not to do anything about them. In a democratic society, several groups are involved in these decisions. Some people will obviously belong in more than one group, but generally they fall into one of three categories: the general public; their political representatives; and experts and managers. In principle, experts gather scientific evidence and give technical advice to the politicians, who then legislate and regulate for the benefit and with the implicit agreement of the general public. In practice, of course, things do not very often work out that way. Measuring things is not always as precise a procedure as politicians and public would like. Politicians may have personal and partisan aims which have a higher priority than the public benefit. The public tends to mistrust both experts

and politicians, and experts are inclined to dismiss public understanding of technical issues as being insufficient for "rational" decision-making.

And overall, this potential for mistrust and misunderstanding lies in the fact that people, whether within groups or as individuals, see things differently from each other. One of the things they see—"perceive"—differently is risk.

When the world was a less complex place, there was less scope for differences in perception of risk. At the individual level, the hazards faced by ordinary people were accepted and coped with on a day-to-day basis: fire, water, cold, heights and so on. Disease and disaster were likely to be seen as acts of God or some other supernatural force and, therefore, beyond reckoning and beyond control. The absence of fast and wide-ranging communications media meant that risks to other people were out of sight and thus out of mind. The risks to worry about were the risks one faced oneself.

Things are very different now. Familiar risks are still faced, but are generally felt to be under voluntary control and for that reason not very worrying. Perhaps as a reaction to a humdrum existence which is too free of excitement, risk may be deliberately challenged by involvement in high risk sports and activities. But the really big change is that as part of the process of technological evolution, *new* hazards have emerged, posing risks which are known to exist, but which do not threaten the individual very directly. Control over those risks has passed completely out of an individual person's control. Their scale and nature are things the individual can only learn about secondhand, by talking to other people and through exposure to the media. And as viewed through tabloid pages and the television screen, the world looks to be a very dangerous place to live in.

When decisions are made and actions taken about risk, whether at an individual level or as part of public administration, it is the way that people *see* those risks that determines what decisions are made and what action is taken, and perceptions of risk can be very different from group to group. The basis of most experts' and technologists' view of risk is the type of analysis mostly used throughout this book: the measure of the various components of risk, the assessment of their probability, measurements of the outcome, of unexpected and unintended events, and the evaluation of probabilities.

Experts like to use statistics. But other people (and most politicians) have a fundamental distrust of statistics and base their perceptions of risk on a very wide variety of other values, philosophies, concepts and calculations. Over recent years, a rather small number of research workers have tried to find out what it is that people mean when they say something is or is not "risky", and what it is that determines their perceptions. This work has clear implications for predicting how people will respond to new hazards and the way they are managed, for improving communication between all those concerned, and for directing public education.

In order to make sense out of complicated issues such as the evaluation of risk, people use a set of mental strategies which in the jargon of psychology are called "heuristics"[1]. The process of reducing difficult mental tasks to easy ones

is not, of course, limited to lay people, but is also used by technologists especially when the statistical data, on which they would normally prefer to rely, is sparse or of low dependability. These rules of judgement can lead to perfectly valid and reliable assessments, but sometimes they can lead to substantial bias and, accordingly, to disagreement with people who have used different patterns of thought to evaluate the same set of facts.

The mental trick with perhaps the most significant implications for the perception of risk is the "availability" heuristic, whereby the situation under review is matched with information which is most readily available and easily recalled. Thus, the more *available* the information on a given event, the more likely it is judged that the event will occur. Things which really do happen often are, of course, easy to bring to mind, but many other factors also influence recall. These include the regular reporting of events which are not truly very frequent, and exposure to dramatic information which is rich in death and disaster. A helicopter crashed into the North Sea in 1986 with the sad death of nearly all the oil rig workers it was carrying. Cries followed for new and more stringent safety measures for helicopters, because of the immediate perception that they "must be" dangerous aircraft. But in 1985 there was not a single fatal helicopter crash in the UK and only six large helicopters were reported to have crashed fatally in the entire world, which would seem in fact to indicate an extraordinarily low degree of risk in helicopter operation[2]. The book *Jaws* was about leaders of a community who wanted to suppress news that a shark was in the vicinity so as to *decrease* the perceived risk, in order that tourists might not be discouraged. In the real world, publication of the book stimulated to an unprecedented extent the fear of sharks which already existed throughout the world.

In the developed world an individual's personal contact with unexpected death is really very rare, and, therefore, people's knowledge of it is gleaned more through the media than from first-hand experience. Because the media concentrate, quite understandably, on the more unusual and dramatic happenings, such events are likely also to be perceived as being the more frequent ones.

This proposition has been tested by several research workers. These include, notably, a group of psychologists in Oregon, who started this line of enquiry by asking rather different groups of people to judge the frequency of

The easier it is to bring events to mind, the more we think the events are likely to happen. The more often, and the more dramatically, that events are reported in the media, the easier it is to bring them to mind. Thus our beliefs about how common events really are might be quite wrong. Dramatic but rare events might appear to be more common—and more worrying—than undramatic but familiar events which, nevertheless, cause more harm.

various causes of death, such as those arising from smallpox, tornadoes and heart disease. These studies showed that while judgements were moderately accurate, in the sense that people generally knew which were the most frequent and least frequent lethal events, there were several seriously wrong judgements and these did seem to reflect bias which was consistent with the "availability" hypothesis[3]. The accompanying graph shows a comparison of the judged number of deaths each year with the actual number as reported in US public health statistics. If the judgements were accurate, points on the graph would fall on the straight line. However, while most of the frequent hazards did elicit higher estimates, there was a clear tendency among participants to over-estimate the incidence of rare causes of death and under-estimate the frequency of the common ones. Accidents were judged to cause as many deaths as diseases, whereas diseases actually account for 15 times as many lives. Murders were wrongly judged more frequent than diabetes and cancer of the stomach. Frequencies of death from botulism, tornadoes and pregnancy were also greatly over-estimated, along with fire and flames and animal bites and

Relationship between the judged and the actual annual number of deaths from a selection of 41 causes

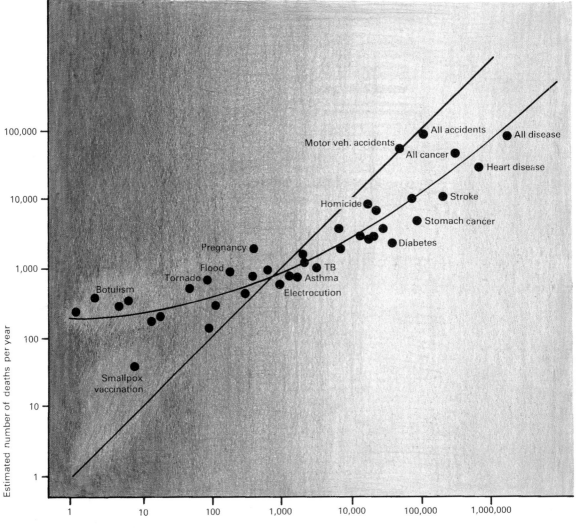

While people have a generally good idea of what causes of death are more numerous than others, there is a tendency to over-estimate rare causes of death and under-estimate common causes. The highest over-estimates are found among the most dramatic events.
Source: reference 3

stings. Studies of newspapers produced at about the same time in America showed, not surprisingly, that the most reported events corresponded with the most over-estimated causes of death.

The researchers in this group have pointed to an important potential effect of the availability heuristic, which is that people may well not be reassured by frequent reiteration of the fact that rare events are rare. If, for example, an engineer wishes to show the rarity of a disaster by stressing the number of safety features built into a power plant, and does so by repeated detailed descriptions of them, it can well result in the perception that the supposedly rare event is, in fact, rather likely, as "proved" by the number of safety features which are needed to prevent it.

A similar study has been performed in England among students, who were asked to give the order which they believed to correspond to the total number of deaths each year in Britain[4]. Like the American groups they did recognize the most serious and least serious risks and they also gave a low risk rating to the use of medical X-rays, presumably because perception of deaths which might occur decades after the X-ray is overwhelmed by knowledge of the immediate benefits of the procedure. Both the American and the British groups rated the risk of death from industrial machinery much higher than is justified by the figures, indicating ignorance of the fact that machinery is responsible for rather a low proportion of industrial deaths. A striking difference between the American and British studies is that in the United States, all but a group of "experts" put nuclear power near or at the top of the list of risks, but the British did not.

Another set of mental manipulations which can lead to misperception and disagreement relates to people's desire for certainty of opinion and over-confidence in their own judgements, whether they are right or wrong. Politicians are notoriously intolerant of scientists whose advice begins "on the one hand" and the average television viewer would much prefer to be told by the forecaster whether or not it is going to rain tomorrow rather than what the chances are of its doing so. This is related to a general tendency among experts and lay people alike to attribute a greater degree of certainty to their estimates than in fact exists. Indeed, few people without statistical training have a good grasp of the general concept of probability and ranges of uncertainty. In a replication of the Oregon studies on misperception, a group in Pennsylvania studied students with a strong professional interest in technology and technology policy and found that their estimates of numbers of deaths for various activities were much closer to analytical estimates, even though there was still the same tendency to over-estimate the frequency of rare events[5]. Like the Oregon students, the Pennsylvania group also wrongly estimated that murder was responsible for a greater number of deaths than suicide. In investigating the *certainty* of this estimation, the Oregon researchers found that about 30% of the study group had given odds greater than 50 to 1 against their being wrong in this ranking. Opinions on risk that are so strongly held are obviously very difficult to change, whatever the arguments.

Yet another way that people handle complicated issues relating to risk is to reject them by saying "it won't happen to me". This is a particularly likely attitude for risks which are familiar and which people believe they have well under personal control. Driving a car is perhaps the supreme example of this and it is one of the more important reasons why people are hard to persuade to wear seat belts. In the future, the extent to which people believe that AIDS does not prevent a risk to themselves could be an important factor in determining the speed of spread of disease.

Examination of the ways in which various groups evaluate risk makes it clear that while experts use statistics and fatality rates in order to assess and rank them, other people do not. They must, therefore, be using some other set of concepts and beliefs in order to do so. "Perceived risk", while it is possible to put numbers on it and predict it, clearly has a multi-dimensional quality. A British group of researchers, having performed a set of studies very similar to those performed in Oregon, have concluded that it is the *qualitative* aspect of risks which is important in determining perceptions, rather than the *quantitative*[6]. These researchers have argued that individuals evaluate potential risk in accordance with conjecture based on images rather than on technical judgements and enumeration.

Three factors, therefore, appear to be in principle most likely to affect the perception of risk: personal experience of the hazardous events; ability to control these hazards; and some concept of them which encompasses "dread", a general feeling that the events are thoroughly nasty things which have the capacity to kill a great many people at one time.

Following up their earlier work, the Oregon group selected a much wider range of hazards, events and activities and asked people to scale them in two respects[7]. The first of these can be termed the *"dread factor"*, which characterizes events which are out of personal control, have potentially catastrophic consequences of global scale with fatal outcomes, are unevenly distributed, posing a high risk to future generations, increasing and not easily reduced, involuntary and with potential to affect the individual. Scaling events on this basis showed a high correlation of perceived risk with a high score on this scale. The higher an activity's score on the "dread factor" the higher its perceived risk, the more people want its risks reduced and (later studies confirmed) the more they want to see strict regulation employed to achieve the desired reduction in risk[8]. The factors encompassing *exposure* to risk and *familiarity* with risk were far less well related to the perception of risk. In contrast, the perception of risk by experts was not found to be related to any of these factors. These studies indicate very strongly that non-experts' perception of risk is governed not by numbers and statistics, but by subjective evaluation.

At the University of Exeter a group at the Department of Psychology critically reviewed these Oregon studies[9], arguing that they were valid only for large groups of people whose composition was reasonably homogeneous and that for individuals and small groups the results might well not be applicable. In order to see whether this technique for studying perceived risk could be used to indicate perceptions of various procedures and activities related specifically to health, ranging from sleep through smoking to heart transplantation, they found that risk perceptions were best explained by ratings of likelihood of mishap, and likelihood of death as a consequence of mishap. Group and individual characteristics were found to be important in influencing perceptions of risk and benefit in certain situations. Once again, actual numbers were relatively unimportant in risk evaluation.

The American studies found that perceived risk was inversely related to perceived benefit. This finding was true also for the Exeter study of health issues, but for individual cases, the assessment of risk did not necessarily predict the amount of benefit perceived and the immediate likelihood of mishap and death was again a potent factor in balancing risk and benefit. This is consistent with the common observation that

huge expenditure will be seen as justifiable to save one indentifiable trapped miner, or a single named fisherman missing at sea, but not to reduce deaths among the scores of generally anonymous miners or fishermen who die every year.

Back in 1969, a pioneering study in this field recorded what people actually did, and used these measures of activity as an index of the risks they are prepared to put up with[10]. It was concluded that the public seems willing to accept risks from voluntary activities (such as skiing) that are roughly a thousand times greater than it would tolerate from involuntarily imposed hazards providing the same level of benefit. But the later Oregon studies have indicated that the extent to which activities are voluntary is closely related to other characteristics, shared with lack of personal control, catastrophic potential, the use of nuclear weapons, terrorism and nuclear power as examples of among the most important. Although perceived risks do appear to be related to "voluntariness", they appear to be much more strongly related to characteristics related to dread.

Clearly then, perception of risk is a very much more complicated matter than the use of statistics would indicate, and depends very much on personal biases and the context in which the risk is introduced into society. Thus, images are drafted which help to determine the perceptions. The use of nuclear power, it can be argued, is associated with images of nuclear bombs and mushroom clouds, and thus with the possibility of the types of nuclear explosions at power plants which experts maintain are impossible. Imagine that petrol, an extremely common source of energy used by everyone day by day, had been introduced into public perception through its use as napalm or a powerful explosive (which it is). Perceptions of the risk associated with carrying the stuff around in a metal tank in the family car could well, thereby, have been very considerably different from what they are now.

When accidents occur, especially if they are of a catastrophic or potentially catastrophic nature, they can act to strengthen perceptions which are already firmly held. For example, a power station malfunctions and automatically shuts down. The technologist acclaims the success of his safety measures. But the non-technologist has his fears of a potential catastrophe reinforced. If, indeed, it is catastrophic *potential* which is the main determinant of the response of society to a threat, then the existence of a perception gap is well nigh inevitable.

People's expressed attitudes to risk also vary with the way that questions are asked and the way that potential outcomes are expressed. A similar idea is encompassed in the old question "is that glass half full or half empty?" In yet another experiment the Oregon researchers asked a study group to estimate the death rates of a number of diseases, but employed several different ways to represent the rates[11]. It was found that while people were quite consistent in getting the ranked order correct, they varied widely in their estimate of actual rates depending, for example, on whether they had been asked how many people *died* or how many people *survived* in a given population in the case of each disease. Similarly, when in another study (already referred to in Chapter 11 in the context of medical risks) two treatments of lung cancer were presented for choice, each choice being equally effective, the choice was influenced by the description of the treatment. The treatment which was described as having a 90% *survival* rate was preferred—both by patients and by doctors—over the treatment having a 10% *mortality* rate, although both measures mean exactly the same thing. That does show, incidentally, that even though doctors may be regarded as technologists, their own perceptions may also be biassed by mental images and other subjective influences.

In a similar experiment, the choice of two medicines was offered, also giving the same expected outcome overall[12]. One medicine was presented as having a definite effect in terms of extension of life, and the other was presented in terms of a balance of probabilities. Respondents consistently chose the drug whose effect was represented as definite, indicating an unwillingness to gamble. However, an extension of the same work showed that when the choice was expressed in terms of loss and adverse effect, people chose the drug whose effects were uncertain. And in another experiment, people were asked to select treatments for an illness, again with one treatment having a definite outcome and the other being something of a gamble. Outcomes were expressed either as pain or as relief of pain. It was found that when the outcome was expressed in terms of pain relief, people were reluctant to take chances; whereas if the outcome was expressed in terms of episodes of pain, then they were prepared to take chances even though the outcomes of treatment were the same.

Thus, our perception of risk depends a great deal on how the facts are presented. Tobacco advertisements focus on the benefits of smoking, not the risks. A factory worker may be worried by a chemical that doubles his risk of getting bladder cancer, but not by one which increases his lifetime risk by 0.002; yet their risk to him is the same.

Research into the perception of risk is in a comparatively early stage, but it has already identified factors which do appear to be important. These include the extent to which the risk is *voluntary*, the extent to which it is under *control*, the extent to which it represents a threat of *catastrophe*, and whether it is viewed as the potential for a *reduction in gains or an increase in losses*. These findings have implications for minimizing disagreements and conflicts between various groups in society.

Public policies on the management of risk will be threatened if they challenge values and opinion which are firmly held, especially when the risk is perceived as being of a potentially catastrophic nature. Formal analyses as performed by scientists and understood by those of a technological inclination are of rather little value. The problem is not that "objective" characterizations of risk and the statistical calculations that accompany them are more correct or more real or more valid than the subjective assessments of risk performed by the majority of the population. It is simply that they are different, and represent the fact that the world is seen in different ways by different people. It is the difference between risk estimation by intuition and risk estimation by using formulae. The "technologists", including "experts", are comfortable with the use of numbers, and believe that the world and its systems are under human control and management. On the other hand, there are those who believe that feelings are more important than numbers, that the world's systems are delicately balanced and should not be upset by human intervention. They are inclined to view experts as arrogant, insensitive and sometimes dangerous: the "mad scientist" mental set. It follows that if any agreement is to be reached on risk-related issues and policies, an understanding of the other person's perceptions is a necessary prerequisite. Disagreements about risk should not be expected to evaporate in the presence of *evidence*, which, if it is consistent with initial beliefs is accepted as being reliable and informative, and, if inconsistent, dismissed as unreliable and unrepresentative.

However, research has also shown that people understand some things quite well, although their conclusions may be reached on a different basis from that used by technologists. When information genuinely is inadequate and experiences biased, educational efforts may help to bridge the gap. As part of the process of policy determination, people's knowledge and attitudes can be studied in order to deduce ways as to how best to narrow such gaps in understanding. Knowledge does not ensure that decisions will reach universal approval, but without knowledge, the extent of disagreement and disapproval will almost inevitably be greater.

An example of how what we know about risk perception can be used in the real world is as follows. People correctly perceive that the risk of being apprehended for a drink–driving offence *on a given trip* is very low, and the risk involved in having a few drinks before taking the wheel is therefore perceived as acceptable. However, the risk of being apprehended for a drink–driving offence, or crashing because of alcohol use, is actually rather high overall, when a *lifetime's*

driving is taken into account. To strengthen this latter perception may reduce acceptance of this particular risk, and help to bridge the gap between an individual's perception and the way that policy makers perceive the risk of drinking and driving. Accordingly, differences in opinion which upset the process of policy making could thus be reduced in this instance if a wider time-scale is used when information is being processed.

In summary, then, risk assessments by technologists should take into account the qualitative and subjective aspects of risk which influence the perceptions of lay people, and seek to find ways to express such aspects in their calculations and proposals. For those who are not technologists, there is a need to understand that information *does* provide a good basis for making decisions; further, that unsupported judgements are unreliable, that perceptions are strongly affected by judgements unrelated to the "real" extent of the problem to an extent of which we may well not be aware, and that new evidence may help us to make better judgements.

THE ACCEPTABILITY OF RISK

Throughout this book we have tended to avoid the words "safe" and "safety", because they imply a zero-risk situation which for practical purposes cannot be attained. In choosing between activities with different levels of risk or in managing a given activity so that risk is to be minimized (see the next chapter), what we are working towards is a level of risk which is "acceptable". It is that level which most people will regard as being "safe", or at any rate "safe enough", which is not to say they are necessarily happy about it. Everyone will prefer less risk to more risk if the benefits stay the same.

Well then, how safe is safe enough? Can the level of risk ever be so low that it is negligible?

As will now be clear from the foregoing discussion on the perception of risk, judgement that a risk is acceptable is not something that depends (for most people) on numbers, but is more usually a subjective determination using value judgements. People in one locality will violently oppose the burying of low-level nuclear waste in their vicinity, despite expert assurances

of safety, while people living under high dams in earthquake areas happily ignore expert warnings of disaster. At the individual level the acceptance or otherwise of a given (sometimes quite high) risk is very much a personal decision, such as choosing whether or not to run a red traffic light, to water ski, or to smoke a cigarette. Some would have it that it is impossible to define a "negligible" risk in numerical terms. Mathematical analysis of probabilities can be used to demonstrate to an individual that the risk of contracting cancer from the water supply is, say, one in a million over the next fifty years, but the actual question he wants answered is, is the water safe, or will it give me cancer?

A working definition in non-numerical terms might be that a situation would be regarded as safe, and the associated hazards negligible, if reasonably informed and experienced people in fact disregard the risk. To then represent the risk in terms of numbers would be a secondary activity, undertaken after the question of negligibility has been decided.

Early work in the field of risk analysis did, in principle, take this line of thought, through measuring what people actually did, then assessing the risks of these activities and drawing conclusions as to what risks were "accepted". But because many of these people were in fact acting in ignorance of the "real" risks, such measurements are rather meaningless. If it is true that it is perception of risk which affects behaviour (including acceptance of risk), and if it is also true that increased access to factual information can change perceptions of risk, then it follows that increased information, including that of a numerical nature, can affect the acceptance of risk and thus what people regard as being "safe".

Some economists have argued that people's acceptance of risk can be represented by their willingness to pay for protection against various hazards. Again, this can only be at least a very indirect measure, because people may well quite wrongly believe that the expenditure of money *can* eliminate a risk, when in fact it can do no such thing. Conversely, people may have no real idea of how much it would really take to reduce a risk to what they would consider to be acceptable levels.

"Health" and "safety" tend to be moral sentiments given high priority, being social imperatives which appear to justify the unlimited application of available resources. As the next chapter will show, the management of risk is very much tied up with the principle that resources are not unlimited, and that the management of risk includes choosing between alternative measures. An "acceptable" risk is the risk associated with the best of the *available* alternatives, not the best alternative we can think of.

In the case of public administration of risks affecting whole communities, people are inherently suspicious of what is done—or what is not done—and measurement has shown that what people are prepared to accept under these circumstances is a level of risk which is very much lower than the level of risk which they accept voluntarily. For these situations, and for the circumstances faced by a worker in a hazardous environment, there is a great deal of difference between a risk which is acceptable and a risk which must be accepted. The degree of risk which is acceptable also depends on the size of the population exposed to it. A large industrial facility might be designed so as not to impose an average risk of death on the population of a country of higher than one in a million. But the same standard could not apply for workers within the facility (industrial accidents), who drive to work (road crashes) after a cooked meal (carcinogens), or for their families who after a visit to the doctor (X-rays) go for a day on the beach (ultraviolet rays from the sun). Society would grind to a halt if individuals were never exposed to risks much higher than the standards required to protect society *as a whole*.

In both public administration and occupational safety, it is now becoming widely agreed that risk levels should be fully disclosed and explained as far as possible to those affected by it, although actual compliance with this principle is more a feature of American administration than British. If a serious effort is made at the communication of information related to risk, then the outcome is more likely to be that a known level of risk becomes accepted (albeit sometimes with reluctance).

At this point, what people will then regard as being "safe enough" depends a great deal on the confidence that they have on the operation of risk management procedures, whether these are applied on the factory floor or to the complex operations of a large industrial facility with the capacity to injure those that live around it[13]. When the management of risk is not under the direct control of the individual it takes a much higher level of confidence to make risk acceptable. It is confidence in management which is at the root of risk acceptability, and it is to the management of risk to which we now finally turn.

Chapter Fifteen

Management of Risk

MANAGEMENT OF COMMUNITY RISK

We may not normally think of it in such imposing terms, but the management of risk is a matter of day-to-day decision-making for us all. At the personal level, as we have seen in many examples in this book, managing risk does not necessarily mean reducing it. The skier who flies to Switzerland for a fortnight on the slopes is choosing not to *minimize* personal risk, but rather to face it and embrace it as part of an attempt to maximize the enjoyment and quality of life. There is no reason for society to intervene. Another example might be the complex set of decisions on perceived risks and benefits which are taken by the car driver with an evening's alcohol intake flowing through his blood and brain as he buckles on his seatbelt before starting his journey home. In this case, while his decisions may be taken with the aim of maximizing his quality of life, they may well have other effects which are not to the public benefit, may impose risks involuntarily on other people, and which do justify society's involvement.

We will return to matters of personal risk management later, but first let us consider how risk is managed at the institutional level with an eye (it is to be hoped) to community benefit. This will include the variety of decisions that have to be made by governments and public administrative bodies, as well as the managers of large public utilities and industrial installations. Risk management is the process of deciding what to do in cases where risk has been determined to exist. It includes integrating risk assessment with feasibility and economic and socio-political realities.

As part of any such process several different groups will be involved, and examples of the ways that such groups may disagree have already been touched upon in this book. Arguments on risk reduction—as part of what will usually be referred to as improvements in safety—are likely to centre on the *feasibility* of introducing the necessary measures, their *cost* and their *inconvenience*.

Institutions which act, in principle, for the overall benefit of the community include the legislature, government departments and administrative bodies concerned with health, safety and welfare, and industrial organizations supplying public utilities such as energy, water and food. The measures they employ include regulatory intervention, common law and self-regulation.

In general, as prosperity and economic standards increase, social and legislative pressures tend to drive downwards the level of risk which is publicly acceptable.

Different countries have different ways of expressing their aims in legislation. In respect to industrial safety, for example, in Norway and Sweden there is an implicit assumption that

Risk can be managed by avoiding or controlling the hazard, blocking it off from people and from vulnerable property, and minimizing the consequences when things go wrong.

safety depends on the environment rather than the worker. The Swiss rely on past experience. In the UK (where the employer is enjoined to ensure "so far as is reasonably practical" the health and safety of his employees) and in the United States (". . . as far as possible . . .") there is a feeling that we can legislate to move towards a goal but not to require its attainment[1]. When it comes to the process of control, again there are substantial differences; for instance, occupational health and safety is much more centrally controlled in the UK than the United States.

Public participation is increasingly part of risk management in large utilities, especially when the production of power is concerned. Participation may be formal, as in public enquiries, or informal, as through pressure of public opinion expressed in the media. Participation raises the risk of confrontation between politicians, public, experts and managers. Lawyers become involved, raising the black-or-white issues of the courts. And all competing groups will differ on the importance to be placed on technical evidence.

The actual techniques employed for managing risks at the societal level include the following[2]:

—avoiding or eliminating the risk, such as prohibiting the use of a potentially dangerous substance or activity;

—regulating the use of the substance or the activity to reduce the adverse health effects, such as controlling pub opening hours and the sale of medicines;

—reducing the vulnerability of people and property, such as by requiring guards on machines and the wearing of pressure suits by airmen;

—developing mitigation and recovery procedures after the event, such as the establishment of search and rescue teams and firefighting services;

—instituting schemes to reimburse and redistribute losses, such as insurance and extra pay for high-risk jobs.

All the above approaches have been used at one time or another throughout the past several centuries.

Taking the control of injury as a specific example of risk management, injury research pioneer Dr William Haddon defined ten strategies[3]. With tactics applicable to traffic safety as examples, they are as follows. The "hazard", it will be recalled, is in this case mechanical energy.

1 Prevent the creation of the hazard

Traffic deaths would never have occurred if, after centuries of managing civilization without it, we had not invented the private car.

2 Reduce the amount of hazard brought into being

Limitation of maximum speed reduces the potential for injurious energy release in crashes.

3 Prevent the release of the hazard that already exists

Roads can be made more resistant to skidding, cars' and lorries' brakes can be made more efficient, drivers can (perhaps) be made more skilled.

4 Modify the rate and distribution of release of the hazard

Seat belts and child restraints transfer the energy of a crash to the human body a great deal less destructively than windscreens and dashboards.

5 Separate the hazard from the human

Pedestrians and bicyclists can be physically separated from motor vehicles by sympathetic land use and town planning. Trees, telegraph poles and other rigid structures can be removed from the roadside.

6 Separate the hazard and the human by a barrier

Opposing lines of traffic can be separated from each other by shock-absorbent barriers. Motorcyclists can wear crash helmets. Inflatable bags can assist seat belts in separating vulnerable people from unforgiving vehicle interiors.

7 Modify the basic qualities of the hazard

The interior surface of vehicles can be made rounded and shock-absorbent. Telegraph poles and light posts can be made to break away on impact.

8 Make the human more resistant to the hazard

The prevention of osteoporosis and the treatment of haemophilia can minimize the risk of fracture or bleeding in vulnerable groups.

9 Immediately counter the damage done

The widespread public knowledge of basic first aid and the provision of emergency roadside telephones permit rapid response to injury.

10 Stabilize, repair and rehabilitate

Prompt and efficient medical care in the early days, and the provision of devices such as artificial legs later, can help even the severely injured to lead normal lives.

Exactly the same set of strategies can be employed for the management of risks posed by any other of the hazards mentioned in this book, from stairs, to swimming pools, to nuclear power stations. Further, the same principles apply if the object to be protected from the hazard is not a human being but rather, say, an animal or a Ming vase.

All the countermeasures and techniques outlined above are readily available. For most risks, the question is, not *how* do we reduce them, but *whether* we reduce them. Risk management does not (to the dismay of some technologists) exist in a social vacuum.

Activist proponents of safety measures may well disregard economic issues, arguing from the moral position that it will always be worth while to save a life and that no one person's life is more valuable than any other. It follows from this argument that it is immoral to delay the introduction of any measure designed to reduce risk. "Safety must be paramount" could well be their battle cry.

Faced by such calls, responsible institutions such as governments, manufacturers and industrial managers are likely to take what seems to be at first glance a rather defensive position. They are able to claim that any single problem is very small compared to all the other threats to life and welfare that exist in our complicated world. In any event, many losses result from behaviour of the consumer rather than the institution. If people drove more carefully, then road crashes would not occur and vehicle safety features would be unnecessary. Further, the technology at present available is not sufficient to reduce most risks to the desired extent, let alone to zero, and even if suitable measures could be developed the cost would be such as to overwhelm the benefits to be sought in risk reduction.

The definition of a middle ground, of what risks can and should be managed, and the need for some balancing of risks, costs and benefits are all matters on which agreement (or, at least, consensus) could bring disputing groups together. But all must agree that it is futile to say that *no* risk should be tolerated. Alternative activities, technologies and substances all have risks. To ban any one of them might eliminate that particular one, but its *lack* carries a risk as well. It is a matter of balance, of comparison.

We have already seen how public confidence in risk management measures can influence the level of risk which is publicly acceptable, so that confidence in management is as important a factor as the actual level of risk in itself. Further, people must believe that risks are being accurately reported to them, especially in the case of "dread" events of very low probability but potentially catastrophic consequence. The trick is to build that public confidence, and there is some evidence that where the safety of consumer products is concerned, formal analysis of risk is preferred as a basis for making decisions over the informal practices which, in general, represent the standard industry approach today[4].

In earlier chapters in this book we have outlined some of the procedures which together make up the formal process of risk analysis. The *estimation* of risk is the essential first step in the process, but we have made the point several times in various chapters that to a widely varying extent, depending on the risk that is being measured, the figures produced through such estimation are necessarily inexact, whether they have been gathered as part of an experimental or laboratory process or through epidemiological measurements of people in the real world. Risk assessment also includes *evaluation*, which takes into account personal value judgements and the public perception of risks. The *management* of risk very much depends on public perceptions and public opinion, and to the extent that objective scientific measurement of risk differs from public perceptions there will necessarily be, as part of that management, a process of interaction between the groups whose perceptions are different.

Public *acceptance* of a risk does not mean that people find the risks *acceptable*. So, for the purpose of management, it is convenient to divide risks into three groups.

—events of very high risk and unacceptable consequences;

—events of very low risk with negligible consequences;

—risks falling between those two extremes which require management for maximum benefit.

Various studies on the acceptability of risk have led to the drafting of guidelines which can help to define the upper and lower levels of probability of risk within which systematic management is called for. These are definitely not strict limits, and they are subject to all the inexactitudes and differences in perception which we have already described. Every individual case will still have to be resolved on its merits, and public action will still depend more on public perceptions than on numerical measurements.

Some risks are so high that decision makers can reasonably expect that practically all individuals would find the risk unacceptable. A continuing risk of death of 1 in 100 each year, imposed over and above risks existing from all other sources, is essentially too high to be publicly acceptable. The more dangerous voluntary sports and activities such as those of professional stuntmen approach this sort of level, and some (Grand Prix racing drivers, for example) exceed it. Some situations such as those faced by young and inexperienced motorcyclists and professional oilrig divers involve higher risks, but these decline with experience or are restricted in duration rather than continuing to exist over an average lifetime.

At the other extreme, in attempting to put numbers on a level of risk which is so small as not to be worth worrying about—to the extent the public funds are invested in its management —there is a view that this level should probably be about that at which individuals who are aware of the risks that they run would not do very much on their own initiative to reduce it[5]. However, this is hard to estimate because few people are in fact aware of the actual magnitude of very small risks, and have little opportunity to demonstrate whether or not they are prepared to reduce them. Several review bodies have speculated that few people would commit their own resources to reduce an annual risk of death that was already as low as one in 10,000 and even fewer would take action at an annual level of one in a million. A one-in-a-million risk is about the same as that from dying from a prescribed drug or a vaccination, or of a meteorite killing a thousand people, or of an aeroplane crashing into an empty football stadium around London, and is lower than the risk of dying from an earthquake in California. A chemical with a one-in-a-million

risk of causing cancer would kill 50 people in Britain in 70 years (a lifetime), or less than one a year.

There is of course—as we have already stressed in other contexts—a big difference between a one-in-a-million chance of killing a million people in a given year, and the chance of one person a year dying every year for a million years. We have made the point that public perceptions of these two outcomes of the same risk are very different so that, for example, the risk of a disaster which is prominent in the public mind (such as the catastrophic disruption of a nuclear reactor) has to be reduced to somewhat below what, for other less "dread" events, would be regarded as acceptably low levels.

The limits within which risks should most appropriately be managed, therefore, embrace a range of between about one in a thousand and one in a million.

For a few already tiny risks it may be the case that they can be reduced even further at very low cost, but inevitably at some point there will be reached a situation where to reduce risk further would necessitate unjustifiable expenditure. It follows that a necessary part of risk management is to take account of benefits and in some way balance them against the risks which are being reduced.

The evolution of safety design features in private cars is an example of risk management at the public level. For the first six decades of the car's history, very few resources were put into the development and construction of safety features as such, and the basic philosophy among public administrators, manufacturers and (generally) the public was that because the basic "cause" of road accidents was the "nut behind the wheel" there was very little that could or should be done about accidents unless this nut's behaviour could be changed. However, accident analysis showed that many crashes occurred because the driver's task was unnecessarily difficult because of design features of the car and the road environment, and that when crashes did occur, completely unnecessary death and injury was being caused to the occupants of the crashing vehicle. Ralph Nader was the most famous (but by no means the only) early exponent of this view[6]. Crash research went on to show many features of vehicle design which could be improved in order to reduce the risk of death and injury, but because the voluntary reaction of manufacturers to this information was rather slow, and was governed more by market considerations than those of risk, safety design standards were introduced so that action was expedited. Because all manufacturers had to do the same things at the same time, marketing inequities were minimized.

However, a point has now been reached where substantial changes in vehicle design for safety are unlikely unless there is a significant public shift in attitudes to the balancing of risks and benefits, despite the fact that driving a car is one of the more dangerous things that we do these days and that the technology is available right now to further reduce death and injury very substantially. The use of this technology would certainly increase the cost of cars and thus the cost of living, adding inflationary pressures which now appear to be undesirable although the benefits to the general welfare could be considerable.

From this brief history of one piece of public risk management, two lessons emerge. One is that perceptions of the causes of loss can actually *prevent* resources being allocated effectively. If people think that because human behaviour is associated with most (say, 75%) road crash injuries, they may also conclude that (at least) 75% of available resources should be allocated to changing road-user behaviour. But if (as is the case) it is much easier and more effective to change *other* parts of the system, namely the (say) 25% contribution of the vehicle and the environment to crash injury, then it makes much better sense to push resources in that direction. Accordingly, perceptions of what risks are most usefully manageable are important and influential.

The other lesson is that for some activities, public perceptions will stall resource allocation at a much higher level of risk than for others. Immediate improvements in street lighting or the fitting and compulsory use of rear seat belts, known to be highly cost-beneficial in reducing injuries, are much less enthusiastically supported than increases in police traffic law enforcement, let alone what is demanded of safety measures for activities such as the production of nuclear power.

The use of what are seen to be impersonal cost–benefit analyses may be unacceptable, particularly where dread events are concerned. In the case of the private car, perhaps the most dreaded event of all is that the vehicle catches fire after a crash, but it is in fact rather a rare happening. After a small Ford car was found in the United States to be relatively likely to catch fire in certain sorts of crashes, there was a public outcry when it was discovered that the manufacturer had used cost–benefit analysis to reject a feature which would only have cost £8, but which would have reduced the possibility of such fires occurring. Specifically, the benefit of preventing 180 deaths, 180 injuries and 2,100 burned vehicles was assessed at £34 million, while the cost of the modification to 12.5 million vehicles was £94 million. Ford used £138,000 as the value of life for their analysis[7]. There is always a danger that prejudiced analysts may push their calculations in the direction of a predetermined outcome. Again, the history of this case shows that while cost–benefit analysis may be used as one of a number of tools to help make decisions, public perceptions and desires may still be of over-riding importance.

It should be clear that there is a difference between cost–*benefit* analysis and cost–*effectiveness* analysis. One simple way of looking at the difference is this. In cost–benefit calculations, the decision is whether to spend money to save lives; this means weighing lives in the balance against sums of money, a process so set about with value judgements that it can be viewed as anything between entirely sensible and essential to immoral and unacceptable. Cost–effectiveness analysis, on the other hand, makes the assumption that resources are available, even if limited, and is used to help decisions on how best to make use of them to solve a problem or limit risk.

The great advantage of cost–benefit analysis is that it does force a line of systematic and rational thought by assigning monetary values to the various factors under consideration. It is in the assignment of these values that difficulties arise. For example, what is the value of restraint of freedom? Does the writing of a motor vehicle safety standard have any cost other than the administrative time involved? And perhaps the most intractable problem of all is that because many of the risks of public interest are most effectively measured in terms of death or, at best, reduction in life expectancy, some monetary value has to be placed, for comparative purposes, on human existence. Further, at that point it is very easy for the discussion to become distorted. For example, the question "how much should we spend per life saved?" is very different from the question which many people take to be an inevitable corollary, namely, "how much is a life worth?" It is *not* necessary to answer the second question in order to cope with the first.

Everyday experience shows us that as a community we are willing to spend far more on some lives than on others, and this has very little to do with how economists might value those lives. Several calculations have shown that far more is spent on safety measures in commercial aviation per life saved than is spent on road accident prevention.

Therefore, cost–benefit analysis is always liable to moderation on a case by case approach, with the importance of the individual generally being believed to be paramount. Unlimited resources would be released to save the life of a miner trapped underground with his plight clearly visible to the nation through the news-hungry media. Yet nearly a miner a week dies in Britain from ''routine'' accidents. Take another rather more complicated example of individual exposure to risk. Imagine that a huge food store required fumigation to prevent the growth of a mould which could result in the death, over the next 20 years, of (say) a dozen people. However, the necessary fumigant chemical (for which there was no alternative) was hazardous to the workers to the extent that one or two would be likely to die within this period. It is unlikely that this fumigant would be permitted for use although there would be a net community gain, because the near certain death of one or two people in a small group is regarded generally as a matter of much greater concern than the possible death of more people but among a very large number.

Because of the importance of the individual in managing the risk faced by workers in the chemical industry, the principle of ''as low as reasonably achievable'' is often written into regulations, indicating a desire not simply to reduce risks to a point where they are exceeded by the benefits but also to continue to reduce them until further reduction would cause an unwarranted drain on resources.

In the case of the reduction of public risks, resources sooner or later come to an end. At some point, a greater improvement in general health and public safety might well be sought from a healthier economy than from continued but individually minor improvements in pollution levels or accident rates. In a situation where outlays are necessarily limited, resources are best devoted to those risks in which the most reduction is achieved for every pound expended. There are, nevertheless, some consequences which are so horrendous that extraordinary measures will be justified in reducing the risks, however small or vague they are. For example,

chlorofluorocarbon aerosol impellers (CFCs) *may* be destroying ozone in the stratosphere, and thus potentially upsetting the earth's entire temperature balance. If they do, it will be too late to do anything about it afterwards. There are alternatives. So, the US government is proposing a ban on them.

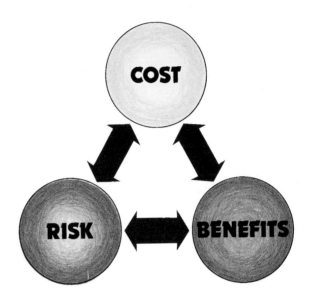

Risk management does not only mean reducing risks. To reduce any risk costs money, drains resources. Sooner or later it costs too much to reduce a risk further, and the money would be better spent elsewhere. Most events, activities and technologies which carry a risk also offer a benefit; if we reduce the risk too far, we may find we have lost the benefit as well. These three elements are always interlinked. One cannot be changed without affecting the others.

Health services have an insatiable hunger for money. It is needed to pay for medical, para-medical and support staff, for buildings and facilities, for the provision of high-technology equipment, and for research. There will always be the dying, the unwell, the disadvantaged—those at risk, in other words. At the individual clinical level, the doctor and other people in the system will, of course, always do the very best they can for the people they see. But because resources cannot ever match demand, there must be rationing of access to care. In health systems under central control, decisions at high political and administrative levels are made to allocate the resources in various directions; if there is not enough money to pay for, say, cataract operations for all who need them, sufferers simply have to wait. In health systems controlled completely by free enterprise, on the other hand, access to care is limited by individuals' ability to pay for it.

Risks to health are of two kinds: to the length of life, and to the quality of life. There is interest now in making rationing more "fair" by combining these elements in order to encompass an overall measure of benefit. This would help to make a choice, say, between spending a given sum on a few expensive operations designed to increase the *length* of life, and a lot of cheap operations designed to increase the *quality* of life. Such considerations can be extended outside the health services: it may be more cost-effective, for example, to fit windscreens with an inside layer of strong plastic than to commit surgical resources to fixing up disfiguring but non-fatal glass injuries to faces.

All groups in society bear some responsibility for the effects of decisions on risks. An individual or pressure group who succeeds in getting a pesticide banned will be responsible for any deaths that might occur (such as through increases in diseases such as malaria) in countries which may be remote from his own. If coal-burning power stations are used to replace nuclear power stations because of the risk of radioactive contamination, and if this results in an exaggeration of the "greenhouse effect" on the world through the continuing release of carbon dioxide, then those responsible for the decision are also responsible for the potentially catastrophic environmental changes which could occur as a result.

As a community in a complicated world, therefore, we must realize that if we assign our priorities in managing risks in a way that has the effect that resources are *not* distributed in a maximally effective manner, then the result is that people will die, and those premature deaths could have been prevented.

MANAGEMENT OF PERSONAL RISK

The "risk-free man" would probably be a very dull fellow. Risk adds spice to life, most people would maintain, but it does seem that many of us spend a great deal of time worrying about small risks over which we have no control rather than large risks which we *can* do a great deal about.

Smoking is the supreme example of these risks, and for those who smoke there is no other single action they can take which would so much reduce the risk of premature death—without any doubt to themselves and possibly to others as well—as stopping[8]. Cigarette smoke is carcinogenic to an extent which eclipses any other substance which is regularly absorbed into our body, and it has many other adverse effects on which it would be repetitive to dwell.

Alcohol use is another potent risk factor over which we have substantial control, although in this case the major risk that arises is that of death and injury through accidents and violence rather than from disease, unless the alcohol intake is exceptionally high. As long as alcohol is not taken before attempting hazardous tasks (such as driving) which require a high degree of concentration and judgement, then drinking that corresponds with the following criteria should not increase the risk of personal harm above existing levels[9]:

—a weekly intake not exceeding 50 units for men and 35 units for women;

—not drinking every day, or alone;

—not using alcohol as an emotional prop or an aid to sleep;

—not drinking quickly or on an empty stomach.

Food is not medicine. Eating it should be fun. The main risks we face in the developed world arise as a result of eating too much of it and creating the hazard called obesity. Despite widespread concern, the evidence is that we are under no significant risk from additives and preservatives. Nevertheless, dietary factors have been identified as affecting the risk of some diseases, and it is clear, overall, that the lowest risk lies in an enjoyable and balanced diet[10] which:

—maintains an ideal weight;
—keeps fat intake to around 30% of total calories;
—increases the ratio of polyunsaturated to saturated fats;
—minimizes dietary cholesterol;
—keeps salt intake to under 10 grams a day;
—limits sugar intake to about 55 grams a day;
—emphasizes food containing lots of fibre.

In respect to *occupational health*, it is difficult these days to be as selective about jobs as perhaps was the case in economically less troubled times, and in any event many individuals are happy to accept the rewards of a high-risk job because of personal satisfaction or extra monetary return. In Chapter 6 are outlined those occupations which do appear to carry a higher risk than others, especially of accidental injury, and there is little doubt that in occupations such as farming there is a great deal of scope for changing individual operating practices and equipment design to reduce the risk of unnecessary injury.

In *transport*, the risks of travelling in publicly administered systems such as commercial aviation and railways are already very low, to the extent indeed that they are near-impossible to reduce further. However, that is not at all the case for road transport, where human behaviour interacts with vehicle and environmental design in a way which makes the use of the roads one of our highest-risk daily activities. Steady community pressure on administrators of road and traffic systems and the manufacturers of cars could steadily change perceptions in cost-effectiveness terms in the way which has been

done, for example, in the case of pharmaceutical preparations and the generation of nuclear power, where far lower levels of risk are demanded. Reliance on human behaviour, the traditional way to improve safety in traffic, is about the worst possible way to reduce public risks.

The constant use of seat belts, in the front and rear seats of cars, and ensuring that children also *never* ride unrestrained by safety seats or harnesses, are simple steps which do more to reduce the risk of death or injury in a crash (of whoever's "fault") than any other single measure.

In the case of risks in the *home* and during *recreation*, personal choices again can largely determine the levels of risk we face, at least in the western developed world. Here again, it is knowledge that is the key.

And it is knowledge which should help us keep a sense of proportion when comparing one risk with another. Of some sorts of risks we appear to have very little knowledge, and these range from the risks of natural and man-made disasters to the risks of medical and surgical treatment. Particularly in the latter case, an informed discussion between the participants in any decision is more likely to lead to an outcome which is satisfactory to all than if risks are blindly entered into on both sides.

There is some risk in everything we do. Risks which we face involuntarily as a result of public decision-making and administration are best managed in a climate of the highest public awareness possible. Risks which we face at a personal level are most effectively managed by us as individuals if we know what the risks really are and how they compare with each other. Then, our personal decisions are most likely to fulfil our desires and expectations. If this book has helped its readers to handle a subject which has been with us for ever, yet which has only recently become the subject of systematic consideration, it will have served its purpose.

Further Reading

For the reader interested in further study of the subject of risk and risk assessment, there has been a recent burgeoning of a hitherto very sparse literature.

Several books offer an overview of risk-related matters. The easiest for the non-technical reader is *Risk Watch*[1], a first-class introduction to the topic and, as we have already noted in this book, a major contribution to discussion on how degrees of risk should be publicly represented. The report of the Royal Society's Study Group on risk, *Risk Assessment*[2] is harder reading, but offers another broad picture and is an essential reference. More technical and theoretical discussion will be found in the textbooks, *An Anatomy of Risk* by W D Rowe[3] and *Acceptable Risk* by B Fischhoff and his colleagues in Oregon[4]. A good conference report, published as a book, is *Societal Risk Assessment*, edited by Richard Schwing[5].

Turning specifically to injury and its control, an unmatched book is *Injury Control* by Professor Julian Waller[6], of the University of Vermont, who surveys the literature on a world wide basis. A more discursive volume is *Injuries*, by Leon Robertson of Yale[7], and Professor Susan Baker's *Injury Fact Book*[8] includes an extraordinarily comprehensive set of American data, of a scope and detail which is sorely required for other countries.

These three books all cover transport risks particularly thoroughly, and are essential reading for those interested in traffic safety.

For the major risk factors, the report of the Royal College of Physicians on smoking, *Health or Smoking?*[9] and the report of the Royal College of Psychiatrists on alcohol, *Alcohol, Our Favourite Drug*[10], are both easy to read, despite their comprehensive coverage and scientific status. Nutrition is the subject of scores of books, but a particularly good combination of readability and scientific validity is *Nutrition, Diet and Health* by Michael Gibney[11].

Also very readable is Professor Fremlin's book *Power Production: What are the Risks?*[12] which contains much comparative information on risks generally. Hugh Crone's book *Chemicals and Society* is another example of how to mix good writing with good science[13].

There are now several multidisciplinary journals publishing scientific papers on risk-related matters, including *Accident Analysis and Prevention* (Pergamon Press), *Hazard Prevention* (System Safety Society Inc.), and the new *Risk Analysis* (Society for Risk Analysis, Plenum Publishing Corp.). These are, of course, additional to the wide range of journals specific to fields such as medicine, engineering and insurance.

References

Note: References to work cited in the text (by numbers in superscript) are listed here in a way which is normally used in scientific literature. Books are described by author or editor, title, publisher, and year of publication. Articles in journals are listed by author, title of paper, name of journal, year of publication, volume number of journal, and number of first page of article cited.

Chapter 1 History and Background: The Times are Changing

1 Hippocrates, On Injuries of the Head, in Adams F *The Genuine Works of Hippocrates*, Williams and Wilkins Baltimore 1939
2 Nriagu J. *Lead and Lead Poisoning*, Wiley Interscience New York 1983
3 Covello V T and Mumpower J. Risk analysis and risk management: a historical perspective, *Risk Analysis* 1985, **5**: 103
4 Office of Population Censuses and Surveys, *Mortality Statistics 1841–1980 England and Wales*, Serial Tables, Series DH1 No 15, HMSO London 1985
5 Office of Population Censuses and Surveys, *Trends in Mortality 1951–1975*, Series DH1 No 3, HMSO London 1978

Chapter 2 The Nature of Risk

1 Royal Society Study Group, *Risk Assessment*, The Royal Society London 1983
2 Thompson M. Aesthetics of risk: culture or content, in Schwing R C and Albers W A (editors) *Societal Risk Assessment: How Safe is Safe Enough*, Plenum Press NY 1980
3 Cotgrove S. Risk, value conflict and political legitimacy, in Griffiths R F (editor) *Dealing with Risk: The Planning, Management and Acceptability of Technological Risk*, Manchester University Press 1981
4 Chief Medical Officer of the DHSS, *Annual Report on the State of the Public Health*, HMSO London 1986

5 International Commission on Radiological Protection, Problems involved in developing an index of harm, ICRP Publication No 27, *Annals of the IRCP* **1977, 1)4)**: 1
6 Gordon J E. The epidemiology of accidents, *American Journal of Public Health* 1949, **39**: 504
7 Haddon W. Advances in the epidemiology of injuries as a basis for public policy, *Public Health Reports* 1980, **95**: 411

Chapter 3 The Measurement of Risk

1 Royal Society Study Group, *Risk Assessment*, The Royal Society London 1983
2 Fox A J. Mortality statistics and the assessment of risk, *Proceedings of the Royal Society of London* 1981, **A376**: 65
3 Urquhart J and Heilmann K. *Risk Watch: The Odds of Life*, Facts on File Publications 1984
4 Whittemore A S. Facts and values in risk analysis for environmental toxicants, *Risk Analysis* 1983, **3**: 23

Chapter 4 Main Causes of Death

1 Vemura K and Pisa Z. Recent trends in cardiovascular disease mortality in 27 industrialized countries, *World Health Statistics Quarterly* 1985, **38**: 142
2 WHO Expert Committee, *Community Prevention and Control of Cardiovascular Disease*, WHO Technical Report Series 732, WHO Geneva 1986

3 American Heart Association Committee Report, Risk factors and coronary disease, *Circulation* 1980, **62:** 449A

4 WHO Expert Committee, *Prevention of Coronary Heart Disease*, WHO Technical Report Series 678, WHO Geneva 1982

5 The Pooling Project Research Group, Relationship of blood pressure, serum cholesterol, smoking habit, relative weight and ECG abnormalities to incidence of major coronary events: final report of the Pooling Project, *Journal of Chronic Diseases* 1978, **31:** 201

6 Gordon T, Kannel W B, and McGee D. Death and coronary attacks in men after giving up cigarette smoking, *Lancet* 1974, **2:** 1348

7 Daly L R, Mulcahy R, Graham I M, and Hickey M. Long-term effect of mortality of stopping smoking after unstable angina and myocardial infarction, *British Medical Journal* 1983, **287:** 324

8 Gloyne S R. Pneumoconiosis: a histological survey of necropsy material in 1205 cases, *Lancet* 1951, **1:** 801G

9 Marmot M G, Rose G, Shipley M J, Thomas B J. Alcohol and mortality: a U-shaped curve, *Lancet* 1981, **1:** 580

10 Hennekens C H and MacMahon B. Oral contraceptives and myocardial infarction, *New England Journal of Medicine* **1977, 296:** 1166

11 Office of Population Censuses and Surveys, *Trends in Mortality 1951-1975*, Series DH1 No 3, HMSO London 1978

12 Doll R and Peto R. *The Causes of Cancer*, Oxford University Press 1981

13 National Cancer Institute, *Decade of Discovery*, NIH Publication, 81-2323, 1981

14 Japanese Radiation Research Society, A review of thirty years study of the Hiroshima and Nagasaki atomic bomb survivors, *Journal of Radiation Research* (supplement) 1975

15 International Commission on Radiological Protection, *ICRP Publication 27*, Annals of the ICRP 1977, **1)4):** 1

16 Grosch D S and Hopwood L A, *Biological Effects of Radiation*, Academic Press NY 1979

17 Dennis J A. The measures and risks of radiation, *Biologist* 1986, **33:** 195

18 Fremlin J H. *Power Production: What are the Risks?* Adam Hilger Ltd 1985

19 Office of Population Censuses and Surveys, *Mortality Statistics 1841–1980 England and Wales*, Serial Tables, Series DHI No 15, HMSO London 1985

20 Elmes P C. Relative importance of cigarette smoking in occupational lung disease, *British Journal of Industrial Medicine* 1981, **38:** 1

21 Doll R and Peto J. *Effects on Health of Exposure to Asbestos*, Health and Safety Commission, HMSO London 1985

22 Waller J A. *Injury Control: a Guide to the Causes and Prevention of Trauma*, Lexington Books, D C Heath and Company 1985

23 Office of Population Censuses and Surveys, *Mortality Statistics: Accidents and Violence*, Series DH 4 No 9, HMSO London 1984

24 National Clearinghouse for Poison Control Centres, *Survey of the Most-Frequent Accidentally Ingested Products*, Department of Health, Education and Welfare 1963

25 Kreitman N. The coal gas story, *British Journal of Preventive and Social Medicine* 1976, **30:** 86

26 Surgeon General's Report on Acquired Immune Deficiency Syndrome, *Journal of the American Medical Association* 1986, **256:** 2784

27 Biggar R J (leading article), The clinical features of HIV infection in Africa, *British Medical Journal* 1986, **293:** 1453

28 Quinn T C *et al.* AIDS in Africa: an epidemiologic paradigm, *Science* 1986, **234:** 955

29 Tillet H E and McEvoy M. Reassessment of predicted numbers of AIDS cases in the UK, *Lancet* 1986, **2:** 1104

Chapter 5   Major Risk Factors

1 Royal College of Physicians, *Health or Smoking? Followup Report of the Royal College of Physicians of London*, Pitman Publishing London 1983

2 US Department of Health, Education and Welfare, *Smoking and Health*, DHEW Publication PHS 7950066, 1979

3 Office of Population Censuses and Surveys, *General Household Survey 1984*, HMSO London 1986

4 World Health Organization, *Epidemiology of Cancer of the Lung: Report of the Study Group*, WHO Technical Report Series 1960: 192

5 Doll R and Peto R. Mortality in relation to smoking: twenty years' observations of British doctors, *British Medical Journal* 1976, **4:** 1525

6 Wald N J *et al.* Does breathing other people's tobacco smoke cause lung cancer? *British Medical Journal* 1986, **293:** 1217

7 Marshall E. Involuntary smokers face health risks, *Science* 1986, **234:** 1066

8 Marsh A. Smoking and illness: what smokers really believe, *Health Trends* 1985, **17:** 7

9 WHO Expert Committee on Smoking Control, *Controlling the Smoking Epidemic*, Technical Report Series No 636, WHO Geneva 1979

10 Royal College of Psychiatrists, *Alcohol: Our Favourite Drug*, Tavistock Publications 1986

11 McDonnell R and Maynard A. The cost of alcohol misuse. *British Journal of Addiction* 1985, **80:** 27

12 Sherlock S (ed). *Alcohol and Disease*, British Medical Bulletin 38, Churchill Livingstone 1982

13 Walmsley R. *Personal Violence*, Home Office Research Study No 89, HMSO London 1986
14 Board of Science and Education, *Young People and Alcohol*, British Medical Association 1986
15 Kozel N J and Adams E H. Epidemiology of drug abuse: an overview, *Science* 1986, **234**: 970
16 Board of Science and Education, *Diet, Nutrition and Health*, British Medical Association 1986
17 Doll R and Peto R. *The Causes of Cancer*, Oxford University Press 1981
18 Gibney N J. *Nutrition, Diet and Health*, Cambridge University Press 1986

Chapter 6   Occupational Risks

1 Office of Population Censuses and Surveys, *Occupational Mortality 1979–80, 1982–83*, Decennial supplement, HMSO London 1986
2 Health and Safety Executive, *Report by HM Chief Inspector of Factories 1985*, HMSO London 1986
3 Office of Population Censuses and Surveys, *Social Trends 15*, HMSO London 1985
4 Schilling R S F. Hazards of deep-sea fishing, *British Journal of Industrial Medicine* 1971, **28**: 27
5 Reissland J and Harries V. A scale for measuring risk, *New Scientist* 1979, September 13: 809
6 Waller J A. *Injury Control: A Guide to the Causes and Prevention of Trauma*, Lexington Books, DC Heath and Company 1984
7 Baker S D et al. *The Injury Fact Book*, Lexington Books, DC Heath and Company 1984
8 Health and Safety Executive, *Agricultural Black Spot: A Study of Fatal Accidents*, HMSO London 1986

Chapter 7   Risks in Transport

1 Waller J A. *Injury Control: a Guide to the Causes and Prevention of Trauma*, Lexington Books, D C Heath and Company 1985
2 Department of Transport, *Road Accidents Great Britain 1985: The Casualty Report*, HMSO London 1986
3 Borkenstein R F et al. *The Role of the Drinking Driver in Traffic Accidents*, Department of Police Administration, Indiana University 1964
4 Campbell B J and Reinfurt D W. *The Degree of Benefit of Belts in Reducing Injury*, SAE Technical Paper 790684, Society of Automotive Engineers 1979
5 National Highway Traffic Safety Administration, *A Report to the Congress on the Effect of Motorcycle Helmet Use Law Repeal: A Case for Helmet Use*, US Department of Transportation Washington DC 1980
6 Department of Transport, Railway Safety, *Report on the Safety Record of the Railways in Great Britain during 1985*, HMSO London 1986
7 Civil Aviation Authority, *Accidents to Aircraft on the British Register 1985*, CAA Report ACP 525, Civil Aviation Authority London 1986
8 Abelson L C, et al. Passenger survival in widebodied jet aircraft accidents vs. other aircraft: a comparison, *Aviation, Space and Environmental Medicine* 1980, **51**: 1266

Chapter 8   Risks in the Home

1 Office of Population Censuses and Surveys, *Mortality Statistics: Accidents and Violence 1983*, HMSO London 1984
2 Office of Population Censuses and Surveys, *General Household Survey 1984*, HMSO London 1986
3 *Accident Facts*, National Safety Council Chicago 1981
4 Accidents in the home, *WHO Chronicle* 1966, 20: 3
5 Robertson L S. *Injuries: Causes, Control Strategies, and Public Policy*, Lexington Books, DC Heath and Company 1983
6 *NEISS Data Highlights: Hazard Identification and Analysis 1980*, 4; Consumer Products Safety Commission Washington DC
7 Waller J A. Non-highway injury fatalities, I: the role of alcohol and problem drinking, drugs and medical impairment, *Journal of Chronic Diseases* 1972, **25**: 33
8 Ducic S and Glezzo H R. Epidemiology of accidental home fires in Montreal, *Accident Analysis and Prevention* 1980, **12**: 67
9 Spengher J D and Sexton K. Indoor air pollution: a public health perspective, *Science* 1983, **221**: 9
10 National Research Council Committee on *Indoor Pollutants, Indoor Pollutants*, National Academy Press Washington DC 1981
11 National Radiological Protection Board, *Living with Radiation*, HMSO London 1986

Chapter 9   Recreational Risks

1 *Hazards in Recreational and Commercial Boating Statistical Bulletin* Metropolitan Life Insurance 1977 **58**: 9
2 United States Coast Guard, *Boating Statistics 1980*, US Department of Transportation Washington DC 1981
3 Hale E. Analysis of fatal drowning accidents which occurred in 1961, *Journal of the Royal Naval Medical Services* 1963, **49**: 233
4 Schuman S H et al. Risk of drowning: an iceberg phenomenon, *Journal of the Americal College of Emergency Physicians* **1977, 6**: 139
5 Harries M. Drowning and near drowning. *British Journal of Sports Medicine* 1983, **17**: 5

6 Fergusson D M and Harwood L J. Risks of drowning in fenced and unfenced domestic swimming pools, *New Zealand Medical Journal* 1984, **97**: 777

7 Barry W, *et al*. Childhood drownings in private swimming pools: an avoidable cause of death. *British Medical Journal* 1982. **285**: 542

8 Dietz P E and Baker S P. Drowning: epidemiology and prevention, *American Journal of Public Health* 1974, **11**: 237

9 Penttila A *et al*. Drunken driving with motorboats in Finland, *Accident Analysis and Prevention* 1979, **11**: 237

10 Kewalramani L S and Kraus J F. Acute spinal-cord lesions from diving, *Western Journal of Medicine* 1977, **126**: 353

11 Burke D C. Spinal cord injuries from water sports, *Medical Journal of Australia* 1972, **2:** 1190

12 Kistler B. How safe is water skiing? in Winterhaven F L *The Water Skier*, American Water Ski Association 1983

13 McAmiff J J. *Underwater Diving Fatality Statistics 1970–79*. Report URI-SSR-80-14. National Oceanographic and Atmospheric Administration 1981

14 Davies D H and Campbell D G. The aetiology, clinical pathology and treatment of shark attack, *Journal of the Royal Naval Medical Service* 1962, **49**: 3

15 Weightman D and Browne R C. Injuries in eleven selected sports *British Journal of Sports Medicine* 1975, **9**: 136

16 Sparks J P. Half a million hours of rugby football, *British Journal of Sports Medicine* 1981, **15**: 30

17 Waller J A. *Injury Control: a Guide to the Causes and Prevention of Trauma*, Lexington Books, D C Heath and Company 1985

18 Schneider R C, *et al*. Football, in Schneider R C, *et al* (editors), *Sports Injuries*, Williams and Wilkins 1985

19 Tong J S, Vesgs J J, Sennett B, and Das M. The National Football Head and Neck Injury Registry: 14-year report on cervical quadriplegia, 1971 through 1984, *JAMA* 1985, **254**: 2329

20 Blyth C S and Mueller F O. *An Epidemiologic Study of High School Football Injuries in North Carolina*, Department of Physical Education, University of North Carolina, Chapel Hill 1974

21 Casson I R, Siegel O, Sham R, Campbell E A, Tarlau M, DiDomenico A. Brain damage in modern boxers, 1984, and

22 Board of Science and Education, *Boxing*, British Medical Association 1984

23 Powell J W. National athletic injury reporting system, *International Ophthalmology Clinics* 1981, **21**: 47

24 Mchatchie G R and Morris M B. Prevention of karate injuries: a progress report, *British Journal of Sports Medicine* 1977, **11**: 78

25 Eriksson E and Johnson R J. The etiology of downhill ski injuries, *Exercise and Sport Science Reviews* 1980, **8**: 1

26 Hughson R L *et al*. Heat injuries in Canadian mass participation runs, *Canadian Medical Association Journal* 1980, **122**: 1141

27 Williams A F. When motor vehicles hit joggers: an analysis of 60 cases, *Public Health Reports* 1981, **96**: 448

28 Mchatchi G R. Equestrian injuries: a one year prospective study, *British Journal of Sports Medicine* 1979, **13**: 29

29 Sports Hazards, *Statistical Bulletin, Metropolitan Life Insurance Company* 1979, **60**: 2

30 Swiss Re (UK) Insurance, *Motor Sport: a Background and Guide to the Assessment of Risk*, Swiss Reinsurance Company (UK) Ltd London 1985.

Chapter 10 Risks and Energy Production

1 Fremlin J H. *Power Production: what are the Risks?* Adam Hilger Ltd 1985

2 Ferguson R A D. *Comparative Risks of Electricity Generating Fuel Systems in the UK*, Energy Centre, University of Newcastle upon Tyne, Peter Peregrinus Ltd 1981

3 Health and Safety Commission, *Report on the Hazards of Conventional Sources of Energy*, HMSO London 1978

4 Black D *et al*. *Investigation of the Possible Increased Incidence of Cancer in West Cumbria: Report of the Independent Advisory Group*, HMSO London 1984

5 Committee on Medical Aspects of Radiation in the Environment, *First Report*, HMSO London 1986

6 Okrent D. Comment on societal risk, *Science* 1980, **208**: 372

7 Cohen A V and Pritchard D K. *Research Paper 11*, Health and Safety Executive, HMSO London 1980

8 Health and Safety Executive, *Canvey: An Investigation of Potential Hazards from Operations in the Canvey Island/Thurrock Area*, HMSO London 1978

9 Chernobyl Report, *Nature* 1986, **323**: 25

10 Inhaber H. Risk with energy from conventional and nonconventional sources. *Science* 1979, **203**: 718

11 Holdren J P, *et al*. Energy: calculating the risks (II), *Science* 1979, **204**: 564

Chapter 11 Risks of Medicine and Surgery

1 Office of Health Economics, *Anaesthesia*, OHE London 1976

2 Office of Health Economics, *A Review of Clinical*

Risks, OHE London 1986

3 Vayda E. A comparison of surgical rates in Canada and in England and Wales, *New England Journal of Medicine* 1973, **289**: 1224

4 de Dombal F T *et al.* Human and computer-aided diagnosis of abdominal pain: further report with emphasis on performance of clinicians, *British Medical Journal* 1974, **1**: 376

5 Office of Population Censuses and Surveys, *Hospital In-patient Enquiry* 1983, HMSO London 1985

6 European Coronary Surgery Study Group, Long-term results of prospective randomized study of coronary artery bypass surgery in stable angina pectoris, *Lancet* 1982, **2**: 1173

7 Harris A A, Levin S, and Trenholme G M. Selected aspects of nosocomial infections in the 1980s, *American Journal of Medicine* 1985, **77 (1B)**: 3

8 Committee on Safety of Medicines, CSM update, *British Medical Journal* 1985, **291**: 1269

9 Speirs C J *et al.* Demography of the UK adverse reaction register of spontaneous reports, *Health Trends* 1984, **16**: 49

10 Inman W H W. Risks in medical intervention: balancing therapeutic risks and benefits, in Worden A *et al.* (editors) *The Future of Predictive Safety Evaluation*, MTP Press 1986

11 *Breast Cancer Screening.* Report to the Health Ministers of England, Wales, Scotland and Northern Ireland by a working group chaired by Sir Patrick Forrest, HMSO, 1987

12 Inuma T A *et al.* Benefit vs risk analysis of stomach cancer mass screening, in Okada S (editor), *Radiation Research*, Proceedings of the 6th International Congress of Radiation Research 1979

13 Sidaway vs Governers of Bethlem Royal Hospital, *Weekly Law Reports* 1986, March 8, 480

14 McNeil B J, *et al.* On the elicitation of preferences for alternative therapies, *New England Journal of Medicine* 1982, **306**: 1259

15 Consumers' Association, Herbal medicines—Safe and effective? *Drug and Therapeutics Bulletin* 1986, **24**: 97

Chapter 12   Natural Disasters

1 Sapir D G and Lechat M F. Reducing the impact of natural disasters: why aren't we better prepared? *Health Policy and Planning* 1986, **1**: 118

2 Seaman J. *Epidemiology of Natural Disasters*, Karger Basel 1984

3 de Bruycker M, *et al.* The 1980 earthquake in Southern Italy, *Bulletin of the WHO* 1983, **61**: 1021

4 Levine R J *et al.* Failure of sanitary wells to protect against cholera and other diarrhoeas in Bangladesh, *Lancet* 1976, **2**: 86

5 Okrent D. Comment on societal risk. *Science* 1980, **208**: 372

Chapter 13   Chemical Risks

1 National Academy of Sciences, *Risk and Decision Making: Perspectives and Research*, National Academy Press Washington DC 1982

2 Doll R and Peto R. *The Causes of Cancer*, Oxford University Press 1981

3 Advisory Committee on Pesticides, *Further Review of the Safety for Use in the UK of the Herbicide 2,4,5-T.* Ministry of Agriculture, Fisheries and Food London 1980

4 Department of Primary Industry, *Report of the Consultative Council on Congenital Abnormalities in the Yarram District*, Australian Government Publishing Service Canberra 1978

5 International Agency for Research into Cancer, *Monographs on the Evaluation of the Carcinogenic Risk of Chemicals to Humans*, IARC Monographs 1982

6 Evatt P. *Royal Commission on the Use and Effects of Chemical Agents on Australian Personnel in Vietnam: Final Report*, AGPS Canberra 1985

7 Hardell L *et al.* Malignant lymphoma and exposure to chemicals, especially organic solvents, chloro-phenols and phenoxyacids: a case control study, *British Journal of Cancer* 1981, **43**: 169

Chapter 14   Perception and Acceptability of Risk

1 D Kahneman *et al.* (editors). *Judgement Under Uncertainty: Heuristics and Biases*, Cambridge University Press NY 1982

2 Civil Aviation Authority, *Accidents to UK Aircraft and to Large Jet and Turbo-prop Transport Aircraft Worldwide in 1985*, CAA paper 86005, Civil Aviation Authority London 1986

3 Lichtenstein S *et al.* Judged frequency of lethal events. *Journal of Experimental Psychology: Human Learning and Memory* 1978, **4**: 551

4 Fremlin J H. *Power Production: What are the Risks?* Adam Hilger 1985

5 Morgan M G *et al.* On judging the frequency of lethal events: a replication, *Risk Analysis* 1983, **3**: 11

6 Green C H and Brown R A. Counting lives, *Journal of Occupational Accidents* 1978, **2**: 55

7 Slovic P, *et al.* Facts and fears: understanding perceived risk, in Schwing and Albers (editors) *Societal Risk Assessment: How Safe is Safe Enough?* Plenum Press NY 1980

8 Slovic P *et al.* Why study risk perception? *Risk Analysis* 1983, **2**: 83

9 Harding C M and Eiser J R. Characterising the perceived risks and benefits of some health issues, *Risk Analysis* 1984, **4**: 131

10 Starr S. Social benefit versus techological risk, *Science* 1969, **165**: 1232

11 Fischhoff B and MacGregor D. Judged lethality: how much people seem to know depends upon how they are asked, *Risk Analysis* 1983, **3**: 229
12 Eraker S A and Sox H C. Assessment of patients' preferences for therapeutic outcomes, *Medical Decision Making* 1981, **1**: 29
13 Starr C. Risk management, assessment and acceptability, *Risk Analysis* 1985, **5**: 97

Chapter 15   Management of Risk

1 Singleton W T. Risk-handling by institutions, in Singleton W T and Horden J (editors) *Risk and Decisions*, John Wiley & Sons 1987
2 Covello V T and Mumpower J. Risk analysis and risk management: an historical perspective. *Risk Analysis* 1985, **5**: 103
3 Haddon W Jr. Advances in the epidemiology of injuries as a basis for public policy, *Public Health Reports* 1980, **95**: 411
4 MacGregor D and Slovic P. Perceived acceptability of risk analysis as a decision-making approach, *Risk Analysis* 1986, **6**: 245
5 Knox E G. Negligible risk to health. *Community Health* 1975, **6**: 244
6 Nader R. *Unsafe at any Speed*, Grossman NY 1965
7 Robertson L S. *Injuries: Causes, Control Strategies and Public Policy*. Lexington Books DC Health Company 1983
8 Royal College of Physicians, *Health or Smoking?* Pitman Publishing 1983
9 Royal College of Psychiatrists, *Alcohol: Our Favourite Drug*, Tavistock Publications 1986
10 Gibney M J. *Nutrition, Diet and Health*, Cambridge University Press 1986

Further Reading

1 Urquhart J and Heilmann K. *Risk Watch: the Odds of Life*, Facts on File Publication 1984
2 Royal Society Study Group, *Risk Assessment*, The Royal Society London 1983
3 Rowe W D. *An Anatomy of Risk*, J Wiley New York 1977
4 Fischhoff B *et al*. *Acceptable Risk*, Cambridge University Press MY 1981
5 Schwing R and Albers W A. *Societal Risk Assessment: How Safe is Safe Enough?* Plenum Press NY, London 1980
6 Waller J A. *Injury Control: A Guide to the Causes and Prevention of Trauma*, Lexington Books, DC Heath and Company 1985
7 Robertson L S. *Injuries: Causes, Control Strategies, and Public Policy*, Lexington Books, DC Heath and Company 1983
8 Baker S P, O'Neil B, and Karpf R S. *The Injury Fact Book*, Lexington Books, DC Heath and Company 1984
9 Royal College of Physicians, *Health or Smoking?* Pitman Publishing London 1983
10 Royal College of Psychiatrists, *Alcohol: Our Favourite Drug*, Tavistock Publications 1986
11 Gibney M J. *Nutrition, Diet and Health*, Cambridge University Press 1986
12 Fremlin J H. *Power Production: What are the Risks?* Adam Hilger Ltd 1985
13 Crone H D. *Chemicals and Society: A Guide to the New Chemical Age*, Cambridge University Press 1986

Index